THE GATHERING STORM

FRANK SIMON

THE GATHERING STORM

A NOVEL

BROADMAN
&HOLMAN
PUBLISHERS

Nashville, Tennessee

0-8054-2577-2

Published by Broadman & Holman Publishers
Nashville, Tennessee

0106 – 92160 – MM

Dewey Decimal Classification: 813
Subject Heading: FICTION

1 2 3 4 5 6 7 8 9 10   08 07 06 05 04 03

b 16359288

For Jan Simon

Acknowledgments

I want to thank the people who helped make this book possible:

My wife, LaVerne, first editor and my sweet helpmate.

Lieutenant Carol Stearns, Operations Officer, United States Coast Guard Group, Grand Haven.

Lieutenant (junior grade) Daniel Leary, Law Enforcement (pilot), United States Coast Guard Air Station, Traverse City.

Warren J. Spencer, Police Legal Advisor for the Plano Police Department.

My friend and agent, Les Stobbe.

Leonard Goss, for his help and encouragement.

Chapter One

Special Agent Barbara Post stood motionless, close enough to the demolished snowmobile to touch it, but touching the mangled heap of steel and plastic was the furthest thing from her mind. She shivered inside her heavy parka as something other than the brisk winter wind chilled her to the bone. She began piecing together how the Polaris had come to this end, claiming the life of U.S. District Judge Nelson Richards. Barbara shivered again when she remembered the crime scene photos of the judge's battered and bloody remains, only too aware of the reddish-black stains on the otherwise pristine white snow.

She heard a tinkling sound behind her as the engine of their double-riding Polaris cooled; however, she was more aware of the National Response Team agent standing beside her. The man seemed wary and suspicious of her, a reaction she encountered from time to time despite working for a federal bureau. Momentary irritation welled up inside her. Some agents apparently expected explosives experts to be of the male gender.

"So, what do you guess did that?" the agent asked her.

"I don't *have* to guess!" Barbara said, before she could check her tongue. The white puff of her breath faded, and a short silence ensued. She clamped down with her internal censor and continued in a more subdued tone. "I knew what it was when you showed me the shells, but I wanted to examine the crime scene myself to make sure nothing was overlooked."

The man seemed to stiffen at this, but it was hard to tell, encased as he was in his bulky parka.

"So, what was it?" he asked.

Barbara felt momentary satisfaction at the agent's obvious irritation. "Forty millimeter M-203 high-explosive grenade rounds, from a launcher mounted on an M-16."

"Something mounted on a gun did that?"

"The M-16 is an assault rifle, but yes, the M-203 is quite capable of this. The high-explosive grenade contains a 35-gram charge that is wrapped with rectangular-shaped steel wires, notched to provide fragmentation on detonation. It makes a real mess of the target." Again she remembered the judge's mangled body.

"But why use grenades?"

Barbara had been wondering that herself. "Good question. The guy obviously had an M-16, which would be easier to use and more than adequate to take the judge out. Maybe the assassin wanted to make a statement."

"Termination with extreme prejudice?"

"Something like that."

"Where do you think the weapons came from?"

Barbara turned from the wreck and looked at the agent's mirrored sunglasses. "The brief I read in Dallas said that Judge Richards was trying a suspected militiaman. I presume the Team is pursuing a connection."

"We are. When apprehended, the suspect was in possession of several kilos of C-4, stolen from an Army National Guard armory in Billings, Montana."

"Which is a violation of the Federal Explosives Law," Barbara finished for him.

"That's a roger."

"What kind of unit?"

"Artillery battery."

"That's probably the source of the weapons then. Artillery would definitely have M-16s and M-203 grenade launchers. However, we can't rule out private dealers. You'd be surprised what's available out there, particularly in states like Montana." The agent said nothing. Barbara suppressed a grin. "OK, so you wouldn't be surprised."

"We *are* in the militia belt." The man paused. "What do you make of the scene outside the Richards' cabin?"

Barbara thought about the comfortable, modern cabin back at the Pahaska Tepee Lodge and the trampled snow roughly two hundred feet away among the fir trees. The response team agents had found three circular depressions forming a large triangle and a heavy metal pin.

"Don't know," she said. "The circular depressions could have been caused by tripod footpads, perhaps an observation device, but more likely a heavy weapon."

"You mean, something to blow up the cabin?"

"That would be my guess. It's consistent with using grenades to kill the judge rather than using the M-16."

"Then why didn't they do it?"

"Who knows? Heavy weapons are complex. Maybe a component failed, or they were missing a part. Perhaps they had second thoughts. That site *is* terribly exposed. Could be they were afraid of getting caught. Ambushing Judge Richards out in the boonies makes a lot more sense."

The agent nodded. "OK. What about the pin?"

Barbara thought about the photos. "It's definitely military, probably used to secure a device inside its storage container. But I've never seen that particular part before. I'll run it through my sources when I get back to Dallas. Will you be sending me copies of the forensics?"

The man nodded. "Of course. It's standard procedure."

"Right. I'm done here. Is there anything else you need me to look at?"

"That's it. Shall we head back to the lodge?"

The agent climbed onto the snowmobile and engaged the electric starter. The powerful engine started immediately. Barbara got on behind and gripped the handholds as securely as she could with her heavy gloves. The grisly details of the crime scene faded a little as they roared over the fresh snow near the eastern entrance to Yellowstone National Park. Dark green fir and spruce trees lined the way, along with stripped aspens. The sun blazed down from the deep blue, cloudless sky. Barbara squinted against the brilliant glare, even though she wore sunglasses.

Snowmobiling was new to her, and she decided she really liked it. Growing up in Marfa, Texas, in the northern reaches of the Chihuahuan Desert, snow sports had not been a high priority in her recreational goals. Perhaps she would have to reconsider, especially with her impending transfer to the Grand Rapids, Michigan, Field Office of the Bureau of Alcohol, Tobacco, and Firearms. That thought brought a pang of anxiety. Bureau representatives had told her before she joined that travel and relocation came with the Treasury Department job, and that had been no lie.

But Barbara was committed to her job and found she really enjoyed it. At twenty-eight, she had recently celebrated, if you could call it that, her fifth year with the ATF, and at the present time wanted to make a career of it. There weren't a lot of other openings for explosives experts outside the military, which did not appeal to her.

The snowmobile roared over a ridge, revealing the Pahaska Tepee Resort. The agent pulled up beside the main lodge and stopped. They dismounted and trudged into the large, A-frame building. Once inside, Barbara pulled off her sunglasses, revealing her brown eyes. The interior seemed dark and dingy after the brilliant snow. The ATF agents had commandeered a storeroom for their command post, since all the cabins were rented. Although the Richards' lodge was empty, it was off-limits until all federal and state agencies were done with their investigations.

Barbara removed her gloves, then unzipped and shrugged out of her parka. The snug hood refused to give up without a fight. She frowned and tried to smooth her short brunette hair with a hand, then realized it was futile. Removal of her bulky coat revealed a petite figure and lithe build. She walked beside the agent, making no attempt to match his long strides.

The agent in charge looked up as they entered the storeroom. He gave them a weary smile as he leaned over a large table, his hands resting on a map of the resort. He made a quick note with a red pen and stood upright.

"What did you find?" he asked Barbara.

"The weapon was an M-203 grenade launcher mounted on an M-16. You found three spent shells. The damage done is consistent with what three high-explosive grenades would deliver. From my observation at the scene," Barbara swallowed. " . . . and the photographs, one round hit the judge in the chest; the other two struck the snowmobile."

"And the site outside the cabin?"

"I don't know. Possible heavy weapon. I'll see if I can track down that pin when I get back to Dallas. I suspect it's a military part, probably army."

"I see. Well, keep me informed."

"I will."

"What are your plans?"

"Head back to Dallas—if you're done with me." She saw the look of surprise in his eyes as he glanced at his watch.

"I think that's all for now, but you're going back today?"

Barbara had already decided she wanted to avoid another night in that dreary motel in Cody. "I better. I'm being transferred to the Grand Rapids Field Office in May, so I've got to finish up my work in progress."

"Need a ride back to Casper?"

"No, thanks. I've got a rental car."

"I appreciate your help." He seemed to hesitate, then shook her hand.

Barbara said hurried good-byes and bundled herself into the white Ford Contour. Although the drive from Pahaska Tepee to Cody was spectacular, she concentrated on keeping her speed up. Fortunately the roads were open, and the forecast was for clear and cold through the weekend. That being the case, she didn't see any problem in making the 4:55 P.M. departure from Casper to Denver. Assuming she made her connecting flight, she would be back at DFW a little after 7:00 P.M. Then claim her baggage, grab the shuttle to the north remote lot, and be home by what time? Not too late, if everything went as scheduled. She said a silent prayer that everything would.

The Gathering Storm

⸻ ⸻ ⸻

It was not until a week later that Barbara finally identified the mysterious pin found near Judge Richards's cabin, not because this was difficult but because other projects ranked higher in priority. Had the part figured in the actual assassination, she would have been in more of a hurry, but it didn't. Still, it was a loose end to tie up, and Barbara had plenty of those to deal with as her transfer date approached.

Suspecting an older weapon, Barbara first looked at back copies of *Jane's Armour and Artillery* CDs and found the part within thirty minutes. In the section on U.S. heavy antitank weapons, she found a picture of the TOW (tube launched optically tracked wire-guided) missile together with its launch container. And there, between the two, was the part in question. It was the hold-back pin that retained the missile inside its container.

Barbara pulled the crime scene photos out and compared them with the picture on her monitor. There could be no question, but to be sure she called an acquaintance at the army's Aberdeen Proving Grounds. After a short discussion with the young armor major, she had confirmation. Further, the man told her that the TOW missile was part of the Army National Guard's weapons inventory. Barbara thanked him and hung up.

So, the militia probably had stolen the missile from the same armory that yielded the M-16 and M-203 grenade launcher. Barbara tilted back in her swivel chair. This was not good news. A missile capable of knocking out a main battle tank could do a lot of damage. Here was yet another worry to add to the bureau's unending list.

The ATF had a wide and somewhat catchall portfolio: regulation of alcohol, tobacco, and firearms trade, and the licensing of explosives distributors and customers. Barbara's work centered mostly on militias and paramilitary organizations, not particularly surprising for an explosives expert. But she knew these groups were a growing concern for the ATF as a whole. Given terrorist activities in recent years, it was to be expected.

Barbara switched to her contacts application and found the mobile number for the National Response Team agent in charge. She punched in the number and waited as it rang. A few seconds later, the agent's voice mail announcement played. Barbara waited for the beep. She left a message telling him the identity of the part and said she would fax the details to his office.

And that's that, she thought to herself as she hung up. It bothered her that a militia would have a TOW missile, but at least this one was not her responsibility. She decided to get a cup of coffee before returning to her duties.

Chapter Two

Lieutenant Craig Phillips wasn't aware of it, but he was wearing his aviator's smile. His blue eyes, hidden behind sunglasses, liked what they were seeing. The young Coast Guard officer enjoyed flying, and a near-perfect day in Traverse City, Michigan, only increased his spirits. At thirty, he had been in the service for eight years and was thinking seriously of making it a career.

Snow blanketed the ground below. The HH-65A Dolphin helicopter clattered onward over the Michigan coast, following a southern course to the Grand Haven Airport. Craig relaxed in the right-hand seat as he operated the controls. Like most pilots, he was tall, trim, and athletic. The assurance of complete control exhilarated him as he relied on his finely honed skills. Then he felt a momentary twinge of conscience—he recognized pride when he saw it. But God *had* gifted him for this job, and for that he was truly grateful.

The early morning sun was still low in the east. Craig's eyes swept the sky to the right. The blue expanse of Lake Michigan stretched out and over the horizon. Down below, snow-mounded homes and buildings dotted the flight path. Cars and trucks traveled along the freshly plowed streets and highways without significant difficulties.

Almost an hour later, Craig pulled back on the stick slightly and reduced power as the helo pad at the Grand Haven Airport came into sight. The trim helicopter began to slow. The pad had been cleared, Craig was glad to see. They could land on snow, but that usually caused a momentary white-out from the rotor blast. There was no point in landing on instruments unless you had to. Craig increased power to bring his aircraft into a hover. Finally they touched down with a gentle bump.

"Don't believe we broke anything, skipper," Lieutenant (junior grade) Joel Foscue said as he began unbuckling.

Craig continued flipping switches, going through the shutdown procedure. The whine of the twin turbines decreased rapidly. He grinned as he glanced at his thin copilot. "I suppose you could do better?"

"Wouldn't think of criticizing my boss," the young man said.

Craig snorted. "Yeah, right."

He finished up and moved aft. Craig removed his flight helmet and ran a hand through his sweaty blond hair. He traded the sturdy brain-bucket for a ball cap and pulled on a flight jacket over his blue dry suit, a heavy garment made of canvaslike material with tight-fitting rubber seals around the neck and wrists. Craig grabbed a traveling bag containing a fresh uniform and stepped out of the helicopter. Joel and the two crewmen joined him moments later.

"What's up, skipper?" Joel asked as they walked toward the waiting car.

"Don't know, exactly," Craig replied. "The CO said I'm to meet with some federal agents from Grand Rapids, and that's all I know."

The two officers got in the back while the crewmen joined the driver up front.

"Sounds ominous," Joel continued.

"I guess we'll find out soon."

The car pulled up in front of Coast Guard Group Grand Haven. Craig got out and led the way inside. After arranging where to meet Joel and the crew, he proceeded to a rest room where he changed into his trops, a light blue short-sleeve shirt with dark blue trousers. His shirt sported ribbons and gold aviator's wings to the left and had shoulder boards with two gold stripes denoting a lieutenant. His name tag rested above the right pocket.

Craig located the second floor conference room. He paused outside the door, took a deep breath, and knocked.

"Come in," a muted voice said from within.

Craig opened the door and looked inside. Somewhat surprising, there were no Coast Guard personnel present. Instead, two men in dark suits stood at the end of the conference table obviously waiting for him.

An overweight, middle-aged man held out his hand. Although he smiled, his brown eyes were sharp and hard. "Lieutenant Phillips—Dan Oliver. I'm resident agent in charge at the ATF Grand Rapids Field Office." He had a large, shiny bald spot surrounded by gray hair flecked with a little of the original brown.

Craig took his hand. They were nearly the same height, but Craig was a little taller. "Pleased to meet you, Mr. Oliver."

Dan turned to the black man at his side. "And this is special agent Sam Green."

"Mr. Green," Craig said, shaking his hand. Unlike his boss, this man had a firm grip.

The agent smiled. His dark brown eyes seemed friendly but reserved. He had close-cropped black hair and a wide mustache. His skin was quite dark. He was obviously younger than his boss, with a trim, medium build that spoke of a better exercise program.

"Mr. Phillips," Sam said with a brief nod.

Craig was surprised the agent omitted his rank. Most civilians addressed him as "lieutenant," but junior officers were addressed as "mister" in both the Coast Guard and Navy. "Were you in the military, Mr. Green?" he asked.

That produced a broad smile. "Navy Supply Corps."

Craig grinned. "Oh, a Porkchop," he said, recalling the usual nickname for Supply Corps personnel.

"That's right. Without supply, you Airdales would be stuck on the ground."

Craig noted the service term for aviators. "Can't argue that."

"Hate to break up the class reunion, folks," Dan said, "but I really *do* have some business to conduct here—if you guys don't mind."

Craig felt the flush of embarrassment. "Sorry, sir."

Dan sat at the head of the table. Craig took a seat opposite Sam.

"Now, Lieutenant, were you briefed on this meeting?" Dan asked.

"Not really. My CO said my orders were to fly down to Coast Guard Group Grand Haven for a conference with some federal agents."

"The lack of detail was intentional. Before I proceed, I've been told you have a top secret clearance. Be advised that what we will discuss today is classified top secret. You may not divulge any of it without my express permission. Are we clear on that?"

Craig stifled his momentary irritation. "Very clear, sir."

"Good. We're here today for two reasons. As you probably know, the current administration is quite concerned about state militias and paramilitary groups. The president has declared this an initiative of his, so the agencies involved are preparing for implementation—the ATF, FBI, and state and local police departments mainly." He nodded at Craig. "And the military—that's why you're here."

"Sir, I fail to see what this has to do with search-and-rescue."

Dan's frown grew even deeper. "If you'll bear with me, Lieutenant, I'm sure the picture will come into focus."

"Yes, sir."

"There are several militias in western Michigan, plus indications that another one is forming near Grand Haven. The Coast Guard has been tasked with providing transportation and other logistics for our operations. This is the first reason for your involvement. The second has to do with the kickoff for the president's initiative." Dan paused, and his expression seemed to slide toward a sneer. "Because Michigan militias are so prominent, the president will announce his program at a speech in Grand Haven. *Air Force One* will fly him into Grand Rapids. From there a motorcade will bring him to Grand Haven. The Secret Service, FBI, and ATF will all be involved, of course. The Coast Guard will provide transportation as required, and that includes your helicopter."

"Sir, you're aware we're stationed at Traverse City?"

"Yes, Lieutenant, I am." Dan pulled out his reading glasses and put them on. He unfolded a paper and scanned it. "You will receive orders in a few months forming a detachment at Coast Guard Air Facility Muskegon. In addition to search-and-rescue duties, you'll be instructed to provide all necessary assistance to the ATF, under direction of my office. Coast Guard Group Grand Haven is also tasked with this operation." He pulled off the glasses and returned them to his pocket.

"I see," Craig said. "Is there anything I or my men need to do to prepare?"

"Not at this time. This is just a heads-up. You can tell your men about the coming detachment, and that they will be assisting the ATF, but that's all."

"With all due respect, sir, I don't understand this level of security. We're used to handling classified information. My men will want to know what we're doing, and I'd feel better if they knew."

Dan's brown eyes glinted. "The president's trip is top secret, and the itinerary will *not* be released until shortly before his arrival. Ever since this initiative was announced, the militias and wackos have been kicking up a stink. Naturally, the Treasury Department is demanding airtight security on the president's visit. You'll be told when you can brief your men."

"Yes, sir."

"After your detachment becomes operational, Sam or I will be your contact with the ATF; however I may add other agents as the time draws near. Any questions?"

Craig shook his head. "No, sir. I will await my orders and your instructions."

The three men stood up.

"Thank you, Lieutenant," Dan said.

Craig shook his hand. "My pleasure, sir." He turned to Sam. "And I'm looking forward to working with you, Mr. Green. It'll give us a chance to trade sea stories."

"I'd like that," Sam replied.

They walked to the entrance together. Craig waited inside while the agents went out to their car. He heard a noise and turned. Joel lounged against the wall, now changed into his uniform. His shoulder boards sported two gold stripes, one wide and one thin.

"So, what's the scoop?" the copilot asked.

"In a month or so we'll be detached to Air Facility Muskegon." He saw the surprise in the young man's eyes.

"Muskegon? What in the world for?"

"We're going to be assisting the Bureau of Alcohol, Tobacco, and Firearms."

"Doing what?"

Craig took a deep breath. "That's all I can tell you right now."

Chapter Three

Barbara scanned the mounds of paper stacked on her desk. It was early afternoon, and she could see no progress since morning. But getting the fax on the TOW missile out yesterday helped some. At least she was done with the Judge Richards assassination. The phone rang, providing an almost welcome distraction.

"Special Agent Post," she said.

"Agent Post, this is Dan Oliver, Resident Agent in Charge at the Grand Rapids Field Office," the man said, speaking rapidly. "How are you?" His last words sounded flat, like an amen tacked on to a perfunctory prayer.

Barbara knew this was her future boss, but she had never met him. "I'm fine, Mr. Oliver, how are you?"

"Peachy-keen," the man grumbled. "Now, as much as I like chitchat, let's get down to business, shall we?"

Barbara's half-buried dread of her transfer sprang forth again. "Oh— of course. Go ahead."

"As you know, the Bureau, in its wisdom, is sending you up here to fill a special agent opening I have. Now, I don't have any say in this, and neither do you, so I guess we'll have to make the best of it."

"Mr. Oliver, if you're concerned about my ability . . ."

"Can it, Ms. Post. Come May, you're mine. Then you'll either do the job or not. This is just a heads-up on what you'll be doing. I understand you're an explosives expert."

Barbara gritted her teeth. "You've seen my service folder. What does it say?" The moment the words were out of her mouth, she regretted it.

"Don't get snippy with me. Of *course* I've read it. If it's not *too* much trouble, could we discuss it?"

"I'm sorry. What would you like to know?"

"Fill in the details."

"Well, my folder covers most of my experience—schools, explosives I've dealt with . . . I'm up on most of them: fertilizer bombs, C-4 plastic explosives, dynamite, and so on. In addition, I'm fairly current on small arms, heavy machine guns, grenades, mortars, and some infantry and artillery missiles." She continued for several minutes, trying to be as complete as possible. She concluded by saying, "Is there something specific you want to know?"

"No, I think that covers it. I understand you assisted one of our National Response Teams on the Judge Richards case."

"Yes, I did. Judge Richards was killed by three 40mm grenades from an M-203 launcher. Actually, *one* of the grenades got him, the other two shredded his snowmobile."

"I've got a copy of your original report in my hand. What about that pin? Did you find out what it was?"

"Yes, and I faxed the NRT agent in charge yesterday. It's a hold-back pin that secures a TOW missile in its container."

Dan's response was slow in coming. "I'm not familiar with that missile. What's it used for?"

"It's a line-of-sight weapon designed to knock out main battle tanks. The acronym stands for tube launched, optically tracked, wire-guided missile. Extremely effective, as long as the gunner keeps his crosshairs on the target."

"It's frightening to think of a militia having one of those."

"Yes, it is. But that's the trend. More and more high-tech weapons are turning up in the hands of militias. The TOW, for example, has a range of 3.75 kilometers—2.33 miles. Anything the gunner can see within that radius, he can hit—and kill."

"Well, I hope we won't have to deal with anything like that around here. As you know, we have more than our share of militias in Michigan. Most are fruitcakes, so they're not much of a challenge. I don't see that changing anytime soon."

"Is that what I'm going to be working on?"

"Initially. I'm teaming you with Special Agent Sam Green. You've heard about the president's initiative against militias?"

Barbara realized it wasn't really a question, and Dan's tone indicated he didn't think much of the program. "Yes, of course I have."

"Well, the policy wonks handed the bureau a special assignment related to that. I can't give you the details now, but you're involved in that too. I'm sure you're totally thrilled."

"I'm serious about doing a good job, if that's what you mean."

"Right, I'm sure you are," he grumbled. "See you in May." The phone clicked dead.

Barbara frowned as she replaced the handset. She felt a momentary twinge of anxiety, thinking about her first impression of her future boss, but this quickly turned to anger. Dan Oliver clearly didn't want her in his organization, only he didn't have any say in the matter. Although she didn't know his reasons, she had her suspicions. Equal opportunity might be the official federal tune, but some bureaucrats didn't know how it went.

But there was something else that bothered her. Dan didn't seem all that worried about the Michigan militias. If so, he was dangerously mistaken. Barbara knew the militia movement was fast becoming a serious national threat. She shivered as she thought about what they could do with their growing arsenals.

Brad Anderson had heard enough. He stood up behind his desk and leaned forward. His balled-up fists rested on the surface as if he were about to jump over it. He was tempted to do just that. His icy blue eyes glared down at his half brother Ed, seated in one of the side chairs.

The two shared last names, but not much else. Brad was six-foot-two and a trim 230 pounds, and he maintained his blond hair in a neat military crew cut. Ed, two years younger, was four inches shorter and had brown eyes and unruly brown hair.

Brad made no attempt to hide his contempt. "That was a stupid thing to do!" he said, almost in a shout. "What did you expect to gain by wasting a judge? You got a death wish or something?"

Ed jumped up and glared back. "He was trying our guy! What was I supposed to do?"

"Your guy was an idiot, or they wouldn't have caught him with the plastic. So now your whole militia is on the run, and you come begging me for help?"

Although both had grown up in Noxon, Montana, Brad had relocated to Grand Haven after his service as a Navy SEAL. The last thing he needed was to have *his* new militia messed up.

"But we have to do something," Ed whined. "The feds are after all the militias. If we don't act, they'll take away every American right we've got. They've been trying to grab our guns for years. They've attacked everywhere—Ruby Ridge—Waco. And they're caving in to the United Nations."

"Shut up! I know all that, but reacting to the feds like you did will get us all wiped out. Fighting them requires a plan, something you know nothing about."

Ed clinched his fists. "You can't talk to me like that!"

"I just did! You wanna have a piece of me, come on!" He watched as the fire in his brother's eyes gradually died away. Brad knew he would back down; he always did. But the problem was, these confrontations never changed anything. That his brother marched to a different drummer didn't cover it as far as Brad was concerned. He was convinced Ed didn't know what a drum was.

"I'm your brother," Ed finally said.

"Don't remind me. Far as I'm concerned, that was Pop's mistake."

Brad saw the insult hurt, but he could tell Ed wasn't going to rise to the bait. Not now.

"You're not sending me away, are you? I brought you the missile and the guns."

"I've already got M-16s and grenade launchers. Besides, you say the TOW is broken."

"You can fix it, can't you?"

Brad considered that. "Don't know," he said. Quite possibly he could, he thought. He certainly had the equipment and technicians. The two brothers stood inside the ostensible office of Anderson's Automotive. More than a front, the garage was actually a thriving business. But only Brad and a few trusted lieutenants knew that the large steel building had a secret basement housing an armory and gunsmith shop. Provided the TOW didn't need a hard-to-get part, Brad knew someone who could probably repair it.

"Maybe," Brad said finally. "But it wouldn't do me much good. I don't have anyone qualified to operate it. Of course, that could change since I'm still recruiting."

"I know how to use it."

"Come on! You were never in the service."

"Our operator showed me how."

"We'll talk about it later."

Ed's eyes took on a hunted look. "Are you going to let me stay?"

Brad waited a long time before answering. Then he pointed his finger. "All right. But you mess up just once, and you're dead meat. You got me?"

Ed stared at him.

"I asked you a question!"

"I won't mess up."

"OK, sit down." Brad settled back in his high-backed executive swivel chair. He hoped he wasn't making a mistake.

Ed averted his eyes. "Thanks. I appreciate you taking me in. I don't know what I'd do otherwise."

Brad sensed resentment leavening this expression of gratitude. "Fine, fine. What say we get down to business. We've got a lot to do. All the stuff is in your van?"

"Yes."

"Are the police looking for it?"

"I don't think so. I was very careful."

Brad stifled what he wanted to say. "We can't be too careful now, can we? I'll schedule your Chevy for a custom conversion. I guarantee even *you* won't recognize it when I get done." He grabbed a blank work order and started filling it out. "I have a few mechanics I can trust to be discreet. Tonight, you and I will unload the van after my regular crew goes home." He paused. "Meanwhile, you got a place to stay?" Brad knew the answer to that, but he asked anyway.

"No."

"You can crash at my place. I just moved, so here's my new address." He wrote it on a slip of paper and handed it to his brother along with a key.

Ed got up. "Thanks. I gotta go buy some things. What time you want me back?"

"You're not taking the van, are you?"

Ed shrugged. "It's the only car I've got."

Brad had to struggle to remain calm. "And what would happen if you had a wreck, or if someone broke into it?" He stopped when he saw the other's look of anguish. "Hold it. Never mind." He reached into his pocket and pulled out a key ring. "Take my truck. It's the navy blue Suburban out behind the shop."

Ed took the keys and turned.

"I need your keys," Brad said, holding out his hand.

Ed gave them to him. "What time you want me back?"

"Around six."

His brother left and closed the door. Brad rocked back in his chair and surveyed his office. On the wall opposite him, above the windows looking out on the garage, hung a selection of photos from his Navy SEAL days, action pictures of him and his teammates in rubber boats or slogging through swamps. Brad smiled as he studied the two posters that flanked the action shots. One was the actual SEAL insignia, a golden eagle clutching a sword, trident, and anchor. The other was a cartoon of a rampant eagle in scuba gear, wings spread, talons gripping a combination M-16/grenade launcher. Centered, in the place of honor, hung the commission of Ensign Brad Anderson. A hand-lettered banner surmounted it all: "Live Free or Die," the name of the new militia. Brad believed New Hampshire's motto entirely appropriate for these difficult times.

He looked at his mementos for a long time. He was proud of his military service. It gave him an appreciation for the defense of liberty, an appreciation shared by his closest associates, most of them former SEALs and Army Rangers. He was well aware that very few members of either service agreed with the militia movement, but that was their problem. Perhaps they would see their error when the feds took over and confiscated all guns. Of course, then it would be too late.

His gaze drifted down to a framed photo on the corner of his desk. A young woman and small boy seemed to peer out at him, squinting into the summer sun. Brad had taken it several years ago during happier times. He wondered yet again why he had kept the picture after his divorce. Unfortunately, his ex had not understood the importance of freedom and what it costs to preserve it.

Brad sighed, got up and opened the mini blinds fully. He went out into the shop and opened the garage door to the empty bay nearest his office. He drove his brother's white Chevy van inside and got out. He stabbed the button to bring down the garage door, shutting out the frigid wind. A warm breeze blew past him, thanks to the powerful overhead gas heaters. Brad checked to make sure all the van doors were locked, then returned to his office.

He waited patiently as the legitimate side of his business closed for the day. Gradually the banging, clattering, and grinding sounds diminished then quit altogether. Around seven, Brad heard the steel door near his office rattle. He went out and peeked through the door's tiny window.

"Hey, Hawk," Brad said, opening the door. "Come on in out of the cold."

Mike Hawkins stepped inside. He was a tall man and quite trim. He removed his beret, revealing short, brown hair. His brown eyes seemed ever vigilant.

"I've finished overhauling the M2HB machine gun. That makes two ready to go, but we're a little light on ammo for all the guns."

"I know. We'll have to do something about that. But tonight, I have something else for you to do."

"Oh? What's that?"

"Fix a TOW missile." Brad grinned at the obvious surprise in his friend's eyes.

"Where'd you get a TOW? Or should I ask?"

"Ed, my brother from Montana, brought it, along with some M-16s and grenade launchers." He paused. "His militia had a little trouble out in Wyoming."

Hawk whistled. "So, he was involved in knocking off that judge. Guess I admire his courage, but . . ."

Brad frowned. "But not so smart if you value your life. Ed doesn't understand the difference between tactical and strategic. You can't cut off the head if you spend all your time whacking at the feet."

"Yeah, the federal buzzard takes a dim view of that. So, where's the stuff?"

Brad nodded toward the van. "In there. We'll unload it as soon as Ed gets back."

"When will that be?"

Brad glanced at his watch in irritation. "He was due back an hour ago."

"Looks like punctuality isn't his thing."

A pair of headlights flashed across the window. A dark vehicle swept past and around the corner, heading for the back.

"Guess that's him now," Brad said.

They waited. Footsteps sounded outside, crunching over the ice and snow. A shadowy face appeared at the window. Brad opened the door just as Ed began tapping on it with a key.

Ed hurried in. "Hi. Sorry I'm late," he said in a rush. "Got to talking to this guy at the convenience store and lost track of the time."

Brad clinched his fists. "What about? Our operations here are secret. You're not authorized to . . ."

"Quit jumping to conclusions!" Ed interrupted. "Give me a little credit, will you? We were only talking about Grand Haven. I'm new here, remember?"

"OK, OK." Brad glanced at Hawk, noting his furrowed brow. "Meet Mike Hawkins. Hawk was a sergeant with the Army Rangers. He's my second in command."

The two men shook hands. "Hi, I'm Ed Anderson."

"So your brother was telling me."

Brad saw Ed's questioning look and decided to ignore it. "Shall we get on with it? Let's get the truck unloaded so I can get my guys started on it tomorrow."

"What are you going to do to it?" Ed asked.

"I think we'll turn it into a weapons carrier."

"I don't know," Ed began.

Brad put his hands on his hips. "Let's get one thing straight, right now. You either submit to my authority, or you can hit the road. What'll it be?"

Ed frowned. "No need to get huffy. I just want some say in this. After all, it is my van."

"Fine! Is it OK with you if I spend my time and money on that old heap of yours so that the feds can't trace it to you?"

Ed remained silent.

"I'm serious," Brad continued. "Are you in or out? If you're in, this is my command." He waited through a few moments of silence. "Well?"

"I'm in," Ed mumbled.

"Good. Now, since I'm putting more money in your van than it's worth, it's only right you make it available for our operations. So, let's get the weapons out of it and down to the armory."

"OK."

Brad pulled out Ed's keys and opened the van's side and back doors, revealing heavy crates stacked high. "Hawk, grab that four-wheeler. Ed and I will hand out the boxes."

They made quick work of it. The first load took about a third of the crates. Hawk spotted some large boxes still in the truck.

"Where'd you get the TOW?" Hawk asked.

"Out of a National Guard Armory," Ed answered, snickering. "Saw it while we were picking up the M-16s and grenade launchers. Thought it might come in handy."

"Man, that's some firepower!" Hawk's eyes lingered. "That might come in handy."

"Let's get this stuff below," Brad said. He closed up the van and locked it.

He led the way to the corner of the shop nearest his office, just past the Coke machine. He unlocked two steel doors and swung them wide, revealing a freight elevator. Hawk and Ed pushed the four-wheeler onto the platform. Brad closed the doors and punched the button marked "B." The elevator lurched and started down. A heavy hydraulic growl seemed to permeate everything. A few moments later the platform stopped with a solid thud. Brad opened the doors and stood back while Hawk and Ed pushed their load into the armory.

Ed stopped and turned around. "Wow! Look at all this stuff!"

The basement was fully as large as the shop above. Steel shelving units ran lengthways, each holding neatly stacked crates of weapons and ammunition. The sharp smell of gun oil and powder filled the air, making it seem almost explosive. Workbenches and machine tools filled the far end. Although the fluorescent lights gave adequate illumination, the concrete walls and gray shelves seemed to drain it away.

Brad started pushing the cart down the aisle. "This is Hawk's domain. He's our gunsmith and armorer. He's been concentrating on weapons while I've been recruiting."

"So, how's it going?" Ed asked, following along behind.

"We've got forty-six now—forty-seven counting you, but my goal is to be able to field several hundred soldiers. We've got a good mix: some SEALs and Rangers, but a lot of ordinary soldiers and sailors as well— patriots who hate what the scumbags in Washington are doing to America."

"Taking our guns . . ."

"That, and all the other petty limits on our freedoms. And all the one-worlders who want to turn America over to the United Nations."

"I hear you."

They stopped beside an empty shelving unit.

"Let's put them here for now," Brad told Hawk.

One by one the heavy crates screeched across the steel shelves. Brad eyed each one, wondering what condition the weapons were in. Unfortunately, there wasn't a lot of ammunition.

"What all do you have in here?" Ed asked.

This brought a smile to the ex-Ranger's face. "We've got a good supply of rifles, pistols, and light machine guns. We currently have enough mortars, percussion grenades, and grenade launchers, but we're still acquiring. I've just started on the heavy machine guns. But we're short on ammo—that and special weapons like your TOW."

"*Our* TOW," Brad corrected. "Assuming you can fix it."

"I'll give it my best shot." He turned back to Ed. "Anyhow, what we've got is adequate for our present needs—except for ammo. But we'll have to add to it as our militia grows. As you can see, we've got plenty of room for more." He paused. "Say, what's wrong with that TOW?"

Ed's expression turned serious. "I don't know. We had it all set up outside Judge Richards's cabin, checked out and everything, then it developed some kind of error in the missile guidance set. We finally had to pack it up and take out the judge with grenades."

"OK, I'll see what I can find. Are all the parts there?"

"All except the hold-back pin. We lost it somewhere."

"I can probably make a replacement. We've got a full machine shop down here."

Brad thought about the antitank missile as they continued moving the weapons down into the armory, the TOW last of all. True, they only had one, but he knew what it could do. It just might come in handy, assuming Hawk could fix it. He glanced at the ex-Ranger, now locked in a reluctant conversation with Ed. If anyone could fix the TOW, Hawk could.

By the end of the week, Brad was ready for a few days off. But as stressful as it had been, a lot had been accomplished. As he had expected, Hawk had been able to fix the TOW missile—and machine a replacement hold-back pin. Also, the van conversion was going well. But best of all, Ed seemed to be fitting in.

Chapter Four

Barbara Post felt a strange combination of excitement and dread as she guided her blue Volvo C70 coupe onto the off-ramp from Highway 131 in downtown Grand Rapids. It was May now, and she was relieved her move was finally over. Actually, it wouldn't be entirely over for a few more days, when the van arrived from Dallas. But the important thing was, she was here ready to start her new job as special agent with the Grand Rapids ATF Field Office.

She turned left onto Fulton and followed it east and turned right on Ionia. And there was her new office, right where the Excite map had said it would be. She smiled. *Found it without getting lost,* she thought. It probably would be best not to be late on her first day. She parked, entered the building, and made her way to Suite 230.

The receptionist looked up from her computer. "Can I help you?" she asked.

"Hello. I'm Special Agent Barbara Post. Would you tell Mr. Oliver I'm here?"

The receptionist offered her a seat, then placed the call. Barbara glanced at the professional journals scattered on the low table but didn't see anything that looked interesting.

"Mr. Oliver is in a meeting," the young lady announced. "He said he'll be out as soon as he can."

"Thank you."

Several times Barbara glanced at the journals as the minutes dragged on. Finally she picked up one and started flipping through it, but she couldn't concentrate. Each time a man approached, she wondered if he was her new boss. But the only attention she received was mild curiosity. Finally a tall black man approached, and his eyes immediately locked on hers. He had a trim black mustache that gave him a distinguished look. *This is Dan Oliver?* Barbara wondered.

The man's smile seemed reserved. "Ms. Post—I'm Special Agent Sam Green. Dan's still tied up, so he sent me out to get you."

Barbara stood and held out her hand. Sam hesitated a moment then took it. "Pleased to meet you, Mr. Green."

There might have been a flicker of amusement in his brown eyes. "Call me Sam."

She nodded. "Sam. And I prefer Barbara to Ms. Post."

"Fine, Barbara. Why don't we go back to my office? I can start filling you in on our operations while we're waiting on Dan."

"Lead the way."

"Like some coffee?"

"Yes, I would."

Sam guided her into the break room, poured two mugs of coffee, and gave Barbara one. "Did you have any trouble finding us?"

"Not a bit," Barbara said. "The Excite maps do a good job of getting you there."

Sam chuckled. "Yeah, what would we do without the Internet?"

"It is rather handy."

Sam stopped outside a small office. "Welcome to my office, such as it is. It's a little cramped since we're tight on space. Please take a seat."

She chose one of the utilitarian side chairs. Sam sat in the plain swivel chair behind his desk. "I haven't heard where your office will be. My guess would be your predecessor's, but that's up to Dan. So, have you found a place to live?"

"Yes. I rented a garage apartment in Spring Lake."

"Oh, so you're out near Grand Haven. That's a nice area. It's convenient to Lake Michigan and not a bad commute. A lot better than living in the city."

Barbara had to listen carefully, since she found it difficult keeping up with Sam's rapid-fire speech. Then there was the matter of his accent.

"It's sure different from where I grew up," she said. "I drove over to Grand Haven yesterday and went up and down the coast. I've never seen anything like Lake Michigan—looks like an ocean. Where I come from, the only water we have is from windmills, stock tanks, and a few piddly old lakes."

A quizzical expression came to Sam's face. "I know you're from the Dallas office. Is that where you grew up?"

Barbara laughed. "Big D? Not hardly. I was born and raised in Marfa, Texas."

"What's that close to?"

"Nothing of any size. Marfa's the county seat of Presidio County, which borders on Mexico. Around three thousand people live there. Presidio is the only other good-sized town in the county. Just lots and lots of wide open spaces surrounded by mountains. El Paso is the closest city, but it's two hundred miles away."

"Desert?"

"Yep. We're in the northern end of the Chihuahuan Desert."

"Sounds desolate."

Barbara shrugged. "Marfa may be out in the boonies, but it does have a few claims to fame."

He arched his eyebrows. "Oh? Such as?"

"We're close to the Big Bend National Park—really pretty down there. McDonald Observatory and Fort Davis are to the north. And Marfa's where the movie *Giant* was filmed—in fact, you can still see the remains of the Reata ranch house on the Ryan Ranch outside of town. Then there's the Marfa Lights."

"What's that?"

"On clear nights, mysterious lights form south of town. They move about, merge, go racing off—weird stuff like that."

"You're kidding."

"No, and it's a real phenomenon. Even scientists don't know what causes it. Of course, the UFO buffs think it's flying saucers. People come from all over to see the lights. There's even a special observation turnout on the highway."

Sam's subdued smile returned. "Nothing like that around here, just pretty countryside, especially along the coast. Lake Michigan is spectacular."

"Are you from around here?"

"Yes, right here in the southeast part of town. My folks moved to Holland when I was fifteen. I went to high school there and graduated from Grand Valley State University in Allendale. That's where I met my wife, Alicia."

"Any children?"

His smile grew more pronounced. "Yes, two. Grace is seven, and Tamara just turned five."

"What beautiful names."

"Thank you. Gracie is as sweet a child as anyone could hope for. Tammie, however, thinks she's empress of the world; however she only has one loyal subject: Daddy. Mommy's wise to her ways."

Barbara laughed. "Yes, I'm afraid little girls are born cruise directors."

Sam glanced at his watch. "I have no idea how long Dan will be. Did he tell you anything about what you'll be doing?"

"He said I'd be working with you on militia projects, and he mentioned the president's initiative. He said he'd fill me in when I reported."

"That's my understanding. In fact, we're supposed to go over to Coast Guard Group Grand Haven at one o'clock to meet with some helicopter pilots. They're going to be providing transportation for us, as needed."

"Will Dan be going?"

"I'm not sure, but I don't think so."

Sam maintained eye contact for a few moments, then looked away, clearly embarrassed. Barbara became aware of the low murmur of office activity around them as she wondered what to do. Dan being tied up couldn't be helped; but she knew Sam probably had work to do, and keeping her company wasn't helping him any.

"Listen, I know you're busy," Barbara said finally. "I'll go out to the reception area and wait for Dan."

This seemed to fluster Sam. "No, that wouldn't be right. I really don't know what's keeping Dan—this isn't like him. Let me introduce you around, and if he's still not free, I'll take you by your office—I mean, it has to be your office—it's the only vacant one we have."

Barbara felt a twinge of misgiving. "Is there any reason why it wouldn't be mine?"

Sam's brow furrowed. "Not that I know of. But I asked Dan about it several days ago, and he said he'd have to think about it. We're scheduled for some remodeling, and I guess that could affect things." He paused. "We are tight on space here, no doubt about that. But still, you're our new special agent."

Barbara forced a smile as she stood up. "OK, Sam. I'm ready for the howdy rounds if you are."

Sam seemed relieved. "Shall we?" he asked.

Barbara did fairly well with her mental filing cabinet as she associated names with faces. She and Sam made their methodical way around the office. All of the agents and staffers were pleasant and seemed pleased to meet her. Most accents betrayed a northern or midwestern background; there was some variety as well, but hers was the only southwestern twang. After completing a final work interruption, Sam led Barbara back along the main corridor.

"That's Dan's office," Sam said as they passed a closed door. Across the hall was a small room. "And this was your predecessor's office." Sam shrugged. "As far as I know, this is your new home."

Barbara forced a laugh. "Well, I doubt anyone will object if I park here temporarily."

"Great. I'll bring you some reports to read. Militia stuff."

"OK."

He hurried away. Barbara entered the cramped office. She checked a few drawers in the desk and peeked in the file cabinet. Everything had been cleaned out. She picked up the phone. It worked. She sat down in the swivel chair behind the desk and looked out through the open door. She could see an edge of Dan's door. It was still closed. A few minutes later Sam brought in a thick stack of reports.

"Enjoy," he said as he plopped them down on a corner of the desk. "Would you like to grab a bite to eat before the meeting in Grand Haven?"

"Sounds good to me. When do you want to leave?"

He looked at his watch. "How about a little after eleven. That should give us plenty of time."

"I'll be ready."

She began sifting through the papers. Most of the Michigan militias she had heard of, but this information was more current and in considerable detail. When Barbara had joined the ATF, she had been surprised at how intensely militia members held their beliefs. Many groups were well beyond the fringe, and quite a few were rabidly racist. But the almost universal common denominator was a deep distrust of the federal government, especially concerning the right to bear arms.

One thin report described an ongoing investigation in Grand Haven. Barbara flipped to the front and saw that Sam had prepared it. Brad Anderson, the owner of Anderson's Automotive, was suspected of organizing a new militia, together with Michael Hawkins. The latter owned a gun store named The Flintlock. Barbara scanned the rest of the report. Mr. Hawkins was a member of a local gun club and had been observed firing licensed machine guns at a firing range. Both had military backgrounds. Anderson had been a Navy SEAL and Hawkins an Army Ranger. Beyond this, there wasn't much in the way of hard facts.

She heard a sound, looked up, and saw Sam.

"It's after eleven. Ready to go?"

"Sure." She grabbed her purse and a notepad.

Sam stopped at Dan's office on the way out and rapped on the door. There was no answer. Sam checked the knob. The door was locked. "That's odd," he said.

He led the way to the entrance. "Agent Post and I are leaving for Grand Haven," he told the receptionist. "I have my mobile phone if you need to reach me." He paused. "Has Mr. Oliver left the office?"

The woman nodded. "Yes, about a half hour ago."

"Did he say when he'd be back?"

"Tomorrow."

Barbara saw Sam's glance. There was no mistaking his confusion. He turned back to the receptionist. "I see. Thanks."

Sam waited until they were outside before continuing. "I suggest we take two cars since it'll be near quitting time before we can get back."

"OK. Where do you want to meet?"

"Follow me. I recommend we eat at Harbor Lights. It's on South Harbor Drive in Grand Haven. Good menu and a great view of the lake."

"Sounds good to me."

They took Interstate 96 out of Grand Rapids, then Highway 104 into Grand Haven, ending up on Beacon Boulevard. Barbara looked down from the bridge over the Grand River where the murky brown waters rippled and swirled. After crossing another bridge, Sam turned right. Large trees dotted the well-kept yards and parks, their thick green canopies a rich springtime green. Roses and tulips bloomed in Technicolor profusion as if celebrating the recent end of winter.

Jackson Street changed to Harbor Drive. They passed the Coast Guard Station Grand Haven on the right, followed by Group Grand Haven. The drive curved around to the south, paralleling the shore of Lake Michigan. Sam signaled for a turn. Up ahead Barbara saw the restaurant's sign. She pulled in and parked, then got out and gazed at the lake's deep blue waters. A fresh cool breeze tugged at her hair.

"Like the view?" Sam asked.

Numerous sailboats traced sedate courses parallel to the shore, sunlight reflecting off their colorful sails. "It's gorgeous." Further out a large ship, indistinct in the distance, plodded along toward the north.

Inside the restaurant, the hostess grabbed two menus and led her guests out on a large wooden deck, seating them near the rail under a red umbrella. Only a few tables were vacant. Harbor Lights was obviously a popular lunch spot. A few moments later a young man with long blond hair appeared. His eyes said he wished he were elsewhere.

"You folks decided yet?" he asked without really looking at them.

Barbara scanned the menu quickly. She considered asking him if they had Mexican food but suspected the young man was probably humor challenged. "I think I'll have the perch. And iced tea to drink."

Barbara looked around at the nautical décor. Nets were artistically draped around the deck perimeter, but instead of fish they held glass floats and seashells. This place was definitely serious about seafood.

"Got it." The beach boy turned to Sam. "And for you, sir?"

"I'll have a hamburger, fries, and a Coke."

The waiter wrote on his pad, took up the menus, and disappeared.

Barbara thought of Sam's order and tried to stifle a laugh but couldn't.

"What?" Sam said, his eyebrows knitted together.

"Here we are at a fish place, and you order a hamburger?"

"I happen to like hamburger. I've lived here all my life. I can have fresh fish anytime I want."

"OK. But why not go to a hamburger joint?"

He smiled. "A hamburger joint wouldn't have this view. Besides, I thought you might like the fish. This place is quite famous for its food."

"That was thoughtful. Thanks."

The waiter reappeared quicker than Barbara expected and placed the platters and drinks. He dispensed his wish that they enjoy, along with a vague promise that he would check on them later. Barbara looked at the lightly battered, deep-fried perch. It looked and smelled wonderful. When she looked up, Sam was giving his fries a generous salting.

At a certain point in her life, Barbara had decided it was important to thank the Lord at all meals, even when eating out. The first few times she had done this, she had felt self-conscious, but she had stuck with it. She bowed her head and gave her thanks in a silent prayer. When she raised her head, she was surprised to see that Sam had his head bowed. As she watched, he looked up.

"Are you a Christian?" she asked.

"Yes. Are you?"

"That's right." She felt embarrassed. "Somehow . . ."

His expression became stern. "You assumed I wasn't."

"I didn't know," she said. "I mean, how could I? We don't wear signs."

"No, but maybe we should. Maybe it should be more apparent."

She sighed. "Probably." Then she brightened. "I'm glad you are."

Sam's smile returned. "Now you don't have to save my soul, is that it?"

"No. It means we have more in common than just working for the bureau."

"Perhaps." He glanced at his watch. "Don't want to rush you, but we better eat. I need to brief you before our meeting, and I can't do that in this crowd."

His words seemed to draw the lakeside vista back in, as the carefree day dissolved into worry over what militias could do to an unsuspecting public. Barbara started eating her perch. Although it was excellent, her thoughts would not let her enjoy it. She recalled Pahaska Tepee, her first experience with a violent death crime scene. Although she had not seen Judge Richards's body, the photos of his mangled corpse were seared into her brain. The shattered, bloodstained snowmobile gave mute evidence to the lethal intent. Barbara shivered.

They finished their lunch and left the restaurant. Sam led the way to a secluded bench facing the beach.

"Did you have time to read the reports?" Sam asked.

"I scanned them."

"What did you think?"

"The more I learn about militias, the more I worry. Many are harmless wackos, but some are real threats."

"Right. Domestic terrorism is on the rise—no doubt about it. The Oklahoma City bombing indicates a trend, not an isolated incident. And if a militia dares to take out a federal judge, where will it stop? These groups are definitely growing."

"I know, and unfortunately, the government has made mistakes too. We did some bad things at Ruby Ridge and Waco, for example."

"True. But these guys are saying it's some one-world, United Nations conspiracy to take away their guns and freedoms. That's just not true."

"I agree. So, what are we going to be working on?"

"Investigating western Michigan militias for now. Later we'll help prepare for the president's visit."

"When will that be?"

Sam looked all around and lowered his voice. "This is top secret. It's tentatively scheduled for the first week in June. The administration will set the exact date in a few weeks. Word has it the Secret Service is having a cow over it. Ever since the president announced his initiative, we've been hearing death threats."

"Are they credible?"

"We're not sure, but I can tell you the bureau's worried about it. Same for the FBI and especially the Secret Service. I believe militiamen pose a credible threat. Our job is to make sure they don't get the chance."

"I see. Are we going to be investigating that new militia?"

"You mean the one in Grand Haven?"

"Yes."

"That will be our highest priority. The older militias could give us trouble, but this one is right where the president's going to be."

"Your report was a little thin on details. Are you sure Anderson and Hawkins are actually organizing a militia?"

Sam hesitated. "I can't say for sure since we've just started the investigation. But I'm convinced they are." He snapped his fingers. "Oh, I heard something about the Judge Richards case you'll be interested in. We found out where the stolen C-4 came from."

"Where?"

"The McAlester Army Ammunition Plant in Oklahoma. The FBI sniffed out who they think the inside contact is."

"Did they arrest him?"

"No. They're keeping him under surveillance in hopes we can find out who his buddies are."

"That would be a nice break."

"Hope so. We sure need one."

Chapter Five

Barbara glanced at her watch as she and Sam entered Coast Guard Group Grand Haven, noting that they were a few minutes late. Sam led the way upstairs to a door near the end of the corridor and knocked.

Barbara looked in as the door swung open. A tall, blond officer wearing a blue uniform faced them, his blue eyes engaging hers for a moment. She felt her pulse quicken. *Nice smile,* she thought. And with his Nordic features, he certainly looked like he belonged up north. The young officer turned to Sam.

"Good afternoon, Mr. Green," he said.

"Hello, Mr. Phillips," Sam replied. "This is my associate, Special Agent Barbara Post."

"Nice to meet you, Ms. Post," Craig said. "I'm Lieutenant Craig Phillips."

She held out her hand. He took it and squeezed gently. "My pleasure," Barbara said with a nervous intensity she didn't intend. She maintained her smile as she groaned inwardly at how that must have sounded to him.

"And is this your copilot?" Sam asked.

"Yes," Craig said, stepping to the side. "Meet my partner in crime, Lieutenant (junior grade) Joel Foscue."

The young man shook their hands.

"Sorry we're late," Sam continued. "Barbara is new in our office, and I was bringing her up to speed on our operations."

"Quite all right, sir," Craig replied.

"Shall we get started?"

Barbara watched as Sam took the chair at the head of the table. After a short hesitation, she sat immediately to his right. Craig sat in the chair directly opposite her with Joel next to him.

"First order of business," Sam said. "I'm Sam, and Barbara's told me she doesn't like being called 'Ms. Post.'" He smiled at her. "Gents, we're going to be working together closely, so I recommend we drop the formality."

"OK by me," Craig replied.

Joel nodded.

"Have you moved down to the Muskegon air facility yet?" Sam asked Craig.

"Yes, sir . . . I mean, yes, we have. We're ready to provide you air transport."

"Good. As Dan Oliver mentioned, what we discuss here is classified top secret. However, since the operation is about to begin, you may brief your crew—but no one else."

"We understand."

"I know you do. Now, you already know about the president's trip. Once that's firmed up, you'll be working with us to augment the Secret Service, FBI, and the state and local police. This will be, as you say, an all-hands effort."

Craig nodded. "Given the circumstances, not surprising."

"Right. But for now, Barbara and I need your help in our ongoing investigations. As you recall, we believe there's a new militia forming in Grand Haven. Needless to say, that makes us nervous, especially with the president's visit looming. So we'll be concentrating on that for the time being."

"When do we start?"

"Sometime this week. Barbara needs a day or so to get settled in, then we'll begin in earnest." Sam paused and looked at her. "That sound OK to you?"

"I'll be ready," she replied.

Sam spent the next hour briefing the aviators on militia operations in west Michigan, emphasizing those around Muskegon, Wolverine, and the suspected new group in Grand Haven. Craig and Joel listened, making notes in small spiral notebooks.

"That's about it," Sam said when he finished. "Any questions?"

"No, this seems pretty straightforward," Craig replied, "and our orders are clear. As you know, we're available for search-and-rescue, but your operations come first." His glance took in Barbara. "You can reach us through either Group Grand Haven or Air Facility Muskegon."

Barbara tucked her notepad into her purse.

"Very good," Sam said as they all stood. "We appreciate your help."

The ATF agents left the building. Barbara smiled as she and Sam walked through the parking lot. The richness of the northern springtime was still new to her. The tops of the stately trees swayed in the gentle breeze, showing off new green growth.

Sam unlocked his car and opened the door. "I'll see you in the morning."

"Right." She gave a nervous laugh. "Maybe I can finally catch Dan and go over my job with him."

Sam didn't reply at once. When he did, it sounded forced. "Sounds like a plan to me."

He ducked into his car and closed the door. He backed out and left the lot. Barbara heard voices approaching as she walked toward her car. Craig and Joel were nearing a fire-engine red Mitsubishi 3000GT.

" . . . you sure she's coming by for you?" Joel asked.

Craig laughed. "She said she was! Course she might get to talking to someone and let the time slip up on her. Go on. I know you're in a hurry to get back. I'll be all right. If she's not here in a few minutes, I'll give her a call."

"OK. See you tomorrow."

Joel slid behind the wheel of his sleek sports car and drove off with a flair not inconsistent with youth and his chosen profession. The powerful engine's roar gradually faded into the more subdued city sounds.

Barbara reached her car and punched the remote. The electric locks opened with loud thunks.

Craig looked around at the sound. He smiled when he saw her. "Oh, hi," he said.

"Hello." She started to open the door then stopped. "I couldn't help hearing. Do you need a ride?"

He walked over. "Thanks for the offer, but someone's coming for me."

"Are you sure? I don't mind. I live near here."

His eyes widened. "You do?"

The phone clipped to his belt chirped. He grabbed it and poked the "talk" button.

"Lieutenant Phillips," he said. As he listened, his smile faded. "No! Don't try anything else. Didn't you see it when you drove in?" He closed his eyes as he listened to the answer. "OK, OK. Don't get excited. The post is up against the left rear; is that right? OK, here's what you do. Turn the wheel all the way to the . . ." He stopped talking, and an exasperated look came to his face. "Wait—now calm down. Sit tight, and I'll be there as soon as I can." He nodded and looked right at Barbara. "No, I won't be long. It'll be all right. OK?" He listened for the reply then said, "Bye. Love you too." He punched the phone off.

Barbara watched as a sheepish grin came to his face.

"Ms. Post—I mean, Barbara. Can I take you up on your offer?"

"Of course. Is something wrong?"

He cleared his throat. "Uh, that was my ride. My mother has managed to get her van up against a telephone pole—she's not the best driver in the world. I told her I'd come take care of it."

"Oh, I see." She didn't really, but it seemed the right thing to say. "Get in."

Barbara started the car and backed out. "Where are we going?"

"Grand Hope Nursing Home. Mom was visiting a friend from church. Take the first right."

Barbara made the turn and followed Craig's directions. Soon she spotted the facility's sign. Four long wings came together at the entrance like a tall "X" lying on its side.

Craig pointed. "It's that silver Chevy van over there."

"I see it," Barbara said. She looked around. The lot was almost full except for a few handicapped slots. Then she saw a space near the end.

"You can just drop me off," Craig said.

"I'll wait until I know everything's all right."

Barbara parked, and they got out. She followed Craig as he approached the van. A middle-aged lady with blonde hair turned her head as she heard them. Her blue eyes looked just like Craig's. She opened her mouth to speak but stopped when she saw Barbara.

Craig took a long look at the black telephone pole, jammed up against the side of the van. He shook his head. "I won't ask how you did this."

The lady smiled. "Thank you, dear," she said. "I thought about taking care of it myself but talked myself out of it." Her eyes shifted to Barbara. "Aren't you going to introduce me to your friend?"

Craig turned a little. "Oh, she's not a friend." He stopped, and Barbara saw his face flush. "I didn't mean it like that. Barbara, this is my mother, Elizabeth. Mother, I'd like you to meet Barbara Post. She's a special agent with the ATF—the Bureau of Alcohol, Tobacco, and Firearms."

"I know what 'ATF' stands for," Elizabeth said. She shifted her eyes back to Barbara. "How are you, dear? So nice to meet you. Please forgive my son's manners. I've tried my best in raising him, but there's only so much a mother can do."

Barbara giggled at the twinkle in Elizabeth's eye. "I'm pleased to meet you, Mrs. Phillips." She cut her eyes toward Craig. His expression said he was long-suffering. "I think your son is a perfect gentleman."

Elizabeth looked doubtful, but the twinkle was still there. "You're very kind, and please call me Elizabeth." She paused. "You have such an interesting accent, dear. Where did you grow up?"

"Marfa, Texas."

"Oh? Where is that?"

"Two hundred miles from anywhere. Marfa's a small town in the desert southwest. El Paso is the closest city."

"How interesting. Have you lived in Michigan long?"

"Only a few days. I'm renting an apartment in Spring Lake. My office is in Grand Rapids."

"How convenient—I mean, the coast is so much nicer. I'm sure you'll enjoy being near the lake."

"Excuse me," Craig interrupted.

Elizabeth looked at him. "Yes, dear?"

"You did want me to do something about this, didn't you?"

She glanced at the offending pole then turned back. "I'd appreciate it."

"This wouldn't have happened if you had parked in a handicapped spot."

"There was only one space when I got here. I was afraid someone might drive in who needed it more than me." She looked away in obvious embarrassment.

"All the more reason to use a handicapped spot."

Her eyes flashed. "I get along quite well, thank you."

Craig rolled his eyes. "Forget I said anything. You want me to drive, or shall I tell you how to do it?"

"I think you should drive."

Craig and Barbara walked to the passenger side. A whining noise started up inside the van. Barbara watched as the driver seat moved back. The side door unlocked and rolled back. Elizabeth raised the right armrest and lifted herself into the adjacent wheelchair. She punched a button on the remote in her hand, and the driver's seat returned to the front. She pressed another button, and the lift moved out and swung down to the ground. Elizabeth rolled clear, then retracted the ramp and closed the door.

She and Barbara followed Craig as he went around, knelt down, and examined the impact site. The telephone pole depressed the van's rear panel but hadn't dented it. A black streak ran forward to the point of initial contact. Craig touched it and shook his head.

"He takes things so seriously," Elizabeth whispered.

Barbara giggled.

"What was that?" Craig asked.

"Nothing, dear," his mother replied. "Carry on with your duties."

He got in the van, rolled down the window, and looked back at the pole. He started the engine, turned the wheel all the way to the left, and backed up slowly. The van's rear panel squealed against the obstruction for a few moments, ceasing as the two came apart. Craig put the van in park, shut off the engine, and got out.

"There you are," he said. "I'll clean off the streak this weekend."

"Thank you, dear," Elizabeth said. She turned and looked at Barbara. "And thank you for bringing him. Will you join us for dinner? We have plenty, and we'd love to have you."

This caught Barbara by surprise. She liked Elizabeth's friendly, straightforward style. And Craig's rugged good looks were only too apparent.

"I'd love to," she said finally.

"Lovely." Elizabeth glanced at her watch. "Oh, my. I'm late picking William up."

"William's my nephew," Craig explained. "He's staying with his grandma . . ." He paused. "Along with my sister-in-law."

"Susan is visiting a friend in Muskegon," Elizabeth said with obvious reluctance.

"I see."

"We can pick up William," Barbara offered.

"That would be a great help, if you don't mind."

"No trouble at all."

"See you at the house, then."

Elizabeth turned her wheelchair and rolled around to the van's side door. She operated the remote control like a conductor, opening the door and lowering the lift. Soon she was back inside and behind the wheel.

"That is some fancy van," Barbara said as she and Craig walked back to her car.

"Yes, it is," Craig agreed. "I don't know what Mom would do without it. It's a custom conversion by Anderson's Automotive. It was expensive, but they really did a nice job."

Barbara waited until they were inside the car. "Do you know Brad Anderson?"

Craig's blond eyebrows arched at this. "I've talked with him a few times. His repair shop has an excellent reputation—the guy really knows what he's doing. He's an ex-Navy SEAL, and that's about all I know. Why do you ask?"

Barbara hesitated. Technically, Craig was not privy to the ATF investigation, but he and his crew could not avoid learning things as they provided transportation for the bureau. Besides, Craig was no dummy.

"This must go no further." She saw the recognition in his eyes.

"I understand. You mean . . ."

She nodded. "We suspect he's involved with the new Grand Haven militia."

Craig shook his head. "That's hard to believe. Brad seems like such a nice guy."

"We're not positive, but I think it's highly likely. Anything unusual about him?"

"Not really, except he's got the best equipped and maintained garage I've ever seen, and he makes his mechanics keep it clean. I was in his office once. He's got all sorts of SEAL stuff on the walls. He's what you'd call gung ho."

"Fits the profile," Barbara said. "What about a guy by the name of Michael Hawkins? He owns a gun store named The Flintlock."

"Don't know him. I've seen the store but never been inside." He paused. "I hate the thought of what's happening."

"It's a growing problem." Barbara started the car and backed out. "Where do we pick up William?"

"School. Turn right leaving the lot."

They made the trip quickly. Barbara inched forward in the long line of cars and minivans picking up children.

"There he is," Craig said. He rolled down his window and started waving. "William! Over here!"

The boy's eyes swept past them several times before he finally connected. He looked at his uncle then at Barbara as if he didn't know what to do.

"Come on," Craig said.

William sauntered over and got in the backseat. He had light brown hair and brown eyes and seemed around eight or nine. He wore jeans, a long-sleeve shirt, and carried a huge backpack.

Craig turned around. "Hey, dude. How was school?"

"Boring." The boy shrugged his way out of the backpack. His eyes darted over to Barbara.

"William, this is Barbara Post," Craig said. "Grandma invited her to dinner."

"Howdy, William," Barbara said, reaching over the seat to offer her hand in a high five.

William's face scrunched up in a questioning look as he gave her hand a perfunctory swipe. "You talk funny," he said.

"William!" Craig said. "That's rude!"

The boy hunched his shoulders. "Well, she does."

Barbara laughed. "Maybe you're the one who talks funny."

"What?" he said.

"Back where I come from, everyone talks like me."

"Really? Where are you from?"

"A small town in southwest Texas."

"Wow. Do you have a horse?"

"No, I'm afraid I don't. But I know how to ride. We've got lots of horses and cattle around my hometown. In fact, we've got all kinds of interesting critters: coyotes, wild pigs, roadrunners, and tarantulas the size of bowling balls."

"Cool!"

Craig cocked an eyebrow at his nephew. "Only cool?"

"Way cool!" William amended.

Craig turned to Barbara. "I haven't seen him that excited since Mom let him operate the van's remote control."

William leaned forward as far as the shoulder belt would allow. "Got any cattle rustlers?"

Barbara laughed. "Actually, sometimes we do. But it's not like the old days. The sheriff doesn't call out the posse anymore."

"How's he catch 'em then?"

"He uses his pickup truck, mostly. Sometimes a squad car."

"You got police cars in Texas?"

"Well, yes. And paved roads, and airports, and even shopping centers and malls."

"Really?"

"Let's not wear our guest out," Craig said.

"But . . ."

"Later."

Craig leaned close. "Wish he'd get that interested in his schoolwork," he whispered.

"I heard that!" came from the backseat.

Barbara grinned and decided she didn't mind Craig being close. She started the car and pulled out into traffic. She crept along until they were out of the school zone. "OK, Lieutenant Phillips, plot us a course."

"Aye, aye, ma'am. All ahead two-thirds and steady as she goes."

She narrowed her eyes. "Roger that."

"Not bad. Maybe you should become a Coastie."

"Think I'll stick with the ATF."

"Pity."

Craig directed her toward the east side of town. Barbara pulled into the driveway behind Elizabeth's van. William jumped out, dashed for the front door, and clattered inside. Craig looked over at Barbara. He didn't say anything, although he looked like he wanted to. A warm sensation stole over Barbara that had nothing to do with the fine spring day. Craig finally turned, stepped out of the car, and came around to her side.

Barbara got out and looked up at the large, two-story house. It was painted white with green shutters.

"Very pretty," she said, quite aware of his nearness.

"Yes, it is. This is where I grew up."

The way he said it told Barbara that it had been a happy childhood. With a mother like Elizabeth, that wasn't surprising.

The front door banged open, and William raced out.

"That kid doesn't walk anywhere," Craig whispered.

"When's Mom coming home?" William demanded, looking up at Craig. "All Grandma would tell me is she's in Muskegon visiting a friend."

"I don't know. Your mother's going through a hard time right now."

"She doesn't love me!" He looked down and kicked at the grass.

"Yes she does. Give her time."

He glared at his uncle. "Then why is she seeing that guy in Muskegon?"

Barbara saw the unshed tears in William's eyes. Her heart went out to him.

"We'll talk about it later," Craig said.

"You don't care either!"

Before Craig could say anything, William whirled around and ran back inside. The front door slammed shut.

"Wish you hadn't heard that," Craig said.

"That's all right. Bless his heart. Lord knows, there's a lot of hurt in this world."

"There's something I guess you need to know. Susan's a widow. My brother, Larry, died in December, so she and William are still getting over that."

Barbara sensed Craig's uneasiness. "I'm so sorry."

"Thanks." He looked toward the house. "Ready to go in?"

"Yes."

His hand brushed against hers as they walked along. He held the door for her. Barbara went inside and looked around at the spacious, high-ceilinged entryway. A thick hooked rug covered part of the dark hardwood floor. An antique marble-top table with spindly black legs sat underneath a springtime landscape oil painting. The spacious living room was on the right.

Craig waved toward the living room. "Please, make yourself comfortable."

Barbara looked around. A large couch sat near the front windows, and chairs circled the room, interspersed with decorative tables. The pieces were old but well-kept. Barbara sat at one end of the couch and looked toward the dining room. Craig stood in the entryway for a few moments then crossed the living room in long strides. After a brief hesitation, he sat in the center of the couch, not close to her but not all that far away either.

"Do you think your mother would like some help?" Barbara asked.

Craig nodded toward the dining room door into the kitchen. "She'd have a fit if you went in there. You're her guest—our guest." He smiled. "That wheelchair doesn't slow her down, if that's what you're thinking. After her accident, we had the entire house remodeled—especially the kitchen."

"How did it happen?" Barbara asked.

Craig hesitated before answering. "Mom and Dad were skiing in Vermont, and she got on an advanced slope by mistake. Dad tried to stop her, but he couldn't catch up. She got going real fast and fell. She slammed into a tree—broke some ribs and fractured her lower spine. It paralyzed her legs, but not her spirit."

"That's easy to see."

"And William is a big help. He doesn't mind as long as he doesn't have to do any sissy stuff." Craig glanced her way. "His words, not mine."

Barbara suppressed a giggle. "Why, Lieutenant Phillips. Are you afraid I might take that as an insensitive remark and hit you with my purse?"

A cautious grin came to his face. "It can be a hazardous subject, and I'm not wearing my flak jacket."

"You can rest easy. Where I come from, men are men, and women like it that way." She paused. "But times change, like it or not. I'm single. After I finished college, what was I supposed to do, wait tables?"

"I understand."

"Do you?" She looked into his eyes and saw only concern there.

"Not perfectly, of course, but I care."

Elizabeth rolled into the dining room with a tray across the armrests of her wheelchair, and she and William began setting the table. A half hour later, she called them to dinner. Craig sat at the head of the table across from his mother. After Craig gave the blessing, Elizabeth started the dishes around.

It was a simple dinner: salad, beef stew and string beans, with apple cobbler for dessert. Barbara enjoyed it thoroughly, and the animated conversation, much of which came from William's curiosity about what he called the wild west. The boy's disappointment was evident when he discovered it wasn't nearly as wild as in the past. However, he perked up when Barbara told him about the bears and mountain lions that were common in the Big Bend. Elizabeth clearly wanted to know more about her guest, but she showed considerable subtlety in her probing questions.

All too soon the dinner was over. Elizabeth rolled back from the table. "Thank you for coming, dear," she told Barbara. "I've enjoyed getting to know you."

"Thank you for inviting me," Barbara said as she and Craig stood. "Everything was delicious."

Elizabeth looked over at William. "I had good help. Now, if you two will excuse us, my assistant and I have things to do in the kitchen."

"But Grandma," William complained. "I'm not done asking about mountain lions."

"Yes, you are."

"But . . ."

"Now!"

He stuck out his lower lip and stomped off into the kitchen.

"Hope to see you again real soon," Elizabeth said.

"I do too," Barbara replied, realizing she really meant it. "Bye."

Elizabeth wheeled around and left the room, closing the swinging door as she went.

"I'd better be going," Barbara said. "I'm still settling into my apartment."

He smiled. "Sounds like fun."

She started for the door. "Do you need a ride?"

"No, thanks. I'm staying here for the summer. I don't want Mom dealing with William and Susan by herself."

"I understand. I'll pray for you all."

"I appreciate it."

The cool, damp breeze made Barbara shiver. She sensed Craig's closeness as they walked slowly toward her car. She chided herself for her heightened awareness, this interest in someone she had only met today. But there was no denying her attraction. She unlocked the doors with her remote.

"I guess I'll see you when we start our investigation," she said.

He cleared his throat. "May I ask you out sometime?"

She felt an icy tingle in her stomach. "Yes, I'd like that." She fumbled in her purse and almost dropped it. She finally located a small pad and wrote down her mobile phone number. "Here."

He took the slip of paper. Barbara got in her car and began the short trip to Spring Lake. She thought about the young Coast Guard officer, wondering how he felt about her.

Chapter Six

Barbara walked into the office determined to talk to Dan Oliver if she had to track him down personally. She was about to ask the receptionist where he was when the young lady spoke.

"Mr. Oliver left word you were to see him immediately," she said.

Barbara felt the heat rising in her face. "Good morning. I'm fine. Thank you for asking!" She closed her eyes and wished she had not lost her temper.

"What?"

Barbara took a calming breath. "Never mind. Mr. Oliver, I presume, is in his office?"

"Why, yes. Where else would he be?"

"I plead the fifth on that."

Barbara hurried away before her interlocutor could respond. She stopped outside Dan's office and knocked.

"Come in," a voice inside said.

Barbara opened the door and looked in. She took in his accusing brown eyes, balding head, and middle-aged spread in a glance. Actually, his middle did a little more than spread. "I'm Barbara Post. I understand you wanted to see me."

"Yeah, I guess you could say that. You apparently think we run a country club here—you know, come and go as you please. I understand you knocked off early yesterday, probably thought it didn't matter being your first day and all."

Barbara gritted her teeth. "What?" she almost shouted.

"Are you hard of hearing?"

"It would have been nearly quitting time before I could make it back. Sam suggested . . ."

"Do you work for Sam or me?"

"For you—of course."

"That's a relief! Thought maybe I was slipping. Ms. Post, let's get something straight right now. I run a tight ship here. I expect performance, and I get it." He threw up his hands. "But I really don't expect a woman to understand that."

Barbara's mind was a whirlwind of anger, but she couldn't decide on what, exactly, she wanted to attack. "If you doubt my performance, I suggest you check my record."

"Hey, I'm not talking about your performance. I'm talking about your attendance. I don't tolerate goofing off."

"I wasn't goofing off."

"What time did you finish your official ATF duties yesterday?"

Barbara hesitated. "I'm not sure. Close to three, I guess."

"My, my. Even bankers do better than that." Barbara started to speak, but he hurried on. "Can it. As I told you before, either do the job or you're out—makes no difference to me either way."

"I can do my work."

"Good. Oh, one more thing. I don't baby my agents, so don't expect any concessions to feminine sensibilities or whatever you call them. Understand?"

"I'm beginning to," Barbara said through clinched teeth.

Dan frowned. "What's that supposed to mean?"

"If you'll direct me to my office, I'll get down to work."

"Oh, yeah. That presents another problem. We're tight on space right now."

"I know. Sam told me."

"Actually, you're arriving at a bad time."

"I'm sorry to inconvenience you."

Dan rocked back in his chair and looked up at the ceiling. When he lowered his head, his scowl was even darker. "That kind of attitude is exactly what we don't need around here. Now get this straight, Ms. Post. Until the bureau approves an expansion, we're short on office space, and to make matters worse, we need a second conference room as well. I've called in a maintenance crew to convert the open office. It won't be as large as I'd like, but it will have to do."

Barbara couldn't believe what she was hearing. "You don't mean the office across from yours?"

"That's the only open office we have." He enunciated each word slowly and clearly.

"But . . . where will I be?"

"I'm having a temporary cubicle built out in the reception area."

"What?"

"Much as I'm enjoying this conversation, you really must excuse me. I've got work to do." He picked up a report and started reading it. Barbara turned. "And close the door on your way out," Dan added.

It took all her self-control, but Barbara managed to close Dan's door without slamming it. She took a few deep breaths as she considered where to go and what to do. Finally she started toward Sam's office and was almost there when he came out. He saw her and smiled, but this quickly faded.

"Good morning," he said with no inflection.

"May I come in?" she asked, not breaking stride.

"Uh, of course. Would you like some coffee? I was about to get some."

"No."

Barbara swept past him and sat in a side chair. Sam hesitated, then closed the door and sat in his swivel chair.

"Is something wrong?" he asked.

Barbara told him what Dan had said about converting the spare office to a conference room. She considered unburdening herself concerning the rest of Dan's outrageous behavior but decided that might not be wise. At the very least, she knew she could not be entirely objective at the moment. Better to wait and calm down.

"What am I supposed to do?" Barbara asked. "I have no idea when the cubicle will be ready."

"I don't know. Would you like me to talk to Dan about it?"

"No, no! Don't do that!"

"Well, you can share my office until we find out."

"No, that wouldn't be right," Barbara said. "It would interfere with your work." She paused. "Dan's got to do something. I mean, I'm one of his special agents. I've got to have a place to work."

"No arguing that. I guess you could use the spare office until the maintenance people start in on it."

Barbara nodded. "Yeah, I guess that's my best bet." She got up. Sam also stood. Barbara tried to smile. "I appreciate you listening."

"You're welcome."

She hurried out and down the corridor. As she approached the spare office, she heard sounds inside. A workman inched out the door guiding the desk on a dolly. She waited until he had it out then looked inside. Another man was tilting a file cabinet up so he could get a dolly under it. On the floor, beside the phone, sprawled a toppled stack of papers—the militia reports she had been reading. The top report had a black oval smear where someone had stepped on it. Barbara hurried in, scooped up the mound, and stood up. The man working on the file cabinet looked around, then resumed his struggles. Barbara turned and saw Dan standing in the doorway. He was looking past her to the worker.

"I see you guys are hard at it."

"Yes. Should be done by the end of the day."

"Good." Dan's eyes swept over Barbara, then he turned and returned to his office. His door closed with a muted thump.

"Excuse me," the worker said as he pushed the file cabinet past.

Barbara followed the man out. Not knowing what else to do, she took the reports out to the front. The receptionist looked up momentarily then lowered her eyes again, as if her curiosity had been satisfied.

Barbara dropped the papers on a low table and sat down. She picked up Sam's report on the new Grand Haven Militia and had to read the first page several times before her anger dissipated enough so she could concentrate. She studied Brad Anderson's profile carefully, then turned to Michael Hawkins's. Barbara knew that militias varied greatly, ranging from ineffective paranoids to paramilitary teams that were frightening in their dedication and abilities. There was no question that the Grand Haven Militia fell in the latter group, judging from these two men.

Barbara looked up at the sound of squeaking wheels coming from the corridor. One of the maintenance men parked the displaced desk near the receptionist. Over the next few minutes the file cabinets joined it. Barbara shut out the interruptions as best she could.

"Excuse me," a voice near her said.

She looked up and saw one of the men holding a cubicle partition. "Yes?"

"Sorry to bother you, but I've got to move the table and those chairs. We're building the new cube in this corner."

Barbara retreated to the other side of the reception area and watched as the men went about their work. It didn't take long. The walls locked together like a giant Lego set. Instead of the ancient desk and file cabinets, the cube came furnished with a wraparound work surface and integrated drawer and file cabinet units. The men finished their work and took away the old office furniture, leaving a single guest chair for the cubicle.

In the ensuing calm, Barbara sorted through the reports, looking for the one on the Muskegon Militia. Again the sound of squeaking wheels interrupted. A thin young man pushed a cart into the reception area. He grabbed a mini-tower computer and set it and a monitor on the cubicle's work surface. He plugged the equipment together and ran a cable to a floorboard jack. Next came the phone. He disappeared momentarily, returning with a steno swivel chair. He booted up the computer, changed a few settings, then logged off to the sign-on screen. He scribbled something on a sticky-note and stuck it to the monitor's screen. Only then did he turn to Barbara.

"Ms. Post?" he said.

"Yes."

"Got you all set up. Are you familiar with networks and Microsoft Office?"

"Yes. I have been in the bureau for awhile."

His laugh was strained. "Yes, ma'am. Just checking. I wrote your ID on the sticky-note. The initial password is the same as your ID. You'll have to change it first time you log on. If you have any problems, call the help desk."

"OK. Do I have dial-up access?"

"Sure." He scribbled on the note. "Dial this number and use your regular ID and password. Should get you right in."

"Thanks," Barbara said, not really sure that she meant it.

"No problem." He grabbed the cart and disappeared into the back.

Barbara picked up her peripatetic papers and carried them into her new office. She sat down at her computer, pulled the sticky-note off the monitor, and signed on, changing her password as she did. After making sure the computer applications worked, she sat back in the steno chair and looked around.

She had almost made up her mind to call Dan's boss in the Detroit office, but on reflection she decided this might not be such a good idea. She was convinced that Dan didn't want a female special agent, and that, if true, was illegal. However, Barbara knew he could give plausible reasons for most of what he had done. She had seen enough of the office to know that they really were short on space. How Dan utilized the space was up to him, and he had provided her with all the office space and equipment she needed to do her job. Proving sexual discrimination would not be easy, and the attempt would almost certainly be messy. Then there was the question of what the Lord would think about it. Barbara felt her righteous indignation begin to fade as she considered her ultimate role model. Her resolve returned. She would succeed, but she would do it the right way.

Chapter Seven

Ed Anderson slouched in Brad's recliner, munching on a sandwich. He reached for his brew and took a healthy swig as he surfed the cable channels. There wasn't anything on he really wanted to see; it was just something to do. The phone rang. Ed considered letting the answering machine get it, but curiosity overcame him. He put down the remote, grabbed the portable phone, and punched the "talk" button.

"Hello," he said.

"Ed—that you?"

He felt an icy chill in the pit of his stomach. "How'd you find me?"

"It wasn't hard. You told me your brother lived in Grand Haven."

"Are you crazy? What if they trace this call?"

"Cool it. I'm calling from a pay phone. Our friend is looking for you."

"I don't care! I told you guys to lay low!"

"I know, but it's been quiet. I don't think the feds are on to me. Anyway, FYI, there's an ammo shipment that's going to the 46th Infantry Brigade in Wyoming, Michigan. You interested?"

Ed thought it over. He knew that Brad was short on ammunition. "I don't know. Guess it wouldn't hurt to check it out."

"OK. Got something to write with? I'll give you the number."

Ed jumped up and hurried into the kitchen. He grabbed a pad and pen. "OK. Shoot." He scribbled rapidly.

"He'll be there at 7:00 P.M.—six o'clock his time," the man concluded. "If you don't call in five minutes, he's gone."

"I understand. But listen. Don't call me again! Understand?"

"Roger that." There was a slight pause. "Don't forget your friends."

"I won't."

Ed punched the "off" button and checked his watch. It was nearly noon. He had seven hours to kill. He considered telling Brad about the call, but decided he would have to think about it.

—◆—◆—◆—

It was around 4:30 when Barbara heard a rap on the cubicle wall. She turned to see a solemn black face peering in at her.

"Hi, thought I'd come by and see how you were doing. May I come in?"

She struggled to smile. "Sure, have a seat. It's a bit snug."

Sam nodded. "Dan's been after the bureau about more space. I'm sure he'll get you an office as soon as he can."

Barbara considered asking Sam if they really needed a second conference room but decided it would be a cheap shot. "We'll see."

"How are you doing on the reports?"

"I'm almost done. These groups are scary."

"Yeah, and they're growing like wildfire. I'm glad the president is trying to do something. I have no argument with the right to bear arms, but we have to come down on the violent element."

"That's for sure."

"Any suggestions?"

"I recommend concentrating on that new militia in Grand Haven. We know the least about them, and this Brad Anderson seems to know what he's doing."

"Yes, and the president kicking off his initiative in Grand Haven shoves things up a notch or two." Sam smiled. "I wish he'd do it some-where else, but he didn't ask my opinion."

"Right." That bosses were often poor listeners was not news to Barbara. But that didn't solve the immediate problem. "We sure don't have much on this militia. In fact, according to your report, we're not even positive that Anderson and Hawkins are actually involved."

"Oh, I'm sure all right; I just can't prove it. But you're right about the lack of evidence."

"So what are we doing?"

"We're it, for now. I'd like to have some wiretaps and FBI assistance, but that's out until we can show it's likely the militia has broken the law."

"Once there's a bombed-out building or a dead body."

"Sometimes it works out that way."

"I know, and I agree with the restrictions. But it sure gives the bad guys the advantage. What have you done so far?"

"The usual. Full search of federal and state files. Got a lot of military info on Anderson and Hawkins—excellent records, both of them. No arrests. I've checked around Grand Haven. They're respected businessmen, well liked. Both of them are loners." He shrugged. "I'm not sure how to proceed."

Barbara leaned back in her chair. A thought had been tugging at the back of her mind. "You know, a gun shop and a garage could be awfully useful to a militia. I presume you've checked them out."

"As much as I can. Both businesses are legitimate. Even though I'm sure of what Anderson and Hawkins are doing, we can't get search warrants on mere suspicion."

"How about visiting The Flintlock as a potential customer?"

"Couldn't hurt." Sam grinned. "However, I doubt Mr. Hawkins leaves his subversive stuff lying about for customers to peruse."

"Probably not. Also, I found out Craig Phillips knows Brad Anderson. His mom is handicapped, and Anderson's garage did the modification work on her van. How about if I investigate his business?"

"OK by me, and I'll see what I can find out about Hawkins."

"Where do we go from here? Do we have any other active investigations?"

"Not for us. We're assigned to investigate western Michigan Militias and prepare for the president's visit. So, time to start the fieldwork. Have you got my mobile phone number?"

"No, better give it to me. Here's mine." She wrote it on a sticky-note and gave it to him. Sam wrote his on a business card.

"I'll give you a call, say, around eleven tomorrow. Then we can decide where to go from there."

"Sounds good to me."

After Sam left, Barbara felt her task begin to close in around her. It was all well and good to say she would investigate Brad Anderson, but how? Living in a democracy put strict limits on police work, for which she was grateful. But it did make getting at the truth difficult.

Her earlier thought returned. At first she rejected it, but the more she pondered the idea the more intriguing it became.

She rolled her chair forward and started Internet Explorer. A few clicks later, she jotted down Elizabeth Phillips's phone number. Barbara looked at the phone, hesitated, then punched in the number. She counted the rings and began to wonder if anyone was home.

"Hello," a woman answered.

"Elizabeth?"

"No, she's not here. Can I take a message?"

"Yes, please. Actually, I'm calling for Craig. This is Barbara Post."

"Oh, the ATF agent. Craig told me about you. I'm Susan Phillips." Her voice was a joyless monotone.

"Oh, I see. How are you?" Barbara winced at her words, thinking them inane, but she couldn't think of anything else to say.

"As well as can be expected, I guess."

"Craig told me what happened to your husband. I'm so sorry. It must be very hard for you."

There was a long pause. "Yes. I just take it one day at a time." She sounded even more sad.

Barbara had to struggle not to judge, especially since Susan's philosophical statement was a pet peeve. What other way could you live but one day at a time?

"That's all you can do."

"Does Craig have your number?"

"Yes. Well, bye."

"Good-bye."

Barbara continued reading reports. About a half hour later she heard someone hurry past. She turned to see Dan Oliver go out the door without looking in her direction. A few minutes later her mobile phone chirped. She pulled it out of her purse.

"This is Barbara."

"Hi, Craig here. Susan said you called. Sorry I wasn't here. I was out with Mom and William at the supermarket."

"That's OK." She watched the animated screen saver on her monitor as she pondered what to say. "I'd like your help on something," she said finally.

"Sure. Related to . . . what you're working on?"

"That's right."

"Anytime. We're used to twenty-four/seven in the Coast Guard. Would you like to meet somewhere?"

Barbara's mind wandered off business for a moment as she thought about Craig. "Yes. But I'm new around here. Where would you recommend?"

"I was going to call you when we got back from the store, only you beat me to it."

"Oh?"

"May I take you out to dinner?" He said it in a hurry as if he was nervous. "We could discuss—whatever you want to talk about, afterward."

Barbara smiled at the prospect. "I'd love to. What time?"

"How about if I come by around seven?"

"Sounds great."

"Wonderful."

She gave him the address of her apartment in Spring Lake. Five minutes later she was out the door for her afternoon commute. She tried to keep her mind on business but was not very successful.

Ed roared out of the Wal-Mart parking lot and into the heavy traffic on East Sherman Boulevard. The dashboard clock said 6:55—he had five minutes to find a pay phone. He hadn't meant to cut it so close, but Brad had given him the third degree about borrowing the Suburban. That was followed by more questions about why Ed needed to borrow a hundred dollars. But he had stood his ground. He didn't have to explain every move. That had earrned another lecture, but Brad finally handed over the money and the keys to the truck.

Ed was pleased with himself. He was being careful—he understood the danger full well, which was why he had decided to get the prepaid phone card in Muskegon. He didn't think the feds had his contact under surveillance, but why take chances? If the calls were traced, all they would get would be the pay phone number and the phone card account. And since he had paid cash, that was where the trail would end.

Ed spotted a pay phone outside a convenience store, pulled off, and parked. He looked around as he approached the phone, making sure he was alone. It was one minute after seven. Ed pulled out the scrap of paper, unfolded it, and placed it on the shelf below the phone. He then punched in the toll-free number on the phone card. At the prompt, he keyed the card's PIN followed by his friend's number. It rang only once.

"Hello."

"I got your message. What's up?"

"Got something to write with?"

Ed pulled a pen out of his shirt pocket. "Shoot."

"The shipment leaves McAlester at 8:00 A.M. next Monday on a Century Transportation eighteen-wheeler, dark blue with light blue stripes. There's one escort. The route goes through Springfield, Missouri, St. Louis, south of Chicago, and on into Michigan."

"Straight through?"

"Except for eating and rest stops. They've got two drivers plus two men in the escort car."

"What's in the shipment?"

"Mainly rifle and machine gun ammo but also some C-4 plastic explosives and flares."

"Man, just what we need. What's their route?"

"They'll be on I-55 through Illinois to I-80. Then they take that to I-94 until it hits I-196, which takes them on into Wyoming, Michigan." The man laughed. "Unless, of course, something happens."

Ed giggled. "I can't imagine what. When will they enter Michigan?"

"I don't know. I got this from the dispatcher. He and I are friends, but I didn't want to press my luck. That's all I have."

"I understand. Thanks. We'll make good use of it." Ed paused. "Are you all right?"

"I think so. I'm being careful. I don't think the feds are watching me, or they would have done something by now."

"I hope you're right. Bye."

"Good luck."

The line clicked. Ed replaced the handset. He walked back to the Suburban deep in thought. Now all he had to do was convince Brad they could do it.

—◦— —◦— —◦—

The FBI special agent waited until the suspect drove off, taking the highway back into McAlester, Oklahoma. The agent hurried to the pay phone and wrote down the number. A few minutes later he was on the phone with a request for information on the call. He wondered if he should recommend pulling the suspect in for questioning. He shrugged. That decision would be made by conference between the FBI and ATF at a level considerably higher than his, and those involved probably wouldn't care for his opinion.

——— ——— ———

Barbara turned her head from side to side as she checked her pearl earrings, deciding they added just the right touch. She selected a blue pantsuit with an off-white wool sweater under the jacket. Barbara tugged at the loosely tied, navy print scarf around her neck. She applied a final light misting of hairspray and dabbed on perfume.

She gathered up her small black purse and went into the living room to wait. At precisely seven, the doorbell chimed. Barbara opened the door.

"Good evening," Craig said.

She liked what she saw as her eyes did a discreet but thorough inventory. His casual tan trousers certainly complimented his trim, athletic build. His long-sleeve sports shirt had the right amount of taper and fit snuggly without being tight. Barbara decided he measured up to Texas standards of manliness.

"Howdy, Craig," she said before she remembered she was far from the Lone Star state.

"You look wonderful," he said. A boyish grin lit up his face. "So, this is what Texas women dress like."

She smiled. "I thought about wearing my buckskins and boots but decided this might be more suitable. You look a tad different yourself—a little less gold braid and no pilot's wings, but I think you'll do."

"Uh, thanks. Are you ready to go?"

"Yep."

Their hands brushed briefly, and he seemed to hesitate. Then his hand closed gently around hers. Barbara found his grip strong but gentle.

They descended the stairs from the garage apartment. Barbara was not surprised when she saw his red Trans Am since she really didn't expect an aviator to drive an Escort. Craig held the door for her, and she got in.

The instruments bathed the snug interior with varicolored lights as Craig drove them into Grand Haven. He was more attentive than most men, as he made polite conversation. He seemed relaxed with perhaps a hint of nervousness.

Craig turned onto Jackson which soon changed to Harbor Drive. They rounded the curve to run parallel to the shore. In the distance Barbara saw the sign for Harbor Lights. Craig pulled into the lot and parked.

"Harbor Lights is the best place for fish in Grand Haven," he said. "I guess I should have asked what you wanted to eat, but their entire menu is quite good."

"I like fish. Sam and I ate here before we met with you and Joel."

"Oh, I'm sorry. Wish I had known. We could have gone somewhere else."

"This is fine."

She saw his look of concern dissolve into a grin.

"You sure? We could hit a burger joint."

"I'm sure."

He grabbed a lightweight jacket, got out, and came around to her side. He opened the door and held out his hand. She took it. They strolled up the steps and inside the crowded entrance. The maitre d' turned as Craig approached. The man made a quick check of the reservations list, grabbed two menus, and led his guests out on the deck, seating them at the rail overlooking the beach and Lake Michigan. The cool breeze made Barbara glad she wore a sweater under her jacket.

The waiter approached, pad in hand. "May I take your drink orders?"

"I think I'll have hot tea," Barbara said.

"Same for me," Craig said.

"Be right back to take your order." The young man made a few notes and hurried off.

"What do you recommend?" Barbara asked.

"If you like fish, I recommend the perch. I think that's what I'm going to have. But their steaks are excellent also." A glint came to his eyes. "However, I'm sure they don't measure up to a Texas steakhouse."

"I'll go with the perch." She decided it was well worth a repeat.

The waiter brought their tea and wrote down their order.

"How is William doing?" Barbara asked after the waiter left.

"Oh, about the same. This is a really tough time for him—and Susan."

"I don't mean to pry."

He smiled, but it was strained. "That's OK. I know you care." He paused. "There's more to Larry's death than I told you. Last December, he got drunk and skidded off the road. His car turned over several times and ended up behind an embankment—you couldn't see it from the road. He was pinned inside and froze to death."

"Oh, no."

Craig's face grew hard. "It gets worse. He and Susan were on the verge of divorce at the time." He looked into Barbara's eyes. "William knew what was going on, and that's one of the reasons why he's the way he is."

"He needs his mother's love—especially now."

"I know. But Susan is too wrapped up in herself right now. Mom's there for William, and that helps." He smiled. "Elizabeth Phillips is pretty good in the loving department."

"And William's got you for a role model."

Craig shrugged. "I try. I want William to turn out right. Sorry to burden you with our troubles."

"We've all got problems in this life."

"That's true. How about telling me something about you?"

"Have you ever been to Texas?" Barbara asked.

"I went through Amarillo on the way to Air Station Los Angeles. That was my first duty station out of flight school."

"That's it?"

"I'm afraid so, just that once. I took the northern route through Colorado and Nebraska when I was transferred to Traverse City."

"Why, all you saw was a little bit of the panhandle. There's a whole lot more to Texas than that. Meaning no disrespect to my home state, but you didn't exactly see the prettiest part either."

"How far is Amarillo from Marfa?"

"Oh, something over four hundred miles, give or take."

"As the crow flies?"

Barbara laughed. "If the crow didn't know where he was going. There is no straight line between Marfa and anywhere."

"Big state."

"The biggest, if we don't count that chunk of ice north of Canada."

"Then let's not count it."

"All right by me."

The waiter brought the salads, asked if they needed anything else, then departed.

Craig waited, then leaned forward and lowered his voice. "Shall I offer the blessing?" he asked.

This surprised but pleased her. "That would be nice."

He reached out to her with both hands. She put her hands in his. Craig prayed, giving thanks for the food. It seemed to Barbara that he was a little slow in releasing her hands after he finished.

She looked out over the lake. The nearly full moon hung over the restaurant, shining its silvery light on the choppy waters.

"What a beautiful view," she said.

"Yes, it is." He pointed toward the north. "See that light?"

"Yes."

"That's the lighthouse on the South Pier. That's where the Grand River flows into Lake Michigan. The red light further out is some ship or boat traveling either west or south."

The light looked like it was standing still. "How can you tell?" she asked without thinking.

"We are talking about my job here," he said with a grin. "That's a port navigational light. Since it's on the left side, we know the vessel's direction within about ninety degrees." He pointed again. "Now that ship over there is going in the opposite direction."

"The green light?"

"Yes. It's on the starboard or right side."

"Is it possible to see the red and green lights at the same time?"

"Usually you see only one or the other, but if you do see both, the ship is coming directly at you."

"Time to get out of the way?"

"If you're out in a boat. However, we're fairly safe here."

Barbara saw the glint in his eye. She liked his gentle sense of humor. Actually, she found herself liking a lot about him. "Collisions between ships and restaurants are rare?"

"Never been called out on one. But, if it happens, we'll be there."

The waiter brought out the main course. Barbara broke off a tender bite of the perch with her fork. She found it excellent. She watched Craig's blue eyes, sensing there was a question behind them.

"Tell me. How does a West Texas gal end up in the ATF?" he asked.

"As a girl, I was fascinated by my dad's jobs. He works with explosives, doing things like blasting out rock quarries and building highways. I used to live for the times he'd allow me to go with him, which wasn't often. I was fascinated by what you could do with TNT and C-4."

"What's your dad's name?"

"Ken, and my mom's is Fran."

"Any brothers or sisters?"

"Nope. I'm an only child."

"Were you lonely?"

"Some. But we're a loving family, and I had lots of friends. Growing up in a small town has its advantages."

"Amen to that."

"Anyhow, after high school I went to Texas A&M in College Station and ended up as a chemistry major. When I was a junior, I found out the ATF had agents specializing in explosives and firearms so I joined the bureau after graduation. After I learned how to be a special agent, the ATF sent me to military schools to train on all sorts of weapons."

He shook his head. "This is so unusual."

Momentary irritation touched Barbara. "You don't think a woman should be doing this?"

Craig's voice became firm. "I don't mean that at all. I think you should do what you want."

She knew he meant it. "Well, thanks. Not everyone feels that way, but I don't want to get into that."

His smile returned. "I guess I should have said it adds to your mystique." He paused. "Which it really does. Am I off the hook?"

She couldn't keep a straight face. "Yep. Now it's your turn. How did Craig Phillips get to be a pilot?"

"My dad was in the Coast Guard, so I guess I inherited his love for our mission. But my interest in aviation I discovered for myself. The Coast Guard Academy accepted my application, so I spent four years in New London, Connecticut, getting a college education and learning how to be a sailor. My first duty station was a high endurance cutter. I spent my next two years in the communications department."

"You weren't a pilot then?"

"No. You have to go to sea before they'll let you into the flight program. After my first tour, I got orders to Navy Flight School in Pensacola, qualified in helos, and reported for duty at Air Station Los Angeles. After that, I asked for a transfer to Traverse City and got it."

"I imagine that pleased your mother."

"Yes." He stopped and lowered his eyes. After a few moments he looked back up. "Especially after we lost dad."

"Oh, I'm sorry. How did it happen?"

His smile was strained. "Dad was a Coast Guard chief—stationed right here in Grand Haven. He was on a search-and-rescue mission during a bad storm when his boat capsized. He was the only one who didn't make it."

"Oh, how horrible."

"Unfortunately, there's more. The boat that sent the SOS had already made it back to port, but the owner failed to notify the Coast Guard."

"That must have been difficult for you to accept."

"Losing Dad was hard, especially for Mom. But we understood his dedication. The modern Coast Guard has all sorts of missions, but the one dearest to us is protecting and saving mariners. That's why I joined." He stopped, and Barbara could tell he was moved. "I'm really proud of my dad."

"I bet he felt the same about you."

"Yes, he did. He was strict, but I never doubted he loved me—and Larry."

Despite the painful topic, Barbara was grateful for Craig's openness and the opportunity to learn more about him. She declined dessert but gratefully accepted a cup of coffee, both to finish off the dinner and to warm her. Craig paid by credit card, and they strolled out of the restaurant.

"I presume you'd like a secluded spot," he said in a low voice.

Despite knowing exactly what he meant, Barbara found her mind exploring in another direction, one she much preferred. She shivered. It was even cooler now.

"Where do you suggest?" she asked.

"Are you cold?"

"Yes. That wind is chilly."

"Get used to it." He took off his jacket and draped it around her shoulders. "Let's walk along the beach."

Soon they were strolling north toward the Grand Haven State Park. There were still a few people out, but by the time they neared the South Pier, they were alone.

Craig pointed to a bench. "That all right?"

"Fine."

They sat down, and although not touching, Barbara was well aware of Craig's nearness. Once she dealt with her distraction, her next problem was how to state her request.

"You needed my help doing something?" he asked.

"Yes, but what I want to do is . . . rather unusual."

"Oh?"

"I'm investigating Brad Anderson. We're convinced he's organizing a new militia, but we don't have much in the way of hard facts. I need to start filling in the gaps. We especially want to know if he and his buds are in violation of firearm or explosives laws."

"OK, but I don't see how I can help."

"Not to put too fine a point on it, I'd like to investigate Anderson's repair shop without him knowing it."

"Uh, I'm not trying to interfere, but is that legal?"

Barbara sighed. "Strictly speaking, I doubt it. But it's not that simple."

"Oh? Tell me more."

"Could you schedule your mother's van for some kind of service? If I hide inside, I could come out after the garage closes, look around, then get back inside and sneak out in the morning. It wouldn't be breaking and entering since I'd be in a customer's vehicle—which happens to be inside Anderson's garage."

"I don't know. That sounds awfully shady."

"I understand, and I agree. It is shady, and I think I know what a judge would say. But listen—we really need something on this militia, and I don't know how we're going to get it. At some point, I plan to question Brad, but I'd rather save that for later."

"If Brad is forming a militia, you could be in danger."

"I know, but this is my job."

"I don't like it. I'd hate for something to happen to you."

That stopped her for a moment. "Well, I guess I'm glad you care."

"I do. But if you get in, what do you hope to find?"

"Proof of what Anderson is doing—and hopefully what their intentions are. All I want to do is look around the garage a little. Will you help me?"

For a long time he said nothing as he looked out on the lake. Then he turned his head toward her. "OK. When do you want to do it?"

"As soon as possible."

He nodded. "I'll see when he can take it tomorrow. I'll call you at work." He paused. "But please think it over. Make sure you're doing the right thing. This worries me."

"I will." She refrained from saying that she was worried also.

Chapter Eight

Barbara connected her laptop modem to the wall jack and sat down at the kitchen table. After setting the communications software to the access number, she connected, then entered her ID and password. The screen flashed, and she was in. Barbara checked her in-box and found it empty.

Her thoughts drifted back to the previous evening. What she planned on doing still worried her, and the nagging doubts would not go away. But every time she thought about the new militia, she sensed a ticking time bomb. They had to get more information on Brad Anderson and what he was up to.

Another distraction popped up. She had thoroughly enjoyed her evening with Craig. He had been kind and attentive. After discussing business, they walked along the beach and out on the South Pier as far as the lighthouse. She began to understand his devotion to the Coast Guard as he described how lights and buoys guided sailors safely in and out of port.

Afterward, Craig had driven her home. She remembered the walk up the steps to her apartment entrance, his hand around hers. He had hesitated only a moment, then gently kissed her. The kiss may have been gentle, but its affect on her certainly hadn't been. She blushed as she forced her thoughts back to business.

She considered discussing her plan with Sam but decided not to. She reasoned that how she investigated Brad Anderson was up to her.

Sam parked in front of The Flintlock and got out. His practiced eye took in the well-maintained, painted brick exterior. It was an older building with a narrow front and had probably served many masters over the years. A harsh buzzer sounded as Sam opened the front door. Massive glass cases lined either wall, displaying a wide range of handguns, some chromed but most either black or blue steel. Rifle racks ran along behind the glass cases. Heavy steel cables were threaded through each weapon, secured at intervals by massive padlocks. A partition ran across the back of the store. On it hung a banner printed in red letters over a blue background:

Amendment II to the United States Constitution
A well regulated militia, being necessary to the security
of a free state, the right of the people to keep and
bear arms, shall not be infringed.

Sam recognized Michael "Hawk" Hawkins from his military photos. The only other person in the store was a middle-aged man examining a Colt 45 automatic. The proprietor turned his head and for just a moment locked eyes with the newcomer. But it was long enough to tell Sam that he was not welcome.

The customer pulled back the slide and peered into the chamber. "Seems to be in good condition, for a used gun."

"Oh, it is," Hawkins said. "I check out every used gun before putting it on sale. This weapon has been well maintained."

The man lowered the heavy pistol to the cloth pad that protected the glass case. "I'd like to think about it."

"Sure thing, but I wouldn't take too long. Used guns don't stay around long."

"Thanks, I'll keep that in mind." The man left the store.

The way Hawkins trained his eyes around on Sam reminded him of looking down the wrong end of a machine gun.

"What do you want?" the store owner demanded as he returned the automatic to the case.

"I'm looking for a handgun."

"How about looking for it somewhere else?"

Sam felt the sting, although he had expected it. "You could find yourself in trouble with an attitude like that. The laws are a little different now."

"Fine. You got a license to carry?"

"Not yet."

"Then I can't sell you a gun. It's the law." His frown turned to a sneer. "They make you take a test. If you don't score seventy percent, no license. Think you can hack that?"

Sam struggled to maintain his composure. "I believe so."

"Well, now, I guess that remains to be seen, doesn't it? Tell you what, come back in with a license, and we'll talk guns."

"How about we talk now."

"What do you want to know?"

"Do you repair guns on site, or do you send them out?"

Hawkins drew himself up. "I'm a fully qualified gunsmith. I can do anything a customer needs, providing it's legal. I also do reloading, carry custom ammo, even deal in antique weapons, including selling black powder."

"I'm impressed. So, what do you recommend for self-protection?"

"Man, there's no right answer to that. Some guys like Fords, some like Chevys. If you want to poke big holes in people, it's hard to beat a 44 magnum, but a Colt 45 automatic also does a fine job, despite a low muzzle velocity. But serious guys usually get one of the newer nine-millimeter automatics. Glock makes a nice one."

"Do you carry any specialty guns?"

Hawkins's brown eyes sliced into Sam. "I don't have time for silly questions." He turned abruptly and disappeared through the partition door.

Sam caught a glimpse of a metal lathe before the door slammed shut. The brief visit confirmed the information in Hawkins's service record. The man certainly knew guns, and he felt strongly about the right to bear arms.

Sam returned to his car and phoned Barbara, asking her to meet him at Coast Guard Group Grand Haven.

Barbara entered the second-floor conference room. Sam looked up from his open laptop computer.

"Good morning," he said. "Anything new?"

"Not really. The first thing I'd like to do is check out Anderson's Automotive—see if it could be a front for gunsmith and weapons work."

"You think he's dumb enough to leave the cookies out in the open?"

"Probably not. But they've got to be doing their work somewhere. Maybe he's overlooked something."

"I guess it's possible. It's a well-equipped garage from what I've heard."

"Right. And besides working on guns, they could easily build custom vehicles and support equipment." She paused. "What I'd really like to know is Anderson's intent. Are he and Hawkins harmless cranks, or are they planning major mayhem?"

"That is the question. Sure can't hurt to check it out, I guess."

"Come up with anything on Hawkins?"

"It's about what I expected. The guy has a first-rate gun store, complete with a gunsmith shop in the back. He even has a banner quoting the second amendment to the Constitution."

"How surprising."

"You got it. Oh, remember that guy in McAlester that the FBI is shadowing?"

"Yes."

"Yesterday evening, he goes out to a pay phone, and someone in Muskegon calls him. The caller was also using a pay phone and a prepaid phone card, so that's all the FBI got."

"Sounds like the suspect is spooked."

"The FBI doesn't think so. They believe he's just being careful."

"Any idea what they talked about?"

Sam frowned. "We can be sure it wasn't the weather. It was probably about an ammunition shipment from the McAlester Plant. The FBI checked and found out that Century Transportation is making a run to Wyoming, Michigan, next Monday."

"Carrying what?"

"A load of ammo, C-4, and flares. They're leaving at 8:00 A.M. bound for the 46th Infantry Brigade."

"Any other shipments coming our way?"

"Not in the near future." He paused. "What do you make of it?"

This seemed so obvious, Barbara wondered if Sam was testing her. "Have you warned the brigade?"

He shook his head. "Haven't had time. I'll be visiting their head-quarters this afternoon."

A wild thought flitted through Barbara's mind. At first she dismissed it, but the longer she considered it, the more likely it appeared. "Sam, what if—whoever it is—ambushes the shipment before it gets there?"

"You think that's likely?"

"You know the trend. The unthinkable is becoming commonplace: the Oklahoma City Bombing, assassinating a federal judge. I wouldn't be surprised if some group hijacked an ammo truck."

"Could happen, I guess. So who was the guy in Muskegon?"

"I see where you're going, but it could be any western Michigan mili-tia. There's one in Muskegon, for instance."

"Dan will want our opinion. You really think it's Muskegon?"

Barbara shook her head. "No. It's more likely the Grand Haven mili-tia. If they're still in the organizing stage, they'll have a greater need for arms and ammunition."

"For what it's worth, I agree. If you were running the militia, where would you hit the truck?"

"Why not ask me something hard?"

Sam chuckled. "You're the explosives expert."

Barbara frowned. "That doesn't help."

"We're going to have to tell Dan something."

"OK. I think they'll strike as close to home as possible—somewhere in Michigan. I presume you've got the route."

"Yes. They have to follow the hazardous cargo routes, so from Illinois they'll take I-55 to I-80 to I-94 to I-196. I-196 goes right through Wyoming."

"Let me study a map. When do we have to report?"

"Soonest."

"OK. I'll get with Craig and see what he thinks."

"Good idea. Maybe you could survey the route from the air."

"That would be even better."

Sam turned off his laptop and snapped the lid shut. "Keep me posted. I've got to visit the 46th Infantry, and after that I have a meeting at the office. I'll check in with you tomorrow."

"Dan called a meeting?"

Sam looked embarrassed. "Yes."

"I wasn't included?" After she asked the question, she wished she hadn't. She knew the answer from Sam's pained expression.

"No, you weren't."

Barbara struggled to maintain her composure. "Well, see you tomorrow."

"Right. Bye." He hurried out.

⚊⚊ ⚊⚊ ⚊⚊

Barbara's call to Air Facility Muskegon revealed two things: there was no need to drive up there, and Craig and his crew had not eaten lunch yet. She made a quick trip to Domino's on Beacon and picked up two large pepperoni pizzas and five Cokes. The orange-and-white helicopter was just touching down by the time Barbara arrived at the YMCA ball field. She parked and hurried out through the swirling grit and dust. Craig met her halfway.

He eyed the boxes. "You're going to spoil my crew!" he shouted over the whine of the turbines.

"It's the least I could do."

He took the pizzas and drinks. They lowered their heads and walked out to the helicopter. One of the crewmen took the food. Craig helped Barbara aboard and got her strapped in behind Joel Foscue. Craig fitted Barbara with a headset, showed her how the intercom worked, then took the right-hand seat. The jet whine increased, and the helicopter lifted off in a cloud of dust.

Barbara looked out the canopy as the ground dropped away. Grand Haven became an orderly grid of streets marking off green and brown rectangles punctuated by trees in their springtime finery. The helicopter hugged the coast as it sped south, gaining altitude. After they leveled off, one of the crewmen passed out the pizza and drinks. Barbara took a slice and handed one to Craig.

"Thanks," he said, taking a large bite. "This is my favorite of the basic food groups." His voice was remarkably clear in her earphones.

Barbara laughed. "Who watches your nutrition?"

"I take care of that now, although Mom is seeking reinstatement for the summer."

"I hope she succeeds."

"I'm going to ignore that. Now, if you'll look over there." He pointed to an approaching town. "That's Wyoming, and beyond it is Grand Rapids. You want to fly down I-196 to Benton Harbor?"

"Right."

"What are we looking for?"

"Places where an eighteen-wheeler could be hijacked."

He looked back in surprise. "Related to . . ."

"The Grand Haven Militia."

"You're sure about this?"

"No, I just want to check it out. At this point, we're not sure of any-thing. A suspect in the Judge Richards case got a call yesterday from someone in Muskegon. We suspect they were talking about an ammo shipment that's going to a National Guard regiment in Wyoming."

"When?"

"It leaves Oklahoma next Monday."

"That doesn't give you much time."

"No, it doesn't. And, as I said, it's only a hunch."

"There's I-196 down there." Craig pointed.

"I see it."

"You guys copy that?" Craig asked.

Barbara glanced back at the flight mechanic and rescue swimmer. Both men were currently more occupied with demolishing their pizza. "Roger, skipper," the mechanic said after a hasty swallow.

"OK. Keep a sharp lookout."

Craig brought the helicopter around onto a southwesterly course. Barbara looked down on the interstate traffic. The cars and trucks looked like toys, and the houses and buildings more like models than the real thing.

"I could get used to this," she said.

"It's a great way to travel, and what a view. There's the lake." He pointed at the deep blue expanse that made up their entire western hori-zon. "I never get tired of looking at that."

"I can see why."

Barbara noted a few rural spots between Wyoming and Holland, but what about traffic? Even in the early hours it wouldn't be light. And what about the escort? How would the militia deal with that? It occurred to Barbara that they might let the shipment get to the armory, then steal what they wanted. But if that was the case, why call beforehand? The more she thought about it the less sure she became.

After flying over Holland, Craig turned south, hugging the coast.

"There's no shortage of rural stretches," Barbara said.

"That's true, especially between here and Benton Harbor. Got any way of narrowing it down?"

"No, except I'd expect them to wait until close to Holland. That would make it easier to haul the ammo to Grand Haven."

"That still leaves a lot of territory."

"I know, and I'm not at all sure we're on the right track." She looked down at the highway. "If Dan approves the operation, can we use your helicopter to shadow the shipment?"

"I think so. We should be able to follow from a distance, as long as the weather isn't too bad. And we can alter our course so it looks like we're going somewhere else. We use these helicopters for law enforcement all the time."

"Good."

They continued on down to Benton Harbor and St. Joseph.

"You want to go any farther?"

Barbara scanned the map. "I don't think so."

Craig brought the helicopter around in a broad one-hundred-eighty-degree turn and headed north for Grand Haven.

He looked over at Joel. "I'm getting out at Grand Haven. Think you can find your way back to Muskegon?"

"I'll give it my best shot. I'll call if I get lost."

"You do that."

Barbara saw his expression turn to concern. "Can you drop me by home?" he asked.

She felt an icy chill, a strange combination of wanting to be with him and anxiety over what she had planned for that evening. "Sure. I'll be glad to."

The helicopter hugged the coast. Lonely beaches and thick stands of trees swept under them as Craig dropped down lower. Soon Barbara saw Grand Haven approaching. Craig circled the ball field and came in for a landing. The helicopter bounced a little on its stubby landing gear.

"It's all yours," Craig said as he unstrapped and got up.

He helped Barbara out of her harness. She followed him out of the aircraft and away from the whirling rotor blades. She squinted to avoid the flying grit. They turned and watched as Joel lifted off.

Craig waited for the helicopter's clatter to die down then said, "I'm supposed to take the van to Anderson's at six. Are you sure you want to go through with this?"

Barbara took a deep breath. "Yes."

He didn't seem happy about it.

Chapter Nine

Barbara almost talked herself out of her special operation as she waited for Craig. But if she quit now, what if this new militia really was planning a terrorist act? Viewed under the lens of recent history, knocking off an ammunition shipment didn't seem all that unlikely. Of course, the ultimate objective would be something entirely different, something worthy of the firepower they were acquiring. She shivered as she wondered about that.

Barbara tied the laces of her running shoes and stood up. She wore a blue blouse and work pants with large pockets, and as an afterthought, pulled on a lightweight navy sweater, just in case. She reviewed her plan once more—she would look around, then get back in the van and wait for morning, hoping to sneak out once the garage opened up for business.

A knock sounded at the door. Barbara picked up a heavy bag containing her 9mm Glock, a flashlight and some snacks, then opened the door. Craig stood there smiling, but he was obviously tense. Barbara found herself momentarily distracted as she took in his long-sleeve sports shirt and khaki pants. He certainly dressed better than most bachelors she knew.

"I don't suppose you changed your mind," Craig said.

She shook her head. "We need a breakthrough, and I'm afraid time's running out."

"I wish you wouldn't do it."

"I know. But I have to."

"OK."

He took her bag. Halfway down the steps he reached for her hand and escorted her to the van's side door, which was open with the ramp down. He helped her up and climbed in himself.

"There's your hiding place," Craig said. He pointed to a large green nylon bag in the back. "That's our camping tent, minus the poles and ground cloth. It'll be snug, but I think you'll fit inside."

"Elizabeth goes camping?" Barbara asked.

"Growing up, it was our favorite thing to do. Mom decided she wasn't going to let her accident stop her, and it hasn't."

Barbara smiled. "She does seem . . ."

Craig's smile echoed hers. "Stubborn?"

"Not exactly the word I was looking for. So, what did you tell Brad Anderson?"

"Oh, the ramp's busted."

Barbara looked at the still-extended mechanism. "Seems OK to me."

"It won't be by the time we get there. I also asked him to put the van inside because of the camping gear."

"Good idea. It wouldn't do me any good being locked out of the garage."

He looked into her eyes. "Last chance."

"Let's go."

He helped her slide in beside the tent, then placed her bag inside. He pulled the zipper up to her neck. "See if you can operate it."

Barbara squirmed around until she could reach the zipper. She tugged on it, moving it up a little. "No problem."

Craig cleared his throat. "Ah, you're going to be stuck inside the garage until morning, so there's a chemical can in the corner."

"Oh, thanks. I appreciate your thoughtfulness."

He smiled. "Comes in handy on camping trips." He looked at her for a few moments. "Take care of yourself."

"I will."

Craig ran the zipper all the way up, and everything went dark. Barbara felt the van shake and heard the muffled sounds of his footsteps. The wheelchair ramp whined, and the side door thumped shut. Something snapped.

"What's this?" Craig asked. "Looks like a busted connector. Better check the ramp and see if it still works. Nope. Boy, sure hope Brad can fix it."

"Very funny," Barbara said, raising her voice.

"There's no one in here but me, so I didn't hear that."

"Press on, Lieutenant."

"Aye, aye, ma'am."

The engine started, and the van lurched a little as Craig backed out of the drive. The trip to Anderson's Automotive was quick but disorienting, since Barbara couldn't see anything. After Craig parked, Barbara wondered if he would say anything else, but he didn't. A sharp click sounded, the van lurched, then a door slammed shut. A short time later a car pulled up and stopped. Someone got in, and the car drove off.

The wind sighed as it blew past the van. After what seemed like a long time, Barbara heard the crunch of approaching footsteps. A door opened and someone got in. The engine started, and the truck moved forward slowly and stopped. The engine quit, and the door clumped shut. Barbara was all alone again.

An electric motor clicked on, and something started rattling—the garage door apparently. Barbara listened to the random sounds as the shop approached the end of its workday. Several times she heard the sharp ping of a tool dropped on the concrete floor, once accompanied by a pungent oath. Other garage doors closed. Finally everything was quiet.

Barbara gripped the inner side of the zipper with her fingernails and pulled it down. The dim light inside the van seemed bright after the bag's darkness. She wriggled out, tiptoed to the back and looked out. All the garage doors were closed. She looked to the left. Against the far wall was the office. Light slanted through the open blinds. There was only one person inside: Brad Anderson. A Coke machine stood at the far end of the office, its lighted panel augmenting the glow from the windows.

Barbara sat down and rested her head against the tent bag as she waited. Eventually she heard the sound she was waiting for when a door opened and closed. She raised up and took a cautious look. Brad was unlocking the outside door next to his office. He went through. A moment later Barbara heard the faint click of the lock.

She sat back down and grabbed a sweet roll as she waited for the right time to move out.

Brad opened the door to his apartment and found Ed waiting for him, which wasn't really surprising since his brother didn't have any wheels unless he borrowed the Suburban. After customizing Ed's van, Brad had told him he couldn't use it because of the unusual modifications required for a command vehicle. That this limited Ed's movements was not lost on Brad.

"We need to talk," Ed began. "I know where we can get a bunch of ammo, but we have to move fast."

"Slow down. What are you talking about?"

"My old militia has a contact inside the McAlester Army Ammunition Plant."

Brad laughed. "You mean the militia that got scattered because you're such a hothead?"

Ed glared at him, and for a moment Brad thought he might lash out. "Someone has to take a stand! Just because you're chicken . . ."

"Shut up! I told you before, we are going to strike, but we're going to do it when we're ready, and we're going to pick a target that really matters."

"So you say."

"So we will, little brother. Now, if you don't like the way I run things, then you can shove off. Are you reading me?"

"But . . ."

"I don't want to hear it. Either do what I say, or go pester someone else."

"Listen! You need ammo! Your armory is coming along, but even Hawk is complaining about the bullets. Unless you stock up, you'll run out first time you're out in the field."

Brad held his tongue. Ed—his brother who was so good at being wrong—was right about this one thing. Brad and Hawk had held many talks about what to do, but so far they hadn't been able to agree on a plan.

"OK, what's your idea?" Brad asked.

"There's an ammo shipment leaving Oklahoma next Monday for the 46th Infantry Brigade in Wyoming. Rifle and machine gun ammo, C-4 and flares—a whole eighteen-wheeler."

"When does it leave?"

"Eight in the morning."

Brad whistled. "That doesn't leave much time. Do you have the route?"

Ed beamed. "I've got it all."

"OK, tell me everything."

⚊⚊⚊ ⚊⚊⚊ ⚊⚊⚊

Barbara decided it was late enough. She slipped the automatic into her pants pocket, turned on the flashlight, and unlocked the back doors. She opened one side and stepped down to the concrete. A dim wash of light came through the office mini-blinds and merged with the glare from the Coke machine. Barbara closed the van's door and thumbed the switch on the flashlight, turning it off. The only other light came from a single fluorescent fixture at the far end of the garage.

Barbara hurried over to the office and tried the door. It wasn't locked. She went in and looked around. The light came from the overhead fluorescents that Brad had failed to turn off. Barbara turned around slowly. Craig's description had been accurate. Brad was clearly proud of his military service. Barbara saw the "Live Free or Die" banner and shook her head. She tiptoed along, careful not to disturb anything. It certainly looked like an auto business.

Barbara returned to the garage and looked down the long line of bays. The center section was concealed in inky darkness. She moved along with great care, periodically checking the tools and equipment with her flashlight. Again, it was exactly what she expected, the only surprise being the cleanliness. Shielding her flashlight, she examined a lathe in detail. Although it could be used for weapons work, it was also required for precision auto machining. Barbara reached the end of the garage and turned off her flashlight. A disassembled transmission sat on a long metal workbench under a fluorescent fixture someone had apparently forgotten to turn off.

Barbara began retracing her steps. Up ahead, the lighted office and Coke machine seemed like islands rising out of a dark sea. She brought her flashlight up and started to press the switch. Her hand froze as she heard a click somewhere up ahead.

Barbara's blood ran cold as she searched frantically for a place to hide. She tiptoed toward the back of the garage, shuffling her feet to avoid tripping in the dark. She rammed into something cold and hard and almost fell. Barbara steadied herself, holding onto an unseen car fender. She eased back behind the car and watched as the door next to the office started opening, admitting a slice of light from outside.

Barbara ducked back out of sight. She heard scuffling sounds as several people came in. The outside door closed, and footsteps echoed through the garage. Something clicked. Barbara eased forward, peered around the back of the car, and saw the office door swing shut.

She felt her way cautiously along the rows of shadowed cars until she neared the office. Her pounding heart seemed audible as she inched along, fearing discovery at any moment. Closer and closer she came to the lighted windows. Finally she could hear the murmur of voices but not what was being said.

Barbara dropped to her hands and knees and crawled past the door, continuing on until she was under the windows. But it was still an incoherent mutter. Barbara turned around so she could face the door. Sprawling on the floor, she pressed her ear against the wall. That didn't help a bit.

—————— —————— ——————

Brad sat behind his desk, listening as Ed told Hawk about the upcoming shipment. As usual, his brother was embellishing his story with the obvious goal of praising himself. So far, Ed had described how his militia had gotten some C-4 and the TOW missile by using the unnamed informant Ed had recruited. Hawk's expression made it clear he was not enjoying the show. Ed paused for a breath.

Hawk's pained expression became a sneer. "Could we cut to the chase? What does this guy in Oklahoma—who shall remain nameless—have to do with us—if anything?"

Ed glared at the ex-Ranger. "I was getting to that!"

Brad sensed a blow-up brewing. "Cool it." He waited until Ed looked his way. "Tell Hawk about the shipment."

"But . . ." Ed stammered.

"The shipment—please." Brad spoke slowly in a calm voice, the opposite of what he was feeling.

"OK, just giving a little background." Ed's tone dripped with self-sacrifice.

"I think we have the picture. Proceed."

"The McAlester Ammo Plant is sending a shipment to the 46th Infantry Brigade in Wyoming next Monday. If we ambush it . . ."

"What?" Hawk interrupted, his voice rising. "Out in the open, just like that?" He snapped his fingers. "That's the most harebrained idea I've ever heard!"

Ed jumped out of his chair, his fists clinched. "If you're so smart, where's all the ammo we're going to need?" he shouted.

Hawk stood up as well.

Brad resisted the urge to join them. "Sit down! Both of you!" Ed turned back to him, followed by Hawk. "We're all on the same side," Brad continued. "Now sit down. We're going to discuss this calmly. Nothing's decided . . ."

"But . . ." Ed interrupted.

"That's enough—I mean it. Now, this is how I see it."

⚊⚊ ⚊⚊ ⚊⚊

Barbara grew dizzy from her extreme concentration. She had caught a few indistinct words when tempers flared. But what really jolted her was when one of the men asked where they would get their ammo. *What did that mean?* she wondered.

Barbara felt something rub against her thigh. She flipped over, her eyes wide with terror, and nearly screamed until she realized what it was. A large gray cat, equally scared, scampered away, dropping a freshly killed rat. The animal's frantic yowl sounded like a siren inside the cavernous garage. Barbara knew the men must have heard it.

An icy jolt shot down her spine. She glanced all around, then turned and started scrambling toward the Coke machine, jumping upright after passing the last office window. Barbara caught a glimpse of the door opening as she ducked into the shadows beyond the tall machine.

"Someone's out here!" a man said.

"What's that?" another asked. After a few heart-stopping moments he continued. "It's a dead rat!"

A dark shadow slinked toward the office from the back of the garage. Barbara lost sight of the cat as the Coke machine cut off her view.

"Hey, it's only the cat."

"Are you sure? It sounded pretty spooked."

"She's a nutty cat but death on rats. If she wasn't, I wouldn't keep her."

"Don't you think we should look around?"

"Hawk! This garage is locked tighter than maximum security. Now, how is anyone going to get in here?"

"Come on, Brad. It can't hurt to check."

There was a long pause. Barbara looked around. There wasn't anywhere she could hide. If they searched the garage, they would surely find her, and how would she explain that to Dan Oliver? Barbara slipped her hand into her pocket and felt the reassuring cold steel of her gun. She said a silent prayer.

"This is wasting time. We've got work to do."

"What work? All we've heard is your brother's screwball idea."

"Hey!"

"Stop it! Now back in the office. I want to talk to both of you."

For a few moments, nothing happened.

"Come on! I mean it!"

Finally Barbara heard the sound of footsteps on the gritty floor. The door opened, then closed. Only then did she relax a little. She groaned inwardly as she realized it was far from over, that she was still trapped and anything could happen.

Barbara discarded the idea of resuming her listening post. She considered sneaking past and reentering Elizabeth's van but decided it was too risky. She would wait them out, hoping they wouldn't have any reason to walk past the Coke machine.

Chapter Ten

Brad looked at Hawk. "Ed's right about one thing. We've got to get some ammo from somewhere. I was going to start checking with other militias or see if I could find a source in one of the armories, but this shipment could solve all our problems, like that." He snapped his fingers. "At least for now."

"I hear you, but this is pretty wild stuff," Hawk said. "Knocking off a semi—out in the open?"

"That was my first impression, but I think we can do it."

Hawk did not look at all convinced. "Won't the shipment be escorted?"

"Yes, but . . . " Ed began.

"Let me handle this," Brad interrupted. "Yes, there's an armed escort, but we can take care of that."

Hawk whistled. "How? Ask 'em to pull over?"

Brad laughed. "You're close. Say you're the escort driver and a state cop pulls up alongside, lights flashing, and motions you to pull over. What would you do?" He watched as the ex-Ranger thought it over.

"You mean . . . "

"I can make a cop car that would fool even a state trooper. Now, if I was escorting a load of ammo, I think I'd pull over if a cop wanted me to." He laughed again. "After all, we're on the same side."

"OK. What next?"

"We stop 'em on a rural stretch. I walk up to the guards. They're curious about what I want, so the driver rolls down his window, thank you very much. Meanwhile, my partner—that's you—is back at the semi. I take care of the guards, while you hammer the truckers. Time it right, and there's nothing to see—just a truck pulled over by the state cops. Then all we have to do is drive off with the ammo."

"That might work. What do we do with the semi?"

"Drive to a secluded spot and transfer everything to waiting vans and trucks. Within a few hours our ammo problems are over."

"OK. Have you worked out the plan?"

"I'll start on that tomorrow. First thing is to get going on the cop car, since that's the most critical item." Brad saw his brother's strained expression. "And Ed can help us with the details."

Hawk frowned at this but said nothing.

"Gents," Brad hurried on, "time is short. I say we proceed assuming it's a go. Then if something comes up, we can always call it off. What do you think?"

"No harm in that, I guess," Hawk agreed.

"So, that's settled. Is there anything else we need to do tonight?"

"There are about a dozen M-16s that need work. The actions are dirty, and I'll probably have to replace a few parts—won't know until I get them stripped down. Could use some help down in the armory." Hawk looked pointedly at Ed.

"Fine with me," Brad said. "I can start making notes on what we need for the operation."

He stood up and followed them out into the garage. Brad looked for the dead rat, but it was gone. Apparently his cat had returned for her prize. All that remained was a small pool of blood illuminated by the Coke machine. Hawk led the way toward the hidden elevator.

He looked over his shoulder at Brad. "Junior won't mind getting his hands dirty, will he?"

Ed grabbed him by the arm. "Why don't you ask me?"

Hawk stopped and faced him, an angry scowl on his face. "That's a good way to lose your teeth!"

Brad tried to step between them. "Stop it—both of you!"

Ed turned to his brother. "I'm just as much a part of this militia as he is!"

"Dream on," Hawk said, his voice low and sarcastic.

"That's enough!" Brad shouted. He waited to make sure they were both listening. "I'm not going to say this again! We're a team, and I expect both of you to work together!"

"But . . ." Ed began.

"No 'buts'! You asked me to take you in. You wanted in my militia. OK, you're in. If you step out of line one more time, you'll regret it." Brad saw Ed was about to interrupt. "Don't say anything! We'll talk about it later." He turned to Hawk. "Let's call it a night. You can work on the rifles tomorrow."

Hawk seemed subdued now. "Yeah, that's probably best. Sorry if I caused you trouble."

Brad shrugged. "That's all right. You know how much I value your leadership, but think about it. The enemy is in Washington, not here among us. Let's focus on that, OK?"

"You're right."

An eerie yowl echoed off the steel walls. The cat paraded across the floor, her tail held high like a battle flag. She paused at the dark spot on the floor, sniffed, then licked it.

"That is some weird cat," Hawk said.

"Tell me about it," Brad replied.

The cat looked up at the men, then flicked her tail and resumed her journey. She disappeared behind the Coke machine and did not reappear.

"Hawk, I'll call you tomorrow after I have a chance to plan this out," Brad said. "Maybe we can get together for lunch and see where we stand."

"Fine by me."

Barbara looked down. The cat butted her head against the agent's leg, her purr clearly audible. Barbara waved her away, but it did no good. She listened as the sound of footsteps diminished. Finally the door opened and closed. Only then did her breathing return to normal.

Barbara waited a few minutes, then hurried over to Elizabeth's van. She opened the back, climbed inside and locked the door. She debated on where to sleep. The carpeted floor was tempting, but inside the tent bag would be safer. She shivered at the thought of someone surprising her in the morning, should she oversleep. Barbara climbed into the bag and zipped it up.

Craig squirmed around as he tried to get comfortable in the front seat of Susan's old Escort. But it wasn't possible, and besides, the inside of the car looked like a dumpster, fast-food wrappers and empty cups strewn everywhere. Had he not been in such a hurry, Craig would have cleaned the car out. Not for the first time, he regretted that his car was in Muskegon.

Susan had picked him up after he delivered the van to Anderson's. Craig had tried to convince himself that Barbara would be all right, but somehow he couldn't dismiss his worries. Later, he asked Susan for her car, enduring her questioning look without answering it. He had arrived outside the garage right at sunset. When the three men showed up, Craig had considered stepping in. He tried to see their faces as they got out and went inside, but the light was too dim. The waiting, not knowing what was happening, dragged on, shredding Craig's nerves even further.

Finally the door opened again. Craig dropped to the seat to keep from being seen and waited until the men drove off. Somewhat relieved, Craig sat up and said a silent prayer for Barbara.

The Gathering Storm

━━━ ━━━ ━━━

Barbara jumped at the sound of a door opening. She had been awake for hours, dreading this moment. A garage door started grinding its way up. She pulled the zipper down a little and looked out. The pale light of morning drifted through the van's windows, bathing everything in pastel tones.

Barbara heard the muffled sound of approaching footsteps. Something scraped on metal, then a click and a door opened. She raised her head and saw a man standing by the driver's door, but he was not looking in her direction. She dropped back down.

"You want me to start on this?" a voice asked.

"Yeah," another man said. "That's Mrs. Phillips's van. Something's wrong with the ramp. I want it out today."

Barbara recognized Brad Anderson's voice.

"Shouldn't be a problem," the mechanic said. "I'll get right on it."

"Good. Oh, and see me later. I've got something special for you."

"Will do."

The van rocked as the man got into the driver's seat. A bell began chiming, then the engine started. Something clicked repeatedly, followed by a rustling sound.

"Ah, ha," the man said.

Barbara froze. Had he seen her? She gripped the zipper with her fingernails and prepared to bolt.

"Connector's busted."

The van moved again as the mechanic got out. The door thumped shut. Barbara waited a few seconds. How long would the man be gone? She eased the zipper down and listened. Two men were talking. Barbara wriggled out of the bag and crept to the back doors. She slowly raised up and peered out. She couldn't see anyone but knew there had to be at least two people inside the garage. She checked the side windows. Still nothing, but it would be easy to overlook someone in the garage's organized clutter.

Barbara opened a rear door, stepped down and closed it. After a quick glance around, she crept toward the open garage door and freedom, expecting with every step that someone would call out. Only when she was outside did she begin to relax. Now the only problem was to get home. She hurried through the parking lot and across the street.

Barbara heard a car door open. She looked toward the sound and saw Craig getting out of a rather forlorn looking car. He waved but did not call out. She checked traffic and crossed the street. His somber expression chilled her.

He opened the passenger-side door. "Are you all right?"

"Yes." Barbara noted the stubble on his chin as she ducked inside the car. She stepped over the trash piled up on the floor. He closed her door and went around.

Craig made a U-turn but didn't say anything until they were several blocks away. "I'm glad to see you," he said finally. "I was worried."

"How long have you been out here?"

"All night. I didn't have peace about you being locked up in there. I borrowed Susan's car and came to wait. I wanted to be here if you needed me."

Barbara felt momentarily pleased that he cared, but other thoughts intruded as well. Did he think she was incapable of doing her job? Then there were her own doubts about the wisdom of what she had done. But, at least she hadn't gotten caught.

"Thank you," she said finally.

"You're welcome. Did you find out anything?"

"Not in the garage, but while I was searching, some guys came in."

"Did you see who they were?"

"No, but I'm pretty sure I picked out Brad's voice; and I heard Hawk's name mentioned. I was really scared."

Craig's concern was obvious. "Scared me too. All I saw was their backs when they drove up, but you're right—Brad had to be one of them. What did they do?"

"After they went in the office, I crawled under the windows, but I couldn't hear much, except when they were arguing." She paused. "One guy asked something about where they were going to get their ammo." She turned to Craig. "What do you think?"

"Well, since they need ammunition, the shipment to Wyoming and the mystery call from Muskegon suggest a connection—maybe. A hijacking is a possibility, I guess."

"Meeting at night plus all the arguments could mean they're planning something."

"Could be, but why not wait until the ammo gets to the armory? It would be easier, assuming they had a contact."

"Is that really what you think?"

He took his time answering. "All things considered, I'd have to go with the hijack theory. I know it sounds extreme, but it's the only thing that fits all the clues."

"And there's no question some of these militias are getting bold."

"Yes. So, what are you going to do?"

Barbara felt a sense of dread. "Get with Sam and tell him what I've done. Then we'll have to bring Dan up to speed."

"Mr. Oliver doesn't seem like the easiest person to deal with."

"Impossible comes to my mind."

The trip to Spring Lake didn't take long. All Barbara could think about was her coming confrontations, first with Sam, then with Dan. Craig parked the car and came around for her. Her preoccupation fell away as she got out and looked into his eyes. His concern was obvious. He had spent a miserable night in that car, waiting for her. He took her hands in his. A huge lump formed in her throat.

"I don't know what I'd do if something happened to you," Craig said, almost in a whisper.

She felt the tears coming and couldn't stop them. He pulled her close. She rested her head against his chest, grateful for the comfort of his arms. He stood perfectly still and stroked her hair. Finally she looked up, pulled a tissue from her pocket, and wiped her eyes.

"Sorry," she said, sniffing.

"For what? I . . . I care about you."

She looked into his eyes and saw his emotion—and what he really meant. In that moment, she realized she felt the same way. The physical attraction had been obvious for some time, but it went deeper than that. As nice as that realization was, it certainly complicated her life at a rather difficult time.

"Do you . . ." He began but did not finish.

"Yes," she said softly.

For a long time he did nothing except look into her eyes. Then he kissed her, slowly and thoroughly. Barbara's response opened up deep wells of emotion that surprised and scared her. There was no mistaking how Craig felt. They stood there breathless when they finally parted.

Craig cleared his throat. "I love you."

She looked into his eyes, adoring what she saw there. He had only said what was all too obvious. Realizing this didn't make the other problems go away, but it did make them more bearable.

"I love you too," she said finally.

His smile grew more relaxed. He pulled her close in a gentle embrace. She rested her head against his broad chest. His beating heart sounded loud and reassuring. A worrisome thought stole in among her warm feelings, unwelcome but unavoidable. What would Dan do when he found out about last night?

Chapter Eleven

Brad looked up as Greg Zach stuck his head inside the office door.

The man looked puzzled. "Got the Phillips' van fixed up, but I need to show you something."

Brad got up and followed him. "What's the matter?" he asked.

"When you gave me the keys you said the van was all locked up."

"That's right. Craig told me there's camping equipment inside, not to mention the custom gear we installed. That's why he wanted it inside the garage overnight."

"Well, after I got done, I found the back doors unlocked."

"Oh? You sure you didn't unlock them?"

"Positive. I only opened the driver's door, since that's all I needed to fix the connector. After I finished, I checked the rest of the doors to make sure they were locked. That's when I discovered the back open."

"Were you away from the van any after you started working on it?"

"Yeah. I had to go find a connector. That was also about the time you asked me if I had installed a heavy-duty suspension in your brother's van during the conversion—which I had."

Brad opened the back doors and looked in. There wasn't a lot of camping gear inside, only a camp potty and what looked like a tent. He crawled inside and examined the carrying bag, noting that the zipper was partially open. He pulled it the rest of the way down and moved the tent components around.

"Looks like the tent poles are missing," Brad said. He turned to Greg. "Did you see anyone hanging around this morning?"

"No. You and I were the first ones here. Since then, all I've seen are the other guys."

Brad zipped up the bag and stepped out of the van. "This sure is strange. I'll ask Craig about it. Got the keys?"

"Right here," Greg said, holding them up.

"Lock it up, and come in the office. There's something else I want to talk to you about."

The mechanic locked the doors. He and Brad walked back to the office.

"You say it was a connector?" Brad asked as he opened the door.

Greg stepped inside. "That's right. A busted connector in the lift motor wiring harness. Only took a couple of minutes to replace it."

Brad closed the door. "Busted? How?"

"Don't know. Defective, probably. Anyhow, it's fixed now."

Brad went around his desk and sat down. "OK. Take a seat." He waited as the mechanic did so. "I've got a hot job for you. I want you to build me a cop car."

Greg's eyes opened wide. "You mean, for . . ."

Brad nodded. "The militia—yes. So make sure all the parts are untraceable, including the car." He opened a desk drawer and pulled out a bundle of hundred-dollar bills. "Here's ten thousand. Will that be enough?"

Greg took the money. "I think so. I know a junkyard that specializes in salvage cars. How quick you need it?"

"By next Monday. Can you do it?"

The man whistled. "That's a little tight, but I think so. I assume you want me to work by myself."

"Roger that. This is top secret."

"I understand." He got up. "I'll keep you posted. You want state police or local?"

"State."

"You got it."

━━━ ━━━ ━━━

Barbara tried to rein in her thoughts as she trudged up the stairs to the Group Grand Haven conference room, but it was hopeless. The revelation of Craig's love and the realization that she loved him too had been wonderful but unsettling. She had avoided facing this truth, but now she had to; and that was nice except for how it complicated her work—especially now.

Barbara yawned. She opened the door and looked in. Sam wasn't there yet, she was glad to see. She sat down at the table, opened her laptop and went over her rough notes. A few minutes later Sam arrived.

"Good morning," he said. He took the chair beside her. "How did it go yesterday?"

Barbara felt a twinge of guilt since all he knew about was the helicopter scouting trip. "It was a good idea. There are lots of places along the highway where they could hijack the truck. But I think the stretch south of Holland is the most likely."

"That seems reasonable."

She hesitated. "There's more. I staked out Anderson's garage last night."

Sam's eyebrows shot up. "You did?"

She took a deep breath. "From the inside."

"What? You mean you broke in?"

"No! Please hear me out. I did not break in."

Sam leaned back in his chair. "OK, you were inside Anderson's garage, but you did not break in. Would you care to explain?"

Barbara took her time, going over what she did and why. Sam's scowl never fully went away, but it did moderate a little. However, after reflection, Barbara wasn't proud of what she had done either.

"Barbara! Dan will have your head for this!"

"I'm sorry. I agree, I shouldn't have done it."

Sam shook his head. "Well, you answer to Dan, not me."

Barbara shrugged. "But we can still use what I found out. What do you make of them saying they needed ammo?"

"Well, I guess it's likely they'll try to stock up sometime. This meeting, coming so soon after that call to Oklahoma, might connect the two. But you didn't hear them talking about a hijacking."

"What else could it be?"

"First of all, we're not sure anyone's planning a hijacking; but if so, we can't assume it's the Grand Haven Militia." A wry smile came to his face. "We do have a few to choose from around here. Did you get a look at the men?"

Barbara shook her head. "No." She paused. "Craig thinks I'm on the right track."

"And you very well could be."

"What's your opinion?"

Sam didn't answer at once, and when he did, Barbara could tell he was worried. "I suspect you're right, and if so, we don't have much time. What do you think we should do?"

"I'd recommend using the Coast Guard helicopter to pick up the shipment once it enters the state. What kind of ground assistance could we expect?"

"Oh, two or three cars and a half-dozen agents; FBI and Michigan state police, perhaps. We can ask Dan about it."

"Good. The more the better. One of the cars could trail the transport, while we position the others up ahead. We probably should give the FBI in Oklahoma a heads up so they can warn the shipping company."

"I agree. That sounds like a good beginning." He glanced at his watch. "Are you ready to brief Dan?"

"I guess so."

Sam's brown eyes bored into hers. "He's not going to like what you did at the garage."

Barbara shrugged. "Yes, I know."

"And you realize Dan doesn't see the militia threat quite like we do. He thinks most of them are ineffective wackos."

"I gathered that. He better reconsider."

Sam shrugged. "Got any suggestions?"

"No, I was hoping you'd take care of it."

"Don't believe I can do that."

Craig settled back in the car seat and tried to make himself comfortable. He was wearing casual clothes rather than his uniform because he would not be going to Muskegon until later. Susan was driving him to Anderson's Automotive to pick up Elizabeth's van.

He tried to concentrate on his task but found that impossible. His mind kept stirring up what he had said to Barbara that morning and what she had said in return. He smiled at these pleasant thoughts, but his reverie hit a little bump as he realized his life was now more complicated.

"Are you and Barbara—you know—involved?" Susan asked.

Craig jumped. He glanced at his sister-in-law. He wasn't sure how to answer or if he wanted to. "What do you mean?"

Her sniff was audible even over the car's rattles. "Do you love her?"

His first impulse was to deny it, but he realized he couldn't do that. He considered telling her it wasn't any of her business, but that wouldn't be right either. "Yes, I do," he said finally.

"Have you told her?"

"I have, and she loves me too."

Susan turned into the parking lot and stopped. Craig saw her intense gaze and the undisguised contempt lurking behind it.

"Moving kinda fast, aren't you?"

Craig clamped down hard on what he was tempted to say. "That is a personal question."

"OK, fine, forget I said anything."

Craig sighed. "Thanks for the ride."

Susan drew herself up a little. "Think nothing of it."

Craig got out and watched as she backed out and drove away. He regretted the torment Susan was going through, but so far she had been unwilling to take practical steps to change her life.

He walked into the garage bay nearest the office and looked around. Brad was coming his way.

"Hi. I'm here to pick up the van," Craig called out. "I promised Mom I'd get it before going to Muskegon."

"That your search-and-rescue station?" Brad asked.

Craig forced a grin. "That's a roger on your last."

Brad slapped him on the back. "You know I appreciate the Coast Guard, Craig. The sea services gotta stick together, right?"

"That we do."

Brad hesitated. "Your mom's van is ready to go. Come on in the office."

Craig followed Brad inside. The din of the garage faded considerably with the door closed.

"What was wrong with the lift?"

"Before we discuss that, I'm a little concerned about something."

Craig's heart jumped. "Oh? What's that?"

"I drove the van inside the garage last night, just like you asked, but this morning my mechanic tells me the back doors were unlocked. Are you sure the van was locked up when you dropped it off?"

"Yes," Craig said.

Brad's frown remained. "I don't know what happened. My mechanic said he didn't open the back, but he did leave the van unattended with the driver's door open. I suppose someone could have gotten inside without us knowing. Tell me again what all you had in there."

"A tent and a chemical john."

"They're still there, but it looks like the tent poles are missing."

"Oh, don't worry about that. I took them out myself. Doesn't sound like anything's missing."

Brad looked a little relieved. "Good, but please check it out. If anything is, I'll file on my insurance."

"I'm sure everything's fine. What was wrong with the ramp?"

Brad's grin returned. "Busted connector." He laughed. "Not going to make much money off you this time." He pushed the bill over.

Craig glanced at it and reached for his wallet. "Very reasonable. Thanks, Brad."

"You're welcome. I appreciate your business."

Craig took out the signed check Elizabeth had insisted on giving him and filled it out. Brad took the check, marked the bill paid, and gave Craig a copy.

On his way home, Craig found himself wondering about Brad. Could this model citizen and respected businessman really be planning to hijack a truck full of Army ammunition?

Barbara followed Sam back to Dan Oliver's office, dreading the coming confrontation. Sam knocked.

"Come in," a muffled voice said.

Sam pushed the door open. Barbara looked in and saw Dan. He was not smiling.

"What is it?" he asked.

"We've got an update on the Grand Haven Militia," Sam replied. He took one of the side chairs while Barbara sat in the other.

"You sure there is one? Anderson and Hawkins don't strike me as your typical off-the-shelf weirdos."

"We believe there is. I paid Hawkins a visit at his gun store, and he fits the profile right down the line. He's a gunsmith and even has this huge banner with the second amendment on it."

Dan's expression turned to a sneer. "That's a heavy-duty indictment if I ever heard one."

"There's more."

"I should hope so."

"The FBI has been shadowing a suspect in the Judge Richards case. Two days ago, someone in Muskegon calls this guy, but they're both using pay phones, so we don't know what they talked about. However, the suspect works at the McAlester Army Ammunition Plant in Oklahoma, and they just happen to be shipping a load of ammo to a guard unit in Wyoming, Michigan."

Dan toyed with a ballpoint pen, spinning it with a finger. "Where exactly is this going?"

"We believe the Grand Haven Militia may attempt to hijack this shipment."

"That's crazy. One, how did you tie the call to them, and two, what makes you think they'd do something that stupid?"

"The FBI thinks this same suspect told a Montana militia where they could get some munitions—a local guard armory that the McAlester plant had recently shipped to."

"I remember the case, but that militia had an inside connection at the armory—it wasn't a hijacking. Besides, those shipments are guarded, aren't they?"

"Yes, but we're seeing a pattern of escalating militia violence. I think what we're suggesting is entirely possible."

"Well, folks, as I look out my window, I don't see any smoking ruins, at least not yet." Dan turned to Barbara. "Is this your doing?"

She shifted uneasily. "I agree with everything Sam said. Based on our investigations, we believe it's possible—perhaps likely—the Grand Haven Militia will try to grab this shipment. I've also discussed it with Craig Phillips, and he's of the same opinion."

"Who said you could talk to him?"

"Per your instructions, he and his crew are assisting us in our operations."

"The Coast Guard is providing transportation and logistics. Lieutenant Phillips is not a trained agent."

"He's in the military, and we're faced with a paramilitary operation. Besides, the Coast Guard is heavily involved in law enforcement. I believe Craig is a valuable resource."

"I agree with Barbara," Sam said. "Of course we can't be sure, but I believe there's enough evidence to justify taking precautions."

Dan crossed his arms. "That's it? You want me to authorize an operation to prevent a militia from swiping this ammo shipment—a militia we're not sure even exists? Not without more proof than I've seen so far."

Barbara felt an icy chill in her stomach. "There's more."

A disturbing gleam came to Dan's eyes. "Oh? And what does our explosives expert have to add?"

"We know the Grand Haven Militia is short on ammunition."

His eyes never moved. "And how do we know that?"

Barbara took a deep breath. "I heard one of the members ask where they were going to get the ammo they needed—they were arguing about it."

"How interesting. And how did you come to hear that?"

"I was inside Anderson's Automotive last night. They were meeting in the office." Barbara saw Dan's stunned look but hurried on, "Please let me explain." She gave him a quick summary of what she had done.

"I don't believe I'm hearing this," Dan said when she had finished. "I suppose you expect me to praise you for what you did. Ms. Post, I could fire you for it!"

"What I did was rash—I admit it, and I regret it. But I did not break and enter. I was inside the Phillips's van, and a garage employee drove the van inside."

"What's your opinion?" Dan asked Sam.

Sam glanced her way. "I don't think it was wise, and I doubt it was legal. But it did yield some valuable information."

"The end does not justify the means."

"You're right, it doesn't," Barbara said. "But at least now we can link Anderson to the Grand Haven Militia, and what I heard—plus the other evidence—suggests they could be planning to grab this shipment."

"Even if you're right about Anderson—which I'm not buying—you still haven't convinced me about the ammo shipment. Nothing you've said points to a hijacking."

Barbara struggled to retain her composure. "I know the evidence is circumstantial, but this is one possibility. What happens if they do and we fail to prevent it?"

"You mean what happens to your stupid boss?"

"No, that's not what I meant. We're all in this together. Why not take a few precautions? If nothing happens, the egg's on my face. But if the militia does strike, we'd be ready."

"What about it?" Dan asked Sam.

"I think it's plausible enough to warrant taking action."

"What kind of action?"

"I'd like Barbara to cover that."

Dan turned to her. "Fine. What do you think we should do, Ms. Post?"

"Basically, set up surveillance units and have the FBI warn the ammo plant."

Dan shook his head. "Nope. This does not leave our office until I know a whole lot more."

"But the drivers could be in danger."

"You still haven't convinced me. What kind of surveillance did you have in mind?"

"Once the truck enters Michigan, I recommend we shadow it by helicopter . . ."

"Time out! What about your bad guys—the ones you're so worried about? Won't they see the 'copter?"

"Not according to Craig. He's been involved in law enforcement operations before."

"Go on."

"I'd also like to station cars along the route. Maybe a half dozen or so agents, augmented by FBI and state police."

"No! I say again: We are not involving any outside agencies unless you can show me a lot more proof than I've seen so far."

"But . . ."

"No 'buts.' The helicopter you can have, plus a car and two agents, but that's all. Besides, how much force does it take to arrest a bunch of crazies?"

Barbara felt the heat rising in her face. "Some militias are capable of extreme violence."

"You haven't produced a smoking gun yet."

"Will you allow us to call up more agents in the event of an attack?"

Dan snorted. "You mean the cavalry riding to the rescue? That'd be a nice Texas touch. I'll think about it. Is that all?"

"Basically. If you approve, Sam and I have a lot to do before Monday."

"Is it a go?" Sam asked Dan.

"You and Ms. Post can plan it, I guess. No harm in that. But keep me informed. I want to think it over before I commit."

Barbara and Sam stood up together.

"Will do," Sam said.

<hr />

A knock sounded on the door. Brad looked up at Greg Zach and hoped it was good news.

"Come on in," he said.

The mechanic did so, closed the door, and sat down.

"How's it going?" Brad asked.

"Not too bad. I located a suitable car with a salvage title. It was caught in a flood, so the insurance company totaled it."

"Yeah, I saw the wrecker deliver it. Will you be able to fix it up in time?"

"No problem. I can't promise all the electrical goodies, but the drive train will work like a champ, and that's all we need."

"Agreed. What about the police gear?"

"I've got a friend who works for Grand Rapids Police Supply. The light and siren package will be delivered tomorrow, with the company none the wiser. Also, Hawk put me onto a guy who works for a specialty print shop. They make decals, among other things. That'll take care of the car's shields and signs."

"Can we trust these guys?"

"Not a problem. I've known Tom for years, and Hawk says his friend is OK."

"Good."

"It'll probably take me all of Friday to check out the drivetrain, but I'll have to wait until Saturday to paint it and install the police equipment. Can't let the regular crew see me doing that."

"Good work. Let me know how it goes."

"Will do."

Brad's eyes followed Greg as he returned to the bay outside the office. He tried to visualize the rusty car with Michigan state livery but failed. But he knew it would look like the real thing come Monday.

Chapter Twelve

Craig glanced at his watch as he put down the phone. It was almost 4:30, and it looked like his day was about to go into extra innings.

"Joel!" he shouted. "Round up the crew. Group Grand Haven communications just handed us a search-and-rescue mission. Missing sailboat."

Craig bolted for the door of the hangar as his copilot went to get the mechanic and rescue swimmer. Outside, he ran across the asphalt tarmac toward the waiting helicopter. Small white clouds dotted the brilliant blue sky, and a cool breeze blew off the lake. Craig heard the sound of pounding feet behind him as he ducked through the helicopter's side door. He hurried forward and jumped into the right-hand seat. Moments later Joel started strapping into the copilot's position.

"What's the mission?" Joel asked.

"A mother called Group Grand Haven and told them her son was overdue. He and his girlfriend took his catamaran out this morning and said they would be back around eleven. The lady is quite upset."

"Any other units?"

The side door shut with a solid thump. Craig initiated the start-up procedure. A low whine sounded above them.

"Yes. Station Grand Haven dispatched a motor lifeboat. They'll be handling the search close in."

He checked with the crew on the intercom and found they were ready. Craig advanced the throttles, and a moment later the helicopter transitioned into forward flight. The ground dropped away as the HH-65A Dolphin turned away from the Muskegon County Airport. After clearing the airport, Craig altered their flight path out over the lake, angling toward their initial search pattern off Grand Haven.

"What's the boat look like?" Joel asked.

"The mother's description wasn't very precise. She said it has white hulls and the sails are kind of gaudy."

"Gaudy? What color is gaudy?"

"She said orange at first, then changed her mind to red."

"Let me guess: she doesn't know how long the boat is either."

"That's a roger on your last. So, look for something white with gaudy sails."

"That narrows it down to a couple thousand."

Craig thought about what it would be like in the water. It might be late spring in western Michigan, but the water was still cold, and the wind would make it seem even colder. "Yeah, but only one is in trouble—assuming this isn't a false alarm."

⁓

Barbara punched in Craig's mobile phone number but got his voice mail. She decided not to leave a message, and instead called Air Facility Muskegon. The man who answered the phone told her that Craig and his crew had just left on a search-and-rescue mission. Barbara thanked him and hung up.

She had wanted to tell Craig how the meeting with Dan had gone and suggest a meeting later to discuss the upcoming operation on Monday, if one could call the limited assets her boss had allowed for an operation. Barbara went to the break room for coffee. The coffeemaker was brewing a fresh pot. As she waited, Barbara had to admit she also wanted to hear Craig's voice.

⚊⚊ ⚊⚊ ⚊⚊

The Dolphin arrived on station, and Craig began the first leg of a standard search box, each leg overlapping the previous one so that nothing was missed. The method was methodical and effective, but most of the time there was little to see, since a lost boat could hide anywhere in the thousands of square miles covered in an average search. Craig was well aware that two young people could be depending on their expertise.

"Not a lot of boats out this far," Joel remarked.

Craig scanned the angry chop below. A brisk wind blew the tops of the waves off, dotting the lake's deep blue with whitecaps. "Yeah. The motor lifeboat is more likely to pick 'em up than we are. Of course, anything's possible."

"Not the most pleasant day to be out sailing. Don't you know it's cold down there with all that wind and spray."

Craig glanced at Joel. "It's not too bad if you dress for it. It can be quite invigorating."

"Not if you capsize."

"Can't argue that." Craig's practiced eye scanned the lake's surface. The wind was from the west, strong and gusty; perfect conditions for what sailors call a knockdown.

Craig brought the helicopter around on a new leg to the west.

A few minutes later Joel pointed. "Hey! I think I see something."

Craig looked. At first he thought it was a long whitecap, but instead of disappearing, the white slash remained perfectly straight.

"I see it!" He cranked the Dolphin around in a sharp left turn.

As they got closer, Craig could see the red sails undulating on the surface. The catamaran bobbed sluggishly on its side, with one hull swamped, the float at the top of the mast the only thing preventing a complete capsize. And there, clinging to the half-submerged boat, were two people. One of them looked up and waved.

"Swimmer," Craig said. "Stand by the hoist."

"Roger," the man answered.

Craig brought the helicopter in from downwind and began a quick descent. The rotor blast beat a circular pattern into the rough waters below.

"I'm hooked up," the swimmer reported.

"Roger," Craig replied. "Let's do it."

He brought the Dolphin to a hover and operated the winch control. Moments later he saw the swimmer descending on the slender steel wire, clad in wet suit and flippers, a face mask and snorkel covering his face. Craig inched the helicopter forward. The swimmer dropped free while still in the air and plunged beneath the water. He surfaced immediately and swam toward the boat with powerful strokes.

Craig lowered the rescue harness until it touched the water and started moving toward the boat. The swimmer grabbed the sling and put it around one of the victims. Craig engaged the winch.

"On the way up," Craig told his flight mechanic.

"I'm ready." A little later the man reported, "She's in. OK to lower away."

The second rescue went just as smoothly. The swimmer hooked up the young man and signaled for Craig to hoist him up. The third lift brought the swimmer back into the helicopter. After he reported the door secure, Craig turned east, applied power, and began hauling for home.

"What's their condition?" Craig asked as he steadied up on the course for Grand Haven.

"Got 'em bundled up in blankets, skipper," the mechanic reported. "They're in hypothermia, but I think they'll be OK."

"Great job. Tell 'em we'll be there soon."

"Roger."

Craig radioed Group Grand Haven, requesting an EMS ambulance meet them at the YMCA ball field and that the mother be called. The shore approached with what seemed like agonizing slowness, even though the Dolphin was making 160 knots. The South Pier and Inner Light appeared on schedule. They roared over the mouth of the Grand River on a direct course for the YMCA. With precise timing, Craig backed off on power and pulled back on the stick. The helicopter slowed and started dropping as it transitioned into a hover. The EMS ambulance was waiting, lights flashing. Craig pulled back further on the stick, increased power, and brought the aircraft down to a swift but gentle landing.

The side door slid open. Craig looked out and saw his swimmer and mechanic helping the bedraggled sailors toward the ambulance. The EMS attendants took over, bundling the smaller figure onto a stretcher. The other victim walked alongside until both disappeared inside the ambulance. The back doors slammed shut, and the vehicle roared out of the parking lot, lights flashing and siren screaming.

"Well done, everyone," Craig said over the intercom.

He increased power and lifted the helicopter off. "Back to the barn," he said to Joel.

—◇— —◇— —◇—

Barbara's phone rang. She picked it up, hoping it was Craig. "Hello," she said.

"Hello, is this Barbara?" a woman's voice asked. It took Barbara a moment to recognize who it was.

"Yes, Elizabeth. How are you?"

"Fine, now that I have my van back. I'm glad Anderson's was able to fix it so quickly."

Barbara wondered what Elizabeth would think if she knew the whole story. "I'm glad too. I know how important it is to you."

"Listen, the reason I called was to invite you to dinner tonight. Craig's on a search-and-rescue mission, but I'm hoping he'll be home fairly soon."

"Is it likely he'll be delayed?"

"It depends on if they find the boaters."

"I see."

Elizabeth laughed, but it sounded a little strained. "It's part of the Coast Guard life." She paused. "I hope you'll say yes. We'd really love to have you."

Barbara thought it over. She would have preferred an invitation from Craig. "Yes," she said finally. "Thank you. What time should I be there?"

"I'm flexible. William and I are here by ourselves. What about around seven?"

"That sounds great. I'll see you then."

She pressed the phone switch then dialed Craig's mobile phone number, but got his voice mail again. She almost hung up without leaving a message, but on second thought said, "Hi, this is Barbara. Please give me a call."

Barbara hung up and checked her watch. She had just enough time to get home. She pulled her mobile phone out of her purse and frowned in disgust as she saw the battery was almost flat. She turned it off and slid it back in her purse. Then she got up and headed for the door.

<hr />

Craig's mind was in overdrive as he guided the helicopter in for a landing, and the familiar white hangar came into view. They were pleasant thoughts—change into his civilian clothes, call Barbara, and play it by ear from there. But then reality intruded in the form of duty, as Craig remembered he was quite delinquent in his paperwork. Maintenance and supply reports were late, and he had official correspondence he had to write. He sighed as his earlier excitement evaporated, but he would take time to call Barbara.

Craig brought the Dolphin to a hover, then landed so smoothly it surprised even him.

"Whoa, skipper," Joel said. "Like to try that again?"

Craig ignored his copilot's silly grin. "Just skill and experience."

"Yeah, right."

The side door behind them opened, and the swimmer and mechanic jumped out and started walking toward the hangar. The pilots finished shutting down, unstrapped, and got out.

"You need me to hang around?" Joel asked.

Craig shook his head. "No. I've got some paperwork to do, but you can hit the road."

"You sure?"

"Yeah."

Inside the hangar, Craig grabbed his mobile phone and punched it on, noting he had a message. He played it back, smiling when he heard Barbara ask him to call her. He considered ditching the paperwork until tomorrow, the prospect of seeing Barbara being a lot more attractive.

"Did you win the lottery?" Joel asked.

Craig turned. "What?"

"Your grin. You know—cat one, canary zero, in sudden death overtime?"

Craig made an attempt to regain what he called his command bearing but had to give up. "Ah, Barbara—I mean Ms. Post—left me a message."

"Whoa, it must have been really heavy-duty." A twinkle came to the young officer's eyes. "Or am I treading on dangerous ground?"

Craig shrugged. He felt sure Joel had his suspicions. "She asked me to call her."

"Uh, huh." Then Joel's grin faded. "You're serious about her, aren't you?"

Craig looked him in the eye, pleased he was a good friend. "Yes, I am."

For a few moments, Joel said nothing. "I'm glad to hear that," he said finally, with none of his usual high spirits. "I hope it works out for both of you."

"Thank you."

Joel finished changing into his sports clothes and left. Craig punched in Barbara's office number and got her voice mail. He hadn't expected her to be there, so he hung up without leaving a message. Next he tried her mobile phone, and again he got her voice mail. He left a message, then dialed her apartment. There he got her answering machine. He hung up, deciding he would rely on the mobile phone message.

"OK," he said to himself. "Zero for three."

He stuck the phone in his pocket and trudged to his cramped office to see how much progress he could make in his paperwork.

⚊⚊ ⚊⚊ ⚊⚊

Barbara parked and rushed upstairs to her apartment. She opened the door and checked her answering machine first thing. No messages. Disappointed, she plugged in her mobile phone to charge it. She glanced at her watch and saw she better hurry if she expected to arrive at Elizabeth's house on time.

She changed quickly and hurried through her preparations, hoping the whole time that Craig would call. But the phone remained silent. She finished, looked at the phone accusingly, and left the apartment.

⚊⚊ ⚊⚊ ⚊⚊

Craig frowned as he surveyed his in-box. It seemed the mound of paper had grown since that morning, and it probably had. He grabbed a stack of requisitions off the top and approved each one after a casual scan. He also signed the routine reports but decided to put off the rest of the paperwork until Friday.

Craig turned to his computer and started composing a letter, a report to his commanding officer at Traverse City covering the surveillance operation with the ATF. But that only caused his mind to wander back to Barbara. He picked up his mobile phone and looked at it, wondering why she had not returned his call. He used his office phone and called her mobile number. When her recorded greeting came on, he decided not to leave another message. He then called her apartment number. The recording came on.

"Hi, this is Craig, returning your call. I'm finishing up some work at Muskegon. You can reach me at the number here or on my mobile phone. Talk to you later." He paused, then added, "Love you."

After several futile attempts at composing his letter, Craig saved the document and shut down his computer. He left his office, told the relief helicopter crew where he was going, and changed into his civilian clothes. He was halfway to Grand Haven before he found out he had left his mobile phone on his desk. *What's wrong with me?* he wondered. But then the answer came just as quickly, as he thought about Barbara. *Where is she?*

Chapter Thirteen

Barbara rang the doorbell more or less on time. William pulled the door open and looked out at her.

"Hello, William," Barbara said. "How are you?"

"OK, I guess." He eyed her cautiously as she came inside.

"Only 'OK'?"

He shrugged. "Grandma says I have to be polite."

"You don't have to hold back with me." Barbara followed the boy into the living room.

The door to the kitchen opened, and Elizabeth rolled out in her wheelchair.

"What do you care?" William asked Barbara.

"William!" Elizabeth said. "That was rude!"

"I do care," Barbara said quietly. "I know you're going through a hard time, and I'm sorry. I'm praying for you."

He frowned. "What good does that do?"

"Maybe more than you think."

"You sound like Grandma."

Barbara glanced at Elizabeth. "There's a reason for that. We're both Christians; so is your Uncle Craig."

He whirled around and dashed for the stairs. "I'm going to my room!"

"William!" Elizabeth shouted. "Come back here!"

His running shoes squeaked on the floor as he slid to a stop. Slowly he turned around. He seemed to shrink under the stern glare of his grandmother.

"Do I have to?" William whined.

"Yes, you do. Now, Ms. Post is our guest. I want you to visit with her while I put the finishing touches on dinner."

"Can I help?" Barbara asked.

Elizabeth's expression faded into a smile. "No, thank you, dear. Please make yourself comfortable."

"Maybe we could find something for William to do."

He looked up at her. "I know what you're doing. I'm not a little kid."

"No, you're not. Know what we'd call you in Texas?"

He squinted his eyes a little. "What?"

"Hombre."

"What's that?"

"An hombre is a tough old dude." She looked him over. "He wears dusty jeans and a raggedy old shirt, scratched-up boots, spurs, and a sweat-stained, plug-ugly hat."

"I don't have any of that."

"Oh, you would if you lived in Marfa."

"But you said things are different now."

"They are, but we still wear western clothes. And we still have our share of tough guys." Barbara glanced at Elizabeth. "And gals."

"You're messing with my mind." William's expression looked like a head-on collision between a sneer and a smile.

"Would I do that?"

"Yeah."

Barbara laughed. "OK, you got me." Then she became serious. "But you enjoy helping your grandmother, don't you?"

"Um, sort of."

"OK. Why don't we sort of help her while we're waiting for Uncle Craig? I could tell you some wild west stories while we're working."

"Like what?"

"Like the time my mom went out in the garage to get the dust mop, only when she reached for it, she found out it didn't have a handle. About that time the mop scampered off into a corner like a tumbleweed in a thunderstorm."

William scrunched his face up. "What?"

"The mop was a tarantula."

"You're kidding!"

"No, I'm not. Tarantulas get mighty big in West Texas."

"What did your mom do?"

"You could have heard her in El Paso. She ran back inside and told Dad to go take care of it. Dad raised the garage door and shooed the critter outside. Mom said that wasn't what she had in mind, but Dad just shrugged. He didn't see what all the fuss was about."

"Wow. Tell me some more."

"Let's mosey on into the kitchen, and I'll see what I can do."

Elizabeth led the way through the swinging door. She assigned the salads to Barbara and William while she checked on the roast, potatoes, and carrots.

"Have you heard from Craig?" Barbara asked as she cut up the lettuce.

"Not from him. Someone called from the Air Facility saying he was going out on a search-and-rescue mission, so there's no telling when he'll be home."

"Does he call when he's on the way?"

"Usually, unless he forgets. I don't think it occurs to him that we might worry." She closed the oven door and turned her wheelchair toward Barbara. "Would you like to give him a call?"

"Yes."

"Why don't you use the cordless phone. I think I left it in the living room."

"I thought you were going to tell me some stories," William said.

"William," Elizabeth called out.

He looked her way suspiciously. "What?"

A twinkle came to Elizabeth's eyes. "When your uncle gets home, ask him to tell you about the time he rescued a flock of chickens."

The boy seemed curious but cautious. "What? The Coast Guard doesn't rescue chickens."

"Not usually, but this time they did. But right now I need some help." She wheeled down to the refrigerator.

"I don't want to," William whined.

"I'm going to pour the chocolate pudding. But, if you don't want to lick the bowl, I guess I can wait until Ms. Post gets back."

William rushed to her side.

Seeing that the bait and switch was successful, Barbara slipped out of the kitchen. She found the cordless phone on a table next to the couch. The man at Air Facility Muskegon told her that Craig had left for home. Barbara thanked him and punched in the number for his mobile phone but got his voice mail. She decided not to leave a message and turned the cordless phone off.

Barbara sat in an easy chair in the living room with Elizabeth at her side, while William squirmed and fidgeted on the couch. Although Elizabeth seemed at ease, Barbara could tell she was concerned. The news that Craig had left the airport over a half hour ago was disturbing since it was less than ten miles from Grand Haven.

The front door swung open, and Craig stepped inside. His eyes locked immediately on Barbara's.

"Where were you?" he asked. "I got your message but never could reach you. I tried everywhere."

Barbara felt a flash of irritation. "I called your mobile number but got your voice mail."

"I left my phone at Muskegon."

"And I called Muskegon, and they said you were on your way home. Where *were* you?"

"Uh, I was worried, so I went over to your apartment. When I saw your car wasn't there, I didn't know what to do."

"Your mother invited me to dinner."

His face became very red. "So I see. Sorry for the confusion. I guess I was distracted."

"Distracted?" Elizabeth said. "My son distracted? Why, what could cause such a thing?"

His flush grew even darker. "Could we talk about something else?"

"We'll see," Elizabeth said. She wheeled around and called to William. "Let's go check on dinner, assuming it's not burned to a crisp."

"But I didn't get to ask about the chickens?"

"Come on. That can wait till later."

"Chickens?" Craig asked.

"Something about one of your rescues," Barbara said.

Craig groaned. "Did Mother tell you about that?"

Barbara grinned. "No, she said you would."

"Great."

William disappeared into the kitchen. Elizabeth paused at the door. "You two sit down at the table. We'll be out shortly."

Barbara saw the friendly glint in Craig's eyes as she turned toward him. She felt her pulse race as he pulled her close and kissed her. She was breathless when they broke.

"I love you," he whispered.

"I love you too," she replied.

He took her hand and led her into the dining room. A few moments after they sat down, Elizabeth came in with a large food tray across the arms of her wheelchair. William placed the platters and bowls with reasonable precision. When they were all seated, Craig offered the blessing.

Barbara started the roast around. "Did you want to ask your uncle something?" she said to William.

"Oh, yeah. Grandma said you once rescued some chickens."

Craig glanced at Barbara. "Thanks," he whispered.

"I can't wait to hear it myself."

"I wish Mom hadn't brought it up. It's not exactly my favorite memory." He looked down the table at her.

"It's a delightful story, dear," Elizabeth said.

"Yeah, Uncle Craig. Tell us about the chickens."

"True story?" Barbara asked.

Craig ladled some potatoes and carrots onto his plate. "Unfortunately," he replied. "It happened about this time last year. Some sailors reported a swamped rowboat with a man inside and some white things about the size of soccer balls; but since it was after dark, they didn't get a good look. Well, they came about but couldn't find the boat again. Group Grand Haven dispatched my helicopter and a motor lifeboat."

"How can you do anything at night?" William asked.

"We have night vision goggles that intensify whatever light there is. They give you a bright picture, in shades of green—sort of like looking through green Jell-O."

"Cool!"

Craig laughed. "Yeah, they're cool alright. But even so, I didn't think we'd find the boat. The estimated location was extremely vague, which made the search area huge. But, we got lucky."

"You found 'em?"

"That we did. And sure enough, there was this swamped boat with what looked like one person aboard. I looked for some sign of life—a wave maybe—but didn't see anything."

"Was the guy dead?"

"Yes and no."

William stopped eating. "What? That's impossible!"

"Stay tuned. I lowered the swimmer, and then a stretcher. I watched my guy, thinking he'd put the victim inside, but instead he began picking up these round things. Well, I hoisted the stretcher up. Next thing I knew, my mechanic was on the intercom. 'What am I supposed to do with these chickens?' he asked me."

"Chickens?" Barbara asked with a snicker.

"You know, those white things that lay eggs."

"What about the guy in the boat?"

"I was wondering the same thing. The swimmer signaled for me to hoist him up. After we got him aboard, he came forward, laughing so hard I thought I'd never get it out of him."

"What happened?" William asked.

"The guy in the boat turned out to be a dummy—a department store mannequin. It and three chickens were the entire crew. About this time one of the chickens came waddling onto the flight deck, giving Joel and me the once-over, like she wanted to know who was in charge. I told the swimmer to strap her and her friends in, which made him stop laughing.

"Meanwhile, I radioed Group Grand Haven and told them we had found the boat and were coming in. They asked if I wanted an ambulance to meet us. I told them no, but they might want to notify Kentucky Fried Chicken."

Barbara giggled. "You didn't."

"Oh, but I did. I told them about our passengers, and for a long time they couldn't decide what to do. I told them to hurry it up because I wasn't about to carry any chickens back to Muskegon."

"What happened?"

"The duty officer met us at the YMCA ball field with a pickup truck and a couple of cardboard boxes with holes punched in the sides. As I was making my approach, our three guests went berserk. Next thing I knew, here was this insane hen flapping around inside the cockpit, squawking like mad."

"I thought they were strapped in."

"So did I, but later the mechanic told me he and the swimmer just couldn't catch them. After a while the chickens had settled down, and my guys decided to cool it and see if the cease-fire would hold. But hostilities broke out again when I increased power for landing, and one of the hens made a break for it. The swimmer tried to tackle her, but she faked him out and raced into the cockpit."

William laughed, leaning back so far Barbara was afraid he would tip over.

She broke up as well. "It's a wonder you didn't lose control," she said.

"It was a little distracting. The hen flapped up in my face, rammed into the canopy, then flopped back down in my lap. She looked up, shook her head, and then started beating me with her wings. Since I was kind of busy, I backhanded her over to Joel. He let out a yell but managed to hold her off while I finished landing, quite smoothly I might add, despite the harassment."

"Oh no!" Barbara said as she struggled to catch her breath. She wiped her eyes with her napkin. "Was that the end of it?"

"I wish. I looked back just as my mechanic popped the side door. He stood back, apparently expecting the chickens to deplane by themselves. Then he turned to me and said, 'What do I do?' I told him to give them to the duty officer. Well, he grabbed one, and she started flapping and squawking and pecking at anything that looked vulnerable. My man hollered and dropped the bird, which promptly scampered out the door. Another hen followed, but the third one hunkered down in a corner. I looked outside. The duty officer was running after one of the escapees while the other hen disappeared into the night."

"What about the one still inside?" William asked.

Craig shook his head. "Since my swimmer didn't seem in the mood for volunteering, I charged in there. The hen saw me coming and ran through my legs and into the cockpit. Well, I came about and followed her. The chicken was sitting in my seat, flapping like mad. Joel held up his hands and leaned away from the fracas. The hen took off, crashed into the Plexiglas bubble, bounced off, hit Joel, then landed back in my seat, looking dazed. Then she did it again. It took several tries, but I finally managed to grab her and dash outside, with her pecking me every step of the way. I thought about trying to stuff her into one of the boxes but finally had to drop her."

"Did you ever catch them?" Barbara asked.

"Nope. I figured if they wanted free that bad, they could have the run of Grand Haven."

"Where did the boat come from?" William asked.

"We never found out, since the boat and mannequin were never seen again. We figured some boys must have found the dummy, put it in an old rowboat, and set it adrift."

"What about the chickens?"

Craig shrugged. "Who knows? Maybe the kids thought the dummy needed a crew."

"I had no idea Coast Guard life was so—I don't know—swash-buckling," Barbara said. She tried to keep a straight face but failed.

"Thanks," Craig said.

"Oh, he has more stories than that," Elizabeth added.

"But not right now."

"Uncle Craig," William said. "I wanna hear another one."

"Later. Eat your food before it gets cold."

"But . . ."

"No 'buts.'" Craig watched his nephew until the boy gave up and started eating.

Barbara saw Craig's eyes swing around to her. The tension was all too clear.

"How did it go today?" he asked.

"It was interesting. That's why I was trying to reach you; to bring you up-to-date." She felt heat rising in her face. "And I wanted to talk to you."

He grinned. "I see. We can discuss it later—both subjects."

"Talk about what?" William asked.

"I don't believe you're included in that conversation," Elizabeth told him.

"What about another story, then?"

"Why don't you give your uncle a rest. I'm sure he'd appreciate it."

The rest of the dinner passed in relative peace, although William made it obvious he was less than pleased. Barbara's heart went out to the boy, but she knew there wasn't much she could do—except pray. She made a mental note to be more faithful in doing that.

Elizabeth and William served the chocolate pudding along with homemade chocolate chip cookies. Barbara reflected on the fact that this northern dinner would have gotten good reviews in Marfa, even if it did lack a southwestern flavor. Chocolate, she decided, did not recognize regional boundaries.

"That was excellent," Barbara said when they finished.

"I'm glad you enjoyed it," Elizabeth replied. "Would you like some coffee? It's decaf."

"Yes, that would be nice."

"Good. Now, I know you and Craig have things to discuss, so if you will excuse me and my able assistant, we'll say good night."

William looked like he wanted to protest, but he didn't say anything.

Craig went to the kitchen and returned with two mugs. "You drink it black, right?" he asked.

"Yes, thanks."

William and Elizabeth finished clearing the table and disappeared into the kitchen.

Barbara followed Craig into the living room and sat beside him on the couch. She sipped her coffee.

"How did it go?" Craig asked.

Barbara shrugged. "Dan was pretty mad over the garage incident, but it could have been worse. At least I didn't get fired." A chill ran down her spine. "Dan still doesn't believe the Grand Haven Militia is much of a threat."

Craig frowned. "I know it isn't any of my business, but that worries me. If that militia knocks off the ammo shipment, it could be a real disaster."

"Well, he is allowing us to plan for surveillance using your helicopter, plus a car with two ATF agents."

"That's pretty thin."

"Yes, I know it is, and he hasn't given his final approval yet, either."

Craig shook his head. "How does Sam feel about it?"

"I think he agrees with us."

"Well, I guess that's something, but I sure hope Dan changes his mind."

Barbara felt the chill return. "I hope so too."

Craig put his arm around her. Barbara snuggled into his shoulder, grateful for the comfort she found there as she listened to his heart beating away. She looked up into his eyes. He kissed her gently. Her worries faded a little for the moment.

Chapter Fourteen

Barbara walked hand in hand with Craig outside Group Grand Haven. He had picked her up at her apartment for the early meeting with Sam to plan the surveillance operation as best they could with the resources Dan had allowed. Craig held the door for her, and they went upstairs to the second-floor conference room. Barbara opened the door and found Sam waiting for them, sitting at the head of the table.

Sam looked up and smiled. "Good morning," he said as he stood.

"Hello, Sam," Craig said, shaking his hand. "How are you?"

"Fine," Sam replied. Then his smile faded. "Are you up for our exciting operation?"

"We're ready to help in any way we can."

"You're very diplomatic."

"I've already discussed it with Craig," Barbara said. "He realizes we're light going into this."

"That we are," Sam agreed. "And we're assuming Dan will approve our final plan."

"I take it Dan still won't let us contact the truck en route."

"That would be a safe assumption." He pointed to the table. "I brought the maps you asked for."

"OK." Barbara turned to Craig. "Shall we start with them?"

"That's what I recommend." He unfolded a map of his own. "I brought along the Chicago VFR Sectional."

"VFR?"

"Visual flight rules. It's the map aviators use when not flying on instruments. The Chicago map includes northern Illinois and part of western Michigan." Craig spread the map out beside the ones Sam provided. "So, what does their route look like?" he asked.

Sam pointed to McAlester on the Oklahoma map. "They're scheduled to depart the ammo plant next Monday at eight in the morning." He glanced at Craig and grinned. "Zero-eight-hundred hours, if you prefer."

Craig smiled. "Civilian time will do."

Sam shuffled the maps around as he showed Craig the rest of the route. "Where do you want to begin surveillance?" Craig asked.

Barbara pointed to the Michigan map. "The hit could come anywhere, but I believe we're agreed it's most likely to happen south of Holland because of the long rural stretches and the fact it's not far from Grand Haven."

Craig looked at his sectional map. "To be on the safe side, why not pick them up when they enter Michigan?"

"That's what I'd recommend," Barbara said.

"When do you estimate they'll get here?"

Sam consulted some scribbled notes. "The total trip is around 920 miles—800 to the state line. They're not stopping overnight, so I calculated the earliest they could reach Michigan would be midnight Tuesday, and on into Wyoming around 2:00 A.M."

Barbara sneered. "Assuming they don't run into any trouble. I wish Dan would let us warn them."

"Yeah, but he won't," Sam said. "So we'll have to do the best we can."

"How long can we stay up?" Barbara asked Craig.

"The Dolphin's max endurance is three and a half hours." Craig glanced at the map. "The driving time from the state line to Wyoming should be around two hours; so that's no problem, assuming our tanks are full when we spot them. We can refuel at the Benton Harbor airport as needed."

"Where do you think we ought to put our agents?" Barbara asked Sam.

"One car doesn't offer us much. I guess our people could follow the truck once it enters Michigan, or they could wait near the most likely ambush location."

"Somewhere before Holland?" Barbara asked.

"That sounds reasonable."

"But it could be on any rural stretch."

"Yes. So what's your preference?"

"I think our people should trail them but stay way back."

"OK. Where should we be?"

"On Craig's helicopter." She turned to him. "Can you take us both?"

"Yes. It means leaving my swimmer behind, but we won't need him anyway."

"Now, what about weapons?" Sam asked. "I'm proficient with my Glock 9mm, but that's it."

"Our personal weapons are a given," Barbara said, "but I'd also like to have an M-16 with a low-light scope. And I think our guys on the ground need some extra firepower."

Sam nodded. "We'll see what the boss says."

Barbara opened up her laptop and turned it on. "Ready to start writing it up?"

"Yes. Dan said he'd come by around two."

"Well, we better get cracking."

Brad stepped out of his office and looked at the large sedan up on the lift. The engine's oil pan was off, revealing the crankshaft, and Greg was in the process of lowering the transmission.

"How's it going?" Brad asked as he approached.

The mechanic stopped and grabbed a rag to wipe his hands. "Pretty good. Engine's fine, but the transmission had water in it. Gonna have to overhaul it."

"Do you have enough time?"

"No problem. The rest of the running gear looks OK, although I haven't had time to check out the electrical systems. The overhaul and paint job will take the most time."

"What about the special parts?"

"The light and siren package and the decals will be here before quitting time."

"You sure?"

"Positive."

"OK. Keep me posted. You need anything, call me."

"Roger that."

Brad watched as Greg pushed the cart with the transmission over to a workbench. Although his militia was still under strength, he had a good group of troopers and was making progress in recruiting. There was no shortage of men concerned about the growing attacks on liberty and the American way of life. The armory was coming along, and soon he would have the infusion of ammo he needed. And once the militia became operational, Brad could begin his strategic planning.

It was almost 2:00 P.M. when Barbara finished reviewing the rough draft of their operational plan, one of four copies printed courtesy of Group Grand Haven's network. The thick sheaf of papers detailed the personnel involved and the equipment and tactics to be used. She waited until Craig and Sam put their copies down.

"What do you think?" Barbara asked.

"Nice draft," Sam replied. "You've covered all the important points." He paused. "I wish we had more assets."

"Maybe Dan will give us more after he reads this."

Sam nudged the plan with a finger. "He won't read it. He'll expect his own copy, of course, but he'll depend on you for a bullet list."

Barbara couldn't help an exasperated sigh. "Maybe I should just create a PowerPoint presentation for him."

Sam laughed. "You think you're kidding. He likes slide shows; and if there were time, it would have been worth doing."

"I can't believe this."

"Get used to it." Sam glanced toward Craig. "You'll have to excuse our dirty laundry."

Craig smiled. "Oh, don't mind me. I'm Swiss."

"What?" Barbara asked.

"I'm neutral. Besides, we coasties have our own share of problems."

"But what we're doing—or not doing—affects you too."

"Don't worry about it. It'll be OK."

"I hope so."

The conference room door opened, and Dan Oliver came in.

"What do you hope, Ms. Post?" he asked as he walked toward the head of the table.

Sam vacated his seat and sat across from Barbara and Craig. Dan sat heavily. His eyes never left his explosives expert.

Barbara felt heat rising in her face. "I hope our operation is successful."

"Assuming I approve it," Dan said.

"Of course."

"This mine?" He grabbed the draft in front of him and riffled through the pages.

"Yes," Barbara replied.

"I don't suppose you have a presentation." His tone indicated he was sure she didn't.

"No. We didn't have time."

"OK. Brief me."

Barbara condensed the plan down into a summary of bullet points.

Dan listened, asking a few inconsequential questions here and there, until she got down to the equipment list.

"Whoa! You want M-16s? Look, Ms. Rambo. Do you really and truly think that ragtag little militia is going to try and knock off an escorted ammo shipment? Come on now!"

Barbara frowned. "Yes, Mr. Oliver, that is exactly what I think might happen."

"You said 'might.' Is your confidence slipping a little?"

"I'm convinced the Grand Haven Militia is serious bad news, and circumstantial evidence points to a possible hijacking."

"Circumstantial . . . possible . . . I think you're giving these local yokels too much credit."

"What about the Oklahoma City Bombing? What about the militia that took out Judge Richards?"

Dan frowned. "Yeah, yeah. I'll grant you that some militias have caused us problems—big-time in a few cases. But even with all the militias we have around here, things are pretty quiet right now. Of course, we've got to keep our guard up, especially as the president's visit approaches."

Barbara picked up a copy of the plan. "So, is it a go?"

"Not so fast. You said you expect the transport to cross the state line around midnight on Tuesday?"

Barbara felt her stomach knot up. "Yes," she said, dreading what Dan might say next.

Dan looked at Sam. "Did either of you contact the McAlester plant?"

"No, we didn't," Sam replied. "The FBI report provided the transport company and departure time. The rest isn't exactly rocket science."

"Don't get smart with me."

"That wasn't my intention."

"Fine," Dan grumbled. "Do you really believe a hijacking is possible?"

"Yes, I do." Sam paused. "Do you approve?"

Dan's frown grew deeper, then seemed to relax into reluctant submission. He turned to Barbara. "OK. You can have the Coast Guard helicopter and two agents, in addition to yourself and Sam."

"What about the weapons?"

Dan shook his head. "You want three M-16s? Don't you think that's a little excessive?"

"No, I don't. If they strike in force . . ."

"You can have one," Dan said, interrupting, "not that you'll need it." He pointed his finger at her. "But I'm going to be watching. If this turns out to be a wild-goose chase . . ."

"That's not fair. I didn't say the militia would strike, only that it was likely. But these guys are dangerous. I'm positive of that."

"So you say. Well, I guess we'll see." He stood up. "If you people will excuse me, I've got things to do back at the office. Keep me posted."

"We will," Barbara said. She struggled against despair as she watched her boss stalk out.

"I thought that went well," Sam said with a deadpan expression, after the door closed.

Sam's sarcasm echoed Barbara's feelings. She believed they were facing a very real threat, but Dan seemed to be thwarting what the ATF should be doing. She shivered as she thought about what a well-armed, trained militia could do—bloodshed and destruction on a grand scale. American terrorism—a nightmare.

"Let's get with it," Barbara said finally. "We've got a lot to do before Monday."

"Right," Sam agreed. "I'd better go back to the office and see who Dan is going to assign us. You want me to take care of the M-16?"

"Please. I'll stay here and work with Craig on the search plan."

"OK." Sam stood up.

"Before you go," Craig said. "The weather wonks tell me we can expect thunderstorms on Monday."

Barbara sighed. "Just what we need. When and how bad?"

"The front is supposed to move through sometime Sunday night. As Sam can tell you, storms around here can be pretty ferocious."

"No argument on that," Sam said.

"Will that ground you?" Barbara asked.

"Probably not, but it could make it hard to track a ground target. Also makes for a rough ride. But we do a lot of foul-weather flying. Don't get a lot of search-and-rescue missions when it's nice out."

Sam grinned and shook his head. "Boaters are so inconsiderate."

"When do you want to get together again?" Barbara asked him.

"How about tomorrow, say around ten or so?"

"Here OK?"

"Fine with me."

After Sam left, Barbara turned back to the maps. Her eyes traced the interstate routes from the Michigan border all the way to the city of Wyoming.

"That's a lot of territory," she said.

"Yes, but it's not nearly as bad as what we cover in a typical search-and-rescue mission. Knowing the exact route helps a lot."

"I guess, but I have a bad feeling about this. Four ATF agents might not be enough if these guys mount a major operation. We're going to be out there without any backup."

"So, what can you do about it?"

She sighed. "Nothing, except prepare the best we can." She paused as something else came to mind. "And pray."

Craig grinned. A little to her surprise, this cheered her.

"Sounds like a good idea to me," he said.

<hr />

Greg stuck his head in the door. "Boss, the special equipment is here. Where do you want to stash it?"

Brad glanced at his watch. It was nearly 4:30. "Better put it in here. We can take it down to the armory after quitting time."

"Right." Greg stepped aside.

Brad stood up as a young man came in with the first box. He had on clean, starched khaki work clothes, and his hair was short and well-trimmed. His blue eyes seemed to miss nothing.

"Where do you want it?" he asked.

"Over in that corner," Brad replied.

The man made two more trips, depositing five boxes without saying another word. Greg entered the office after his friend left.

"You want to check it over?" Brad asked.

"I'll do it tomorrow. But I won't find anything wrong. That guy doesn't miss."

"Good."

Greg returned to his workbench and the overhauling of the transmission. Gradually the outside activity wound down, accompanied by garage doors closing as the legitimate side of Brad's business prepared for the weekend. Eventually Greg was the only one still working. He waved to Brad as he walked past the office. Moments later the remaining garage door rattled shut.

A few minutes later Brad heard a tapping sound. He went to the outside door, opened it, and let Hawk in.

"Got our uniforms," Hawk said.

"Let's take a look," Brad said.

Inside the office, Hawk pulled out two sets of state police uniforms, complete with hats, belts, and badges.

Brad whistled. "Nice. Looks real."

Hawk laughed. "Except for the badges, they are real. The badges are close copies with altered numbers. A good customer of mine is a state cop."

"Can we trust him?"

"No problem. He's sympathetic to the cause. Might even be able to recruit him."

"Good. You ready to go to work?"

Hawk rubbed his hands together. "You bet. Picked the location?"

"Yes." Brad unfolded a Michigan map. "Look at this." Hawk came around behind the desk. Brad pointed to a spot south of Holland. "Right there," he said. "We follow from Benton Harbor and pull 'em over just before this exit. I'll handle the escorts while you whack the drivers." He indicated an east-west road. "Our trucks will be waiting at an abandoned farm, right about here. Ed drives the semi to the rendezvous, we off-load, and then we're on our way back to Grand Haven."

"Ed? Why Ed?"

Brad stifled his own concerns on this point. "Do you know how to drive a semi?"

"No."

"Well, neither do I, but Ed does."

"But . . ."

"Cool it. I'll watch him, OK?"

Hawk shook his head. "It's your decision."

"That's right. Now, don't worry. This'll work out fine."

"Hope so," Hawk replied. "We sure need the ammo."

Chapter Fifteen

Brad pulled into the parking lot of Anderson's Automotive just after 8:00 A.M. on Saturday. After parking his Suburban, he and Ed got out and entered the garage. Brad relocked the door and looked around. The only other person inside was Greg, who was painting the salvaged car. The mechanic hung the spray gun on a hook and raised his respirator, revealing a flesh-colored oval in the over-spray spattering his face.

"How's it going?" Brad asked.

"Great," Greg replied. "I wanted to get the painting out of the way so it can be drying. I'm still working on the transmission, but I'll have that done by early afternoon."

"Good. What about the decals, lights, and siren?"

"I'd like to wait until Sunday, to give the paint a chance to get hard."

"OK. Hawk was planning to take the car to his place late Sunday. That a problem?"

Greg shook his head. "Shouldn't be."

"I'll tell him, but I think we'll wait until after dark. No sense in taking chances."

"I hear you. Well, I better get back to work."

Brad and Ed entered the office. A half hour later Hawk came by. Brad grabbed a map and several sheets of paper, and the three men took the elevator down to the armory where they pulled tall laboratory chairs up to a worktable. Brad sat in one and put his feet on the steel ring attached to the chair's legs. Hawk and Ed sat on either side. Brad unfolded a Michigan road map and placed it on the table surface. A red circle around an "X" marked a section of Interstate 196 south of Holland. He placed several detailed Excite maps to the side.

Brad looked at Ed. "Hawk and I went over this yesterday. This is where we decided to pull 'em over."

Ed shrugged. "OK. You know this area better than I do."

"Right. You'll be in the cop car with Hawk and me. Once we take care of the guards and drivers, you'll drive the truck here."

Brad's finger followed the interstate exit to the secluded east-west road.

"What about traffic?" Ed asked.

"Should be light that time of night. About a mile to the east is an abandoned farmhouse that belongs to a relative of one of my men. We'll pull the semi up into the barn and unload it there." Brad turned to Hawk. "Have you got the trucks lined up?"

"Yes. Counting your Suburban, we have six assorted trucks and vans plus a large rental truck from Muskegon."

Brad looked at him sharply. "I thought we decided not to do that. What if it's traced?"

"I didn't forget, but we really need it. We can't haul all that ammo with only six vehicles. Don't worry. The feds won't be able to trace it."

"Explain."

Hawk grinned. "I'd rather not go into details, but the rental company is sort of donating the truck's use. They'll never even know it's gone, provided I return it right away."

"What about the odometer?"

"That's for them to figure out. My guess is they'll assume it's poor record keeping, but I don't care. If we keep the truck clean, there's no way it can be traced back to us."

"OK," Brad replied after he thought it over. "Make sure the guy driving it wears gloves."

"Already taken care of. For that matter, everyone will be wearing gloves."

"How long do you estimate for the entire operation?"

"Oh, half hour to an hour, maybe a little longer. I figure we'll load the rental truck with the heavy stuff first, then use our trucks for the rest. We should be back here in plenty of time; unload everything, then disperse."

"Weapons? Lights?"

"Besides personal weapons, I'll be providing Uzis and an M-60 machine gun, but I doubt we'll need them. We'll have three heavy battery lanterns plus six flashlights. So, when do we start?"

Brad consulted his notes. "We don't have a detailed schedule, unfortunately." He glanced at Ed. "They leave the ammo plant at eight in the morning on Monday, and they're driving nonstop except for meals and rest stops. So, I figure they could cross the state line as early as 11:00 P.M. on Monday, depending on their average speed."

"What about weather?"

"The forecast is for thunderstorms starting late Sunday, but I doubt that will slow them down much. They won't run into rain until somewhere in Illinois."

"How will the weather affect us?" Ed asked.

"Probably make it unpleasant," Brad replied, "but it won't keep us from carrying out our mission. It could be an advantage since it'll make it harder for enforcement to spot us." He turned to Hawk. "What do you think?"

"On the whole, I think it's a plus," Hawk replied.

"Have you got the roster?" Brad asked.

Hawk pulled a sheet of paper out of his pocket and unfolded it. "Right here."

"OK. Let's go over the operation, step-by-step."

⸻ ⸻ ⸻

The weather was so nice that Barbara decided to wait for the others outside Group Grand Haven. A light breeze blew down the Grand River from Lake Michigan. Overhead, brilliant white clouds drifted toward the east through the deep blue sky. So far, there was no indication of bad weather; however, Sunday night was more than twenty-four hours away.

Barbara adjusted the laptop against her hip. The fact that it was light didn't make it any less bulky, and the addition of her generous-sized purse resulted in a significant bother. She was considering setting her burdens down when she saw a familiar red Trans Am pull into the parking lot.

Craig waved as he and Joel walked toward the entrance.

"Hi, is Sam here yet?" Craig asked.

"No," Barbara replied. "He's bringing the two agents Dan assigned." She glanced at her watch. "It's almost ten. They should be here soon."

"OK. Want to wait out here?"

"No, let's go on up. I'd like to put my stuff down."

Craig held the door for her. She led the way up to the conference room and picked a chair near the end of the table. Craig sat beside her, and Joel took the chair beside his CO.

Barbara opened her laptop and started the boot-up process.

"Aren't we supposed to be on the other side?" Joel asked. "We're sitting with the ATF."

Barbara looked at Craig, then leaned forward so she could see Joel, but he was not looking at her. Barbara saw Craig blush a little.

"I'm leaving room for the other agents," Craig said finally.

"They could just as easily sit where we are," Joel continued.

Craig turned to him. "I got first choice."

"Oh. I see."

The door opened behind them, and Sam came in, followed by two men Barbara remembered meeting on her first day. She stood up along with Craig and Joel.

"Craig—Joel," Sam said. "I'd like you to meet special agents Pete Singleton and Roscoe Carter."

Craig and Joel introduced themselves. Roscoe Carter was a tall, solidly built, middle-aged African-American. Pete Singleton was thin and not quite as tall as Roscoe. They shook hands with the aviators and nodded to Barbara.

"Glad you'll be working with us," Barbara said. "Has Sam briefed you on the operation?"

"No," Roscoe said.

"I wanted to wait until we were all together," Sam explained. "Why don't we go over what we have so far? Then we can discuss what we want Roscoe and Pete to do."

Barbara opened her Word document. "OK." She reviewed the plans for the agents, and the two men took careful notes.

"Where do you want us?" Pete asked when she finished.

"You're going to tail the shipment as soon as it crosses the state line," Barbara said.

Pete scanned his notes. "OK. Hope we don't spook the militia—assuming the hit is really on."

"Stay as far back as you can."

"Right. What weapons will we have?"

"Just your service automatics." Barbara turned to Sam. "Did you get us the M-16?"

"I did, fitted with a low-light scope. I had an agent check it out for me at the gun range."

"Good."

"That's it?" Roscoe asked. "Our automatics and one M-16? What if these guys show up with some real firepower?"

"That's all Dan would let us have," Barbara said, trying to keep her irritation from showing. "To answer your question, we'll have to do the best we can with what we've got."

Roscoe's frown remained. "OK. What does the route look like?"

Barbara brought out the maps, and they started reviewing possible ambush locations. The more she thought about their limited resources and the force a modern militia could field, the more uneasy she became.

Chapter Sixteen

Barbara hurried through the morning routine of putting on her makeup, saving her hair for last, knowing it was going to be difficult. She arranged it the best she could and applied a liberal amount of spray, hoping to limit the damage.

She felt a jolt when she glanced at her watch. Craig was due at any moment. Her mind drifted back to yesterday's planning session and the concern they all had about Monday's operation.

The doorbell rang.

Barbara slipped into her shoes, hurriedly filled her purse, and headed for the door. She pulled it open and smiled when she saw Craig. Her earlier thoughts drifted into the background.

"Good morning," Craig said.

"Isn't it," Barbara agreed. The air was nippy, but the weather was gorgeous. A heavy dew lay on the grass. Fluffy white clouds covered most of the sky, leaving only patches of blue and no sign of the forecast rain.

"Enjoy it while you can. I checked with Group Grand Haven before I left, and the storm's right on schedule."

"When will it get here?" Barbara asked as she slipped on her light jacket.

"Around nine or ten tonight. Looks like we're in for a few days of spring nastiness."

He turned, and Barbara made sure her hand was available. Craig smiled, took it, and walked her down to his car. He held the door while she got in. They drove to the middle of Grand Haven, to a brick church with a modest-sized white steeple. Craig parked, and they went inside.

Barbara spotted Elizabeth and William immediately. She couldn't hear what the two were saying, but she could tell from the boy's expression that he was unhappy about something.

"Good morning," Barbara said as she and Craig approached.

Elizabeth turned in her wheelchair and beamed. "Good morning, dear. I'm so glad you're worshiping with us. I hope my son didn't twist your arm too much."

Barbara gripped her hand. "No, he didn't. I'm looking forward to it." She saw that William was making a point of ignoring her. "Hi, William. How are you?"

He stuck out his lower lip. "I'm only here 'cause Grandma made me come."

"You need to be with kids your own age, dear," Elizabeth said.

"I don't fit in. The other kids make fun of me 'cause . . ."

"Why?"

"Because of my mom."

"I'm sure your teacher wouldn't allow that."

William ground his shoes on the tile. "He doesn't see everything! Listen! The other boys hassle me all the time!"

"Lower your voice. Now, who is your teacher?"

"I don't remember his name."

"I'll catch up with you two later," Elizabeth told Barbara and Craig. She started wheeling toward the educational wing. "Come with me," she said to William.

"No-o-o-o-o, Grandma!"

"Let me take him," Craig said.

Elizabeth stopped and turned around. "Thank you, dear."

"Why don't you and Mom go in," Craig said. "I'll find you when I get back."

"OK," Barbara said. William's look of anguish touched her. "See you later, William," she said.

He looked right at her but didn't say a word. Craig shrugged.

"Come on," he said to William, placing his hand on the boy's shoulder. William tried to shrug it off, but Craig persisted. The two walked off.

"I feel so sorry for him," Barbara said as soon as they were alone.

"We all do," Elizabeth replied, "but this is where he needs to be."

"Oh, yes, I know. I meant the whole situation. . . ." She stopped, afraid she had overstepped.

"Susan—and Larry before he died—weren't the best parents. I know that." The light seemed to go out of her eyes. "Craig and I are trying to reach William—and Susan—but we're not making much progress."

"Well, don't give up—and keep praying."

A weak smile came to her face. "We are. Believe me, we are." She paused. "And I'm glad. . . . I'm pleased you've come into our lives, dear."

"Me too," Barbara said.

They went into the sanctuary and found seats in a pew near the back. Barbara helped Elizabeth get seated. An usher rolled the wheelchair out of the way. A few minutes later Craig appeared and slid in beside Barbara.

"How did it go?" Barbara whispered.

"I talked with the teacher. I think he'll watch out for William—he really cares. But kids can be cruel, even the ones that come from Christian families."

"I know. But you and your mother are doing the right thing. William needs decent friends."

"And help in finding God."

"The most important thing of all."

Barbara put her arm through his. He took her hand and squeezed.

"Hang in there," she whispered.

He smiled. "I'm trying."

"I'm sure you are."

The first hymn began a few minutes later. The cares of the week started to fade, and by the time the pastor began his sermon, Barbara found she was ready to worship. The service was a little different from what she was used to but not in any way that mattered. Marfa might be a lot different than Grand Haven, but it was the same God.

Afterward, Craig collected William, who seemed a little less truculent than earlier. Barbara accepted Elizabeth's invitation to lunch and Craig's suggestion that they take a walk on the beach later.

It was around two in the afternoon when Craig parked near the South Pier. They got out and started walking along the sandy shore. Sailboats plied the lake close in, heeled over in the high wind. A solid gray overcast had replaced the earlier blue.

"Looks like the front is right on time," Craig said. "It'll be raining before nightfall."

"That's going to make things difficult tomorrow."

He shrugged. "Don't worry. Joel and I are used to flying in bad weather. Besides, it'll be worse for the militia, assuming they actually go ahead with it."

"Yep. Of course, that's the big question. Are they really going to hit that shipment?"

"Having some doubts?"

She looked into his eyes. "I'm concerned. It would be nice to be sure, but that's not possible."

"Better safe than sorry."

Barbara shivered as she thought about the mangled remains of Judge Richards. "Amen to that."

<hr />

The roar of the rain against the garage's metal roof made it difficult to hear.

"Is the car ready to go?" Brad asked, raising his voice.

"All except for the driver's window," Greg said. "It had a bad motor, and after I replaced it, it still wouldn't work. Probably corrosion somewhere, but I just didn't have time to fix it."

"I can live with that." He grinned. "You did a great job. If that pulled up alongside me with flashing lights, I think I'd pull over." He turned to Hawk. "What do you think?"

"Looks like the real thing to me."

"Well, I'm going to call it a day," Greg said as he wiped his hands on a rag. "You need me for anything else?"

"Don't think so," Brad said. "Are you squared away on the plan for tomorrow?"

"Roger. I'll be riding with you over to Hawk's, right?"

"You've got it." Brad slapped him on the shoulder. "I appreciate all the work you put in." He walked Greg to the exit. "Now, don't get wet."

The man laughed. "Yeah, right." He zipped up his jacket.

Brad opened the door. A wind gust blew in a chilling swirl of spray. Greg dashed out into the pounding rain, fumbled with his keys and finally got his car door open. The engine started, barely audible over the roaring hiss of the rain. The car's lights came on, and Greg drove away.

Brad relocked the door and returned to look over the car. It certainly seemed authentic, from the lights to the shiny decals on the body panels.

"You ready to drive it home?" he asked Hawk.

Hawk glanced at his watch and saw it was after midnight. "I guess so. I suppose there's not much chance of being seen in all this mess."

Brad shrugged. "Don't sweat it. If someone does, they'll think it's a state cop on patrol."

"I guess so. See you tomorrow."

Brad operated the garage door and let his friend out.

Chapter
Seventeen

Otto Kaufmann stood on the concrete dock and watched as the forklifts roared around loading the Century Transportation semitrailer. He yawned and took a gulp of coffee while he thought about the long trip from McAlester, Oklahoma, to Wyoming, Michigan. He wondered absently what would happen if they had an accident and all those tons of explosives went off. He shivered. All the more reason to stay alert and be careful. Although he had been with Century for more than two years, these army runs were still far from routine. He drained the last of his coffee and refilled his cup from the coffeemaker inside the warehouse office.

When Otto returned to the dock, he saw the loading was complete. He watched as an ammunition plant bean counter moved about inside the trailer, checking the load against the manifest. The driver saw a movement off to the side. Turning, he saw Isaac, his young assistant, approaching in his obviously new, freshly starched Century Transportation uniform.

Otto looked at his watch. "I was wondering if you were going to show up."

"Sorry," Isaac replied. "I overslept." He glanced at the trailer. "Are we ready to pull out?"

"Shouldn't be too long. What do you think about our load?"

Isaac shook his head. "I just hope it doesn't explode." He paused. "How dangerous is it?"

Otto was tempted to tease him but decided the question deserved a straight answer. "Actually, it's quite safe, although we still have to stay on the hazardous cargo routes. The only danger is a really hot fire, and if that happens, we probably won't be around to worry about it."

"I'd rather not think about that."

"No argument on that."

The loading supervisor stepped out of the trailer and waved his clipboard.

"Looks like it's show time," Otto said. "Wait here."

He entered the long trailer with the supervisor and walked toward the front. He felt a chill as he smelled the faint scent of gunpowder.

"Ready to check 'em off?" the supervisor asked.

"I guess."

Otto accepted the clipboard and followed along as the other man noted each box and crate. The whole tedious process took nearly a half hour. They stepped back onto the dock when they finished.

"OK, lock it up," the supervisor ordered.

One of his men closed and padlocked the trailer doors. Then he applied a car seal to the handles and noted the number on the manifest.

"Sign here, and it's all yours," the supervisor said with a grin.

"Thanks a bunch." Otto dashed off his signature and accepted his copies.

"Have a nice trip."

"Hope so."

The supervisor disappeared into the cavernous interior of the warehouse.

Otto walked over to his assistant. "You ready?"

"Let's do it."

"OK. I'll take the first leg."

Otto led the way to the steps leading down to the pavement. Over to the side he saw a rather plain-looking car with emergency lights mounted on the roof. The two men inside got out and came over. They were wearing blue uniforms with silver badges, and each had a holstered automatic. Both were overweight. Otto wondered how effective they would be if the shipment ran into trouble, but shook that off. What could go wrong?

"You guys ready?" Otto asked.

"Anytime you say. What's our first stop?"

"Let's try for Joplin, unless the coffee gets to us first. If I change my mind, I'll radio you."

"OK."

The guards returned to their car. It pulled out ahead of the truck and stopped. Otto walked up to the driver's side of the Kenworth tractor, mounted the steps, opened the door, and slid into the seat. The other door opened, and Isaac joined him.

Otto started the powerful diesel and let it idle for a few moments as the exhaust covers pinged atop the pipes.

He picked up the radio mike. "OK, take us out."

"Roger," the radio speaker crackled.

The escort car pulled out. Otto sighed as he pulled the heavily loaded semi in behind, and the convoy headed for the gate. It was going to be a long trip.

Barbara tried to relax as she sat in Craig's cramped office inside the hangar at Coast Guard Air Facility Muskegon. But the rain pounding on the metal roof made that hard to do. She glanced at Sam. The incessant noise didn't seem to be affecting him. She envied his relaxed appearance.

Barbara's blue coveralls with the bright yellow "ATF" lettering made her feel self-conscious. Craig was trying to get caught up on his paperwork, but Barbara often caught him looking at her. This pleased her, and she found herself distracted at times, despite what they might be facing later in the day. Joel was in and out, checking on the weather with Group

Grand Haven. Barbara eyed the M-16 propped in the corner, wondering if they would really need it.

A tall, blond-haired man stuck his head in the door. "Excuse me, Mr. Phillips. I went ahead and changed that tire. It's got a slow leak, and I didn't want to take a chance on it."

The young man wore a blue working uniform with two red chevrons on his shoulder denoting a second-class petty officer. Barbara hadn't seen him before.

Craig looked up. "Thanks, Jackson. I think that was wise."

The petty officer started to leave.

"Oh, Jackson, hold up a second," Craig said. The smiling face returned. Craig stood. "Barbara—Sam, this is Petty Officer Arthur Jackson, our new flight mechanic and hoist operator. He just reported for duty this morning."

Barbara stood and shook his hand. "Special Agent Barbara Post. Nice to meet you, Arthur."

The man's grin grew even wider. "Please call me Art, ma'am. Arthur's way too formal."

Barbara returned his smile. "OK, Art."

"Hi Art, I'm Special Agent Sam Green." Sam reached past and shook the man's hand.

"Mr. Green."

"Did Craig—did Lieutenant Phillips brief you on our mission?" Barbara asked.

"Oh, yes ma'am. Don't worry, ma'am, my lips are sealed."

Barbara suppressed a giggle. "Well, that's good."

Art's expression became a little more serious. "Mr. Phillips briefed me this morning after I got my gear squared away. I'll be happy to help you and Mr. Green in any way I can."

"Thank you."

Art looked back to Craig. "Is that all, sir?"

"Yes. Carry on."

Barbara and Craig sat back down.

Barbara glanced at her watch. "About 9:10. The shipment should be on its way."

Sam smiled. "That means what—only another fifteen or so hours to go?"

Craig tossed a thick folder into his out-basket with a sigh. "Are you sticking with the planned launch time?" he asked Barbara.

"I don't see any reason to change it. Are you sure we'll be able to see the truck through this rain?"

"I think so, unless we're in the middle of a downpour when they come through, and that's not likely since the forecast is for moderate thunderstorms. We should do fine with our low-light goggles."

"So, now we wait."

"Not much else to do right now. Like a doughnut? Joel brought some in."

She thought about the calories but decided the circumstances warranted it. "Yes, I would."

"Sam?" Craig asked.

He grinned. "Don't get in my way."

<hr />

Otto stretched and tried to get comfortable as Isaac guided the heavy semi through the broad turn taking them from I-44 to I-55. Otto knew this was the young man's first trip as a long-haul driver; but other than a little nervousness, Isaac was doing quite well. And he seemed serious about doing a good job, not like a lot of young people. Otto glanced at his watch and saw it was almost 4:30. They were right on schedule. Up ahead the afternoon sun glinted off the Gateway Arch on the banks of the Mississippi River.

"Wow, that's really something," Isaac said.

"Your first time in St. Louis?" Otto asked.

"Yeah. I've seen pictures, but it's not the same as being up close and personal."

"I agree." Otto pointed off to the left. "That's Busch Stadium over there."

"Cool." The young man scanned the road. "Where do we cross the river?"

"About a mile up ahead. Interstates 55, 64, and 70 cross just south of the stadium."

"And we stay on 55?"

"Right, all the way to Joliet."

"Where do you want to stop to eat?"

"I was thinking around Springfield. That OK with you?"

The young man grinned. "Hey man, I can eat anytime, but it's your call."

Otto smiled as well. He remembered what it was like to be young. "Sure you can make it that far?"

"I'll be OK."

"Good. Don't want your death on my hands."

The escort turned onto the ramp leading to the bridge. Soon they would be in Illinois.

Barbara shifted in her chair beside Craig's desk. It was 7:00 P.M. now, and she was beginning to regret coming to Muskegon so early. Even if nothing happened, she would be up past 2:00 A.M.; and if the militia did strike, she would be on her feet well over twenty-four hours. But Barbara knew she couldn't have stayed away. She glanced at Craig and had to admit there was another reason for her early appearance.

The outside door near Craig's office banged open, throwing echoes through the hangar and admitting wind-borne spray. Barbara got up as she recognized Roscoe Carter and Pete Singleton. Sam walked toward the agents, carrying a steaming mug of coffee and a limp slice of cold pizza, the remains of their earlier dinner.

"'Bout time you two showed up," Sam said with his mouth full. "Have any trouble getting here?"

Pete shook his head. "Nope. It's nasty driving, but at least the traffic's light."

His eyes flicked across Barbara, but he did nothing more than nod. Roscoe struggled out of his raincoat.

Barbara decided she was not going to be ignored. "Pete—Roscoe. You guys ready for the operation?"

"As ready as we can be," Pete replied. "Do you really think that militia is gonna knock off the ammo shipment?"

Barbara glanced at Sam but couldn't read his expression. She turned back to Pete. "We certainly believe it's possible, or we wouldn't be here. Do you have any problem with that?"

Pete shrugged and a sly smile came to his lips. "Dan says it's your call."

"Our call. Sam and I planned this together."

"Whatever. Any change in plans?"

"No. We'll be taking off around 8:30. Got your radios?"

He frowned in obvious irritation. "Yeah, we got our radios and our guns. If that's all, we better hit the road. We certainly don't want to be late arriving on station."

Barbara turned to Sam. "Do you have anything to add?"

"No."

"We'll radio you from the air," Barbara told Pete.

⚊⚊⚊

Brad slowed his Suburban as he approached Hawk's house. The view was black and blurred even though he had the wipers on high. Strong gusts rocked the truck, and the rain pounded a strident tattoo on the roof.

The narrow drive was difficult to see even in daylight, hidden as it was by trees and overgrown brush. At night, in a downpour, it was almost impossible.

"There it is," the man beside him said. Greg pointed to the narrow track. "Hope we don't get stuck."

"We won't," Brad said. "There's a layer of gravel on the drive."

He turned onto the trail. The heavy truck splashed through the deep puddles, and Brad took great care to follow the ruts as the path wound its way through the trees. Finally the rambling house came into view. The truck's headlights illuminated the detached garage through the slanting rain.

"Where's Hawk?" Ed asked from the backseat.

As if in answer, the garage door started going up, revealing what looked like a state police cruiser and a uniformed trooper in rain gear. The car faced outward and seemed poised for action. Brad stopped, put the Suburban in park, and turned around.

"Ready to make a run for it?" he asked Ed.

"Yeah."

Brad threw open the door and splashed through the puddles with his brother right behind him. They dashed into the shelter of the garage. Greg turned the truck around and drove slowly away.

"You got some mud on your uniform, trooper," Hawk said with a nervous grin.

Brad looked down to where his pant legs extended below his raincoat. "Well, what do you expect on a night like this?" He looked Hawk in the eye. "But I don't think we're scheduled for an inspection."

"Sure hope not."

"Did you get the extra weapons?"

"You know I did," Hawk said, sounding a little peeved. "Two Uzis in the backseat and an M-60 machine gun in the trunk, with three, one-hundred-round ammo belts, not that I think we'll need all that."

"I hope not, but you never know. Well, let's get rolling."

"You want me to drive?"

"Yes." Brad turned to his brother. "OK, get in the back, and stay down when cars go by. We don't want to attract any attention."

"I know what to do."

Brad forced a smile. "Good." He turned to Hawk. "Let's do it."

Hawk opened the door and slid into the driver's seat while Brad sat beside him. Ed got in the back and shut the door, rather hard, Brad thought, but he decided not to notice. Hawk started the car, flipped on the lights, and pulled out. Hard rain blurred the windshield instantly. Hawk switched on the wipers and jabbed the button to close the garage door. Then he cursed.

"What's the matter?" Brad asked.

"I forgot the window doesn't work. Here. Toss this out your side." He gave Brad the garage door opener transmitter. "I don't think the cops could trace us if they found it, but why take chances."

"Right." Brad rolled down his window and threw the control out.

Hawk guided the car over the sodden trail with calm assurance. A few minutes later he turned south on Highway 31, headed toward Holland.

<hr />

"It's time to preflight the aircraft," Craig said. "Want to come with me?"

"Sure," Barbara said, glad for something to do.

"Sam?" Craig said.

The agent looked up from the issue of *Proceedings* he was reading and smiled. "I'll pass. Call me when it's time for my row to board."

"Typical Supply Corps attitude," Craig said with a grin. "They're never around when duty calls."

"Watch your mouth, or your CO will hear from me. Besides, I suspect Ms. Post would prefer not to have me along."

Barbara stared at him. She knew she hadn't discussed Craig with him. "What?"

"I've got eyes," Sam said. "Now get on with your preflighting."

Barbara followed Craig out into the open area of the hangar. Art Jackson was fastening the latches on the port-side engine cowling.

"Is the aircraft up?" Craig asked.

The mechanic looked down from his perch on the ladder. "Yes, sir. All systems are go."

"You still have to check it?" Barbara asked.

"Yes," Craig replied. "It's my responsibility."

Barbara followed him around as he examined all the flight controls, landing gear and tires, inspected for leaks, and the other actions necessary to be sure the helicopter was ready to fly. Most she didn't understand, but she found herself wanting to since she shared his fascination with flying.

"Well?" she asked when he was done.

"We're good to go," Craig told her.

"I'll get Sam." Barbara hurried back to Craig's office.

"We're boarding all rows," she told Sam.

He put the magazine down, grabbed his raincoat, and got up. "I'm coming."

Barbara pulled on her raincoat, picked up the M-16, and left the office. A chill wind slashed through the cozy interior as the mechanic and another enlisted man opened the hangar doors. Then Craig, Joel, and Art pushed the helicopter outside.

The crew boarded as Barbara ran across the slick tarmac. She ducked her head and jumped up into the helicopter. Art helped her in and to the side to make room for Sam.

"I think the skipper wants you up front," Art shouted in her ear as he handed her a headset. Barbara gave Sam the M-16 and went forward where Joel helped her strap in and attached the intercom plug. Both pilots donned their low-light goggles. Overhead a jet engine started to whine, and soon both were running. Craig called the Common Traffic Advisory Frequency (CTAF) and heard there was no traffic at the airport.

"Hold on to your hats," he said over the intercom. He looked back at Barbara. "Ready?"

A sudden uneasiness came over her as she stared past him into the forbidding blackness, but she nodded anyway. Reassurance returned when she remembered what a good job the goggles did. She had used similar devices a few times and had trained with low-light rifle scopes as well.

Wind gusts shook the helicopter, and the slanting rain made the cockpit bubble a shiny blur. Lightning briefly illuminated the airport like a strobe. Craig applied power and transitioned to forward flight so quickly Barbara's stomach lurched. She immediately became disoriented as she lost sight of the ground. A few moments later she was sure the helicopter had entered a steep turn.

"Are we all right?" she asked.

"We're fine," Craig replied, keeping his eyes fixed on the instruments. "Does it feel like we're turning?"

"Yes. How did you know?"

"It happens when you lose visual references. That's why we have to trust our instruments."

"Do you feel it too?"

"Yes. Relax. We're doing OK."

The helicopter shook and bounced as they flew through the storm. After a few minutes the turbulence decreased. Barbara looked out through the canopy bubble. The rain slacked off but did not quit.

"We can see the ground now," Craig said.

Barbara looked out the side. Below them was a sea of blackness with pinpoints of varicolored lights marking the towns. Sparse whites and reds dotted a road below, with a few headlights coming north and even fewer taillights going the other direction.

"That's Highway 31," Craig said. "Holland is a couple of minutes up ahead."

Barbara tried to make out the cars but couldn't. "Can you see the traffic?"

"No problem. As long as the rain doesn't get worse, I think we'll be able to identify the truck. The weather wonks are predicting further moderation."

Lightning illuminated the ground for a moment, etching each detail like a black-and-white photo.

"Be nice if it would quit."

"Yeah, but that won't happen until sometime Wednesday."

"Are you OK, Sam?" Barbara asked over the intercom.

"I'm fine. Can't say I'm crazy about the ride."

"This is how we earn our flight pay," Craig told him.

"I won't argue that."

"You've got it," Craig told Joel.

"I've got it," the copilot confirmed.

Craig turned to Barbara. "Would you like a pair of goggles?"

"Yes."

He handed her a spare set. Barbara fitted the bulky device over her eyes, flicked the switch, and looked down at the ground. It was as if someone had turned on a green spotlight. The image was a little grainy but a great improvement over inky shadows. Even though Barbara had used low-light devices before, their effectiveness still surprised her.

"Can you see?" Craig asked.

"Clear as day."

"With a green sun."

She lifted the goggles. The light from the instrument panel provided barely enough light to see the outline of his face. She could tell he was grinning.

"Carry on, Lieutenant," she said.

"Aye, aye, ma'am." Craig faced forward and positioned his goggles. "I've got it," he told Joel.

"Roger." The copilot took his hands away from the controls.

Barbara lowered her goggles again and looked down on the highway. The green image bloomed suddenly, turning almost white as lightning flashed through the night sky. The sharp clap of thunder came a few seconds later and rolled on for quite a while.

<hr />

The unmarked government sedan plowed through the rain south of Benton Harbor. Pete was driving, and the traffic was light, for which he was grateful. He switched the wipers on high as he passed a semi that was blinding him with spray.

"What do you think of the operation?" Roscoe asked.

"I'm not sure, but Dan isn't making any bones about his opinion." He paused, wondering if his partner would misunderstand. "He believes Ms. Post was assigned to our office because she's a woman."

"Did he really say that?"

Pete laughed. "He didn't have to. Besides, you know how he is."

"I'm gonna 'no comment' that. But you didn't answer my question. What do you think?"

"A local militia is going to hijack an Army ammo shipment?" He weighed his answer carefully. "I'd hate to think things are getting that bad. But the federal building in Oklahoma City isn't where it used to be. On the other hand, we don't have any hard evidence that this new militia is planning something."

Roscoe chuckled. "Man, what a waffle."

"OK, so what's your opinion?"

"The circumstantial evidence is disturbing. Sam and Barbara could be onto something, but I sure hope not."

"That makes two of us."

━╫╫╫━ ━╫╫╫━ ━╫╫╫━

"We should be in radio range of your ground unit," Craig said without taking his eyes off the instruments. They had passed Benton Harbor ten minutes ago.

"I'll bring you the radio," Sam said over the intercom.

A few moments later he came onto the flight deck and handed Barbara the radio.

"Kinda snug up here," he said, peering through the canopy.

"Dolphins aren't very roomy," Craig agreed. "Want some goggles?"

"No thanks. I'll wait for the action to start."

Barbara made sure the frequency was correct and keyed the transmit button. "Linebacker, this is Quarterback, do you read, over."

"Quarterback, this is Linebacker. I read you five-by-five."

"We are nearing your position. What is your ETA on station?"

"Estimated time of arrival is 9:30. Will advise."

"Roger. Quarterback out."

"Do you want to stick with the refueling schedule?" Craig asked.

"I don't see any reason to change," Barbara replied. "Once Linebacker is in position, that should cover us in case the transport is making better time than we thought."

"OK. So we'll head for Benton Harbor at 2300. About a half hour on the ground, then we should be back on station before midnight with full tanks."

"That should work. Now comes the waiting."

Brad watched the mile markers as Hawk drove back north toward Holland at a leisurely pace. They had turned around a few minutes ago.

"OK, pull over here," Brad ordered. "We're about five miles from our exit. That should give us plenty of time to catch up and pull them over."

Hawked slowed, then pulled over onto the shoulder. He put the car in park and shut off the engine. Brad grabbed the bag at his feet and pulled out three bulky objects.

"OK, put these on," he ordered.

Brad gave one pair of low-light goggles to Hawk then donned his own. He turned in the seat and saw Ed waiting expectantly. Brad handed his brother the device and turned back around. He picked up his Glock 9mm automatic, checked to make sure the clip was fully loaded, then screwed on the silencer. Hawk did the same with his gun. Brad heard metallic sounds in the backseat.

"What are you doing?" he asked.

"Checking the Uzis," Ed replied.

Brad turned around. His brother had removed the magazines from both submachine guns and was inspecting the breach on one of them.

Brad stifled what he wanted to say. "Are they ready?"

"Looks good to me."

"OK, then insert the magazines and put the guns on the floor. They're reserve anyway."

Ed frowned. "Just wanted to be sure." He jammed the magazines into place with more force than necessary.

"And now we are, so put them down."

Ed reached down and placed them on the floor.

"Now, help us watch for the shipment."

Ed turned around and looked out the rear window.

Chapter Eighteen

Barbara looked out the left side of the canopy as the helicopter completed another wide orbit of the agents on the ground. She had no trouble seeing the traffic on the interstate, which was quite light as eleven o'clock drew near. She was confident they would have no trouble identifying the transport, and she was ready for it to arrive. The long wait had taken its toll on her nerves.

"I recommend we refuel now," Craig said.

"How low are we?" Barbara asked.

"We can stay up about an hour longer, but if we do it now, we can be back on station before midnight."

"Sam, what do you think?" Barbara said into the intercom.

"I say now. If we delay, we might be forced to refuel at a bad time."

"The truck might cross while we're gone."

"Craig, how long will we be on the ground?" Sam asked.

"Thirty minutes, max."

"I think we have to depend on Pete and Roscoe. Let them know what we're doing, and let's get on with it."

"OK," Barbara said. "Craig, are we going to Benton Harbor?"

"Roger. That's closest."

She picked up the radio and pressed the transmit button. "Linebacker, this is Quarterback. We're going to refuel; back in thirty. Over."

"Roger, Quarterback."

"Will advise when departing Benton Harbor. Quarterback out."

Craig increased power and pushed the stick forward as he brought the Dolphin around to a northerly course. Barbara watched as their path gradually intersected the coast of Lake Michigan. About five minutes later Craig spoke into his mike.

"Benton Harbor Traffic, Coast Guard Rescue 5915 is five to the south, inbound to the airfield at one thousand feet. Any traffic in the area? Please advise."

"Don't they have a tower?" Barbara asked.

"No, Ross Field is an uncontrolled airport."

The radio crackled. "Coast Guard Rescue 5915, this is Benton Harbor Traffic. No traffic reported."

"Roger, Benton Harbor."

Craig called in a minute later and again when he had the helicopter on short final to the aircraft ramp. Barbara looked past Joel and saw a man in a slicker waiting for them, fuel hose in hand.

"I'm impressed," Barbara said.

"They know the drill. Lives could depend on how quickly they get us back in the air; and on a night like this, we really appreciate it."

Craig brought the Dolphin into an abrupt hover and touched down quickly. He shut down the engines. One of the side doors clattered open, and Art jumped out into the rain.

"I'll do the preflight," Joel said as he started unbuckling.

"I won't fight you for it," Craig said.

By 11:15 P.M. the refueling was complete, and Craig paid by government credit card. Joel and Art climbed back aboard and shed their raincoats. The young copilot clambered back onto the flight deck.

"Everything looks shipshape, skipper," he said as he began strapping in.

"Very well. Thanks."

"Don't mention it. I'll just add it to your tab."

"Better not forget I write your fitness report."

"And I'm sure this will reflect positively on it."

Craig shook his head. "I don't know what the officer corps is coming to. How about giving our hosts a shout and let 'em know we're departing?"

Joel glanced out to the side. "You're clear to start engines." He then faced forward and keyed the radio. "Benton Harbor Traffic, Coast Guard Rescue 5915 on the ramp, ready for south departure. Any traffic? Please advise."

"Coast Guard Rescue 5915, no traffic."

"Roger, Benton Harbor. Thanks."

A high-pitched whine came from one engine, joined moments later by the second. The overhead rotor began to turn, throwing up spray from the slick tarmac. Craig checked instruments and controls as Joel read the checklist.

"I think we're ready," Joel said.

Craig applied power. The helicopter lurched forward and into the sodden night sky. A few minutes later Barbara picked up her tactical radio.

"Linebacker, this is Quarterback approaching your location. Request status report, over."

"Quarterback, this is Linebacker. Traffic light; rain is moderate. No contact as yet."

"Roger, Linebacker. Quarterback out."

"It's still early," Sam said over the intercom.

"Yeah, I know," Barbara said. "But waiting is hard."

"I know. Hang in there."

That was easy for him to say, Barbara thought. In her mind's eye she could see Dan out there, somewhere, examining and criticizing her every move, just looking for a reason to get rid of her. She clamped down on that worrisome thought. She and Sam could have misinterpreted the evidence, she realized, but wouldn't it have been irresponsible to do nothing? Perhaps the answer depended on what your true motives were.

She glanced at her watch and saw it was almost 11:30. Soon they would know for sure.

The Gathering Storm

Otto was driving again and not enjoying it. They had run into the fore-casted rain around Springfield, and it hadn't let up since, although it had moderated in the last hour. A few minutes ago, they had followed the escort around the ramp leading to I-80. Soon they would be in Indiana and not long after that, entering southwest Michigan. But they were still over two hours from Wyoming, and that didn't include the time it would take to get the guard bean counters to sign for the shipment. He frowned as he anticipated that it would be a slow process.

Otto guided the Kenworth into a right curve. Up ahead the escort braked suddenly and swerved toward the right shoulder.

"What . . ." Otto began.

He hit the brakes a little harder than he intended and felt a shudder behind them. He immediately got off the brakes, knowing he had locked the trailer's wheels.

"Something's in the road!" Isaac shouted, pointing to the left.

Otto angled as much to the right as he dared, hoping to avoid a jack-knife. He glanced out his side mirror and saw the trailer was skidding into the left lane. Dark, angular objects flashed past in the roadway below. A moment later he felt the trailer lurch as the left-hand wheels ran over whatever it was. Loud explosions carried into the cab despite the road noise and rain. The trailer lurched again, but its skidding stopped. Otto headed toward the shoulder. He honked at the escorts but saw they were already slowing.

"What was that?" Otto asked as he flipped on his blinkers.

"I'm not sure," Isaac replied. "Looked like metal scrap to me. How bad is it?"

Otto shook his head. "Won't know until we park and take a look, but we blew at least one tire." He knew from the way the truck was handling that it had to be more than that.

He eased the truck onto the broad shoulder, checked his side mirror to make sure the trailer was clear of traffic, and stopped. He set the emergency brake and started pulling on his raincoat. Isaac slipped into his with the agility of youth and the absence of a middle-age spread. Up ahead the escort backed toward them on the shoulder, emergency lights flashing. Otto considered telling his assistant to stay in the cab but decided this was part of his training.

"Let's check out the damage," he said.

"OK."

Otto grabbed a flashlight, opened his door and began his cautious climb down to the pavement. One of the guards approached from up ahead.

"Did you hit it?" the man asked.

Otto's anger flashed hot. "No, I decided to stop and do a little sight-seeing!" He paused as he struggled for control. "What do you think I stopped for? Of course I hit it!"

"Sorry," the man mumbled.

"Never mind. Come on."

Otto turned around and stomped back toward the end of the trailer. A semi roared past a few feet away, blinding him with spray. Otto swayed in the turbulence and almost fell. He flicked on the flashlight and played the beam over the left side duals. He shook his head. One tire, maybe two, he was prepared to handle, but not this. Isaac came around the end of the trailer and stared. The flashlight revealed four shredded black ovals, barely recognizable as tires.

"Isaac?"

"Yes."

"Go get the reflectors and put them out. We're going to be here awhile."

"Right." He disappeared around the back of the trailer.

"I need to use your radio," Otto told the guard.

"OK."

The guard turned and led the way back to the escort car.

⁂

The thunderstorms had finally drifted away to the east, leaving a steady rainfall that showed no signs of ending. Barbara resisted the temptation to do a radio check with the agents on the ground. There was absolutely no need, since nothing had changed. Barbara was sure the transport had not slipped past unless they had come by before 9:30, and she didn't think that was possible. But where were they? It was nearly one o'clock, and the adrenaline surge she had felt around 12:30 was now gone.

"How are we doing on fuel?" Barbara asked Craig.

He glanced at the gauges. "We can stay up about an hour and a half longer. Do you want to top up?"

"No, I don't think so. Sure as we do, the truck will come through."

The radio in Barbara's lap crackled to life. "Quarterback, this is Linebacker, over."

She picked up the radio. "Linebacker, this is Quarterback. Go ahead."

"Nothing going on down here. How much longer are we going to stay out here?"

The question surprised Barbara. Rather than reply, she spoke into the intercom. "Sam?"

There was a pause before he spoke. "Yes?"

"We covered that in the briefing, didn't we?"

His sigh was audible in her earphones. "We did, and besides, those two are way out of line, and they know it. Want me to talk to them?"

Before she could answer, the radio came to life again. "Quarterback, this is Linebacker. Did you receive my last?"

Barbara gritted her teeth. "Linebacker, wait one." Then she spoke to Sam. "It's your operation, but I think this is aimed at me."

There was a long pause. "I think some operational instruction is in order. Would you handle it?"

"I will." She picked up the radio. "Linebacker, this is Quarterback. This operation will conclude upon direction of the agents in charge, and you will be notified at the appropriate time. Further, this tactical network is for official communications only, not idle chatter. Do you copy?"

The radio crackled, indicating that the ground operator had keyed the transmit button, but no words were spoken. Then the radio speaker came to life again. "Quarterback, this is Linebacker. I copy. Out."

Barbara heard a chuckle over the intercom.

"That put some starch in his knickers," Sam said.

"It would be nice if we could stay focused on what we're out here for."

"I know, and I agree. You're doing fine."

Barbara resumed scanning the sparsely traveled interstate below. Where was that truck?

Ed turned around and looked at Brad. "What time is it?" he asked.

Brad tried to hide his irritation. "Will you knock it off? I'm tired of you asking me that."

"Well, where are they?"

"Now how would I know that? Obviously they've been delayed."

"Any chance they went a different way?"

"No. They have to stay on the hazardous cargo routes. Now settle down."

Ed, looking strange wearing his low-light goggles, continued to stare at his brother for a few moments, then turned back to look out the rear window.

Brad lifted his goggles a little and punched the illumination light on his watch. It was a little after one. He slipped the goggles back in place and saw Hawk looking at him. Brad shrugged. They both turned around to resume their vigil.

Otto watched in admiration as the mechanic finished mounting the back dual on the left side. The man stepped back and carefully lowered the hydraulic jack. The huge tires settled onto the pavement with an audible crunch. It was almost 12:30—two hours wasn't bad for getting out on a rainy interstate in the middle of the night and replacing two duals. Not bad at all. Of course, it was around 1:30 in Michigan, and this would put them over two hours late getting into Wyoming.

The mechanic wiped his hands and returned to the heavy-duty tow truck. Otto reached for his wallet to get the company credit card, anticipating the "how did you want to pay for that" question.

"Credit card?" the man asked from up in the tow truck cab.

Otto handed it up.

The mechanic processed it, completed his paperwork, and stepped back down to the pavement. He extended the clipboard and duplicate receipt to the driver. Otto signed the work order and credit card charge.

"Thanks," the mechanic said.

"Thank you," Otto said, really meaning it. "We appreciate you coming out on such a nasty night."

The man glanced at the hazard signs on the long trailer. "I figured it was either that, or have a huge crater in I-80."

Despite his discomfort, Otto couldn't help laughing. "I commend your civic service."

"No problem. Hope you don't have any more trouble."

"Thanks."

The man climbed back into the tow truck and backed up, lights flashing. A few moments later he pulled out into traffic and was gone.

Otto turned to his assistant. "You want to take it on in?"

Isaac grinned. "You bet."

"OK. Climb aboard while I go talk to the guards."

The young man loped away and climbed up into the Kenworth's cab. Otto checked the traffic behind them. It was moderate, but then they were inside the urban sprawl of greater Chicago. The traffic would drop way off once they entered Michigan. He turned and walked slowly along the semi. The guard who was driving got out and met him.

"We're ready to roll," Otto said.

"OK. I'll be glad when this is over."

"Yeah, me too."

Barbara turned her head as Craig started speaking.

"Group Grand Haven, this is Coast Guard Rescue 5915. Go ahead." He listened for a few moments then switched over to the intercom. "Barbara, it's Dan Oliver. Communications has patched him through to us. He wants to talk to you."

Barbara felt a jolt of anxiety. "Oh? Did he say why?"

"No. I'm switching him to the intercom—now."

Barbara's earphones crackled and popped. "This is Agent Post," she said.

"Agent Post, this is Resident Agent in Charge Dan Oliver. Where's that truck?"

"I don't know. Delayed, I guess."

"You guess. Seems like you do a lot of that. How much longer do you guess you'll be tying up government assets?"

"How about letting us contact the guard? Maybe they know why the shipment has been delayed."

"I told you no! Not on the flimsy so-called evidence you showed me. Now answer my question."

Barbara clinched her teeth. "We'll stay as long as it takes," she said, struggling to keep her temper under control.

"Oh no, I don't think so. You are to release agents Singleton and Carter at once. Your little operation is over as of now."

"But . . ."

"Did you hear what I said?"

Barbara closed her eyes. "Yes," she said in barely a whisper.

"And I expect to see you and Sam in my office first thing tomorrow. Got that?"

"I've got it."

"Good."

The connection popped, then a new voice came over the radio. "Coast Guard Rescue 5915, this is Group Grand Haven. Your caller has disconnected."

"Roger, Group Grand Haven. Coast Guard Rescue 5915 out."

"Sam?" Barbara said into the intercom.

"Yes?"

"I'm going to call Pete and Roscoe."

"Right. I'm sorry."

"Yeah, me too." She picked up the radio. "Linebacker, this is Quarterback, over."

"Quarterback, this is Linebacker. Go ahead."

"You are released. The operation is over."

"Quarterback, say again."

Barbara could hear the glee in Pete's voice and knew he had heard her the first time. "Linebacker, this is Quarterback. The operation is over; you are released. Out."

Barbara heard movement behind her. She turned and saw Sam standing at the entrance to the flight deck.

"Don't let it get you down," he said. "We did the best we could, and I still think it was the right thing to do, under the circumstances."

"But we still failed, and that shipment's going to come through sometime. What if the militia strikes then?"

"We'll address that when and if it happens. Meanwhile, it's time to head for home. Much as our hosts enjoy flying, I'm sure they're ready to call it a day."

"I know." Barbara turned to Craig. "OK, it's all over."

Chapter Nineteen

Craig continued flying toward the Michigan state line. "Do you think it's still possible that the militia will hijack that ammo shipment?"

Barbara considered it, wondering what difference it made, then looked around at Sam. "I don't know about Sam, but I do."

"Nothing's changed as far as I can see," Sam said. "The delay doesn't change the equation. Either the Grand Haven Militia is planning to knock off the shipment, or they aren't. Our intelligence seems to suggest that a hit is likely."

"What are you getting at?" Barbara asked.

"I don't see anything that requires me to fly back to Muskegon," Craig said. "My standing orders are to provide transportation to the Bureau of Alcohol, Tobacco, and Firearms, under the direction of duly assigned special agents. The way I read it, that's you and Sam."

"But . . ."

"Dan Oliver ordered you to release the agents on the ground, and you've done that."

"He also said that my 'little operation' was over."

"Is the investigation of western Michigan militias an ongoing operation?"

"Yes, of course it is."

"Aren't we up here investigating?"

Sam cleared his throat. "Mr. Phillips?"

"Yes, Special Agent Green?"

"Are you a lawyer in your spare time?"

"Perish the thought. But what about it?"

"What do you think?" Barbara asked Sam.

"Dan would have a cat, and you know it."

Barbara frowned. "He'd probably have a whole litter, but what happens if we pack up and the militia grabs all that ammo?"

"I don't like being put in that position."

He said it with some heat, which Barbara understood. "I know. I don't either."

"OK," Sam said finally. "I think we can maintain our surveillance, at least for a while. We have the authority to investigate anything related to local militias, and I think this qualifies."

"Thanks," Barbara told Sam.

"Right." He returned to the crew compartment.

<hr />

Otto tried to get comfortable in the right-hand seat, but the early hour and what they had been through made that impossible. He was ready for this particular trip to be over.

"How are you doing, champ?" he asked his assistant.

"Great," Isaac replied, obviously enjoying himself. "How about you?"

"Not bad for an old guy, but I'll be glad when the guard signs for this stuff so I can get some shut-eye."

They were past Gary now, and up ahead Otto saw a sign giving the distance to Chesterton. They were almost halfway through their short trip across Indiana. Although they wouldn't be in the eastern time zone until they entered Michigan, Otto decided to change his watch now. After all, it wouldn't be that much longer, around 2:15 by his estimation.

⟨⟩ ⟨⟩ ⟨⟩

Brad listened to the never-ending rain as it rattled on the roof over his head. Where was that shipment? He shivered as he imagined what might happen if they were spotted by a real police patrol. Local police would probably leave them alone, he thought, but he wasn't so sure about a state cop. So far, they had not seen any police, and he sincerely hoped it remained that way.

"How long are we going to wait?" Hawk asked.

"As long as it takes!" Brad snapped.

"Don't bite my head off. What if they've had a breakdown or an accident? I mean, we can't stay out here forever."

"I know, I know. Sorry." Brad couldn't bear the thought that the truck might not be coming at all, but he had to consider the possibility. "If it's not here by five, we'll call it off."

He turned and looked out the rear window.

⟨⟩ ⟨⟩ ⟨⟩

Craig relinquished the controls to Joel and turned around. "Time to start thinking about refueling," he said.

Barbara tore her eyes away from the highway and looked at him. "How long can we stay up?"

"About a half hour longer."

"The truck could come through at any time. I'd sure hate to miss it."

"I know, but if we wait too long, we might be forced down at a bad time. It's 2:00 now. If we hustle, we can be back on station in about an hour."

"Sam?" Barbara said into the intercom.

"Let's do it."

"I've got it," Craig told Joel.

He increased power and brought the helicopter around in a steep turn, rolling out on the northerly course for Ross Field. The incessant rain pounded against the canopy as the Dolphin lanced through the night skies at almost two-and-a-half miles a minute.

Joel monitored the approach closely. Ten minutes later he changed the radio frequency and spoke into his mike, "Benton Harbor Traffic, Coast Guard Rescue 5915 is five to the south, inbound to the airfield at one thousand feet. Any traffic in the area? Please advise."

"Coast Guard Rescue 5915, this is Benton Harbor Traffic. No traffic."

"That was snappy," Joel remarked.

"Yeah," Craig said, "I'm impressed. Let's hope the pump jockey is equally sharp."

"Right."

Craig began a gentle descent. Joel called in again at two miles and then on final approach.

Barbara sat up in her seat and watched as Craig began slowing the helicopter. Down below she saw a figure in a slicker waiting for them. She sighed in relief. There would be no delay.

"Skipper!" Joel said, his voice rising. "I have an engine chip light on the Warning Caution Advisory panel."

Barbara felt an icy jab in her stomach. "What's wrong?"

"Possible engine damage," Joel told her.

Craig pulled back on the stick, bringing the Dolphin into a hover. He set the aircraft down quickly and shut down the engines.

"Which engine, skipper?" Art asked as he pulled on his raincoat.

"Port."

"I'm on it." Art hurried to the door, rolled it back, and jumped out.

"Does that mean we're done?" Barbara asked.

"If it's for real, yes. However, it could be a false indication."

Sam appeared. "How serious do you think the warning is?"

"Don't know. All I can say is we get a fair number of false alarms. In a way I'd be surprised if it's real because this aircraft has a good maintenance history, and we don't have a lot of hours on the engines. We'll just have to see."

Barbara looked outside. Art was up on a ladder. Below him, the fuel attendant connected a hose and opened a valve. Barbara watched the rain splatter against the dark tarmac. Sheets of water streamed down the bubble canopy, blurring the view. Somehow, that reflected how she was feeling at the moment.

Isaac turned his head, a broad grin on his face. "We're in Michigan now," he said.

Otto smiled. "Well, how about that, and you found it all by yourself." His impression of the young man had improved considerably during the trip. "Sure you can handle it the rest of the way?"

"No problem. This is fun."

"It'll wear off—believe me."

"Hope not. I like this job."

"For what it's worth, I'm impressed. I appreciate having you along."

This seemed to please him. "Thanks."

"You earned it."

"We hit 196 at Benton Harbor, right?"

"Yep. And that'll take us on into Wyoming."

Otto yawned and wished for a cup of coffee. He had drained the last of his thermos during the wait outside Chicago. Up ahead the escort car drove through the rain, its tires plowing two temporary troughs on the slick pavement. Otto's watch read 2:25.

Barbara heard the door behind her open and looked around. Craig stepped inside and pushed the door shut. He peeled off his raincoat and came into the cockpit. Sam appeared in the doorway.

"So what's the verdict?" Joel asked.

"Loose plug on the engine chip detector," Craig said. "No sign of actual damage, but we'll test the port engine just to be sure."

He settled down in the right seat and started flipping switches. A few seconds later a low moaning sound started and quickly became a high-pitched whine. Craig ran the engine up to full power.

"Looks OK," Joel said, eyes on the instrument panel. "The chip light is out."

"Good," Craig said as he began the start-up procedure on the other engine.

The door behind them opened, and Art boarded. A few moments later he came on the intercom. "How does it look, skipper?"

"That got it," Craig replied. "Outstanding work, Jackson."

"Just doing my job."

"Are we all buttoned up?"

"Roger. We're ready to roll."

Craig glanced at his copilot. "Get on the horn and tell Benton Harbor Traffic we're departing."

Joel made the call and was advised there was no traffic.

Barbara felt an adrenaline surge as Craig pulled the helicopter up into the dreary night sky.

⋙ ⋙ ⋙

Otto looked at his watch. It was 3:10 in the morning, and Benton Harbor was behind them now. Ahead lay South Haven, Holland, and finally their destination.

"Won't be long now," Isaac said.

"Yep, and I'm ready for this day to be over."

The tires hummed over the wet pavement as the powerful diesel ate up the roadway.

"How long do you think it will take to unload?"

"Your guess is as good as mine. They'll probably take their time checking it out, and we can't leave until they sign for it."

"Is it possible they won't sign?"

Otto heard the young man's concern and was tempted to pull his leg. "Oh, it's possible but not likely."

"Have you ever had it happen?"

"A time or two. I try to be careful and make sure I've got everything I sign for. But mistakes sometimes happen."

"What then?"

"You note the discrepancy and everyone initials."

Isaac was silent for a while. "Do they make you pay for it?" he asked finally.

Otto laughed. "No. Let's just say that management suggests you be a little more careful next time."

"Boy, hope that doesn't happen to us."

Otto shifted, trying to get comfortable in his seat. "Don't worry. It won't."

⌇⌇⌇ ⌇⌇⌇ ⌇⌇⌇

"South to the state line?" Craig asked.

Barbara looked down at the intersection of Interstates 94 and 196, now quite familiar to her. Momentary anger flashed as she thought about Dan's preemptory cancellation of the operation. Without the agents on the ground, she knew is was possible the truck could already be past Benton Harbor.

"Yes," she said finally. "Then let's fly back up to Holland."

"Roger."

Barbara scanned the highway as they sped south. There was less traffic now. One by one the Dolphin swept past the sleepy towns of southwest Michigan. A few minutes later she spotted Grand Beach, the last checkpoint on their lonely orbit.

⌇⌇⌇ ⌇⌇⌇ ⌇⌇⌇

Ed sat bolt upright and pointed. "Hey! Here they come!"

Brad adjusted his low-light goggles and looked through the rain-spattered rear window. *Yes, it does look like the shipment,* he thought. An escort car was speeding toward them trailing a semi. With the traffic so light, it couldn't be anything else.

"Crank it up," he said to Hawk, "but don't turn on the lights yet."

The powerful engine rumbled to life.

"Get down, Ed!" Brad ordered. "We don't want them seeing you." He turned back around and glanced at Hawk. "Off with the goggles," he added as he removed his and laid them on the seat within easy reach.

"OK," Hawk said.

"Hit your headlights as soon as the truck is past. We have to be sure."

"Right."

Brad felt his heart rate increase as adrenaline coursed through his veins. He glanced back. The escort was close now, and it would pass them in a matter of seconds. *It's about time,* Brad thought in irritated relief.

A sheet of spray covered the fake police car as the escort swept by. The car rocked when the truck passed.

"Now!" Brad shouted.

Hawk turned on the headlights and pulled the gearshift into drive. The tires spun as they pulled out behind the truck. Brad had no trouble making out the sign on the trailer's rear doors: Century Transportation.

"OK, Officer Hawkins," Brad said with glee. "Do your duty."

"Roger that, Officer Anderson. Stay down back there."

"I know what to do!" Ed griped.

"Just making sure."

"Easy, Hawk," Brad said. "We've got work to do."

Hawk had to let up on the accelerator to stop a skid as they raced after the truck.

"I think it's time to let them know we're here," he said.

"Right," Brad agreed. He laughed. "The state has some official business to take care of."

Hawk turned on the flashing lights and siren and pulled into the left lane. He flipped the wipers up on high as they entered the spray from the trailer. They roared past the high aluminum wall and drew even with the tractor. Hawk pulled in behind the escort.

"I think they got the message," he said.

The car ahead slowed down and began edging toward the shoulder.

"What's the truck doing?" Hawk asked.

Brad turned around. "They're pulling over also—just like we planned."

"So far."

Brad put on his peaked hat and zipped his raincoat partway up, making sure he could reach his shoulder holster.

The escort rolled to a stop. Hawk pulled close, then turned off the siren but left the lights flashing. He opened his door. Brad looked over at him, illuminated by the car's interior lights, now painfully bright. He nodded, and Hawk got out.

Brad opened his door and stepped down into a deep puddle. He cursed as water spilled over his shoe tops, drenching his socks. He closed the door and walked toward the escort car. The driver's window whined down as Brad approached.

"What's the problem, officer?" the guard asked.

Brad looked back and saw Hawk take a step up on the tractor. He turned back to the guard. "We've received a report that your shipment might be in danger."

"Oh? What's wrong?"

Brad looked past the driver, making sure his partner was in the open. "This," Brad said.

He reached inside his raincoat, yanked out his silenced automatic, aimed, and pulled the trigger. A yellow flash illuminated the red circle that appeared in the center of the guard's forehead. A gush of blood shot out as he slumped forward, dead instantly. Brad shifted aim and fired again. The other man jerked once, then keeled over.

The Gathering Storm

⤙⤙⤙— ⤙⤙⤙— ⤙⤙⤙—

Otto frowned as he looked out through the truck's windshield, his view alternately clear then bleary as the wipers did their weary work. Past the police car's distracting lights, one of the cops was standing beside the escort on the driver's side. Otto pondered the two yellow flashes that had briefly illuminated the car's interior. A sense of unease tugged at the back of his mind. In that brief glimpse, it looked like the cop was holding something.

Otto began turning his head, vaguely aware that Isaac was rolling his window down. The other cop was standing on the steps outside the driver's door, his head and upper torso dimly lit by the truck's instruments. Otto's mouth went dry. The officer reached inside his raincoat, and Otto knew what was coming even as the sinister black shape began to emerge. Without thinking, he threw his door open and started out. An ominous plop sounded. Out of the corner of his eye, Otto saw the back of Isaac's head explode, spraying the cab with something dark and wet.

Hunched over, Otto aimed for the unseen steps below, hoping he would not slip and fall. He hit the muddy ground and began running. Behind him he heard scrambling sounds.

"Brad!" the man shouted. "I need your help!"

The highway shoulder ended in a ditch, and beyond that the truck's headlights revealed a forest and tangled undergrowth. Sodden branches tugged at Otto's uniform as he dashed into the woods. The flickering glow behind him dropped off rapidly as dark shadows hid the countryside.

Otto ran into an unseen tree and fell. He scrambled to his feet and felt his face. It was warm and wet. His chest heaved as he drew in deep wracking breaths, painfully loud in his ears. He looked around but couldn't see a thing. Back there somewhere, hidden in the darkness, someone was crashing through the brush.

"Hurry!" a nearby voice shouted. "He's getting away!"

Otto staggered forward and felt the path start descending. Somewhere ahead he could hear the sound of splashing water. Otto's mind raced. Whatever these two men were, they weren't cops. Otto knew what would happen to him if they caught up with him.

Chapter Twenty

Brad turned at Hawk's shout and cursed as he caught a glimpse of a dark shape disappearing into the trees. Hawk jumped down from the truck and raced around the massive fenders, his raincoat flapping. Brad holstered his gun and ran for the fake police car. Reaching the back door, he pulled on the handle but found it was locked.

"Come on!" Brad shouted through the glass.

Ed tugged on the inside handle and pushed with his shoulder. The car rocked. Then he reached up and lifted the locking post. He pulled again, and the door flew open striking Brad in the shins.

"Watch it!" Brad shouted, closing his eyes a moment while the pain subsided.

"Sorry. What happened?"

"Never mind! Get that truck out of here!"

"But . . ."

"Do as I say! Hawk and I will take care of the driver."

Ed hesitated a moment then ran for the truck, Brad limping along after him. He reached the cab and stopped. The door was hanging open. Ed turned when he saw the young man's body.

"Push it out of the way!" Brad ordered.

"There's blood all over the seat!"

"You're wearing a raincoat! Now move it!"

Ed ascended the steps, paused at the top, then shoved the limp corpse across the seat. He then sat down gingerly and closed the door. A few moments later the truck's air brakes hissed, and Brad stepped back. The semi lurched forward, the massive wheels crunching through the rocks and mud, then angled onto the highway and began accelerating.

Brad ran back to the car, opened the driver's door, and got in. He turned off all the lights and the engine. Up ahead the escort's headlights shot white beams toward the north. Brad grabbed a pair of low-light goggles and got out. After killing the lights on the escort, Brad slipped on his goggles and turned them on. The woods sprang into grainy, green life, but he couldn't see Hawk or the escaped driver. Brad listened for a moment to get a bearing on the crashing sounds of pursuit. Then he drew his gun and entered the dense undergrowth.

⚊⚊ ⚊⚊ ⚊⚊

"Benton Harbor is abeam," Craig said.

Barbara looked down at the intersection of Interstates 94 and 196. "I see it."

"How far north do you want to go?"

She did a mental calculation. "Near Wyoming, I think, then start backtracking."

"You got it."

The helicopter clattered on through the rain.

⚊⚊ ⚊⚊ ⚊⚊

Ed slowed down as he guided the semi down the narrow exit and onto the frontage road. Up ahead he saw the country road that went to the abandoned house. He brought the truck to a complete stop and looked all around. The steady rainfall drummed on the top of the cab. There was no traffic in sight.

Ed tried to make a wide right turn but misgauged it. The right side of the trailer started scraping along the stop sign. Ed stopped and looked in his side mirror. He cursed when he saw the sign pressed against the side of the trailer. He considered backing up but decided that would only make matters worse.

He straightened the wheels and pulled forward, trying to ignore the squeal of metal. He stopped again and looked back. There was no way he could clear the obstacle and keep the tractor out of the ditch on the far side of the road. Ed cranked the wheel all the way and began his turn. He watched the stop sign bend to the right and start slipping under the trailer. Moments later the rear duals flattened the metal post and continued on through the shallow ditch. The trailer tilted to the right, and for a moment Ed thought it might topple. But it righted once the tires regained the road.

Ed breathed a sigh of relief and accelerated down the narrow road. He scanned the left side, looking for the overgrown drive. He had been to the site once during the day, but the countryside looked different through the goggle's green lenses. A break in the foliage appeared. Ed slowed and then stopped. It was about the right distance from the highway. He looked toward where the house and barn were supposed to be, but the trees hid everything.

Deciding this had to be it, Ed started a wide left turn into the drive. He felt relieved when he saw fresh parallel tracks through the weeds. Low-lying limbs brushed over the top of the cab and scraped against the trailer as the drive gently rose. Finally Ed saw the barn and knew he was in the right place. A large rental truck sat to the left, surrounded by vans and pickups.

The rain cut off abruptly when Ed drove the truck through the wide opening. The tractor rumbled through the barn and out the rear doors, back into the rain. A man appeared up ahead, holding a flashlight. Ed watched the narrow cone of light until it winked out. He stomped on the brakes, and the semi lurched to a stop. Only then did Ed look at the corpse that had shared the ride with him. It looked like a man sleeping, except the back of its head was blown away—that and the blood which drenched the seat.

Ed shivered, opened the door, and climbed down from the tall cab.

A man ran up to him. "Why the big delay?"

"Don't know," Ed replied.

"Where are Brad and Hawk?"

"We had some trouble. One of the drivers got away."

"What?"

"We can talk about it later!" Ed snapped. "I'm sure they can take care of it." He said it to get the man off his back, but Ed was not at all sure things were under control. And if the driver escaped, what then?

Ed reached the end of the trailer. A man held a flashlight beam on the padlocks while his partner lifted a long-handled tool. The jaws closed over the steel hasp and cut through it with a sharp ping. Soon the other lock was off as well. The man climbed up on the trailer and swung the doors wide.

The rental truck backed toward the trailer, the hydraulic lift level with the bed. Two men stood inside holding a steel ramp. The truck stopped about a foot away. The men dropped the ramp in place, bridging the gap. One grabbed a pallet jack and pulled it into the trailer.

The man standing beside Ed looked inside. "OK, get some lights in there. Put the heavy pallets in the rental. Move it! We haven't got all night."

Ed stood to the side since this wasn't part of his job. He was to wait until the unloading was done, then dispose of the truck.

The rain streaked Brad's goggles as he tramped through the wet brush. His blood ran cold as he thought about what would happen if the driver got away. It would ruin everything, and Brad could not allow that to happen.

Hawk had not called out again, which was good, since he had to know that Brad had joined in the search. Brad heard faint rustling sounds and angled toward them, but all he could see were bushes and trees. The ground began to drop away.

Brad followed a trail downward through the brush. Somewhere up ahead, he could hear the sound of running water. Over to the right he saw movement in a dense stand of trees. He stopped, turned, and brought up his automatic. His finger began tightening on the trigger when he caught a glimpse of a peaked hat. Brad relaxed his finger. It was Hawk.

Brad considered going over to him but realized it was a good way to get killed. Without goggles, Hawk couldn't see him, and besides, Brad didn't want to take a chance on warning the driver. Better to angle away and continue the chase. He continued down the draw and lost sight of his partner. The sound of running water grew louder.

⚊⚊ ⚊⚊ ⚊⚊

The tangled undergrowth tugged at Otto's legs as he groped his way through the blackness, hands outstretched to avoid the trees and bushes. He was moving more cautiously now, but still his breath came in hot, ragged gasps. He had lost track of his pursuer, but off to his right he heard the sound of running water. He snagged his foot on something, stumbled, and almost fell.

Otto reached out. Feeling the rough bark of a tree, he began edging around the trunk when the ground suddenly gave way, causing him to slide down a slick slope into the terrifying darkness. Icy water surged around his legs up to his knees. He gasped in shock and stood there shivering. Knowing he couldn't stay there, he groped around along the unseen bank until he found a root, then pulled himself up the muddy incline. Reaching the top, Otto stood still for a few moments and tried to catch his breath.

⚊⚊ ⚊⚊ ⚊⚊

Hearing a splash, Brad continued downhill until he spotted a rain-swollen creek. He turned to the right and began following the bank. Then he thought he saw a flicker of movement. He stopped and waited. He began to wonder if he had imagined it when he saw a bulky shape almost totally hidden by the intervening bushes and trees. It was definitely a man, but who?

Brad brought his gun up. Something crashed through the brush on the ridge above the creek. Brad turned and saw a figure disappear behind a bush. But in that brief glimpse, Brad had seen a peaked hat. It was Hawk, which meant that the man by the creek had to be the driver.

Brad turned back around. The man had disappeared, but Brad knew he couldn't be far.

"Hawk!" Brad shouted. "Stay where you are! I've got him!"

The movement on the ridge stopped. Brad slipped cautiously through the brush, watching for any sign of movement. He held his automatic up, sighting along the barrel.

Otto dropped to his belly as something colder than the rain shot down his spine. He had heard something off to the left and then a shout from up ahead. These men, whoever they were, had him cornered. He squirmed around and started crawling, angling toward the creek. Sooner than he expected, his left hand plunged into a void. Otto reached down and felt the mud of the creek bank. He pulled himself to the brink and listened to the raging water below. Not knowing what else to do, he slid down the bank and into the water.

The torrent grabbed Otto and bore him swiftly downstream. His feet bumped along the bottom, and he glanced off unseen rocks before finally tumbling into an unseen pool. The powerful current dragged him along then slammed him into an unseen obstruction. Countless sharp objects jabbed through Otto's thin uniform, causing him to cry out. The pressure of the water held him fast.

Brad spun around. He skirted the wild tangle of growth along the creek and made his way downstream. Up ahead the banks narrowed above a small rapids. Beyond lay a natural dam of tree limbs and brush that formed a small pool. And trapped against the dam was the driver.

Brad rounded a tree and stood on the bank. He raised his automatic, took careful aim, and pulled the trigger. The dying man thrashed around but did not cry out. The echoes slowly died away.

"I got him!" Brad shouted.

"Well come and get me! I can't see a thing."

Brad hurried up the slope and found Hawk.

"OK," he said, "follow me."

Brad guided Hawk down to the creek and using a branch pulled the body over to the bank. Getting out with their burden seemed to take forever, but finally they reached the highway. Leaving the body on the shoulder, Brad ran to the escort car while Hawk went for his goggles.

Brad opened the driver's door and grabbed the keys.

"Car coming!" Hawk warned.

They hid in the bushes until the northbound car went past.

"Come on!" Brad said. "Help me get the guards into the trunk."

"Right!"

Brad opened the trunk then ran around to the left side. He saw headlights coming south, but they were some distance away. He reached inside, grabbed the body, dragged it out and back to the trunk. He heaved the deadweight inside as Hawk arrived with the other body. A moment later it was inside as well.

"Hurry!" Hawk said. "Close the trunk."

Brad slammed it, and they hid behind the car. Two cars roared by in a cloud of spray.

Brad and Hawk ran back for the driver's body and hauled it to the car. Brad opened the trunk.

"I'll drive this car," he said. "You take ours."

"OK."

They threw the body inside. Brad slammed the trunk and yanked out the keys. Slick with rain, they sailed out of his grasp and landed with a splash.

"Help me find them!" Brad shouted.

He ran back to a puddle, knelt down, and began feeling around.

Hawk turned to the south. "Hear that?"

"What?" At soon as he said it, he recognized the sound as well. A helicopter was approaching, and that had to be bad news. Through the streaks in his goggles, Brad could see the aircraft speeding toward them.

"Come on!" he shouted.

"What about the car?"

"We don't have time! Now move it!"

Brad ran for their fake cop car, jumped inside, and slammed the door. Hawk swung into the driver's seat, cranking the engine as he shut the door. He yanked the gearshift into drive and pulled out.

"If they land, we've had it," Hawk said.

"I know that! Now keep your eyes on the road!"

Brad reached into the back and retrieved the two Uzis. He checked each one carefully.

—— —— ——

"We're approaching Holland," Craig said.

Barbara scanned the ground below as they sped along. Below them, a car pulled out on the highway. "What's that?"

Joel looked. "State cop. Probably stopped to check out that car parked on the shoulder."

"How far do you want to go?" Craig asked.

"How long to Wyoming?"

"About eighteen minutes."

"OK. Let's go to the outskirts, then back to the state line."

"Roger."

The Dolphin whined north through the steady rain.

Chapter Twenty-one

"That was close," Hawk said.

"Watch for the exit!" Brad said. "We can't afford to miss it."

"I'm watching! Now take it easy."

A mile further on, Brad saw the green sign he was looking for. "There it is."

Hawk slowed and took the off-ramp to the access road. Brad scanned the intersection up ahead.

"Man, someone sure flattened that sign," he said. Then he spotted the deep impressions, now filled with water, and realized what had happened.

Hawk whistled. "Well, at least he didn't get stuck."

A car roared by above them on the interstate. Brad looked all around. There was no traffic down here, for which he was grateful. Hawk turned right.

Brad leaned forward, watching the left side of the road. The green image in his goggles blurred as the car sped along. He wished he had checked out the site at night, but it was too late to worry about that now. Up ahead he saw something familiar.

"Slow down!"

Hawk hit the brakes, causing the heavy car to slide. He backed off and steered into the skid. The car straightened out.

"There!" Brad said, pointing to the nearly hidden drive.

Hawk turned onto the narrow track. Weeds and brush scraped along the bottom of the car. Up ahead he saw a dim glow. They entered the clearing in front of the barn. Hawk parked, and they got out.

Brad hurried toward the open trailer. "We have to kill those lights," he said. "They can be seen from the air."

"But we don't have enough goggles for the entire crew," Hawk said.

"Can't help that. If that helicopter finds the car, they're going to come after us." He approached the rental truck and saw Ed standing beside the trailer. He had his goggles on and was looking the other way.

"Why aren't you helping?" Brad asked.

Ed snapped his head around. "My job is to get rid of the semi."

"Your job is what I say it is. Now, where do we stand?"

"The rental truck is almost full. We're breaking up the other pallets now and loading the vans and pickups. It's going fairly well."

"Good." Brad put his fingers to his lips and blew a shrill whistle. "Gather round, everyone!" He looked up into the trailer. Two large battery-powered lanterns bathed the interior with a harsh glare. Several flashlights bobbed toward him as his men approached.

"Kill the lights!" Brad said.

A man jumped up into the trailer and turned off the lanterns. The flashlights winked out.

"OK, now listen up. We ran into some trouble. One of the drivers got away. We caught him, but we had to leave the escort car up on the interstate."

"Oh, no," someone said.

"On top of that, we saw a helicopter, so I think we have to assume that the feds will be looking for us soon."

"How did they find out?" Ed asked.

"Who knows! Now pay attention. We haven't got much time. Divide up the low-light goggles and pair up. The men with goggles will be the eyes for the ones without any."

A man tugged at Brad's arm. "I'm all loaded," he said, pointing to the rental.

"Good," Brad said. "Pull on out. I've got a crew waiting for you back at the garage."

"OK."

"Hawk will guide you down to the road." Brad turned to his second in command. "Stay down there and keep a sharp lookout. If you see any trouble, hightail it back here."

"Roger," Hawk said.

"Be careful," Brad told the driver. "Make sure you're not followed."

"I hear you."

The two men hurried to the truck and got in.

<hr />

"There's Wyoming," Craig said.

Barbara looked past him and saw a luminous grid of lights covering the ground like a net, merging with the even larger grid that was Grand Rapids.

"Might as well turn around," she said. "They couldn't possibly have come this far."

"I agree." He brought the helicopter around in a tight right-hand turn.

"Craig?"

"Yes?"

"I'm beginning to suspect they've stopped somewhere for the night. How much longer can we keep this up?"

"That's up to you. We'll provide transport as long as you need it."

"Sam?" Barbara said into the intercom.

He appeared at the doorway. "I've been thinking the same thing," he said.

"Yeah, but I'd sure hate to quit five minutes before they come through."

"I know, but we've got to stop sometime."

"What do you suggest?"

He looked out through the rain-spattered canopy for a few moments. "Let's make one more trip to the state line," he said finally. "That OK with you?"

She nodded. "Yes."

"Hang in there. For what it's worth, I think we did the right thing. Unfortunately, not all operations work out."

Barbara looked down at the interstate as the helicopter sped along toward Holland. She appreciated Sam's kind words, but they did not take away the sting of failure. She shivered as she imagined how Dan would review the operation. He rarely smiled, but this would probably do the trick.

They made an arcing left turn at Holland, following I-196 as it paralleled the shore. The small towns clicked off one by one as they approached Benton Harbor.

"There's that abandoned car," Joel said.

Barbara examined it as they flew past. "It has something on the roof."

"Yeah. Looks like lights."

"Police car?"

"Could be, or some other emergency vehicle."

Barbara watched until the car disappeared behind them.

Brad stood by the trailer's open doors. More than half of the trucks were gone now, and it looked like he had gauged it about right. The two vans and two pickups that remained would hold the last of the ammo. The loading was going slower than he wanted, but they would be finished in another twenty or thirty minutes. And so far, their luck was holding.

Ed walked over. "What do you think of my idea now?" he asked.

Brad tensed but then relaxed. His brother was wearing goggles and should have been helping with the unloading, but things were under control. Besides, Ed had one last job to do, and Brad wanted him focused for that.

"It was a good idea," Brad said. "We really need the ammo, and it looks like it's going to work out." He paused. "Thanks."

"Just want to be useful."

A driver approached. "I'm ready to go, but I need some eyes to get down to the road."

Ed turned to his brother. "I'll do it."

"No, you stay with the semi," Brad said. "You're vital to the success of this operation."

"Oh, OK."

"Come on," Brad told the driver. "I'll take you down."

They walked together to the loaded van and got in. Brad guided the driver down to the road where Hawk stood like a silent sentinel.

"OK, stop here," Brad said. "It's all yours."

"Thanks," the man said.

Brad got out and shut the door. He watched as the van drove off. A few moments later its lights came on, and the driver picked up speed.

"How's it going?" Hawk asked.

"We're almost done. One van and two pickups to go. It looks like we're going to get it all."

"Good. I'll sure be glad when this is over."

"Me too."

"You think Ed will have any trouble ditching the truck?"

"No. He didn't have any difficulty driving it here."

"If you don't count mauling that stop sign."

"Cool it! We've got to work together on this."

"OK, forget I said anything. What about the escort car?"

Brad sighed. "I wish we could do something about that, but we better leave it alone. Too much danger of getting caught."

"Yeah, I guess you're right."

"And getting rid of that car wouldn't buy us much time anyway. The feds will be coming out of the woodwork in a few hours no matter what we do."

"OK. Then why hide the semi?"

"No point in making it too easy."

"Just a thought. It'll delay our return to Grand Haven."

"I know that."

<hr />

Twenty minutes later, Brad guided the last pickup down the long drive, then he and Hawk hurried back up the hill to where Ed waited.

"OK, let's saddle up," Brad said to his brother. "All clear on the plan?"

"Yeah." Ed's voice carried more than a hint of irritation.

"Super. Now, give me a quick read-back, and we'll be on our way."

"I've got it, Brad!"

"Humor me."

"OK! East about a mile, then north to the road that goes to Allegan, where we take A-37 north. At Hudsonville we go under the interstate and turn west. The abandoned foundry is on the right just before we get to Borculo. I hide the semi inside, then we drive back to Grand Haven in the cop car. Satisfied?"

"That's great. Now, let's execute the plan. Need any help backing the truck up?"

"No, I can handle it, but what about the body?"

"Leave it where it is. Hawk and I will follow you to the foundry."

Brad hurried back to the car and got in. He tugged at his raincoat, trying to get comfortable, but his uniform was clammy and chaffed his skin. He would be glad to get out of his wet clothes and into a hot shower.

Hawk got in, backed the car in a tight arc, and started down the drive. Reaching the road, he stopped and backed the car down the road to make room for the truck. The windshield wipers flicked at the rain while the two men waited.

"Here he comes," Hawk said.

The semi backed slowly down the drive until the trailer drifted off onto the grass and the brake lights came on. The diesel roared as Ed pulled forward for another try. This time he started his turn before the trailer reached the road.

"He's going to hit the culvert!" Hawk said.

Brad watched helplessly. The left side duals rolled into the ditch, causing the trailer to tilt precariously. Ed stopped and tried to pull forward, but the driving wheels spun on the wet grass.

"Oh, great!" Hawk said, pounding the steering wheel. "Now what?"

Brad threw his door open. "Come on!"

The two men jumped the ditch and ran toward the truck. Brad jumped up on the running board and pounded on the door. The wheels stopped, and Ed lowered his window and looked down.

"Stop!" Brad yelled. "You'll never get it out that way!"

"What can I do?" Ed asked.

"Don't do anything!" He jumped down and turned to Hawk. "Come with me!"

Brad ran through the weeds and brush. When they topped the rise, he stopped and pointed. "Get a pallet."

He picked one up, wincing as a wood splinter drove itself deep into his palm. Hawk grabbed another, and they struggled back down the hill. Brad dropped his pallet and pushed it up against the tractor's wheels.

"Hawk, are you ready?" he asked.

"Do it!" Hawk replied.

Brad looked up at his brother. "OK, now take it easy. Come on forward."

Brad stepped back. The air brakes hissed, and the driving wheels began to spin.

"Wait!" Brad shouted. He jammed the pallet against the tires, hard. "Try it again."

The tractor inched forward, and the tires bit into the wood. The pallet slats groaned then collapsed with splintering crash. Brad breathed a sigh of relief. Ed stopped when the trailer stood on the drive again.

Brad looked up. "OK, now don't turn so sharp!"

"I have to! It's a narrow road."

Brad hesitated, not sure how hard to press. "All right, but don't get stuck!" He stepped down and joined Hawk.

"Think he'll make it?" Hawk whispered.

"I sure hope so."

The air brakes hissed. Ed started back down, this time applying more throttle. The rear duals dropped into the ditch but bounded back up as they climbed up the far side. The trailer rocked alarmingly. Ed continued until the trailer rolled into the ditch on the far side of the road. There he stopped with the tractor not quite clear of the drive. Brad held his breath as his brother cranked the wheel hard to the right and started forward. The tractor's left wheels rolled across the soft shoulder, then up on the pavement.

"That was close," Hawk said.

"Come on!" Brad said.

They ran back to their car and got in. They caught up with Ed and followed as the truck crept along at a speed that made Brad extremely uncomfortable.

"Man, it's going to take us forever at this rate," Hawk said.

"Let me worry about that!" Brad snapped.

"OK, OK! But we've still got a long way to go."

Brad said nothing. He was tormented by exactly the same thought.

Chapter Twenty-two

Barbara's mood dropped ever lower as the helicopter sped north toward Holland. They had traveled this course repeatedly, but this time they would continue along Lake Michigan's shore rather than following I-196 to Wyoming. It was over, and the operation was a complete failure, something she imagined Dan would point out with glee. Well, why not? It was true.

"There's that car," Craig said.

Barbara looked down. Something tugged at the back of her mind. She tried to remember the last time she had seen an abandoned emergency vehicle on the road, and she couldn't. But the police knew about it, so why worry. Then she remembered that the ammo shipment had an escort.

"Craig?" she said.

"Yes?"

"Would you mind checking out that car down there?"

"You want me to land?"

"I hate to ask, but yes."

"It's your show."

There wasn't any hint of irritation in his voice, for which Barbara was grateful. "Thanks."

Craig slowed the helicopter and brought it around in a broad circle, coming into the wind east of the interstate. Picking a broad section of the shoulder, he guided the aircraft into a hover and landed.

"What are you thinking?" Sam asked. He stood at the door bracing himself with both hands.

Barbara pointed to the car. "What if that's the shipment escort?" She winced at how lame that sounded.

"Let's check it out," Sam replied. He stepped back and started pulling on his raincoat. Art handed him a pair of low-light goggles.

Barbara struggled into her raincoat and met her partner at the side door. Art pulled it open. Barbara stepped down into the mud and ducked her head as she ran out from under the whirling rotor blades. She approached the driver's door, peered inside, then cautiously opened the door. There was something dark on the seats. Barbara reached in, touched the fabric and felt something sticky. She rubbed her fingers together and sniffed. The metallic, sweet smell told her what it was.

"Sam. I need a flashlight."

"Be right back."

Barbara felt a sudden chill that had nothing to do with the rain. She leaned in and peered into the backseat but saw nothing there. Sam returned with the flashlight.

"Thanks," Barbara said.

She took off her goggles and clicked on the light, wincing at the sudden brightness. She squinted her eyes and played the beam over the front seat.

"There's blood all over," Barbara said.

She turned off the flashlight and put on her goggles. She glanced at the waiting helicopter, then looked south along the highway shoulder, keeping her eyes on the ground as she walked along. Then she saw it—deep tracks in the mud.

"Here's where the semi stopped," Barbara said.

Sam stood at her side. "Sure looks like it. But where is it?"

Barbara frowned as she turned back to the car. "And where are the guards?

"Sam, would you see if Art has something to pry with. I want to see inside the trunk."

Barbara examined the trampled ground around the back of the car. She could make nothing of the countless boot tracks, but then her eyes followed the two mud furrows that trailed off into the brush. Sam returned carrying a heavy steel bar with a curved end. What it was Barbara had no idea.

Sam wedged the tool under the trunk lid and pulled. The tool slipped and fell to the ground with a splash. Sam grabbed it and tried again. The sheet metal groaned. Sam pulled harder, and something broke with a dull snap.

Barbara took a deep breath and opened the trunk. A cold clammy feeling came over her. Three bodies lay sprawled inside. The one on top seemed to look up at her through sightless eyes. She pushed up her goggles and turned on the flashlight. Her eyes went right to the Century Transportation uniform patch.

"There's the driver," Barbara said. She played the beam over the other two bodies. "And the guards." She felt a sickening sensation in her stomach. Even though she had seen many gory photos, this was her first actual contact with dead bodies. She swallowed hard.

"Wonder where the other driver is?" Sam asked.

"Who knows." She turned around. "Come on!"

They ran to the helicopter and climbed aboard. Barbara hurried forward and began strapping in.

"The militia has the truck," she told Craig. "They killed the guards and one of the drivers."

"What do you want to do?" Craig asked.

"Start searching. We can't let them get away."

"Roger."

"I'll contact Dan once we're in the air."

Craig began applying power. Moments later they lifted off.

Ed held the big wheel tightly. He tried to relax, knowing that the operation was almost over. It hadn't gone perfectly, but at least they now had all the ammo they needed. His idea had proved valuable, regardless of what Hawk thought. And they also had a TOW missile, thanks to him.

The sign marking the city limits of Allegan appeared ahead, along with a lower speed limit. Ed took his foot off the accelerator. He certainly didn't want to attract the attention of some sleepy cop, not while driving a stolen truck. He glanced at the dead body wedged against the opposite door. Ed would be glad when they got to the foundry. It would be a relief to say good-bye to the truck and his silent passenger.

"Back off," Brad said. He didn't want to get too close to the truck.

"Hope he doesn't miss the turn," Hawk said.

Brad decided to ignore the comment. They were on the east side of town now. The trailer's turn signals started blinking. The truck slowed and turned north on county road A-37.

"All right," Hawk said. "I'll be glad when we're out of town."

"Me too," Brad agreed.

Back routes might keep them away from prying eyes, he thought, *but they also made the trip longer.*

Barbara struggled to keep focused, but it was not easy. She had just finished an unpleasant conversation with Dan Oliver, relayed through Group Grand Haven communications. He had demanded to know why they were still on patrol after he cancelled the operation and had not backed off until Barbara told him about the hijacking. Barbara could tell he was still angry; but angry or not, he had promised to contact the FBI and the state and local police. Before signing off, he repeated his demand that she and Sam be in his office at eight sharp.

Sam had been standing behind her the whole time. Afterward, he shrugged and returned to his observation post by the door.

"I may have something," Joel said.

"Where?" Barbara asked.

He pointed. "That intersection down there. See those deep ruts and the bent-over traffic sign? Could be from an eighteen-wheeler."

"Oh, yes. Looks fresh." Barbara turned her head to the right. "What's up that road?"

"Not much," Craig said. "Farms and a few houses."

"Let's check it out."

Craig banked to the right and started down the road at a high rate of speed. Barbara scanned the pavement and shoulders. She considered asking Craig to slow down, but knew that could work against them. If the trail grew cold, they would never catch the militia. A few minutes later, a trampled patch appeared on the left shoulder, next to a culvert.

"I see something," Barbara said. "Can you put us down?"

"No problem," Craig said.

He pulled back on the stick to slow the helicopter, then landed in the center of the road. He unstrapped and followed Barbara out of the cockpit.

"I'll help you," Craig said as he pulled on his raincoat.

"Thanks." She accepted his help with her coat.

Sam was already at the door.

"You want to check down here while Craig and I go up the hill?" Barbara asked him.

"OK by me," Sam replied.

Art pulled the door open for them.

Barbara stepped down, walked out from under the rotor wash and stopped at the culvert. She looked down at the deep ruts that cut through the shoulder, leading up the overgrown drive.

Sam stooped down to get a closer look. "Has to be that semi," he said.

Barbara pulled out her automatic and began jogging up the slope. She saw the crushed pallets but decided to leave them for Sam. Once over the rise, a tall structure came into view.

"It's a barn," Craig said.

"Yep. Guess they wanted some shelter."

The ground in front was a tangle of tire tracks and boot prints. Barbara knew what had happened here and not long ago. The semi sitting there in the barn with trucks parked all around; transfer everything, then drive off into the night, ditch the semi somewhere, and disappear. Barbara set her jaw. Not if she could help it.

"What's that?" Craig asked.

Barbara looked where he was pointing. Something rectangular lay partially submerged in a puddle. She walked over and picked it up.

"It's a box of military flares," she said. "Come on."

Barbara ran down the hill. Sam looked up when he heard them approaching.

"There's a barn up there!" Barbara shouted as she gasped for breath. She held up the flares. "Look. This is where they transferred the ammo."

"See those tracks," Sam said. "I think they headed east from here, probably going to ditch that truck."

Barbara examined the deep gouges then looked up. "Come on! We still might catch them." She ran for the helicopter.

Sam jogged alongside. "Maybe so," he said. "These tracks are still fresh."

Barbara ducked her head and ran beneath the still turning rotor blades. Craig pulled open the door for them. Barbara followed him into the cockpit and waited impatiently while Craig and Joel got the helicopter airborne. She looked out the canopy at the road ahead.

"Where do you think they'll go?" she asked.

"Assuming they're going to Grand Haven, they'll probably head for Allegan, then turn north," Craig replied. "From there they could take Highway 40 to Holland or A-37 to Hudsonville."

"Which one?"

"The highway would be quicker, but A-37 would keep them away from the larger towns. We could cover both—fly up 40 first and, if we don't find them, come back down A-37."

"OK. Do it."

A few minutes later Craig brought the helicopter around in a broad left turn to follow the highway to Holland.

Ed resisted the urge to go faster. Despite their success so far, he couldn't shake his anxiety, and his silent companion wasn't helping his nerves any. The image of the abandoned escort car kept popping up in his mind. Sooner or later some cop was bound to find it. And what about the ordinance people at the guard armory? How long would they wait before reporting the truck overdue?

Ed wished the distance to the foundry would somehow melt away. He estimated they were halfway between Allegan and the interstate, so they had a ways to go. He didn't like coming so close to Wyoming, but there wasn't anything he could do about it since he wasn't calling the shots. But once they made the turn at Hudsonville, a few more miles would bring them to the foundry. And then it would be over.

Ed glanced in the side mirror and saw a single set of headlights hanging several hundred feet back. He was grateful for the light traffic.

"There's Holland," Craig said. "I don't think they took 40."

"Could they be further up ahead?" Barbara asked.

"Not likely. Our delay in Benton Harbor may have caused us to miss the truck but not by much. It had to take quite a while to unload, so they can't have much of a lead."

"I hope you're right. OK, let's check out A-37."

"I suggest starting at Hudsonville."

Barbara looked down at the tapestry of lights below, wondering if they were on the right track. Craig sounded upbeat, but she couldn't really say she felt the same way. "OK," she said finally.

The trip to Hudsonville took only a few minutes. In the distance, Barbara could see the larger sea of lights marking Wyoming and Grand Rapids. Craig hauled the helicopter around in a sharp right turn, heading south again. The lights near the interstate disappeared behind them as they flew over the countryside. Barbara sighed. Soon they would know.

"I see some headlights," Craig said a few minutes later. "Two sets, actually."

Barbara leaned forward. She felt a dim ray of hope as she spotted the two vehicles, then chided herself. There wasn't any point in jumping to conclusions.

Brad cursed when he spotted the red and green navigational lights coming towards them. "Helo—inbound!"

"I see it!" Hawk said. "What do we do?"

"They've got to be looking for us!"

"I know that! Now, what do you want to do? Come on! They're almost on us!"

Brad watched the helicopter's lights as it drew closer. *What could they do?* he wondered.

"Come on, Brad! Talk to me!"

A thought flitted through Brad's mind. He almost rejected it, but on reflection it seemed the only thing that offered hope.

"Hit your siren and lights!" he ordered.

"What? Are you crazy?"

"Do it! The state cops are probably out looking for us by now. So, we're going to pull over that suspect up there."

"Oh," Hawk said, "I see."

"I hope so. Now, as soon as Ed stops, get the machine gun out of the trunk and set it up. Dead men can't tell tales."

Hawk reached down and flipped on the lights and siren. "This ought to give Junior a thrill."

Chapter
Twenty-three

Ed took a long hard look in his side mirror. "What does he think he's doing?"

When he first heard the siren, he thought it was a cop, but there was only one set of headlights behind him. Then he wondered if Hawk had done it accidentally; but not only did the flashing lights stay on, the car was coming up fast, exactly as a trooper would. Ed finally tore his eyes away from the mirror and saw what was happening. His heart beat like a trip hammer when he spied the sinister shape hurtling toward him barely above the treetops.

Did Brad really want him to pull over? Ed wondered. Despite the urge to run, he knew there was no way they could elude a helicopter. Then he understood—their only hope was to kill the threat. But what kind of armament would the helicopter have? If it was an army model, he knew they could be in deep trouble. Tank killers wouldn't have any trouble handling a semi and a fake cop car.

Ed took his foot off the accelerator and began angling toward the shoulder.

⚞ ⚟ ⚞ ⚟ ⚞ ⚟

"That's it!" Barbara shouted. The trailer's Century Transportation sign stood out like Day-Glo.

Sam appeared at the door. "So it is, and it looks like we've got some help. State cop."

"It's about time something went right."

"Want me to land?" Craig asked.

Barbara looked to the right and saw an open field. "Yes. But let's wait until the trooper stops them." She looked back at Sam.

"I agree," he said. "No point in us being a distraction."

The semi rolled to a stop. The patrol car parked about twenty feet behind, and a man stepped out and put on his hat. Then the passenger door opened.

"He's got a partner," Barbara said.

"Good," Craig said. "I hope they know who they're messing with."

"They should."

Craig set the helicopter down. It bounced a little, then settled as he backed off on the power. "Looks like the cops are holding a little confab."

"Don't blame them," Barbara said. "I'd be cautious too."

She unbuckled her harness and joined Sam at the side door. One of the troopers approached the semi while the other walked back to the rear of the cruiser.

"What's he doing?" Sam asked.

"Good question," Barbara said. "He should be backing up his partner. I know I would if I thought I was dealing with a militia." She felt a sense of uneasiness creep over her. This didn't feel right. She glanced back. "Would you get me the M-16?"

Sam handed the rifle to her. Barbara nodded to Art, who pulled the door open. Barbara checked to make sure a round was chambered. She turned the low-light scope on, removed her goggles, and brought the rifle up to her shoulder, centering the crosshairs on the trooper standing behind the cruiser. The man opened the trunk, reached inside, and pulled out a long thin object. Then he grabbed something else.

"What's the other cop doing?" Barbara asked.

"Looks like he's talking to the truck driver," Sam replied.

"Does he have his gun drawn?"

"I'm not sure, but I don't think so."

"I don't like this."

Barbara steadied the M-16 against the door frame and centered her eye behind the scope. The trooper was holding what looked like a weapon that trailed something long and flexible, and he was facing the helicopter. Panic gripped Barbara as she finally realized what he had in his hand.

"He's aiming a machine gun at us!" she shouted. Barbara turned her head toward the cockpit. "Get us out of here! It's an ambush!"

Barbara was vaguely aware of the increased jet whine as she flipped the M-16's safety off and centered the scope on the gunner. The machine gun opened up, causing her magnified view to blossom with green fire. The helicopter lurched into the air. Glowing tracers stitched a luminous trail that swept around toward the accelerating helicopter. Barbara sighted on the deadly flashes and pulled the trigger five times in rapid succession. The tracers cut off abruptly.

"Did you hit him?" Sam asked.

"Don't know."

Barbara heard Craig on the radio with Group Grand Haven. It was some comfort knowing help would be coming, but they would have to deal with the militiamen until then.

"What is he firing?" Sam asked.

"Got to be an M-60," Barbara replied. "That is one nasty weapon. We were lucky to get away."

"If you hadn't fired, we probably wouldn't have."

The helicopter's movements caused the image in the scope to jiggle. The lethal flashes erupted again, this time coming from the other side of the patrol car. The tracers arced upwards, drawing ever closer.

"Do something!" Barbara shouted to Craig. "He's opened up again!"

She aimed as best she could and fired, pulling the trigger with swift precision until the clip was empty, but she knew that hitting the man would be sheer luck. She heard a sharp pinging noise somewhere behind her. The gunner had their range. Barbara's stomach felt funny, like she was in an express elevator going down. She looked forward but couldn't see anything without her goggles.

"What's happening?" she asked Sam.

"We're down on the deck. Looks like we're going to fly under the trees up ahead."

"What? Can we make it?"

"I sure hope so."

The helicopter's clatter increased suddenly then dropped off.

"We're through," Sam said. "I think the rotor tips hit some branches, but we're still in the air."

Barbara ejected the M-16's spent clip. Sam handed her another one. She inserted it and jacked a round into the chamber.

"Keep it low!" Barbara yelled into the cockpit.

"You don't have to tell me twice!" Craig responded.

They were south of the firefight now. The helicopter traced a wide turn to the left, coming around on the east side of the road, giving Barbara an excellent view. The semi was pulling out.

"The truck's getting away!" Barbara shouted.

"I see it!" Craig said. "What do you want to do?"

"Pull up beside it, but stay away from the cop car!"

"Roger that!"

Despite Craig's cautious approach, tracers reached up toward them as they flew north. Craig dropped lower, putting a line of trees between the helicopter and the gunner. Sweeping past the last tree, he angled toward the road, flying so low Barbara wondered if they would crash. She lined up on the truck, then shifted to the right-hand driving wheels and started firing. Dark objects exploded outward as the tires blew apart. The helicopter drew ahead. Barbara put two shots through the windshield.

"He's pulling over," Craig said.

The truck rolled to a stop, listing a little to the right. Craig guided the helicopter around in a broad left turn.

"Where to now?" he asked.

"Can you approach from the north and still give me a field of view?"

"Yes, but be careful."

"Don't worry, I will."

Craig dropped the aircraft down on the deck and flew it slowly sideways toward the car. Barbara swung her scope around. She saw two dark shapes edging along the side away from the road. The helicopter's motion caused the crosshairs to dance around. Barbara pulled the trigger four times. The shapes disappeared.

"They're coming up the other side!" Craig warned.

"I see 'em!" Barbara replied.

She got off three more shots. The men dropped but then sprang back up. Tracers erupted from the machine gun, reaching out for the helicopter. Craig lowered the helicopter's nose and turned hard to the right, almost causing Barbara to fall as they raced away. Heavy slugs raked the bottom of the aircraft.

"Craig! Turn around so I can shoot back!"

"Negative! They'd hit you for sure!"

Barbara slipped her goggles on. The ground rushing past seemed only inches away. She steadied herself with her left hand while she gripped the M-16 with her right, ready for when Craig would swing back around.

"We've taken a hit in the port engine!" Joel said. "I'm shutting down."

"Roger," Craig replied. "Hey! They're running! I'm coming back around!"

"Recommend you find a place to set down!"

"Later! They're stopping at the truck!"

Barbara looked forward.

"Gimme a clip!" she shouted.

She ejected the partially used magazine and inserted the one Sam handed her. "Craig! Turn!"

The helicopter skidded sideways. Barbara pulled off her goggles and thrust the M-16's muzzle through the door, laying the crosshairs on the car. The passenger side door flew open. Barbara lined up on the roof and began squeezing off shots, then moved to the driver's window and door. Round black holes erupted in the sheet metal, and windows exploded. The door closed, and the car lurched backward, turned and came to a sliding stop sideways in the road. It then lunged forward, backed again, and roared off to the south.

"Hold on, everyone!" Craig shouted.

He set the helicopter down hard. It rolled a few feet and stopped. He and Joel began rapidly flipping switches. The remaining engine began winding down.

"Everybody out!" Craig ordered.

Barbara replaced her goggles and inserted a new clip in her rifle. Art reached past and threw the door open. Barbara jumped down into the rain with Sam right behind her. She began trotting cautiously toward the semi.

"He's making a run for it!" Sam shouted.

The driver's door flew open. The man jumped down and began running north on the shoulder. After he cleared the truck, he began angling toward the woods. The sound of a siren drifted toward them, faint and distant but obviously coming closer.

"Come on!" Barbara said. "We can't let him get away."

She saw flashing lights in the north as they crossed the road. The fugitive was nearing the trees. Barbara removed her goggles, raised the rifle and fired one shot, expecting the man would keep on running. To her surprise, he stopped, held his hands up, and turned around.

"OK," Sam said. "Let's go get him."

They approached cautiously, but it was obvious to Barbara that the man was done fighting. She held the rifle on him as Sam recited the prisoner's rights.

"What militia are you with?" Barbara demanded when Sam finished.

The prisoner looked down and shook his head.

A police car slid to a stop facing the truck. The door swung open, and the officer started loping toward them.

"What's going on here?" he demanded as he approached. He held his service revolver in one hand and a large flashlight in the other.

Barbara turned to where he could see the yellow "ATF" on her drenched coveralls. "And you are?"

"Deputy Sheriff Davis, Ottawa County Sheriff's Department."

"Deputy Davis, I'm ATF Special Agent Barbara Post. My partner is Special Agent Sam Green. This man is a federal detainee, and we need the county to hold him until we can transfer him to a federal facility."

The man seemed flustered. "Oh, I've never done that before. I'm new on the force."

Barbara suppressed a smile. "We'll help. Do you have backup on the way?"

"Uh, yes, ma'am. I was patrolling near Hudsonville when I got the call. Dispatcher is sending another car from the jail. Should be here in a few minutes."

"Good." Barbara turned. "These gentlemen with us are Coast Guard aviators. Their helicopter is disabled, so can your backup take them to Grand Haven?"

"Sure, don't see why not."

Barbara turned to Craig. "I presume that's where you want to go."

"That'll be fine. But we could wait for you."

Barbara shook her head. "No need for that. I don't know how long it'll take us to get this guy booked. No sense in you guys standing around doing nothing. After all, it's been a long day."

"It has been that."

Deputy Davis put handcuffs on the prisoner. "Did you read him his rights?"

"I did," Sam replied.

The deputy escorted the man toward the cruiser, and Barbara and Sam followed along behind. Craig, Joel, and Art hung back. Another police car roared up and stopped. The officer inside jumped out and ran toward them. Davis explained what the ATF agents wanted done.

"I'll call you tomorrow—I mean today," Craig said.

"Thanks." She glanced toward the Dolphin. "Sorry about your helicopter."

Craig shrugged. "That goes along with the job. Don't worry. It's repairable." He paused. "I hope your meeting with Dan Oliver goes OK."

Barbara looked down. "I do too."

She watched as the Coast Guard crew got in the other car. The officer turned around and drove off. Deputy Davis helped the prisoner into the back of the squad car, then opened the trunk. Barbara set the M-16 inside. She and Sam joined Davis in the front seat.

The drive to the West Olive jail didn't take long. The officer on duty was more experienced than Deputy Davis and processed the prisoner for the ATF agents without a hitch, despite the fact that the alleged militia-man refused to talk. The officer recorded him as "John Doe" and escorted him to a cell. Barbara decided to let Sam call Dan and bring him up-to-date.

Within a half hour of arriving at the jail, Deputy Davis pulled out of the parking lot with Barbara and Sam snug in the front seat beside him. It was nearly 6:00 A.M., and Barbara and Sam still had to meet with Dan at 8:00. She sighed.

＊＊＊

Brad watched the car drive away. They were parked down the street behind a delivery truck under a burned-out streetlight. Brad took off his low-light goggles and turned to Hawk. "Let's go. It's now or never."

"I don't know. This is awfully risky."

"I know that! But if we don't get Ed out of there, all our plans go up in smoke!"

"He's probably already spilled his guts."

Brad shook his head. "No, he hasn't. Look, Hawk—you may not like him, but he's stronger than you realize. He can be a real pain at times, but he is loyal."

"If you say so."

"I do say so! But if we leave him hanging in the breeze, the feds will eventually get us. Do you really want to rot in a federal pen?"

"Are you sure this will work?"

Brad was not at all sure, but it was the only hope they had. "I believe we can do it," he said finally. "But we have to strike now. Look. We're two state cops working on this case, and we have every right to interrogate this prisoner." Brad knew that wasn't exactly true but hoped whoever was on duty could be persuaded.

"OK. Let's do it." Hawk opened the door and got out.

Brad kept his eyes on the jail as they hurried through the steady rain. He patted his raincoat and felt the reassuring bulge of his silenced automatic. They started up the front walk.

"We must look like a pair," Hawk muttered.

"Cool it. We look like troopers after a hard shift." He straightened his hat and opened the door.

It seemed to Brad that everything slowed down. His vision, normally acute, swept the room with the precision of a gun sight, missing nothing. Every sound registered sharp and clear. A single uniformed officer stood at a counter, his head coming up and around to see who was there. The man smiled. *Good,* Brad thought. This guy wasn't going to hassle two fellow cops.

"Morning gents," the officer said.

"Hi," Brad said. "I'm Sergeant Lowell, and this is my partner Sergeant Thomas."

"I'm Deputy Ellis. What can I do for you?"

"We're assigned to the militia investigation, and we need to question the prisoner you're holding for the ATF."

The man's smile disappeared. "Oh, well, that's kind of irregular."

Brad laughed, hoping he sounded natural. "Tell me about it. Look, I know he's the ATF's prisoner, but Michigan has jurisdiction also. We've got ongoing militia investigations all over the state, and I need to question this guy."

"I don't know . . ."

"Look, you can be present if you want. Just a few questions and we'll be on our way."

The man shrugged. "Guess that can't hurt anything. Just a minute." He punched a button.

"Yeah?" The intercom speaker squawked.

Deputy Ellis frowned. "Do you think you could be a little more professional?"

"Sorry. This is Deputy Ivey. How may I help you?" There was no mistaking the man's irritation.

Ellis rolled his eyes. "If it's not too much trouble, would you bring the John Doe to the interrogation room. The state police want to talk to him."

"OK, be right there."

Ellis let up on the button. "You'll have to excuse him. He's a new hire."

"We all have our burdens," Brad said.

He stepped back from the desk, and out of the corner of his eye, he saw Hawk move to the side. He rested his right hand as close to his open raincoat as he dared.

The heavy door leading back to the cells clicked and began to open. A man wearing an orange jumpsuit appeared, shuffling along in front of Deputy Ivey. Ed blinked in surprise, opened his mouth, then closed it. Ellis looked puzzled and started to say something. Brad thrust his hand inside his raincoat, jerked out his automatic and brought it to bear.

Ed dropped to the floor as Brad brought his left hand around to steady his grip. The iron sights came into alignment, the front blade and back notch centered on Ellis's forehead. Brad pulled the trigger. The heavy automatic jumped a little and emitted a soft plop. The deputy dropped as if poleaxed, a round red circle painted on his forehead. Brad swung his gun right, but Hawk fired first. Ivey dropped to the floor. A crimson pool appeared beneath his head and spread outward rapidly.

Brad jammed his gun back into its holster.

Ed beamed. "Am I glad to see you guys!"

Brad helped him up. "We weren't going to leave you in here." He looked at Hawk. "Get his cuffs off!"

Hawk rolled Ivey over and searched through the man's pockets until he found a key ring. He fumbled through all the smaller keys, trying each one, but without success.

He looked up. "None of these work! It's probably in the back somewhere."

Brad cursed. "We don't have time for this!" he said. "Let's go!"

Ed started to move. Brad grabbed his arm. "Walk between us," he said. "You're supposed to be our prisoner."

Ed giggled nervously. "Oh, yeah. Right."

They walked out into the rain. Brad looked both ways as they reached the street. A chill wave of fear washed down his spine when he spotted headlights approaching. Ed stiffened, but Brad forced him to keep walking. The pickup truck swept past and kept on going.

They made it to the car and got in. Hawk drove them out of West Olive and turned north on Highway 31. A short time later they were inside the city limits of Grand Haven. Brad sighed. The operation had taken a little over eight hours, but it seemed like a week. Weariness stole over him as his adrenaline high began to wear off. All he wanted to do was go home and crash, but that wasn't possible. There were a few more things to take care of.

"Where do you want me to drop you off?" Hawk asked.

"The garage. Have to get these cuffs off Ed—and check on the crew. And you've got to get rid of this car."

"Roger that."

A few minutes later Hawk pulled into the parking lot and stopped. It was still quite dark, even though official sunrise was already past. The rain, though moderating, was still steady. Brad looked all around before getting out. Except for one thing, the shop appeared deserted. Every window was black, but a trace of light showed under one of the garage doors. He would take care of that soon enough.

Brad looked over at Hawk. "You did all right. Good job."

"Thanks. I'll check with you later in the day."

"Right."

Brad and Ed got out. Brad opened the door, and they went inside. After locking the door, Brad turned around. Almost every bay held a van or pickup. Men staggered past carrying boxes of ammo to the secret elevator. The rental truck was gone, Brad was relieved to note. He decided to take care of the light leak himself rather than disturb the unloading process. He pushed the scrap of canvas firmly into place then turned to his brother.

"Come on over here, and I'll take care of those cuffs."

Brad selected a heavy bolt cutter. "OK. Hold 'em out."

Chapter Twenty-four

It was around 7:30 A.M. when Barbara finally collapsed into her chair before her computer. She yawned and sipped some coffee, but the caffeine seemed to have no effect. On her way into work, she had heard a news report on the jailbreak, which destroyed the one bright spot of the operation. Now all she could think about was somehow getting through her meeting with Dan and going home. She shivered.

Barbara booted her computer and logged onto the network. She opened Outlook but found her in-box empty. *That figures,* she thought. *Guess that shows what everyone thinks of me.* Then another thought drifted by, reminding her that true worth was measured differently. She leaned back in her chair. *Yes, but I still have to face Dan.*

She jumped when a strident bell sounded. An Outlook window popped up informing her of her meeting at 8:00 A.M. She confirmed the message and closed the window.

Barbara waited until just before eight then stopped by Sam's office, but he wasn't there. She returned to Dan's office, knocked, and opened the door. He scowled at her from behind his desk. She looked around at Sam. He seemed very uncomfortable.

Dan glanced at his watch. "So nice of you to drop by, Ms. Post. I guess I should count my blessings that you occasionally do what I say."

Barbara waited for him to invite her to sit, but he didn't. Her face grew hot as she took her seat. She checked her impulse to defend herself.

Dan's eyes drilled into hers. "Your behavior last night is totally unacceptable—what you did goes right over the top." He paused. "Is the bureau chain of command in any way unclear to you? Do you know who your boss is—or care?"

Barbara struggled for control. Besides the almost irresistible urge to strike back, she knew she was on the verge of tears. She lowered her eyes. "Of course I do," she said.

"Well, I sure am glad to hear you say that. So, how do you explain last night?"

"The militia did hit that ammo shipment."

"We'll get to that. What about my order? Was it in any way unclear to you?"

"We released Pete and Roscoe."

"What about the Coast Guard helicopter?"

"Craig . . . Lieutenant Phillips was providing transportation to help us in our investigation of local militias—according to established guidelines."

Dan slammed his fist down. "Wrong! You knew you were going against the intent of my order! I terminated your operation, and you flat disobeyed me! Ms. Post—I will not tolerate insubordination in my office! Do you hear me?"

"But what about the hijacking?"

"I said we would discuss that later!" He paused and his scowl changed to a sneer. "In what way would things be different if you had done what I said?"

"Uh . . ."

"Let me help. I'll grant you that the hit would have taken place. I'll also grant that said militia would now have a large store of ammo and that the perpetrators would not be in custody. Now, as I compare that to how things really are, I see what? No difference, except that the Coast Guard lost one of its helicopters and two policemen are dead."

"But we captured one of the perps."

"Who is no longer in custody."

"That's not my fault! The county was responsible for holding him until we could arrange a transfer!"

"Don't you lecture me, Ms. Post! You disobeyed my order, and the fact that the militia hit the shipment is beside the point! The end does not justify the means!"

Dan's words hit Barbara like a slap in the face. What he said was true, and there was no way she could rationalize her way out. She stared into his angry eyes. "You're right," she said, her voice low and shaky. She remembered Dan had accused her of this before, and he had been right then as well.

Dan looked surprised. "What did you say?"

"You're right. The end doesn't justify the means. I was wrong." Her throat tightened up. "Please forgive me."

Dan stared at her as if he hadn't heard correctly. He glanced over at Sam, then turned back to Barbara. "Well, thank you for your honesty."

He cleared his throat. "Next order of business is what we're doing about the hijacking. The FBI and state and local police are trying to identify the perp we had for a while. We've put out his mug shots, plus we should have an FBI report on the fingerprints sometime today. If the guy's got a rap sheet, we'll get a positive ID."

"What about the Grand Haven Militia?" Barbara asked.

Dan's sneer returned. "I'm not familiar which such an organization, Ms. Post."

Barbara gritted her teeth, but knew she had to play his game. "Sam and I are convinced Brad Anderson and Mike Hawkins are forming a militia in Grand Haven. We believe they were the ones who hijacked that shipment."

"I wondered how long it would take for Anderson and Hawkins to pop up. Look, I've told you before. Michigan is crawling with militias, and you haven't shown me one scrap of evidence pointing to Grand Haven. You say there's a militia forming there, but what about established militias? What about Muskegon? What about Wolverine? Just to name two."

"A new militia needs firearms and ammo."

"So do existing ones."

"But . . ."

"You seem to think I'm ignorant of your investigations. I do read the reports, you know. Both Brad Anderson and Mike Hawkins are respected Grand Haven businessmen. They have excellent military records, and neither has a criminal history. You're going to have to show me a lot more than you have so far to convince me that they did it."

"Can you get us search warrants?"

"Search warrants? For what?"

Barbara took a deep breath. "For starters, Anderson's garage and the gun store."

"Anything else? Perhaps the town of Grand Haven?"

"I'm serious."

"I am too, Ms. Post. Perhaps you missed this in your training, but judges require an affidavit claiming probable cause. There must be a reasonable belief that criminal evidence is present."

"I'm well aware of that. But . . ."

"Hold on! You may think your escapade at Anderson's garage gives us probable cause, but it doesn't." He stopped and shook his head. "What do I tell the judge when he asks how you came upon your so-called evidence? Uh, your honor, my agent just happened to be inside the garage after it was closed, and she heard them say they needed ammo for their militia. Come on! He'd throw me out. Besides, all militias need ammunition."

Barbara glanced at Sam, but he seemed to be avoiding eye contact. She focused again on her boss.

"Where do we go from here?" she asked.

"Our office will assist in the hijacking investigations. And there's no change in what you and Sam are doing—investigating western Michigan militias and getting ready for the president's visit." Dan pointed his finger at her. "But let me make one thing crystal clear. Next time you disobey me, you better have your resumé up-to-date. Understand?"

It took all Barbara's willpower to rein in her anger. "Yes."

"Very well. You may go."

Barbara and Sam stood up.

"Stick around, Sam," Dan said

The agent sat back down. Barbara hesitated.

"Please close the door on your way out," Dan told her.

Barbara returned to her cubicle. She considered going home but decided to wait until she could talk to Sam.

Sam finally came by a half hour later and sat down. His smile was strained. "I imagine you're glad that's over with."

"I suppose. So where do we stand?"

"We continue as before, except Dan said we have to investigate all western Michigan militias rather than concentrating on Grand Haven."

"But . . ."

"There's no point in arguing about it. Dan was quite specific."

"Which doesn't rule out Grand Haven."

"That line of reasoning will get you and me in a lot of hot water. Look, I understand your concerns, but we have to play this thing Dan's way—he's in charge. And believe me, he's going to be watching everything we do."

"How do you feel about that?"

Sam sighed. "Not that it really matters, but I'm still suspicious of the Grand Haven Militia. But that doesn't change anything."

"OK."

"Have you heard the latest news?" Sam asked.

"What about?"

"The national press coverage is getting brutal, particularly about the jail break. Rumor has it the White House is taking some heat."

Barbara shrugged. "Well, I can understand that. This is serious business."

"Yes, it is."

It was with a sense of dread that Barbara composed her next question. "Sam—where exactly do I stand in this office?"

Sam's tense expression changed subtly. "I can't comment on that," he said finally. "Look, I know you're beat. Go on home and get some rest. I'll see you sometime tomorrow."

Barbara nodded.

Sam got to his feet and walked out.

Brad's alarm clock went off at 1:00 P.M., and although he wanted to go back to sleep, he knew he couldn't. He rolled out of bed, padded over to the spare bedroom, and opened the door.

"Ed! Wake up!"

His brother moaned and turned over to face the wall.

Brad walked over and shook him. "I mean it! I've got to go to the garage, but we have to talk first."

"Can't it wait?"

"No, it can't. I'm going to fix a pot of coffee and something to eat. Want anything?"

"No."

"Suit yourself. I'll be back in a little bit."

There was no answer to that. Brad got dressed and hurried through the process of brewing coffee. He made himself a peanut butter and jelly sandwich and grabbed a handful of chocolate chip cookies. After placing these on the kitchen table, he returned to Ed's bedroom.

"Get up!" Brad roared.

The way he jumped, Brad knew his brother had actually been awake. Ed turned over and looked up.

"Now get dressed," Brad said with a little less volume. "We have to talk about what happened last night. Understand?"

"Yeah."

"Well, get a move on. I'm meeting Hawk at the garage at 2:00."

Brad returned to the kitchen and sat down at the table. He picked up his sandwich, took a bite, and washed it down with a swallow of coffee, which besides being hot, tasted vile. Ed finally wandered into the kitchen.

"What do you want to talk about?" he asked. He took the chair opposite Brad.

"Give me the details on your capture."

"I already told you."

"Tell me again! I have to be sure what we're up against. If there's any way they can identify you, we're dead."

"They can't!"

"Review it for me again."

Ed leaned back in his chair. "After you and Hawk cut out, I got out of the truck and ran, but they were right on me—I didn't stand a chance. After that, this deputy cuffed me and . . ."

"Back up," Brad said. "Now give me the details."

"OK, OK. These two ATF agents came up, a black guy and a white woman. The woman was carrying an M-16 with a night scope. Then this deputy sheriff arrives . . ."

"Did you hear their names?"

"Yeah. Let's see. The black guy's name was Green—I don't remember his first name. He read me my rights. The woman's name was Barbara Post, and the deputy was a guy named Davis."

"What about the helo crew?"

"There were three of them, but I didn't hear any names."

"Did you tell anyone your name?"

"No."

"You're sure?"

"Absolutely! I didn't say anything!"

Brad nodded. "Now, have you ever been arrested before?"

"No."

"Ever had your fingerprints taken?"

"No."

"You better be telling me the truth."

"I am, Brad! There's no way they can ID me—I swear!"

"I hope so. A lot depends on it."

Ed looked hurt.

Brad glanced at his watch. "I've got to go see Hawk at the garage. Now stay inside. We can't take a chance on someone seeing you."

"I know that."

"Good." Brad paused. "Look, I know this is hard on you, but I have no choice. We'll talk about it when I get back."

⚊⚊ ⚊⚊ ⚊⚊

It had finally stopped raining, and patches of blue were showing through gaps in the gray clouds. Brad pulled into the lot and parked. Hawk's car was already there. Brad went inside to his office and shut the door. The mini-blinds were already closed.

Brad sat behind his desk and looked over at Hawk. "Sorry I'm late. Debriefing Ed took longer than I expected."

Hawk frowned. "Are we in trouble?"

Brad took his time in answering. "I don't think so. I don't believe the feds can identify Ed."

"You sure?"

"He claims he never told them a thing, and I believe him." He paused. "I know Ed's a funny guy, but when he sets his mind on something, you can't budge him no matter what you do."

"I hope that's true. He tell you anything else?"

"Yes. He was arrested by two ATF agents, a woman named Barbara Post and a black guy by the name of Green. Deputy Davis was the officer who took him to the jail."

"Hm. There was a black dude came by my store a few days ago asking all kinds of nosy questions. Wonder if that was Green?"

"Could be, I guess. Now, what about the car?"

"I left it at Greg's house. He's taking it apart as we speak." Hawk's solemn expression changed to a grin. "Oh, and the rental truck's back where it's supposed to be, with the owners none the wiser."

"Good." Brad leaned back in his chair. "This may work out all right after all."

"We'll see."

"Yes, but we're going to have to be careful. I've been thinking. The feds may not be able to ID Ed, but they've seen him."

"So send him back to Montana."

Brad shook his head. "No, that would be more dangerous than keeping him here. Besides, he could be useful to us."

Hawk sneered. "Oh, really? How?"

"He knows how to operate the TOW."

"What? No way!"

"Hold on. The TOW operator at his old militia showed him."

"You believe that?"

Brad took a deep breath. "Yes, I do. Look. Ed's fascinated by things like that, and he's good at learning complicated procedures. At any rate, we don't have anyone else qualified to operate it."

"Your call. I just hope we can keep him from getting caught."

"My thought exactly. Which brings me to this: I need to ask a favor."

"Oh? What?"

"It would be safer for us all if Ed stayed out at your place . . ."

Hawk shook his head. "Time out! Ed and me aren't exactly best buds. No can do."

"Come on! Can't you do it for the cause?"

"Brad! I know he's your brother, but this is too much!"

"Be fair. He did get us the ammo we need."

Hawk frowned. "Yeah, I know."

"And he's the only one we've got who can operate the TOW."

"But . . ."

"Please give it a try—at least for a few days."

"OK, but you owe me big time."

"Will you be working tonight?"

Hawk glanced at his watch. "Yeah, but I'm going home to crash for the rest of the afternoon. Figured I'd come back around 9:00 and start checking the ammo."

"Good. Ed and I will help. Then . . ."

"I get the picture," Hawk interrupted. "I'll take Junior home with me when we're done."

"Please try and get along. You know he doesn't like you calling him that."

Hawk nodded. "All right, all right. I'll be good."

"I appreciate it."

<hr/>

Barbara got up around 4:00 P.M. and put a kettle on the stove to brew some tea. While waiting for the water to boil, she grabbed her portable phone and punched in Sam's home number. A woman answered the phone.

"Mrs. Green?" Barbara said.

"Yes?"

"This is Barbara Post. Is Sam there?"

"Oh, yes. Let me get him for you."

After a short pause he came on the line. "Yes, Barbara."

"Just checking in. Any news?"

"Nothing good. The perp's prints aren't on file. Apparently the guy has no rap sheet, and DOD says he wasn't in the military. The FBI is still checking mug shots, but it doesn't look like they're going to find a match either. I don't think we're going to be able to ID him."

"That's discouraging. How do you want to proceed?"

"Let's meet at 9:00 tomorrow in my office. We need to start revising our plans."

Barbara expected that. "I'll be there. Bye."

"Bye."

The kettle started whistling. She put a tea bag in her mug and poured the boiling water. The phone rang. Barbara returned the kettle to the stove and picked up the portable.

"Hello," she said.

"Barbara, this is Craig."

Her gloom dissipated like the sun coming out after a rain. "Craig, how are you?"

"Fine. I said I'd call."

"Glad you did. I was feeling kind of blue."

"Thought you might be. Sorry to hear about the breakout."

"Well, nothing we can do about it now. Are you back at work?"

"Yeah. Joel and I are hard at it. I'm up in Traverse City handling some paperwork. We're sending a truck down to haul the helicopter back up here for repairs."

"Oh, when will you be back?"

"Tomorrow. Joel and I will be flying a replacement down to Muskegon in the morning. I'll call you when I get in."

"I'll look forward to it." She paused. "You have no idea how glad I am you called. I miss you."

"I miss you too."

"Bye."

⚊⚊ ⚊⚊ ⚊⚊

Barbara sat down to watch the evening news, still not sure what she wanted to do about dinner. She thumbed the remote and watched as the network news logo appeared, only to be replaced by a medium close-up of the news anchor who hurried through a summary of the world's current travails. The Michigan hijacking was the second segment, edged out by a fire on a cruise ship that claimed one life. A commercial came on, showing the miraculous effects of a new prescription drug for arthritis, concluding with audio fine print describing possible side effects.

Barbara muted the sound and went into the kitchen where she phoned in an order for pizza and started preparing a salad. When she returned to the living room, the cruise ship segment was running. She waited impatiently for it to finish and endured the ensuing commercial.

Then the talking head returned, announcing the daring hijacking on Interstate 196, thought to be the work of a Michigan militia. Barbara watched the video of the abandoned escort car as the voice-over told of the three bodies found inside the trunk. Raindrops and camera-shake blurred the graphic images. The next scene took place at the abandoned farm, with yellow tape sealing off the barn. After displaying the stricken semi and the disabled Coast Guard helicopter, the final scene covered the jailbreak at West Olive. This last gory shot segued smoothly into a commercial for a supplemental source of dietary fiber.

Barbara turned off the TV. She had seen all she cared to see.

Chapter Twenty-five

Barbara yawned. She hadn't slept well the previous night despite her exhaustion. She finished reading E-mail—there was only one—then noticed it was a little past 9:00 A.M. She grabbed her notepad and went back to Sam's office. His door was open, and he looked up as she approached. He smiled, but seemed strained.

"Come in," he said, standing.

Barbara sat in a side chair while Sam resumed his seat.

"Are we going to be involved in the hijacking investigation?" Barbara asked.

"Yes, and we'll have lots of help. We're scheduled for meetings with the FBI and the state and local police later today."

"What's our focus?"

"We'll be investigating the western Michigan militias."

"Without concentrating on the Grand Haven group."

Sam looked a little exasperated. "What did you hear Dan say?"

"Essentially that."

"Then that's what we're going to do. He's the boss."

Barbara felt bitterness welling up inside. "Yeah, and he never lets anyone forget it."

Sam looked at her, apparently unable or unwilling to comment.

Barbara's resentment finally boiled over. "It's obvious Dan wants me out of here. Is that the way you feel? Are you on his side?"

Sam's expression changed subtly. "I have nothing to say. Those are inappropriate questions."

Now that her flash of anger was over, Barbara could see he was right; but the damage was done. Worse, her eyes were brimming with tears, and she had left her purse in her cubicle. She brought up a hand and wiped.

"I'm sorry." She meant it.

"Shall we get on with our work?"

"Yes."

"Besides the hijacking, we also have to start planning for the president's visit. That's a little over two weeks away, and we have a lot to do. The Secret Service has the lead on this, with ATF, FBI, and police providing support."

"When do we begin?"

"Actually, some of the procedures are already in place. We have a general checklist, plus reports from various agencies. We'll probably have our first meeting with the Secret Service sometime next week. They're already hard at work, of course."

"I would imagine so. What do you want me to do?"

"Review the hijacking reports as they come in. Tomorrow, we'll probably start investigating the militias." He pointed to a stack of papers on his desk. "There are some preliminaries to get you started."

"Thanks."

She took them and returned to her cubicle. She picked up the top report. It was from the Ottawa County Sheriff's Department, detailing the breakout of "John Doe" and the murders of Deputies Ellis and Ivey. Barbara had to read the first page several times until her anger dissipated enough for her to concentrate. Then morbid fascination drew her in. Not much was known outside the obvious escape and two homicides. Each deputy had been killed by a single 9mm slug through the forehead, with the predictable gory results. Forensics said the slugs came from different weapons, so that meant at least two perps in addition to "John Doe." But at present, the sheriff had no leads. Barbara wondered if the men in the fake cop car were involved. More to the point, was Brad Anderson one of the perps?

Barbara spent a quiet morning in her cubicle and around noon went out for lunch by herself. Upon her return, she checked her Outlook in-box and found two messages announcing meetings. The first was for a conference with an FBI special agent at 2:00 P.M. Then at 4:00 she and Sam would be meeting with representatives of the Michigan state police and the Ottawa county sheriff. All in all, Barbara was glad her afternoon was planned out. It left less time for brooding.

<hr />

Brad turned into the narrow drive and followed the ruts through the brush and trees until Hawk's house and garage came into view. Last night, the work at the garage armory had gone surprisingly well, with Hawk and Ed working together in what seemed like a spirit of cooperation. At one point Hawk had asked about the TOW, and Ed opened the equipment cases and explained how the weapon worked. Brad could tell that Hawk was both surprised and impressed. The truce seemed to be holding when the two men left for Hawk's house.

Brad hoped it still was. He got out of his Suburban and walked over the soggy grass to the porch. He punched the doorbell, and a moment later Hawk opened the front door.

"Come on in," Hawk said, stepping aside.

"How's it going?"

"We're doing fine."

Hawk's subdued reply spoke beyond his words, but he appeared committed to peace, for which Brad was grateful. They were, after all, facing a common enemy.

Brad lowered his voice. "Thanks."

Hawk nodded. "I just brewed a pot of coffee. Want some?"

"Sure."

"I'll get it."

Ed came in from the kitchen holding a mug. A wide grin creased his face when he spotted his brother. "Nice to see something on the armory shelves for a change, isn't it?"

"Sure is," Brad said, knowing what was required. "I'm glad your plan worked out."

"Now maybe we can start planning some operations."

Hawk returned carrying two mugs of coffee. Brad accepted one and took a sip. He noted his friend's strained expression and hoped for the best.

"Thanks," Brad said.

"Sure. Want anything to eat?"

"No."

They went in the den. Hawk settled into his recliner while Brad and Ed sat on the couch.

"So, what are we going to do now?" Ed asked.

That really was the question, Brad knew, but he didn't appreciate his brother prodding him. While the militia had been in the forming stage, there had been no reason to think of the future except in general terms. But now they had the arms, and although Brad was not done recruiting, he had enough experienced men to conduct an operation, providing a suitable target came along. But he would not commit unless it had strategic value, something like the Oklahoma City Bombing, for instance—something that would send a real message to the traitors in Washington.

"I'll decide that when we go operational."

"When will that be?"

Brad gritted his teeth. "When I say so!"

<hr />

It was 3:45 by the time the meeting with the FBI broke up. Barbara hadn't learned anything new, although hearing about FBI procedures had been worth the time. Now she had fifteen minutes before the conference with the state police and the sheriff. She sat down and checked her in-box. *Nothing.* Her phone rang.

"Barbara Post," she said, picking it up.

"Hi, this is Craig," said a cheery voice.

Her earlier gloom dissipated. "Craig. I'm so glad to hear from you. Are you back in Muskegon?"

"I wish. That's why I'm calling. We're still up in Traverse City. The engines on the replacement helicopter were due for a major overhaul, so we're stuck here until they get changed out. The mechanics are almost done, so we should be on our way in a little bit."

"Good."

"How is your day going?"

Barbara sighed. "I cannot tell a lie. It's been hard."

"Well, I guess that's what you expected."

"Yes."

"Hang in there."

"I'm trying."

"The other reason I called: Mother asked if I would invite you to dinner."

Barbara smiled. "I'd love to. What time?"

"Around 7:00. I'll come by for you."

"OK. See you."

"Right, bye."

"Bye." She hung up and finished getting ready for her meeting.

<hr />

Less than an hour later, Barbara was back at her cubicle. The state police and the sheriff were serious about their investigations, but their approaches were not all that different from the FBI and ATF. And so far, there weren't any hot leads. She glanced at her watch and saw it was about time for her commute to Spring Lake. She heard a sound and saw Sam approaching. She groaned inwardly, hoping her day was not about to go into overtime.

"Hi, glad I caught you," Sam said. "I called Alicia a few minutes ago."

"Oh?"

He seemed nervous. "Uh, we'd like to invite you and Craig to dinner on Friday."

Barbara sat there, not knowing what to say.

"Unless you've got other plans," Sam added. "We'd certainly understand."

"No," Barbara stammered. "I mean, I don't have any plans, but I don't know about Craig." She paused. "Yes, I'd love to, but let me ask Craig—I'll be seeing him tonight."

"Good. Here's the address." He gave her a sticky note. "Listen, if there's a conflict, we could do it another time."

"OK. I'll let you know tomorrow."

"Right. Well, you have a nice evening."

He turned and left.

— — —

At forty-seven, Harold Mitchell wasn't the youngest United States president, since that honor belonged to Teddy Roosevelt, who was forty-two when President McKinley was assassinated. Then there was John F. Kennedy, only forty-three when he was elected. But Mitchell had taken a lot of criticism from his opponent during the campaign—accusations of immaturity and lack of experience. Serving two terms in the House as a Michigan representative apparently counted for little in the eyes of some.

The president dropped the summary paper he had been reading onto his Oval Office desk and leaned back in his executive swivel chair. He focused his eyes on his chief of staff, Vincent Walters, former captain of industry, now considered by many to be a stabilizing influence in the administration. Harold struggled to hide his irritation.

"What do you make of it?" he asked.

"The ATF and FBI have it pegged, Mr. President. A Michigan militia hit that ammo shipment. The operation is quite consistent with what we've seen in various state militias recently."

"Exactly! Which is why I came up with my initiative. We have to deal with these people!"

Vincent nodded gravely. "I understand, Mr. President."

Since they were alone, Harold knew his chief advisor was waiting for the cue to go informal. "Talk to me, Vince. You know the flak I'm taking on this. And now a militia in my home state knocks off a National Guard ammo shipment. So, what am I supposed to do—turn a blind eye?"

"It's a matter of priorities, Hal. No one questions the need to address the militia movement, but where does that fit in with, say, international terrorism, Social Security, national defense, environmental concerns, and so on? The administration has a lot on its plate right now. Are you sure launching the initiative at this time is the way to go? We could postpone it."

"Vince—we're both from the same state. You know what the Michigan militias are like."

"Yes, and there are also groups in Montana and elsewhere. It's a growing problem, no doubt about it. But couldn't we consider a brief delay in implementation—just until things cool down a little?"

Harold shook his head. "No. We have to go ahead as planned."

Vince sighed. "As your chief of staff, I support you fully—you know that. But there is one other thing . . ."

The president frowned, since he knew what was coming. "Let's hear it."

"I wish you would reconsider the venue for your kickoff speech, especially in light of this hijacking. No announcement has been made. You could do it anywhere."

"No, I'm not changing my mind. Michigan is my home state." He rapped the paper on his desk. "As far as I'm concerned, this only confirms my decision. I'm going to send these jerks a message they can't ignore, and then we're going to crush them."

"I'm only thinking of your security." Vince paused. "The secret service is quite concerned."

"If the president of the United States is afraid to make a speech in his home state, then something's very wrong in America. I will not give in to these traitors!"

"Yes, Mr. President. Is there anything else we need to discuss?"

Harold glanced at his watch. It had been a long day. "No. That will be all. Thank you."

Vince got up and left the Oval Office.

Barbara felt her spirits lift when she opened the door and saw Craig's smile. He held out his hands, took hers, and pulled her gently to him. She tilted her head back. The kiss started out gentle but didn't stay that way. She felt herself responding to his intense emotions and was breathless when they broke.

"I believe you mean that," she whispered.

"I do." His voice was husky.

They turned, and he took her hand.

"That's nice," Barbara said. She squeezed his hand.

The drive to the house was pleasant, with the springtime finery reemerging after the recent drenching. Craig seemed unaffected by the recent fiasco, but Barbara was still struggling to put the dark thoughts out of her mind. Right now, all she wanted was to enjoy this evening with— what? Her man? She shivered at this electric thought.

"Cold?" Craig asked.

She smiled. "Not on your life." She caught the puzzlement in his eyes before he returned his attention to the road.

"Hm, OK." His grin returned. "Memo to self. I don't understand women."

"That's the way it's supposed to be, sailor."

"Aye, aye."

"Carry on."

Barbara settled back in the seat. Minutes later, Craig turned into the drive at his mother's house and parked behind Susan's Escort. Barbara felt a twinge of distaste, since she didn't enjoy being around Susan, but this was replaced by guilt. Susan needed love and compassion, not judgment.

Craig came around and opened the car door. They walked hand in hand to the door. It opened as they approached, and William peered out.

"Hi, William," Barbara said. She offered him a high five, which he returned with enthusiasm. "How are you doing?"

"OK! Grandma said you were in that shootout. Did you have to use a gun?"

"She can't talk about that," Craig said.

"But . . ."

The door to the kitchen swung open, and Elizabeth rolled out in her wheelchair. Her blue eyes twinkled. "Barbara, how nice to see you. I'm so glad you could come."

"I'm pleased to be here. Thank you for inviting me."

"Not at all. You're welcome anytime, dear."

"You're very kind."

Barbara spotted Susan in the living room. Her sullen expression made it clear that something was bothering her.

"Hello, Susan," Barbara said.

"Hi."

"How are you?"

"Oh, about the same."

Barbara struggled to maintain her smile. "Well, I've been praying for you."

"Thanks," Susan said without enthusiasm.

"Make yourself comfortable," Elizabeth told Barbara. "Dinner's almost ready." She said something to William, and they returned to the kitchen.

Barbara felt self-conscious under Susan's gaze as she sat down beside Craig on the couch. Their conversation was stilted and brief. Fortunately Elizabeth's prediction was accurate, and five minutes later she called them all to the table. Craig offered the blessing, and Elizabeth started the platters around.

"Is there really nothing you can say about what happened?" Susan asked.

"Not a lot. Another agent and I are investigating Michigan militias—with Craig's help."

"With the Coast Guard's help," Craig said.

Barbara grinned. "Don't think I asked for your input, pardner."

"Excuse me."

"Anyhow, that's what we were doing when the hijacking went down."

"Think you'll catch them?" Susan asked.

"I sure hope so." Barbara turned to William. "Say, hombre. How are you doing in school?"

William shrugged. "OK, I guess." Then his eyes grew very round as he trained them around on her. "Uh, oh!"

"Is something the matter?"

William's gaze made a lap of the table, starting with his mother and ending up with Craig and finally Barbara. "I forgot something," he said.

"What?" Craig asked.

"We have career day on Friday. We're supposed to invite adults to come in and tell us what they do."

"Well, you could ask your Uncle Craig," Susan said. "He certainly has an interesting job."

The boy glanced at Craig, then turned back to Barbara. "Yeah, but he's not out chasing the militia." His brown eyes bored right into Barbara's. "Would you come?"

"Me?"

"Yeah. It would be so cool."

"I don't know."

"Please!"

"Don't pester Ms. Post," Craig said.

William looked down and pouted. Barbara's heart went out to him. "I'd be glad to, William." She had no idea how Dan would react to this, but she couldn't say no.

"Really? Thanks! Can you bring your gun?"

Barbara stifled a laugh. "No. I don't think your teacher would like that."

"Aw, I'm sure it would be all right."

"No gun."

He frowned. "Can you wear a uniform?"

"ATF agents don't wear uniforms—at least not like your Uncle Craig's. Tell you what. How about if I wear my coveralls?"

"Coveralls?"

"Yes. They're blue and have 'ATF' in big yellow letters. I'll also wear my bulletproof vest."

"Cool! I can't wait."

"That's very kind of you," Susan said but without any warmth.

"Not at all."

Now all she had to do was convince Dan.

Chapter Twenty-six

Barbara tried to relax as Susan drove them through Grand Haven to William's school. Her bulletproof vest made her hot, and she felt self-conscious in her blue ATF coveralls. Yesterday, she had worried all day, wondering what she would do if Dan refused her permission to participate in career day. Finally, she had stuck her head in his office near quitting time. When she had finally gotten out her request, he had simply shrugged and said, "Fine."

Up ahead, Barbara saw the school, and she realized she had no idea what she could say to a bunch of third-graders. Susan turned into the parking lot.

"You know, it's nice of you to do this," Susan said. She paused then added, "Thanks."

For a moment Barbara wasn't sure what to say. "I want to do it. God's given you a fine son, Susan." She hesitated, knowing she was near a sensitive area. "Life's hard on kids nowadays. I'd like to see William succeed. He's worth it."

Barbara half expected a reaction to that, but Susan only nodded. They got out of the car and entered the building. Barbara had called William's teacher the day before and had agreed to meet outside the classroom a few minutes before the class began.

"That must be William's teacher," Barbara said.

A slim young woman waited near the end of the hall. She had long, silky blonde hair and wore a suit that seemed to be a compromise between practicality and style, with style coming out a little ahead. Her large blue eyes, well-framed in blue shadow and liner, observed the two women as they approached.

"Hi, I'm Barbara Post," Barbara said, holding out her hand.

The teacher took it. "Hello. I'm Renée Villers-Northcutt, William's teacher." She turned. "And you must be Susan Phillips. So nice to meet you."

"Yes, well, it's nice to meet you too," Susan said.

Renée smiled and turned to Barbara. "Thank you for coming, Barbara. It's important for the class to see successful women in responsible jobs." Her eyes flicked over the coveralls. "Not any way they can miss who you work for."

Barbara laughed. "I guess not. But I'm impressed with what you're doing. Teaching children is so important."

Renée looked down. "That's kind of you to say so." Then she looked up with a gleam in her eye. "But I've got my sights set on higher things. I have my master's degree, and I'm working on my doctorate. I plan to get on with the National Education Association. That's where real education begins."

"I see," Barbara said. "But I imagine teachers will continue to serve some purpose, at least for a while." She struggled to maintain her smile.

Renée laughed. "I like your sense of humor."

"It's a gift, I suppose."

The teacher's expression turned serious. "The reason I wanted to see you before class was to go over the guidelines for career day. I'm delighted to have a female ATF agent, but I'm a little concerned about the violence aspect, especially guns. I mean, we all know how much of a problem this is today, especially easy access to handguns."

Barbara cleared her throat. "Uh, I work for the Bureau of Alcohol, Tobacco, and Firearms, and my specialty is working with the illegal possession and use of guns and explosives."

"OK. You might emphasize the illegal aspect, then. But what we really need is to outlaw all guns."

Barbara set her jaw. "I disagree."

"What?"

"I see nothing wrong with law-abiding citizens owning and using guns, for things like hunting and self-defense."

A curious light came into Renée's eyes. "I see. Your accent . . ."

"Yep. I don't hail from around these parts."

"Where exactly is your home?"

"Southwest Texas."

"How—interesting."

"I think so."

"Hm. There's just one more thing. As I'm sure you know, the separation of church and state forbids any discussion of religious topics. So, I mean, this may not apply to you, I don't know, but if it does . . ."

"If you're asking if I'm a Christian, I am. I accepted the Lord as a girl, and I haven't changed my mind since."

Renée seemed flustered. "I'm sure that's valid for you, but you realize we have to respect the sensitivities of others."

"I believe you're saying I can't tell the children I'm a Christian."

"That, or anything else concerning religion."

"I understand."

"Good. Now, if you'll excuse me, I have to meet with the other guests."

Barbara and Susan stood out of the way. Two men and a woman approached Renée and were joined in the next few minutes by another woman and four more men. Barbara didn't know how large William's class was, but it was evident that not all students would have a guest. Besides Barbara, two other people wore uniforms, an attractive female Coast Guard lieutenant and a fireman. The teacher greeted them as a group and went over what was permissible. Then Renée returned to Barbara.

"Would you like to lead off?"

"It would be my pleasure."

"Good. I'll ask William to introduce you."

Renée held the door. "I've arranged chairs for everyone along the front."

Barbara and Susan sat beside the windows. Soon the class began filtering in. When William entered, he grinned at Barbara on his way to his desk near the back of the room. Renée called the class to order and took roll. Then she walked around her desk and gestured toward the adults seated in front of the whiteboards.

"Class, we have a real treat today. As you know, this is career day, and these people up here are going to tell you what they do for a living. Now pay attention. This may give you ideas about what you'd like to do when you grow up." She looked toward the back of the room. "William, would you like to introduce your guest?"

William stood and looked toward Barbara, his face very pale. "Uh, this is Barbara Post. She works for the ATF—that stands for 'alcohol, tobacco and firearms.' She's been working with my Uncle Craig on Michigan militias and they . . ."

"William," Renée interrupted. "You should let your guest tell her own story."

"Oh, sorry. Anyhow, here she is." He started to sit, then stood back up. "Oh, and my Uncle Craig likes her."

Renée cocked an eye at Barbara. "That was quite an introduction. The floor is yours."

Barbara's twinge of embarrassment shifted to amusement. "Thank you, William. That's the nicest introduction I've ever had." He blushed, but only Barbara saw it.

"As William said, I work for the ATF as a special agent. Does anyone know who's in charge of the Bureau of Alcohol, Tobacco, and Firearms?"

Only a few raised their hands. "The FBI?" a girl on the front row asked.

"No, but the ATF works with the Federal Bureau of Investigation."

A boy near the back held up his hand. Barbara nodded.

"The secretary of the treasury."

"Very good," Barbara said. "A lot of adults don't know that. Yes, the ATF is actually part of the Treasury Department, and we enforce federal laws concerning the manufacture and consumption of alcohol and tobacco products, and we also regulate the usages of firearms—guns— and explosives. That's my job. I'm an explosives and firearms expert, assigned to the Grand Rapids ATF office."

Quite a few hands shot up.

"Are you working on that truck shooting?" one boy blurted out.

"Yes, but I can't discuss it. Sorry."

She turned so they could see the front and back of her coveralls. "This is how we dress when we're out on a case. The 'ATF' tells other law enforcement officers who we are so they won't chase us off." The students tittered. "And this is what protects us if someone shoots at us." Barbara unzipped the coveralls. "This is a bulletproof vest, and it has saved many lives."

"Does it hurt if a bullet hits it?" a boy asked.

"Yes, it does. I've never experienced it, but it's like being punched real hard in the chest. It leaves a large bruise, but that's better . . ." Barbara glanced at Renée and saw her look of disapproval. "It's better than the alternative."

"Why don't you tell them how you chose your career."

Barbara gave them the short version of growing up in Marfa, Texas, and being fascinated with what her father did for a living, and how this had led to Texas A & M and finally the ATF. She explained that her home was in the middle of a desert, over five hundred miles from where she went to school.

Barbara concluded and sat down. Her presentation had been a hit, judging from the excited faces around the room. But what touched her the most was William's grateful smile.

Susan was quiet as she drove Barbara back to Elizabeth's house. When they got there, Barbara started to get out.

"I appreciate you taking time off to do that for William," Susan said.

Barbara turned to her. "You're welcome. I think your son is a fine kid."

Susan smiled. "Thanks. And . . ."

"Yes?"

"I hope things work out between you and Craig."

Barbara knew she was blushing. "That's very kind of you, Susan. Thank you. Well, bye."

"Bye."

Barbara got out and went to her car to begin her commute to Grand Rapids.

⁂

Barbara tried to relax, now that her long day was over. She looked all around as Craig drove along. She had seen Wyoming from the air but not from the ground.

Craig turned onto a street of modest-sized houses. "Nice area," he said.

"Yes, it is," Barbara said. She watched the house numbers as they drove along. "There it is."

Craig pulled over and parked at the curb. Barbara looked up at the house as she waited for Craig. She got out, and they stood for a moment on the sidewalk.

"Sam didn't say why he wanted us to come to dinner?" Craig asked.

"No, he didn't. It was kinda out of the blue."

Craig took her hand, and they approached the front porch. "Interesting." He pressed the doorbell.

Sam opened the door. "Come in. Craig, I'm glad you could come on such short notice." They shook hands. He turned to Barbara and grinned. "Hope this isn't messing up your Friday plans."

"Not at all."

"Good."

A woman looked in.

"Alicia," Sam said. "Come and meet Barbara and Craig."

The woman stepped into the entryway. Her skin was a rich brown, lighter than her husband's. She greeted them politely and then looked to Sam.

"Honey, what time did Bill say he would be by for the girls?"

Sam glanced at his watch. "Hm. He should have been here twenty minutes ago. Must have been delayed by traffic." He looked at Barbara. "Bill's a friend from church. He and his wife have kids the same age as ours."

A little girl charged in and slid to a stop when she saw the strangers. A slightly older girl followed a moment later. Sam knelt down. "Come on. Give Daddy a hug." They ran into his arms, and he looked at each one. "I want you to meet some of Daddy's friends from work." He stood up and introduced Barbara and Craig.

"This is Gracie," Sam said.

The older girl smiled. "My name's actually Grace," she said sweetly.

Sam faked a look of distress. "Well, ex-c-u-se me." She giggled. Sam turned to his younger daughter, who seemed on the verge of taking flight. "And this is Tamara, Grand Empress of the East."

"Daddy!"

He looked at her in mock seriousness. "Did I get your title wrong?"

"Can I take a video along?"

"Mom already said no," Grace announced.

Tamara shot her sister a hot look. "I was asking Daddy!"

Sam looked at Alicia, then back down at Tamara. "Your mother's right. The Nelsons will have plenty for you to do at their house."

Tamara stamped her feet. "No-o-o-o-o-o!"

Sam's expression grew stern. "Tamara—stop that."

The doorbell rang. Sam went to the door and opened it. "Bill, come on in. I want you to meet some friends of mine."

An overweight black man came in but seemed to hang back when he spotted Barbara and Craig. He was polite, and he nodded to Barbara and shook hands with Craig. His smile came to full brilliance when he greeted the girls. He wasted no time in corralling and ushering them out the door.

"Bill works for the Post Office," Sam said after the door closed. "We've known the Nelsons for . . ." He turned to Alicia. "How long?"

"Since before the girls were born—nine or ten years." She turned to her guests. "Dinner is ready."

She led the way into the dining room. After they were seated, Sam offered the blessing. Then Alicia started the platters of roast beef, potatoes, and carrots around. That she was an excellent cook, Barbara noticed at once. Conversation languished as they ate. It was partly because of the good food, but Barbara also had trouble coming up with things to talk about.

After dinner, they retired to the living room and sat around a coffee table. Alicia brought out bowls of peach cobbler and coffee on a tray. Barbara tasted the cobbler.

"This is wonderful," she said.

"Thank you," Alicia said. "It's Sam's favorite."

Sam grinned. "No doubt about that." He tried his and took a sip of coffee.

Silence fell again as they enjoyed their dessert. When the last bowl went down, Sam picked up his coffee cup and sat back, and he looked at Barbara. Alicia's smile faded.

"Remember what you asked me on Wednesday?"

Barbara felt an icy pang in her stomach. "I think so."

Sam nodded. "I think you do too. Please forgive me, but Craig needs to know what we're talking about." He turned to him. "We face certain—challenges in our office. I can't go into detail, but Barbara asked me if I was, essentially, engaging in office politics against her."

"Sam . . ." Barbara began.

"Please let me finish. What you said hit me hard, and for a lot of reasons, I didn't really want to say anything. But I've thought about it and finally decided your accusation deserves a reply. But how? It isn't something we can discuss in the office—some of it we can't discuss at all.

"Then there's the question of whose business it is. Craig is aware that we've got problems in our office." His smile returned briefly. "And unless I'm mistaken, you two are pretty good friends."

Barbara felt heat rise in her face. "Yes, we are."

"For what it's worth, I think you make a fine couple."

"Thank you."

"So, Alicia and I talked it over, and I invited you and Craig to dinner so we could air things out a little." He paused. "May I proceed?"

In a way, Barbara dreaded it, but she also wanted some resolution. She nodded. "Yes, please."

"You believe you're the object of discrimination because you're a woman, and you asked me if I was a party to it."

It took all Barbara's willpower to maintain eye contact. "That's right."

"Do you really believe I'm prejudiced against women?"

Barbara blinked, and it took a few moments to organize her thoughts. "You're difficult to read, Sam. For a while, I wasn't sure where you were coming from. But, having worked with you—and thinking about it, no, I don't think you are."

He nodded. "Thank you for that. I'm not against women serving in the bureau, but you know, there was a time when men of my color weren't welcome."

"I understand."

"Do you? Do you know what racial prejudice looks like through my eyes?"

"Well, no, I guess I really don't."

A sad smile came to his face. "That's right, there's no way you could. And I don't know what you've been through. I guess the question is: how do we see each other as persons—or how should we?"

"'Love your neighbor as yourself.'"

Sam's smile turned warm. "Good place to start, and right from the Lord's lips. So, do you think we can trust each other?"

"Yes." Barbara looked at Alicia then back at Sam. "And I would like to know you both better."

"I feel the same way about you—and Craig, since he seems to figure prominently in your future."

Craig reached over and squeezed Barbara's hand. "Thanks. And I don't think we should let it stop here. I feel the same way about this as Barbara."

Later, on the way home, Barbara felt grateful Sam had decided to confront the issue, rather than let misunderstandings continue. Whatever Dan was up to, she couldn't do anything about it. But what really worried her was: what was the militia up to?

Chapter
Twenty-seven

Barbara had to try on several outfits before deciding on blue jeans and a long-sleeved denim blouse. She debated whether to take along a sweater or a more practical jacket. The sweater won, and she draped the heavy, off-white wool garment over the back of the chair beside the door. A plastic cooler containing salad, bread sticks, and Cokes sat on the floor, her contribution to the picnic. She was glad the week was finally over and she could take a break from investigating the hijacking.

Barbara got to her feet when she heard footsteps on the stairs outside. The doorbell rang. She opened the door and saw Craig standing there grinning. The late afternoon sun touched his blond hair, giving it a golden tone she hadn't seen before. Barbara's eyes traced his tan short-sleeved sport shirt and khakis, and gave his outfit a silent seal of approval.

"Ready to go?" Craig asked.

"Yep," Barbara replied.

He picked up the cooler while she grabbed her sweater. They walked hand in hand down the stairs to Craig's car. He opened the trunk and set the cooler beside his. An unmistakable odor drifted out.

"Um, fried chicken," Barbara said. She searched his eyes. "Homemade?"

Craig closed the trunk and opened the door for her. "My dad used to say, 'You don't have to answer all the questions people ask you.'"

She got in. Craig closed her door and walked around. Barbara watched as he folded his long frame into the driver's seat. She saw the twinkle in his eye.

"I'm sure he didn't have someone like me in mind," Barbara said. "Fess up."

Craig started the car and began backing up. "Uh, the Colonel had something to do with it."

"I thought so. It's hard to hide those eleven herbs and spices."

"But I heated up the baked beans myself."

Barbara giggled. "Oh, well, I stand corrected."

His grin returned. "I should hope so."

"What is it we're going to see?"

"The Musical Fountain. The city touts it as the world's largest; however I suspect the mayor has his fingers crossed. Still, I have to say, it is spectacular, and quite popular—with residents and tourists."

"What kind of show is it?"

"It varies. Sometimes it's pops, other times classical or big band. There are fireworks on the Fourth. During the summer they even do worship services on Sundays."

"Where is it?"

"On the north bank of the Grand, near Bicentennial Park—that's where we're going to watch it."

Craig slowed down where Michigan 104 approached U.S. 31. Instead of turning south to cross the Grand River, he went north and began working his way west and finally south on North Shore Drive.

"I haven't been over here," Barbara said.

"There's not a lot here." He pointed to the left. "Over there is the Kitchel-Lindquist Dunes Preserve, which takes up most of the area along the north bank of the Grand."

"Doesn't look like an easy place to get to."

"It is rather out-of-the-way." He slowed and turned back to the east. "We follow this around past the marina to Bicentennial Park. The city recommends watching the fountain from Waterfront Stadium, but the locals prefer the park."

"Will they let in someone from West Texas?"

He grinned. "I'll vouch for you."

"Thanks."

Craig pulled into the lot and parked. "Would you like to see the fountain while it's still light?"

"Why not? Can't say I've ever seen a musical fountain up close."

Barbara waited as he came around. Craig opened her door and helped her out. She felt a tingle as he took her hand and they started walking through the park. Up ahead Barbara saw a shallow depression about the size of a football field. In the center lay the fountain's pool, where hundreds of water nozzles of all sizes and shapes pierced the surface.

"That thing's huge," Barbara said.

"Wait until you hear the sound system."

They strolled all around the pool, stopping on the side nearest the river. A young man approached from the direction of the park. He walked to the edge of the pool and cocked his head as if he were listening to something only he could hear. Barbara watched him for a few moments then turned to Craig.

"What's this evening's show?" she asked him.

"Tonight's classical," the young man said, looking their way.

"Thank you," Barbara said. "Do you know what pieces?"

He laughed. "I should. I do the programming for the fountain. It's an all J. S. Bach show. The first work is his *Toccata and Fugue in D minor,* followed by the first movements of the *Brandenburg Concerti,* numbers one and two." A twinkle came to his eyes. "I can give you the BWV numbers if you like."

Barbara smiled. "No, thank you. I like classical music, but I'm not a fanatic."

He shook his head. "Pity. Are you folks familiar with the fountain?"

"Not really," Craig said. "What can you tell us?"

The man grinned. "More than you'd probably care to hear, but I'll give you the CNN version."

He swept his arm around the pool. "The fountain has over three hundred valves and thirteen hundred nozzles and requires forty thousand
gallons of water for each performance. The nozzles vary in size from
three-sixteenths to one inch in diameter, and the big ones shoot jets a
hundred and twenty five feet high. The total lighting output is 125,000
watts with every color under the sun, and the speakers are rated at twelve
thousand watts. The speakers are JBL—thirty-two subwoofers at six hundred watts each and twelve high-frequency horns, driven by fourteen
power amplifiers."

"Wow," Barbara said.

"Yeah. You couldn't stand it up this close. The sound level at the shoreline is 130dB."

"We'll be watching from Bicentennial Park."

He nodded. "That's the best place."

"Thank you for telling us about it. Much obliged."

The man looked at her curiously. "Ma'am, your accent is fascinating.
You from Oklahoma?"

Barbara put her hands on her hips. "Move your sights south about five
hundred miles, pardner."

He grinned. "Ah, the Lone Star state. Well, excuse me."

Barbara laughed and shot a glance at Craig. "I try to make allowances
for the folks up here, seeing as you don't have much opportunity to come
by and say howdy."

"Thanks. I appreciate you cutting me some slack." The young man
glanced at the fountain then back at Barbara. "Uh, I have a thought. I just
finished mixing a new CD for an Aaron Copland show we'll be doing
later this summer—songs from Rodeo: 'Hoe-Down,' 'Buckaroo Holiday,'
'Corral Nocturne,' and 'Saturday Night Waltz.' Would you like to hear
that instead of the Bach?"

"Well, I guess so, but won't you get in trouble with your boss?"

"Depends on whether we get any complaints. I usually have a pretty
free rein on how I do the shows."

"In that case, I'd love to hear it."

"Thought you would."

Barbara looked into his impish eyes. "And why would that be?"

"Uh, the story—you know, the romantic adventures of a cowgirl, and . . ."

"I get it—I get it."

"Then, I better go change the CD. You folks enjoy."

"We will," Craig said. "Thanks."

"Not a problem."

The young man walked off. Craig took Barbara's hand, and they returned to the car. He opened the trunk and pulled out the coolers while she grabbed the blanket. Craig selected a spot among a sparse gathering of families and couples.

"View should be pretty good from here," he said.

Barbara spread the blanket then took charge of the coolers. Craig sat beside her.

"That kid was closer than he knew with the cowgirl reference," he said.

Barbara stopped unloading the salad and looked at him. "What's that supposed to mean?"

"Uh, you're from Texas and a firearms and explosives expert and all." He paused. "And the romantic element—especially the romantic element." He leaned over and kissed her gently on the cheek. "I kinda fancy my cowgirl."

Barbara blushed. "I'm glad. It so happens I'm kinda fond of my aviator."

She finished preparing their salads. Craig took her hands and offered the blessing. They ate their salads and then started working their way through the Colonel's original recipe and Craig's beans.

When the sun finally dropped below the western horizon it seemed to take the day's meager allotment of warmth with it. Barbara pulled on her sweater, and Craig put on his jacket. They finished their dinner and snuggled together as they waited for the show to start. The western yellow-orange glow faded slowly to a deep, sullen red. The sky's palette went from ultramarine all the way to black overhead in one smooth continuum, speckled with the first stars.

A few minutes later a blue flume of water shot up from the fountain, and an amplified voice boomed out of the night, "Welcome, I am the voice of the Musical Fountain." Then came the stirring chords of the first few bars of "Also Sprach Zarathustra." After a brief pause, the familiar strains of Copland's "Hoe-Down" provided the background for a spectacular water ballet.

"What do you think of Grand Haven now?" Craig whispered in Barbara's ear.

She snuggled even closer. "I'm liking it more and more." Despite everything, Barbara knew she was happier than she had ever been in her life.

Chapter Twenty-eight

Barbara reviewed the ammo hijacking report as she waited for the office coffeemaker to finish brewing. Only a week had passed since that fateful Monday, but it seemed much longer. Both the ATF and the FBI had launched large-scale investigations, covering all of Michigan and the surrounding states. Barbara and Sam had been quite busy investigating the militias in western Michigan, although Barbara believed it made more sense to concentrate on the most promising leads. She finally had to surrender to Dan's demand that they include all militias. He was, after all, the boss.

Barbara filled her mug and continued on to Sam's office. She entered and sat down.

"Good morning," she said.

Sam smiled. "Good morning. Did you have a nice weekend?"

"I did. Craig and I took in the musical fountain on Saturday. It was really something."

"It is, isn't it? Been a while since Alicia and I have seen it; kids kind of limit what you can do as a family. Gracie likes the fountain, but it's not exciting enough for Tamara." He rolled his eyes. "I'll never forget the last time we went. Tamara darted around like a mosquito, whining that she was bored and why couldn't we go get an ice cream cone. There's more, but let's just say a good time was not had by all."

"That's too bad."

He shrugged. "That's part of life." He paused. "I suspect you'll find that out—someday."

Barbara felt herself blushing. "I guess that depends on if the right one comes along."

Sam's grin grew even wider. "Somehow, I suspect that's going to happen."

Barbara took a sip of her coffee. "Thank you for inviting us to dinner. We really enjoyed it."

"You're welcome. Alicia and I were glad you could come. We don't often get the chance to entertain."

Barbara hesitated, not knowing exactly how to express what she felt. "I'm also grateful we had the opportunity to—talk about things."

He grew serious. "Prejudice—of various kinds."

"Yes. I've thought a lot about—everything. I want to get to know you and Alicia better because I like you both."

Sam's smile returned. "I think the Lord would bless that. I have to confess, Alicia was apprehensive when I suggested inviting you and Craig to dinner. This is a painful area, even among believers. She and I talked about the evening before we went to sleep. We'd like to see this go forward, but you do realize it will be difficult, don't you?"

"Well, yes, and I understand I haven't had your experiences, so there aren't any shortcuts."

"That's right, you haven't. And we haven't had yours."

"But I'm willing to learn. I want to."

"Good. Then I suggest we invest the time and see how things go."

"Let's."

Dan stuck his head in the door. "I need to see you ASAP," he told Sam. He glanced at Barbara then walked off.

"My, he's in a jolly mood," Barbara said.

"Have you been following the news reports on the hijacking?"

"Of course."

"The overall tone is getting pretty nasty. The media priests are demanding to know why we haven't apprehended the hijackers—you know, like we're idiots or something. So now we're beginning to get pressure from above, and Dan doesn't react well to that."

"Pressure from where?"

"The short answer is the secretary of the treasury. But I suspect the ultimate source is the president. The hijacking doesn't put his militia initiative in a very good light."

"But the initiative hasn't been implemented yet."

"Doesn't matter, as far as the public is concerned. Right or wrong, they view the president as the supreme handyman. If something's wrong, he has to fix it; and if he doesn't, it's his fault."

"Yeah, I suppose that's right. So, what do we have on tap for today?"

Sam got up. "More of the same. I'll get with you after I see what Dan wants."

"I'll be in my cubicle."

It was a little after 5:00 P.M. when Barbara made her last stop of the day, the Grand Haven State Police Post, which included Muskegon within its district. Sam's meeting with Dan had resulted in a new work schedule for the week: Barbara would investigate militias in the Muskegon area while Sam concentrated on Wolverine.

That settled, Barbara had spent a busy but unproductive day. She started with visits to local gun stores and pawnshops, where her reception had been less than lukewarm. Her hopes for having lunch with Craig were dashed when she found out he was on a training exercise. After a rather dreary lunch, Barbara paid a visit to the Muskegon County sheriff. It was obvious he lacked any real leads.

Barbara pulled up at the state police post and parked. She sighed. One more call, and it would be time to head for home.

Craig felt a gentle bump as the landing gear touched down. He and Joel went through the shutdown procedure, securing the helicopter after the long training mission. The side door behind them thumped open, and the swimmer and mechanic stepped down and started walking toward the hangar.

Joel watched them. "On behalf of our flight crew, I'd like to thank you for flying with us today on Coast Guard Airlines. Please check under your seat and in the overhead bins for the items you brought aboard. Thank you for allowing us to serve you, and we hope to see you again real soon, aboard Coast Guard Airlines, where service isn't our motto; it's an afterthought."

"Very funny, Mr. Foscue," Craig said. "Thinking of a career in the airlines?"

"What, and leave all this behind? Hey, this may have been only a training exercise, but last week we almost got blown out of the air."

"The times are changing."

Joel shrugged. "Yeah, I guess they are. See you inside." He unstrapped and got up.

Craig finished his checklist and left the aircraft. Inside the hangar he went to his office and sat down at his desk. He eyed his in-box but decided the contents could wait until morning. Then he remembered something he had noticed on Sunday. He reached for his phone and punched in a number. It rang twice.

"Hello," the cheery voice said.

"Mom," he said, "this is Craig."

"Hello, dear. How are you?"

"I'm fine. Listen, your van is due for service. Would it be convenient for me to drop it off at Anderson's tonight?"

"Do we have to?"

"Your serpentine belt has fifty thousand miles on it. I want them to replace it, and it's also time to change the transmission fluid."

"Well, whatever you think best."

"Good. I'll call Barbara and see if she can drive me home after I deliver it."

"What a nice idea. Why don't you ask her to dinner?"

"Thanks, but I was thinking of asking her out to Harbor Lights."

"I understand, dear. You go right ahead."

"I'll be there as soon as I can get away—shouldn't be too long. Bye."

"Bye."

Craig glanced at his watch. It was approaching 6:00 P.M., so there was no way he could make it before the garage closed. He thought about calling Brad but decided it wasn't necessary. He regularly dropped cars off for service by depositing the keys and instructions through the mail slot in the door.

Then his mind explored another reason. Craig really didn't want to talk to Brad. The ex-Navy SEAL had been on his mind a lot during the past week, as Craig tried to reconcile this respected businessman with the image of a murdering terrorist. Craig had even considered taking the van to another garage, but he didn't know of another shop he trusted. And there wasn't any real proof that Brad was involved in the ammo heist.

<hr />

Barbara opened the freezer door and looked inside, reviewing her inventory of gourmet entrées. Nothing looked good, and she was too tired to cook something from scratch. She considered making a fast-food run, but that wasn't appealing either. Miniature clouds of frigid air rolled out of the freezer while Barbara pondered her limited options.

Her mobile phone chirped. She closed the freezer, picked up her phone, and punched the "talk" button.

"Hello."

"Hi, this is Craig."

Barbara felt a surge of joy. "Hi."

"How was your day?"

Barbara wasn't sure how to answer that. "Routine, I guess. How was yours?"

"Long and tiring. We just got back from a difficult training mission."

"I know. I called the hangar around 11:00 to see if you wanted to go to lunch."

"Oh, sorry. Wish I'd been there."

"Yeah, me too."

"Listen, maybe I can make it up. How about dinner at Harbor Lights?"

"I'd love to."

"Um, I also need to ask a favor." The note of joy seemed to leave his voice.

"Oh, what's that?"

"I have to drop Mom's van off at Anderson's for service, so I'll need a ride. Do you mind?"

"No, of course not." She paused. "But are you sure you want to use Anderson's?"

"I don't know—I was wondering the same thing. What do you think?"

A thought popped into Barbara's mind. "Actually, it wouldn't hurt. I'd have an excuse to see the garage."

"It'll be closed."

"Oh, well, I still see no reason not to. Want me to meet you there?"

He didn't answer immediately. "No, I'll come by your apartment."

"OK."

"I'll see you in a little bit." He paused. "Love you."

"I love you too."

Barbara hurried off into her bedroom to change.

❦ ❦ ❦

Barbara's doorbell rang about a half hour later. She opened the door. Joy melted the remaining residue of her day when she saw Craig standing there.

"Hi," he said with the self-conscious grin she found so endearing.

"Hi yourself, pardner."

He pulled her into a gentle embrace that quickly became quite warm.

"Whoa, I think I like that," Barbara said.

He grinned. "Me too. You ready to go?"

"Let me grab my purse."

Craig took her hand and walked her downstairs.

"See you at Anderson's," he said. He held onto her hand for a few moments before letting go.

Barbara got into her car and waited while he backed the van out, then followed him out of Spring Lake and into Grand Haven. She felt a shot of adrenaline when she spotted Anderson's Automotive up ahead.

Ed sprawled on the bench seat of Hawk's red Dodge pickup, out of sight in accordance with his brother's orders. Even though he understood the need for caution, it still irritated him, and Hawk seemed to take delight in telling him when he had to duck down.

Hawk stepped on the brake. The truck slowed abruptly, then stopped.

Ed frowned. "Are we there?" he asked.

"Hold your horses. Looks like a customer is dropping off a van."

"But the garage is closed."

"I know that, Einstein. But sometimes customers leave their cars after hours. Think I'll go around the block."

"Let me see." Ed started to sit up.

"Get down, you idiot!" Hawk made a grab for him but missed.

Ed took a quick look. He felt an icy jolt in the pit of his stomach when he recognized the man getting out of the van. Then he saw the woman.

"Get down!" Hawk shouted.

Ed dropped to the seat. "That's one of the ATF agents!" he said.

Hawk glanced at him. "What?"

"She's the one who arrested me! Name's Barbara Post. And that guy with her was on the helicopter."

"You sure?"

"Course I'm sure! What are they doing here?"

Hawk took a quick look. "I don't know. We'll see what Brad says."

The pickup turned the corner.

"I'll poke this through the slot, and we'll be on our way," Craig said as he stuck a note and the van's keys in an envelope and sealed it.

Barbara watched as a pickup truck drove down the side street, rounded the corner, and disappeared. She turned back to the garage and thought she caught a movement out of the corner of her eye. Were the blinds in Brad's office moving? She stepped closer. The light inside was on, but then it had been on the night of her ill-advised investigation.

"Anything wrong?" Craig asked.

Barbara turned and saw him looking at her oddly. She shook her head but didn't answer. Craig looked puzzled as he walked with her to her car.

They got in, and she drove out of the lot. "Are you sure there's no one in the garage?" she asked.

"Far as I know. I didn't try the door, but I've never known them to be open this late. Why do you ask?"

"I thought I saw the office blinds move."

"Well, I guess Brad could be working late."

Barbara smiled. "You think I'm being paranoid?"

"Hm. Think I'll plead the Fifth on that."

"Harbor Lights, you said?"

"That's a roger on your last."

She found his banter relaxing. "As you were, Lieutenant."

"Yes, ma'am."

The Gathering Storm

Brad waited several minutes before peeking through the blinds again. Had the woman seen him? He didn't know who she was but obviously Craig Phillips did. He hoped they hadn't noticed Hawk's pickup, but what did it matter if they did? His friendship with Hawk was well-known, and Ed should have been out of sight.

Brad walked to the outside door, picked up the envelope, and opened it. The requested maintenance was strictly routine. But what had Craig meant by asking if anything was wrong? Had the woman noticed something?

Hawk's pickup turned the far corner and slowly approached. Brad pressed the button to open the garage door. The truck entered the lot and drove into the bay. Brad lowered the door. Ed popped up and got out.

"Do you know who that was?" he asked breathlessly.

"I should. Craig Phillips is a friend—one of my best customers."

"No, I mean the woman! That's Barbara Post—one of the ATF agents! And your friend was on the Coast Guard crew."

"I don't like the sound of that. Come in my office. We have to talk."

Brad waited until they were seated. Then he looked at his brother. "You're sure about this?"

"Absolutely! She and that black guy—Green—were the ones who arrested me."

Brad turned to Hawk. "So, now we know who the helicopter pilot was—one of them anyway." Brad looked at his brother. "Have you seen that agent any other time?"

"No. Just when she arrested me."

"How about Craig? So help me, if you've been careless . . ."

"No! I swear it!"

Brad could see that his brother was getting mad, but he was also obviously afraid. "OK. Then the question is: does the ATF suspect me?"

"I don't think so," Hawk said. "If they did, they'd have searched the garage by now."

"Maybe, maybe not. Have you noticed anything unusual over at your shop?"

"Not recently, but, as I said before, a black dude came snooping around awhile back. Wouldn't surprise me if he was the other ATF agent. But there's no way they could be onto us." He stopped and looked at Ed. "Unless they find something on your brother."

Ed slammed his fist down on the desk. "No way! I have a clean record!"

"Knock it off, you two!" Brad said.

"So, what do you want to do?" Hawk asked.

"How are things down in the armory?"

"Under control. The ammo is all stowed, and I'm almost through checking out all the M-16s. We'll need some more of those soon, to keep up with our growth, and I'd like to get a spare M-60 barrel if I can." He smiled. "Gotta hand it to you, Brad. The militia is shaping up nicely. Looks like we'll be operational before too long."

"I agree. But I'm still worried about that agent. If she suspects something, we could be in real trouble. Shouldn't we consider taking her out?"

Hawk shook his head. "Your call, Brad, but I don't think so, at least not yet. I think the ATF would have acted by now if we were in trouble."

"Yeah, I guess you're right. I sure hope so."

⚙⚙⚙

Harold Mitchell sat propped up in bed, flipping through the cable news channels trying to find one that didn't have a bias against his administration. He frowned. If there were such a channel, he wasn't aware of it. Of course, the reporters would insist they were only doing their jobs, as protected by their first amendment rights. And naturally they claimed to be objective—who would dare to suggest otherwise?

He glanced at Nancy. The first lady seemed to be absorbed in her novel, but Harold couldn't recall her turning a page recently. He turned back to the TV. His one shining hope had been the new initiative; but before he could launch it, a militia had hijacked an ammo shipment, making the ATF and FBI look like fools. It was almost too much to bear. The familiar video clip of the abandoned escort car flashed on the screen. Harold thumbed up the volume.

" . . . bodies of three men were found inside the trunk. So far, the ATF and the FBI have reported no leads, although it has been almost a week since the hijacking. All officials will say is that they suspect a western Michigan militia is responsible for the crime. The White House press briefings have been surprisingly quiet about the situation, saying only that the president's militia initiative is still on track. To this, one reporter asked: 'What initiative?'

"In the Middle East today, further violence broke out. . . ."

Harold jabbed the off button, and the smiling news anchor contracted into a colorful dot and then vanished. He dropped his hand to the covers and stared at the blank TV screen.

"What do they want?" Harold said in exasperation. "They imply I don't know what's going on and that my initiative is nothing more than a lot of hot air." He turned to his wife. "What am I to do?"

Nancy edged toward him. Harold lifted his arm so she could snuggle against his chest.

"What really matters?" she began. "What they're saying, or what's in your heart? Are you giving it your best?"

"Of course I am!" he said with a heat he knew was misdirected.

She took his hand and squeezed it. "And I know you are too." She looked into his eyes. "I love you, dear. You know I'm with you—in everything."

He did know that. Nancy had always been in his corner, and he was grateful for the strong marriage they had shared throughout the years. Many wondered if his wife had a life of her own, suggesting that Nancy was in his shadow. But then, a lot of people didn't know what made a marriage strong. Without mutual love and respect, marriages didn't last. Besides, Nancy was very much her own person. He chuckled.

"What's funny?" she asked.

"Oh, just thinking about how difficult it must be for you, living in my shadow."

She pinched him. "Take that, Mr. President."

He turned toward her. "Good thing the Secret Service didn't see you do that."

"So? They also have to protect the first lady."

"I'm not sure you need protecting." He caught a whiff of her perfume. "You're distracting me," he said. He kissed her gently. The way she returned it left no doubt what was to come next.

Chapter Twenty-nine

Barbara yawned as she sat at her kitchen table, sipping on a second cup of coffee. It was nearly 7:00 A.M., and she was done with the Grand Rapids paper. The hijacking was still front-page news, but the article was only a rehash of the scanty facts ending with a statement of the obvious: there were no suspects. Barbara threw the paper away in disgust. Soon she would be on her way to Muskegon to continue her investigations.

It was Monday again, with not much to show for the previous week's work. She frowned as she considered the pressure the administration was putting on the ATF, pressure that Dan felt free to transmit down to her level.

Barbara gathered up her purse and headed for the door. Then she smiled. That evening she and Craig would be exploring Chinook Pier, visiting the shops and eating at one of the restaurants. She opened the door and walked out into the cool morning.

⚊⚊ ⚊⚊ ⚊⚊

Harold Mitchell sipped coffee from the delicate White House china cup, putting off what he had steeled himself to do. Finally he returned the cup to its saucer, leaving his cinnamon roll untouched. He looked at Vincent Walters over the broad expanse of his Oval Office desk, noting the tension in his chief of staff's eyes. Vince probably knew what was coming and didn't like it, Harold thought. Well, that was just too bad.

Harold nodded toward the two newspapers sitting on his desk. "Have you seen *The Washington Post*?" he asked.

"I always read the *Post,* Mr. President."

Harold knew that was true and noted the hint of exasperation. His chief of staff was an awesome fact-processor. The president touched the thicker paper. "*The New York Times* is saying essentially the same things— and all the news channels and all the squawk shows. Why can't the combined might of the federal government nail those hijackers?"

"We've been through this before, Mr. President."

"Yes, we have, and now it's time for action. Have you seen the most recent polls?"

Vince's jaw muscles bunched up. "Of course I have."

Harold felt the heat rising in his face. "Let me summarize them for you: The administration is twiddling its thumbs while the militias run amok—it's Rome burning, with yours truly playing the part of Nero. Vince! We look like a bunch of incompetents!"

"That's not true, Mr. President. The ATF and FBI have extensive investigations underway; the FBI director and the secretary of the treasury are both excellent managers. We're doing everything we can."

Harold shook his head. "Not everything. I'm calling a press conference this morning. I'm going to announce my trip to Grand Haven and give my critics a little preview of how this administration is going to fight domestic terrorism."

The color left Vince's face. "Sir, I wish you'd reconsider. The Michigan trip is only a week away. Why not delay the announcement until next Monday, like we agreed?"

"The public wants answers now."

"I know, I know. Unfortunately, answers to complex problems take time. What will we gain by announcing the trip now?"

"It will focus attention on my campaign promise to do something about the militias, and that as of next Monday, we begin. Then maybe the media will get off my back."

"What about security, Mr. President? You know the Secret Service is worried about the Grand Haven speech. The director will have a fit if you announce the trip beforehand."

"Hang the Secret Service! I'm the president, and it's my decision!"

"Yes, sir, I know that, but why make their jobs any harder than they already are?"

That gave Harold pause. He appreciated the Secret Service and didn't want to burden them. But . . .

"The decision's made," he said in a softer tone.

"Yes, Mr. President. When do you want to do it?"

"As soon as you can arrange it."

"In the Oval Office?"

"Yes."

Vince got to his feet. "I'll take care of it."

Harold nodded. "Thank you, Vince. I appreciate it."

━╥╨╥━ ━╥╨╥━ ━╥╨╥━

Harold endured patiently as the makeup artist dabbed powder on his face. After countless TV appearances, he still hadn't gotten used to this ritual. He glanced at Vince without moving his head. His chief of staff had arranged the special announcement in record time. At 11:30 A.M., eastern time, he would be answering his critics and sending a message to those who felt themselves above the laws of the United States.

The woman finished with her sponge and went to work with an eyebrow pencil. Harold squinted under the brilliant glare of the TV lights. The cameraman looked rather bored. Beside him, the soundman played with his control board.

He looked up. "Could you give me a test, Mr. President?"

Harold cleared his throat and tried to smile. Mike tests always made him feel self-conscious—what could you say that didn't sound silly? "My fellow Americans: two weeks ago—on a day which will live in infamy—the United States of America was suddenly and deliberately attacked by the combined forces of the state militias. I ask that the Congress declare, that since the unprovoked and dastardly attack by these terrorists on this date, a state of war has existed between the United States and the various militia movements."

The soundman looked up and smiled. "Thank you, Mr. President. That bit about 'infamy' has a nice ring to it."

Harold struggled to maintain his smile. "Um, actually I lifted it from another presidential speech."

"Really, sir? Which president?"

"FDR—Franklin Delano Roosevelt."

"Man, that was a long time ago."

"Yes, it was."

"What speech was it?"

Harold sighed. "It doesn't matter, I guess." Then a thought occurred to him. "Your recorder wasn't on, was it?"

The man looked sheepish. "Well, yes sir, it was. But don't worry. It's not going anywhere. It was just a test."

"Mr. President!" the director interrupted. "We go live in fifteen seconds!"

The makeup artist glared at the man, took one more look at the president, then stepped aside. Harold picked up his notes and willed his hands not to shake. The director continued his countdown. When he reached zero, the camera's red light winked on.

Harold smiled at the camera lens. "My fellow Americans. I come to you this morning with a heavy heart. My prayers go out for those killed in the Michigan hijacking and their families, and with this concern, my resolve that such lawless acts of terrorism will not go unpunished. America was founded upon the rule of law, not men; and as your president, I promise you that the federal government will enforce the laws of our great land. Let those who scoff take note.

"As I promised during the campaign, my administration is about to launch a counteroffensive against the militia movements. Next Monday I will fly to Grand Rapids, Michigan, and announce the details of my initiative at Grand Haven.

"But I'd like to give you a brief preview now. The various militia movements are growing more and more violent. Who can forget the Oklahoma City bombing or the Judge Richards assassination, and now this Michigan hijacking. To counter these threats, I will expand the size of both the ATF and FBI and task them with bringing these terrorists to heel. Further, I will ask Congress to pass legislation requiring that all state militias be registered with the Department of Defense, placing them under the chain of command of the joint chiefs of staff and the president, as commander in chief. Militias failing to do so will be disbanded and their weapons confiscated."

Harold put down his notes. "I know that those who hijacked the ammunition shipment are hearing this. As president of the United States of America, let me assure you, I will not rest until each of you is arrested and convicted for these brutal murders.

"To the law-abiding citizens of our great country, I hear your concerns; and as your president, I promise you: I will act."

Harold continued to stare into the camera lens until the red light winked off. Then the camera crew started packing up, paying him no more attention than if he were a piece of furniture. Harold glanced at his chief of staff. Vince was not happy.

⸻ ⸻ ⸻

It was nearly 2:00 P.M. by the time Barbara finished talking to the owner of Muskegon Guns, who claimed he knew nothing about the hijacking. She left the store and mentally reviewed her schedule. She thumbed her remote to unlock her car, got in, and set her purse on the passenger seat. A muted chirp sounded. Barbara pulled her phone out and punched the "talk" button.

"This is Barbara Post," she said.

"Hi, this is Craig."

Barbara's day seemed to brighten. "Well, hello. Nice to hear your voice."

"Likewise. Did you hear the news?"

"You mean the president's announcement?"

"No, the recording made before he went on the air."

"What?"

"Apparently they were testing his microphone, and someone got a copy of it and posted it on the Internet. It's being E-mailed everywhere, and all the talk shows are yammering about it."

"What did he say?"

"It was a parody of FDR's 'day of infamy' speech—the president said he was asking Congress to declare war on the militias. He was obviously joking, but you wouldn't know it from some of the reactions, especially around here."

"Great! That's all we need on top of everything else. Sam called and said the Secret Service is having a fit about the president announcing his trip."

"I can understand that."

"Since canceling the trip is out, now they want him to take a helicopter from the Grand Rapids airport to Grand Haven."

"That seems reasonable."

"The president didn't think so. He wants to make a speech at the Grand Center convention hall and then ride in a motorcade to Grand Haven."

"That could make security dicey."

"Yes, especially since the parade plans have already been released to the media. There's no going back now."

"Will this affect you?"

"Not right now, but I'm sure it will when Sam and I start preparing for the president's trip."

"There's another reason I called. We didn't set a time for our trip to Chinook Pier. How does 7:00 sound?"

"Fine. I'm looking forward to it."

"Great. I'll see you then. Bye."

"Bye."

Barbara pressed the "end" button and put the phone back in her purse.

The armory under Anderson's Automotive was unusually quiet, the only sound coming from an M-16 round that Brad was pushing around the worktable. Hawk and Ed sat across from him, waiting. Brad felt an icy chill in the pit of his stomach. It seemed as if his destiny had suddenly been thrust upon him, crystal clear and full-blown, the reason for his militia's existence.

"We've been handed a golden opportunity," Brad began, "thanks to the enemy." He looked Hawk in the eye. "You know I've been waiting for the right mission. Well, here it is. If the president's going to bring the war here, I say we show him we're not going to roll over and play dead."

Hawk cleared his throat. "Exactly what did you have in mind?"

Brad's laugh was sharp and sarcastic. "What do you think I mean? Send Harold Mitchell home in a box for what he's trying to do to us! The militia movement is growing, guys. This could be what starts the war— the second American revolution."

Ed nodded and smiled. "I like it!"

Hawk scowled at him. "You would!"

Ed turned on him. "What's that supposed to mean?"

Brad pounded the table. "Cool it—both of you!"

"Assassinate the president?" Hawk asked. "How?"

"That's why we're having this meeting." Brad glanced around the armory. "We've got the weapons, and we've got enough troops. It's only a matter of coming up with the right plan."

"You thinking of using the entire militia? Take out the president with a frontal assault?"

Brad shrugged. "Don't see why not. The more firepower the better, far as I'm concerned."

"Wrong!"

Brad frowned. Hawk's reaction irritated him, but he valued the man's opinion. "OK, talk to me."

"Look, the feds know they're walking into the lion's den. Security will be so tight you wouldn't be able to get a cub scout troop near the president. Have you got any idea how much firepower it would take? He'll be in the middle of a heavily armed motorcade inside an armored limo; and when he gets here, he'll be surrounded by tons of security."

"Well, what do you suggest?"

"I don't know. It's a tough problem."

"Are you scared?"

Hawk glared at him. "What do you think?"

"Sorry, I didn't mean that. But there must be something we can do. We can't let this slip past us."

Ed tapped his brother on the arm. "I know what we could do," he said.

"Who asked you?" Hawk said.

Brad held up his hand and turned to Ed. "What?" he asked.

"Take him out with the TOW."

Hawk rolled his eyes. "Whoa, now why didn't I think of that? What's the plan? Set the TOW up out in the audience and blow him away when he steps up to the podium?"

"Let him speak!" Brad interrupted before Ed could respond. He turned to his brother. "Go on."

Ed glared at Hawk. "I'm not an idiot! You're right. A direct attack won't work. What we need is real power—stand-off power. If a TOW can knock off a tank, it can sure punch a hole in an armored limo."

"Those things are kinda obvious," Hawk said. "Don't you think the Secret Service might notice?"

"Not if it's hidden inside an official vehicle, say a phone company truck."

"That won't work!" Hawk said.

"Not so fast!" Brad said. "An official-looking truck just might do the trick. What kind of range does a TOW have?"

Ed thought for a moment. "Around two miles, I think. I can check the tech manual."

"That should be plenty."

"Time out, folks," Hawk interrupted. "We have a slight problem here. That thing would fry you if you fired it inside a truck."

Ed's laugh was pointed. "Wrong! The TOW has a starter motor that burns out inside the launch tube. The main rocket motor has two nozzles that fire a little to the side, and it doesn't ignite until the missile is about thirty feet away."

"Are you sure?"

"Hawk—they fire TOWs from Jeeps and Humvees!"

"Those are open vehicles."

"I know that! But the blast is minimal." Ed looked at his brother. "Could Greg modify a truck to vent the exhaust out the side or roof?"

"Don't see why not. In fact, your van would be perfect, since we've already modified it as a command vehicle." He paused. "I think this could work. A single telephone truck shouldn't arouse any suspicions, and the Secret Service certainly won't be expecting a strike from over a mile away." He turned to Hawk. "What do you think?"

Hawk's gaze lingered on Ed for a few moments. "It's possible, I guess. You sure you know how to fire that missile?" he asked Ed.

"I can do it!"

"It's your militia," Hawk told Brad.

Brad leaned back in his chair. "OK, I think this could be a go."

⚞ ⚞ ⚞

By 5:00, Barbara decided it was time to head for home. Her investigations weren't revealing much, but she was getting a better feel for the militia mentality. And after the recent events, she sensed a growing hostility. At one gun shop, the owner, after glancing at her ID, had said: "I don't have to talk to you! Get out of here!"

Barbara's discouragement faded as she reached her car. Soon she would be getting ready for her date with Craig, and job worries could wait for morning.

Her mobile phone chirped. She fumbled with her purse and pulled the phone out. "Barbara Post."

"Ms. Post, this is Dan Oliver. Where are you?"

Barbara sighed. "Outside a gun store in Muskegon."

"Good. Go get Lieutenant Phillips and pick me up in his helicopter. I want to see that motorcade route from the air."

"OK. Where are you?"

"I'm approaching Gerald Ford International as I speak."

"I'll need your number."

Dan rattled it off. Barbara wrote it down and stuck her notepad back in her purse. "I'll call you."

"Move it! It's getting late."

Barbara heard a click and frowned as she put her phone away. "Thanks, Ms. Post. Oh, you're very welcome, Mr. Oliver. Don't mention it." She opened the car door and got in.

The trip to the Muskegon County Airport didn't take long, since Barbara had been on the south side of Muskegon when Dan called. Craig was walking toward the hangar when she drove up and parked. She got out and waved.

"Hi," Craig said. "Didn't expect to see you until later."

She smiled. "I can leave if you want."

He circled his arms around her. "Too late."

"I give up."

His kiss was gentle but carried strong feelings, which she returned.

"So, what brings you here?" Craig asked.

Barbara's smile faded a little. "Dan wants—Dan ordered me to come get you. He wants to see the president's motorcade route from the air."

"Now?"

"Immediately, if not sooner."

Craig arched his eyebrows. "Well, I guess we better get it in gear. Where is he?"

"At Gerald Ford International. Where can we pick him up?"

"I'd recommend Northern Air. They're a fixed base operator at the airport. They provide fuel and aircraft services, sell light planes, give flying lessons—stuff like that."

"Dan will need directions. Should I give him a call?"

"No, I'll radio him once we're airborne. Go on out to the helicopter while I round up the crew."

In a few minutes Craig came out of the hangar with Joel and Art Jackson.

"Hello, Joel, Art," Barbara said as they approached. "Ready for an exciting mission?"

That brought a smile to Joel's face. "Hope it's not like last time."

"Rest easy. We're only going to fly over the president's route."

"Yeah, Craig told us."

Art opened the side door. Craig led the way forward into the cockpit and helped Barbara get strapped in. Joel settled into his seat and began going over his checklist. Moments later the twin turbines began spinning up. Craig lifted off and set his course for Grand Rapids, then called Group Grand Haven communications and had them patch a call through to Dan's mobile phone. Craig gave him instructions on how to locate Northern Air.

Their course followed Interstate 96 into Grand Rapids. Barbara looked out and saw the intersection of two highways up ahead.

Craig keyed his mike. "GRR approach, Coast Guard Rescue 5934 is fifteen west for landing at Northern Air."

"What's GRR?" Barbara asked.

"It's the code for the Grand Rapids airport. We're talking to approach control now. We'll contact the tower when we're about five miles out."

"Coast Guard 5934, GRR approach, squawk 4157. Altimeter two-niner-niner-five, wind two-eight-zero at five, active runway is two-six left."

Barbara watched as Joel leaned forward and adjusted something.

Craig turned his head. "Approach control told us to enter 4157 into our transponder—a special transmitter that tells the FAA radar who we are and what our altitude is." He pointed to an instrument that looked like a clock. "They also told us the barometric pressure so we can adjust our altimeter, the wind direction and speed, and that planes are currently landing toward the west on the main east-west runway."

Barbara shook her head. "I don't see how you can understand all that. It sounds like gibberish to me."

Craig laughed. "Just something you learn. Communication has to be brief and precise."

The radio crackled over the intercom. "Coast Guard 5934, radar contact fifteen miles west."

"Coast Guard 5934, roger."

A few minutes later, Craig changed frequencies. "Gerald Ford tower, Coast Guard 5934 is five west. Request landing instruction for Northern Air."

"Coast Guard 5934, you are cleared to land at Northern Air. Be advised a Beech King Air is on short final to two-six left."

"Coast Guard 5934, roger."

Craig brought the helicopter around for a northern approach to the airfield. He pointed Barbara to the left. "See that twin-engine plane?" he asked.

"Yes," Barbara replied.

"That's the one the tower warned us about. We won't come anywhere near it, but it's important for us to know where the other planes are. A midair collision would ruin our whole day."

"Is that a sample of aviator humor?"

"Such as it is."

Craig began a rapid descent toward a row of aircraft parked in front of some low buildings, landing between a business jet and a twin-engine propeller plane.

Dan walked toward them, ducking his head as he approached. Art opened the side door. A few moments later Dan appeared in the cockpit.

"Not much room up here!" Dan shouted over the noise of the engines and rotor blast.

"It is a little snug," Craig agreed. "My mechanic will help you get strapped in."

Dan turned to Barbara and jerked his thumb toward the back. "I need to see, Ms. Post."

Barbara felt her face grow hot. "Oh, of course. Sorry."

She unstrapped and hurried back to the cabin where Art helped her get buckled in. Barbara looked forward and saw Craig assisting Dan. Moments later Joel checked in with the tower, and they were on their way.

"What is the president's route?" Craig asked Dan.

Dan didn't respond. Craig leaned over and showed him how the intercom worked and repeated his question.

Barbara heard Dan over the intercom. "After *Air Force One* lands, the governor meets the president, and they drive downtown to the Grand Center for a short speech—no more than twenty minutes. Then the motorcade takes U.S. 131 to I-96 and down that to where it intersects 104, which they take to Grand Haven."

"OK," Craig said. He pointed to the highway below. "That's I-96. They'll probably take that to 196 and get off at Ottawa Avenue, which is a few blocks from the Grand Center."

A few minutes later Dan asked, "Is that the center down there next to the river?"

"Yes. Do you know where they plan to leave?"

"That hasn't been firmed up yet."

"There are several ways to get to I-96. They could go back to 196, but my guess is they'll take Pearl to 131 and up that to the interstate."

"I see."

Barbara looked out the side as the helicopter flew south of the center, then along Pearl Street and across the Grand River. Then they trailed the commuter traffic north on Highway 131. Soon they were over Interstate 96 where it bent around to the west, into the sun that was now low in the sky, bathing the earth in reddish tones.

"Not much down there," Dan said.

"That's right," Craig said. "It's mostly rural until you get to Grand Haven, and there really isn't any other way to go, unless they want to take country roads."

"Yeah." He turned his head and looked back at Barbara. "What do you think, Ms. Post?"

"It could turn out to be a real security nightmare."

"Tell me about it. But fortunately for us, it's the Secret Service's responsibility. We only support."

"Where do you want Sam and me?"

"I haven't decided yet, but I'll probably assign you to Lieutenant Phillips's helicopter since you've worked with his crew before." He paused. "I assume you have no objections."

What did he mean by that? Barbara wondered. "No, that would be fine. Whatever you say."

"Did I hear correctly, Ms. Post? You're agreeing with me?"

Barbara gritted her teeth. "Yes, Mr. Oliver."

Dan turned back to Craig. "I've seen enough. Take me back to the airport."

"Aye, aye, sir," Craig said.

⚊⚊ ⚊⚊ ⚊⚊

Barbara glanced at her watch and saw it was almost 8:00. Despite Craig's promise to move things along, it had taken awhile to finish the absolute minimum paperwork. Finally they left the hangar, and he took her hand as they walked toward their cars.

"Dan's little outing sure put a dent in our evening," Barbara said. "Sorry."

He squeezed her hand. "There will be other evenings. Besides, this one isn't exactly over."

They arrived at her car, and Barbara turned and faced him. She was only too aware of her wrinkled pants suit and the attention her face and hair needed. "But I look a mess, and . . ."

He pulled her close and kissed her gently. "You look fine to me," he whispered in her ear.

She looked up into his eyes, and a reluctant grin came to her face. "You're distracting me."

He kissed her again, and she returned it with an emotion that surprised and delighted her.

"What say we head for Grand Haven?" Craig asked.

"It's too late for Chinook Pier, isn't it?"

"Probably. I'm not sure how late the shops stay open. But let me introduce you to Fred's."

"What's that?"

"Fred's is a Grand Haven institution. It's a hole-in-the-wall diner near the waterfront, owned and operated by Fred, a retired charter boat captain. It doesn't look like much, but he keeps it clean and the menu is excellent. And Fred has an unlimited supply of stories, some of them true. What do you say?"

The last of her concerns drifted away as she relaxed in his arms. "Sounds like fun."

Chapter Thirty

The next morning, Barbara caught Sam placing a note on her computer monitor.

"Hi," he said. "I was leaving you a message." He peeled it off and handed it to her.

"We have E-mail," Barbara said with a smile.

"Yeah, I know, but this is harder to ignore. Come on back. We've got work to do."

She followed him back to his office.

"The Secret Service has been busy," he said. "The president's itinerary is complete, and we've been given our marching orders—FBI as well, from what I've heard. Dan wants us to get with it since we've got less than a week." He handed her a thin report.

Barbara glanced through the first few pages. "This is pretty much what Dan said yesterday, except it's got the times. So, at 9:10 the governor greets President Mitchell, then they proceed to the Grand Center via I-96 and 196, taking the Ottawa Avenue off-ramp. After his speech, the president departs at 9:50, taking Pearl Street to Highway 131, then I-96 to 104 and on into Grand Haven." She flipped to the last page. "I see the kick-off speech is at the Grand Haven State Park pavilion. Nice location."

"Yes, it is," Sam said.

"What will we be doing?"

Sam handed her another sheet of paper. "We'll be with Craig, orbiting the Park from 9:30 until the president's motorcade is on its way back to the airport."

"That's surprising. I assumed we'd be patrolling the highways leading into Grand Haven."

"Dan thought so too, but the Secret Service say they have that covered."

Sam pushed a bulging file folder toward her. "Here's what we have on the fair city of Grand Haven—brochures and reports on the various parks, the YMCA, Coast Guard Group Grand Haven, and everything else near the speech venue. We've got six days to get to know that area thoroughly."

"I'm already fairly familiar with it."

Sam smiled. "Now why does that not surprise me?"

Barbara's face grew warm. "Thank you for your observation, Sam."

"You're welcome. We'll be spending most of our time in Grand Haven the rest of the week, looking the area over, talking to people who live or work near the park."

"Anything else?"

"Not right now."

Barbara picked up the hefty folder. "If you need me, I'll be in my cubicle trying to stay awake."

<hr />

Brad looked up as Greg Zach entered.

"You wanted to see me?" he asked.

"Yes, please close the door."

Greg did so and sat down in front of Brad's desk.

"Got another hot project for you. Remember the custom work you did on my brother's van?"

"You bet. That's one fine command vehicle, but you sure can't tell it from the outside."

Brad nodded. "It is, but I need a modification."

"Oh, what's that?"

Brad paused. He considered hiding the mission from Greg but realized that wasn't possible. Fortunately, he knew the mechanic was completely reliable.

"This can go no further," Brad said finally.

"You can trust me."

"I understand. You know that TOW Ed brought with him from Montana?"

"Yes."

Greg's puzzled look changed to surprise.

"I want you to mount it in the van," Brad said.

"You mean . . ."

"We're going to take out the president. I need your help, but this is an all-volunteer mission. Do you want in?"

"You bet I do!"

Brad smiled. "Good. Now, can you mount the TOW and vent the exhaust outside?"

"Don't those things burn pretty hot?"

Brad shook his head. "Ed says the blast from the starter motor is minimal."

Greg's serious expression eased a little. "I guess so, but I'll need someone to show me the missile so I can get some idea how to mount it."

"Ed is down in the armory." Brad saw the look of surprise in Greg's eyes. "He comes in with Hawk before we open so he can study the TOW training manuals. You can get with him after we close."

"Roger. Anything else?"

"Not for now."

Greg left the office.

⁂

Around 5:00 P.M., Barbara heard someone approaching. She rolled her chair back and looked. Sam was hurrying along carrying his laptop computer.

"Come on," he said. "Dan wants a briefing."

"But we just got started."

"I know." He tapped the laptop. "I've been working on a PowerPoint presentation as a background task. Don't worry. He only wants some reassurance that things are on track—nothing in depth."

Barbara shrugged. "OK. Where are we meeting?"

"The large conference room."

Sam led the way past the receptionist to a room behind a wall of glass. He opened up the laptop, plugged it into the large TV-like monitor, and started the boot-up process. Soon an introductory slide popped up on the monitor, jittered a moment, then steadied.

"Nice," Barbara said.

A grin replaced Sam's serious expression. "I thought you'd like it."

Two bright red lighthouses rested on stone foundations above the restless blue waters of Lake Michigan. The one closest to the shore was a tall, conical tower while the more distant one looked much like a small barn. A meandering pier atop tall pilings connected the two structures to the beach at the mouth of the Grand River. Whitecapped waves crashed on the rocky shore in the foreground. Above the lighthouses, emblazoned in gold letters, Barbara read: "Grand Haven Speech."

Dan hurried into the room and shut the door. His gaze swept over Barbara before focusing on Sam. He sat at the head of the table facing the monitor. "OK, people, what have you got?"

Sam pressed the room's dimmer switch and started the presentation. The lighthouses dissolved into a bright scene of people strolling along a broad path flanked by old-fashioned, iron lampposts, followed by a slide showing a beach pavilion.

Sam pressed a key to pause. "This is the pavilion at the Grand Haven State Park. Next Monday, Barbara and I will be orbiting over it the entire time the president is there. We'll be spending the rest of this week in Grand Haven conducting interviews, looking over the park, and surveying the town from the air."

"Good," Dan said. "Be sure you cover everything."

Sam resumed the presentation. "Oh, we will. Now here's the route the president's motorcade will take."

An aerial picture of Gerald Ford International flashed on the monitor, then dissolved into a shot of the VIP ramp where *Air Force One* would arrive. The next slide showed a map of Grand Rapids, with the president's route to the Grand Center animated in red.

Sam used his laser pointer. "President Mitchell is scheduled to arrive in Grand Rapids at 9:10. The governor and mayor will greet him, and they'll drive to the Grand Center for a speech, departing for Grand Haven at 9:50."

The animated map continued, tracing the motorcade route from Grand Rapids, through the countryside, and on into Grand Haven. The final slide was an aerial view of the Grand Haven State Park shot from north of the river.

"Is that the pavilion down there?" Dan asked.

"That's it," Sam replied.

A caption slid onto the screen from the left: "10:30—President Arrives."

"How long will the speech be?"

"Twenty minutes, followed by a half hour of pressing the flesh and finally the VIP luncheon."

"When does the president return to the airport?"

Sam flipped a page in his notes. "One o'clock."

Dan sighed. "I can't wait."

Sam nodded. "You and the Secret Service and the FBI."

Dan got up. "OK. Keep me posted."

"You know we will."

Dan hurried out.

"How's your research going?" Sam asked.

"I've waded through most of it. Can't say I learned all that much, but it's good background information."

"I think so." He grinned. "I expect we'll see a lot of dark suits and sunglasses once we get to Grand Haven. You can bet the Secret Service and FBI will be checking it out also."

Barbara frowned as a stray thought intruded, unwelcome and disturbing.

"Something wrong?" Sam asked.

Barbara took her time answering. "I know the president's trip is important, but I'll be glad when we can get back to the hijacking." She hesitated. "And something else bothers me."

"What's that?"

"The militia that stole the ammo shipment has to be connected to the one that knocked off Judge Richards. But how? And why?"

Sam shrugged. "OK, I agree the circumstances suggest it, but so what? The militia movement is close-knit. Could be the Oklahoma suspect has a friend up here."

"Maybe when we scattered that Montana group, some of the members moved here. If so, we know what they were like."

"That's a disturbing thought, but knocking off a federal judge is one thing—assassinating the president of the United States is quite another. This particular visit is going to be well covered."

"I sure hope so." Barbara paused. "And maybe when we get back to investigating around Grand Haven we can prove who hijacked that ammo."

"Could be, but to be fair, we don't know that Anderson was behind it. It could be another group."

Barbara shook her head. "Maybe, but I don't think so, and if he's that brazen, what if he decides to take out the president?"

"I don't see how he could possibly do it. Security is going to be air-tight." Sam laughed, but it sounded forced. "I bet there'll be more government agents in that park than ordinary citizens."

Barbara sighed. "So you're saying I need to adopt a positive attitude."

"Might help, and then remember who's really in charge."

She looked at him and smiled. "You're right. Thanks. Do the best you can . . ."

"And leave the rest to God," he finished for her. He disconnected the laptop and shut it down.

Barbara followed him out of the conference room and returned to her cubicle. She sifted through the reports and brochures for a while, selecting the ones she wanted to study further and stuck them in a folder. Then another thought lodged in her mind, and like an ember with adequate fuel, it began to spread. *What ever happened to that TOW missile?* she wondered.

⚙ ⚙ ⚙

Anderson's Automotive was closed for the day. Brad and Greg waited by the door near the office. Finally a familiar red pickup drove into the lot and parked.

"Glad you could make it," Brad said as he let his friend in.

"What's up?" Hawk asked.

"Come on down to the armory. We've got some planning to do."

Brad led the way to the hidden elevator, unlocked the doors, and followed his friends inside. He then closed the doors and punched the button for the basement. The elevator throbbed to life. Brad stepped out when the doors opened and looked down the long aisle. Ed came around the end of the worktable.

"How goes it?" Brad asked.

"Fine," Ed replied. "I've checked the TOW out completely—twice. It's ready to go."

"You're positive you know how to fire that thing?"

Ed's eyes narrowed in obvious irritation. "Yes, I'm positive!"

Brad held up his hand. "Take it easy. You know how important training is. So tell me how you're doing with the operator's manual?"

Ed waved his hand toward the large book sitting on the worktable. "I've read it and reread it, and the technical manual. You show me a target within line of sight, and I'll make it a smoking hulk—guaranteed."

"Good, that's what I wanted to hear. Now, how about we sit down and start planning this thing." He waited until they all got settled at the worktable. "Any comments to start out with?"

"I've got one," Hawk said. "I'm concerned about our cover."

"Oh? What's wrong with using a telephone company truck?"

"Nothing, as long as it fakes out the feds. But what if they decide to investigate? If they check our IDs, they'll bust us for sure."

Brad frowned. "What if we wait until the last moment?"

Hawk shook his head. "That won't help. We've got to have enough time to set up the missile. Do you really think the Secret Service would pass up a truck that's on the president's route?"

"OK, what do you suggest?"

"What about including Paul French in the operation? He works for the phone company, so his ID would check out. If the feds swoop down, we hide inside the truck and let Paul front for us."

"What if they search the truck?"

"I don't think that would happen. Once they verify Paul's ID, it's perfectly reasonable for him to be out there—he's working on the phone lines."

"Sounds OK, and Paul has plenty of reason to hate the feds."

"Why is that?" Ed asked.

"From when he was a naval aviator stationed in San Diego. The Navy court-martialed him for buzzing the beach in front of the Hotel del Coronado."

"Bummer."

"Major bummer. Because of that, he's never been able to land an airline job, which is why he's working for the phone company. Paul's a good man and as brave as they come." Brad turned to Hawk. "Where did we put that Michigan map?"

Hawk pushed back from the table. "I think it's in here." He opened a drawer, pulled it out, and handed it to Brad.

"Thanks." Brad unfolded it and smoothed it out. "To get to Grand Haven, they have to take I-96 to Highway 104. Question is, where do we hit 'em?"

"I'd say just east of Spring Lake. There's a long, straight stretch of open road—over a mile."

"What's the best range for the TOW?" Brad asked Ed.

Ed leaned forward and examined the map. "Between one and two miles, as long as the target's in line of sight."

"What's the firing procedure?"

Ed leaned back in his chair and smiled. "After checking all systems, the operator raises the arming lever, places the crosshairs on the target, and pulls the trigger, which activates the missile's batteries and spins up the gyro. The launch motor fires a little over a second later, ejecting the TOW. The missile coasts about thirty feet, the main rocket motor fires, and the target's history—as long as the operator keeps the crosshairs on the target."

"The entire time?" Brad asked.

"Yes. Remember, that missile was designed in the 1960s. Even so, it's still an effective antitank weapon." Ed snickered. "It won't have any trouble punching through an armored limo."

"I don't like it. We're sitting ducks until the missile impacts."

"Not for long. The missile's flight takes only twenty seconds or so."

Brad thought it over. "We can live with that, I guess." He nodded toward the mechanic. "Greg needs help in modifying the van."

"What sort of help?" Ed asked.

"First of all, Brad wants me to put in a vent for the TOW's exhaust," Greg said.

"That not a bad idea, although the launch motor blast is minimal. What did you have in mind?"

"I was thinking of cutting a hole in the roof and installing a deflector behind the TOW, then camouflage the hole with a plastic insert that blows away when the missile fires."

Brad snapped his fingers. "What about the missile itself? We can keep the rear doors closed until we spot the motorcade, but then we have to open up to fire. If the Secret Service spots the TOW, we're dead."

Greg thought a moment. "I think I can do something about that. There's a fine-mesh plastic screen that's sort of like a one-way window.

You can see out through it, but people outside can't see in. The exterior surface is normally black, but with a little paint I can make it look like the inside of a telephone truck."

"Won't the paint block our view?"

"No. I'll spray it on real light."

"Sounds like that should work."

"Next, I need to take some measurements of the TOW so I can prepare mounts for the van," Greg said.

Ed pointed toward a side aisle. "No problem. I've got it set up over there."

Greg glanced toward Brad.

"You two go ahead," Brad said. "That's all we can do until I can get Paul in here."

⚊⚊ ⚊⚊ ⚊⚊

It was nearly ten o'clock when the knock on the door came. Hawk and Ed had left hours ago, and Greg had worked on the van until around 9:30. Brad went out and saw Paul French standing under the harsh glare of the security light.

"Hi, Paul," Brad said, opening the door. "Thanks for coming by on such short notice."

"No problem," Paul said. "What's up?"

"Come on in my office. I need your help on something."

Paul sat across from Brad. The young man certainly looked like an aviator. He was tall and had the trim build of a serious athlete. Brad could well believe that he had been one, formidable fighter pilot.

"We have a top secret operation coming up, and I'd like to offer you a piece of it. But before I go on, nothing we talk about can leave this office. Are we clear on that?"

"You've seen my record?"

Brad nodded. "I have, or you wouldn't be sitting there."

"Then you know I held a top secret clearance while I was in the Navy."

"That I do. But you know the drill. I have to be sure."

Paul gave a sardonic laugh. "I wasn't kicked out of the Navy for loose lips, Brad. I can keep your secrets."

"Fine. Let me fill you in on what we're planning."

Paul's intense gaze never wavered as Brad gave him a summary of their objective and how the militia planned to achieve it, ending with Hawk's concern about their cover.

"So, what do you think?" Brad asked when he finished.

"The objective is great, and believe me—I want in." For a few moments an unusual animation lit his eyes. "I'm no ground-pounder, but I see no reason why a TOW wouldn't work. However, I agree with Hawk. A phone company truck would be an excellent cover, but there's no way the Secret Service goons will overlook you, and without valid IDs, you're dead meat."

Brad sighed. "OK, OK, I'm convinced. So can you help us?"

For a few moments he said nothing. Finally he nodded. "I think so. My ID will certainly pass muster, and I'm pretty sure I can arrange a real work order for a cable along Highway 104, in case the secret boys want to snoop into that."

"What happens if they search the truck?"

Paul's expression became very serious. "Better hope they don't." He paused. "Actually, I don't think that's likely. Who's doing the work on the van?"

"Greg Zach—the guy who did our cop car."

Paul smiled. "Oh, yes. That was really nice work. Well then, I expect your van will look like the real thing. We've got quite a variety of trucks, so all he has to do is get the color and signage right."

"You can count on that."

"OK. That being the case, I doubt the truck will get searched. My ID will check out, as will the work order. The feds don't have time to do more than that, or they'd still be investigating when the pres is on his way back to Washington." Paul laughed. "Only he won't be going back to Washington, will he?"

Brad laughed as well. "Oh, yes he will, just like JFK did."

"Oh, yeah! Right!"

"So, are you in?"

Paul's eyes grew very hard. "I wouldn't miss this for the world."

Chapter
Thirty-one

By Friday, Barbara felt like she had questioned half of the people in Grand Haven, under the assumption that Sam had taken care of the rest. But there was one particular person neither agent had interviewed as yet, not by their decision but because Dan had been micromanaging the Grand Haven investigation.

Barbara looked up as Sam entered the Coast Guard Group Grand Haven conference room. She pushed her laptop computer to the side. "So, is Dan going to let us talk to Anderson or not?"

Sam sat beside her. "Oh, yes, there was never any question about that. He was just making sure we covered everything else, rather than concentrating on the hijacking."

Barbara gritted her teeth. "That's not what we were doing!"

"I know that; you know that, but Dan's kind of fixed in his ways."

"Is that a late-breaking news flash?"

A flicker of a smile touched Sam's lips. "Remind me not to get on your bad side, Ms. Post."

Barbara felt the heat of embarrassment. "Sorry, I shouldn't have said that."

Sam only nodded.

"So, who gets to do the dirty deed?" Barbara asked.

Sam hesitated. "Dan said for me to do it."

"He did?"

"But I told him we were a team, and we'd work it out together."

"I see. Well, thank you—I guess."

Sam's smile returned. "You're welcome."

"So who gets to do it?"

"We haven't discussed it yet."

"Sam! OK, how do you want to handle this? Draw straws? Flip a coin?"

Sam's smile changed into a grin. "Would you like to interview Mr. Anderson?"

"With pleasure!"

"Now that that's out of the way, anything new to report?"

Barbara shook her head. "No. Not a thing."

<hr />

Brad and Paul French stood outside the office, watching as Greg finished applying another coat of primer to Ed's van. The mechanic made one final sweeping pass, set the spray gun down, and removed his mask. Brad waved him over, and the three men went inside the office.

Greg closed the door and sat beside Paul. Brad settled into his chair.

"Is everything set?" Brad asked Paul.

"For the most part. I checked out that stretch of Highway 104 east of Spring Lake, and it looks perfect. You won't have any trouble picking off the president's limo. I also located a cable junction box nearby." He grinned. "I've got the strangest feeling that something's going to happen to that cable on Monday."

"How do you know they'll assign the work to you?"

"No sweat. I swapped with another guy so I'll be on call for Spring Lake. I'll be getting that work order."

"Good." Brad turned to Greg. "How are you doing with the van?"

"I'm right on schedule. I've installed the TOW's mounting brackets, along with the exhaust deflector, and the roof vent is in and camouflaged. I'm done with the primer coat, but I have to wait until tomorrow to spray on the paint." Greg snapped his fingers. "Oh, better have Hawk contact his print shop friend. I'll need the phone company decals by sometime Sunday."

"I can get you the real thing," Paul said. "The maintenance shop has a supply of them."

"Great," Brad said. "You and Greg can work out the details."

"Will do."

"Now, what about that screen for the TOW?"

"I have the material," Greg said. "I'll paint and install it Sunday after I apply the decals."

"You sure it'll hide the missile?"

"I'm positive. You can't see through it from the outside; and once I've sprayed it, you won't notice anything unusual unless you get right up on it."

"That's what I want to hear. Anything else we need to discuss?"

Greg stood up. "Don't think so," he said.

Brad remained seated while Paul and Greg filed out. Once the door closed, he leaned back in his chair and scanned the SEAL photos hanging above the shop windows. Soon his militia would be embarking on what would surely be its last mission, but it was well worth doing. It would be a blow for freedom, and Brad only hoped that other patriots would then answer the call.

⟨⟨⟨⟩⟩⟩ ⟨⟨⟨⟩⟩⟩ ⟨⟨⟨⟩⟩⟩

Barbara waited until late afternoon before driving to Anderson's Automotive. She shivered as she walked toward the open bay where she had hidden inside Elizabeth's van. She looked at the van that stood there now. A mechanic saw her and dropped his sandpaper.

"Can I help you?" he asked.

"Yes, I'm looking for Brad Anderson."

"Should be in his office." The mechanic walked past, knocked on the door and opened it. "Boss? Some lady out here to see you."

Barbara peered past the mechanic and saw Brad looking out at her. His expression seemed strained. He got to his feet and came out into the garage. The mechanic returned to his work.

"I'm Brad Anderson. What can I do for you?"

Barbara pulled out her ID and showed it to him. "I'm Special Agent Barbara Post, Bureau of Alcohol, Tobacco, and Firearms. I need to ask you some questions."

His eyes took on a hard glint. "Let's go in my office."

Barbara followed him in. Brad closed the door and circled around his desk. Barbara sat across from him.

"OK, shoot," Brad said.

Barbara had debated with herself on what tack to take and had finally decided on a direct approach. She cleared her throat. "We have reason to believe you are in violation of federal explosives and firearms regulations." She watched his eyes carefully and saw surprise there, which was normal, but there was something else.

"That's absurd!"

"Then you're telling me you are not in possession of illegal explosives and firearms."

"That's exactly what I'm telling you!" He waved his hand around. "I run a garage, Ms. Post, and I don't appreciate federal busybodies coming in here and snooping around."

"Are you a member of a Michigan militia?"

"I don't have to answer that. Now, I've got work to do." He came around the desk and opened the door.

Barbara got up and walked out of the garage. She turned and looked back inside. Brad stood near the van and glared out at her. Barbara returned to her car, wondering if she had done the right thing.

The last embers of sunset were resting on the western horizon when Brad unlocked the door and let Hawk into the garage.

"I came as soon as I could," Hawk said. "What's up?"

Brad relocked the door. "I'm not sure—maybe nothing. Come on down to the armory."

They took the elevator down and found Ed waiting for them.

Ed spoke first. "It's about time you guys showed up. I'm getting tired of hiding down here all by myself."

"Have you got those manuals memorized yet?" Brad asked.

"Near enough. Look! I know how to operate that thing."

"Fine, now pipe down. Something's come up that we have to talk about."

They gathered around the worktable and sat down. Brad told them about the brief interview with Barbara Post.

As Brad expected, Ed was the first to say something. "She's on to us! What are we going to do?"

"Will you shut up!" Brad yelled. "We're not here to jump to conclusions!" He saw the hurt in his brother's eyes and regretted giving in to his temper. Brad continued in a calmer tone, "The feds are not on to us. If they were, we'd be in jail by now. Isn't that obvious?"

"I'll buy that," Hawk said. "Then what do you make of her visit?"

"I'm not sure," Brad said. "It probably has to do with the president's trip. You know the feds have to be worried about that."

"Could be part of the hijacking investigation."

"Yeah, I suppose. But either way, we're not serious suspects, or we wouldn't be here jawing about it. So I say we hang tight. The mission's on track. If they haven't caught us by now, they're not going to."

"I hope you're right." Hawk turned to Ed. "You ready to head for the house?"

"No, I've still got some work to do."

"I thought you said you had it all down," Brad said.

"I do. But just to be sure, I want to make one more system check."

Hawk frowned. "Look, it's been a long day, and I'm hungry."

"Go on home," Brad told him. "I'll bring Ed by after he finishes."

Brad let his friend out. When he returned to the armory, he found Ed on his knees beside the TOW, peering intently at the technical manual.

"How long is this going to take?" Brad asked.

Ed looked up. "At least an hour. Why don't you go get us something to eat?"

"OK. Pizza all right with you?"

"Yeah, and get me a regular Coke."

"Be back in a bit."

"No hurry."

Brad took the elevator up to the garage, let himself out, and walked to his Suburban.

⎯⎯ ⎯⎯ ⎯⎯

Ed knew he had to move fast, since it wouldn't take Brad long to get their dinner and return. He tried information and found, as he expected, there was no listing for Barbara Post. Then he called Paul and told him that Brad needed the agent's address. Paul seemed surprised but said he could get it from the phone company database. He called back a few minutes later. Ed wrote down the Spring Lake address and hung up.

He grabbed an M-16 with a low-light scope and two ammunition clips and dashed for the elevator. Up in the garage he looked around in the dim light, then went to his van and opened the driver's door. To his relief, he saw the keys were in the ignition. Ed laid the M-16 on the floor along with the ammunition, opened the garage door, and backed out.

After a moment's thought, he returned to the garage, punched the button to close the door, and ran back to his truck.

Ed's heart was pounding as he sped through Grand Haven, since he expected to see Brad coming after him at any moment. Only when he reached Highway 104 did he begin to relax.

The drive to the Spring Lake apartment was short and uneventful. He parked across the street. Then he saw the parking spot beside the stairs was empty and wondered if the agent was home.

Ed looked all around. There was no traffic. He grabbed the M-16, inserted a magazine, jacked a shell into the chamber, and flipped the safety on. He jumped out of the truck, ran across the street and up the stairs to the apartment. Pausing only briefly to catch his breath, he rang the doorbell. The wait seemed an eternity as he listened for footsteps. Finally deciding there was no one there, Ed raced back across the street and climbed into his van. After a moment's thought, he drove off and turned right at the next street, stopping when he was sure he could not be seen from the apartment. Then he slipped the spare magazine in a pocket, picked up the M-16, and got out.

━◆━ ━◆━ ━◆━

Barbara drove along the familiar route to her apartment. Her last interview of the day had been with the owner of a gift shop near the Grand Haven State Park, strictly routine. She thought back to her face-off with Brad Anderson. That hadn't yielded anything either, so why did she still have the feeling he was planning something? He certainly didn't seem afraid. But then, unless Barbara came up with a smoking gun, he had no reason to be.

Her eyes swept the instrument panel, then she looked again. The gas gauge was sitting on a quarter. She almost ignored it, since to her mind, a quarter of a tank was plenty of gas. Then she grinned as she remembered what Craig had once said when riding with her: "You shouldn't let it drop that low." Rather than get into a Venus versus Mars argument, she had done as he suggested, but she was by herself now. Up ahead she saw a mini-market with its lighted fuel pumps. After a moment's hesitation, she turned in.

Brad parked, got out and trudged over to the door lugging a large pizza box and a bag holding the soft drinks. After setting the bag down and fumbling with his keys, he let himself in and started toward the elevator. Then he stopped in mid-stride and turned, hoping his eyes were playing tricks on him. They weren't. Ed's van was gone. Brad felt an icy chill run down his spine as his mind raced ahead to what he suspected.

He dropped the food and hurried down to the armory, cursing the elevator for its leisurely pace. The basement was deserted. Brad rushed back to his office, sat at his desk, and punched in Hawk's number. He waited impatiently as it rang.

"Hello," came the crisp answer.

"Hawk, this is Brad! Is Ed there with you?"

There was a slight pause. "No. Isn't he at the garage?"

"Would I be calling you if he was?" Brad struggled for control. "Sorry. I think we have a problem. I went out to get our dinner, and when I got back, Ed was gone and so was his van."

"You don't suppose he's gone after that agent?"

"That's exactly what I think! It would be just like him to pull a crazy stunt like that."

"Want me to come over there?"

"No, I better handle this myself."

Brad hung up and started to call directory assistance but stopped and punched in Paul's number instead.

"Hello."

"Paul, this is Brad. Listen, is there any way you can get me someone's address?"

"Sure. Who?"

"Barbara Post?"

Greg paused. "I already gave that to Ed—didn't he tell you?"

"Ed called you?"

"Why, yes. What's going on?"

"I don't have time! Give me the address!"

Brad wrote it down and hung up. He returned to the armory for his Glock automatic and a pair of night vision goggles, then rushed out to his Suburban, hoping he wasn't too late.

━━━ ━━━ ━━━

Ed worked his way along the side of the street opposite the apartment, cutting through a yard that was deep in shadow. To his left, a two-story house sat well back on the large lot surrounded by tall trees and overgrown shrubs. A single lighted window on the second floor provided the only sign of life. Ed stopped, turned on the low-light scope, swept the M-16 all around, and spotted a high hedge lining the sidewalk. He hurried over, dropped to his stomach, and crawled up to the tangled branches and roots. Through a gap, he saw the apartment across the street. *Excellent,* he thought.

Ed slid the rifle's barrel through the branches and brought the scope up to his right eye. The crosshairs danced a little as he moved them across the drive and up the stairs to the apartment's front door. He smiled as he realized he couldn't ask for a better position. Ed pulled the gun back and began his vigil.

━━━ ━━━ ━━━

Barbara took the receipt from the gas pump and got back in her car. Soon she was on Highway 104 and wondering what she would have for dinner. She sighed as she did a mental inventory of her refrigerator's freezer compartment. Whatever she selected, its principal ingredient would be salt, along with generous helpings of chemicals with long and curious names.

Traffic was light, with only a few cars coming west toward Grand Haven. Barbara glanced in her rearview mirror and saw only one set of headlights. Then she looked again. Whoever the eastbound driver was, he was certainly in a hurry. The lights loomed large, then swept to the left as the vehicle started to pass.

—————— —————— ——————

Brad cursed as he roared around the blue Volvo. Although he couldn't be positive, he felt sure it was Barbara Post's car—he had seen her drive away from the garage that very afternoon. *So now what?* he wondered. He had assumed she would already be at her apartment, not on her way home.

Brad saw the reflection of a street sign up ahead. He slammed on his brakes and made a skidding turn to the right. He continued up the unlighted street several hundred feet, stopped, and flipped off his lights. A few moments later the agent's car drove past and was gone.

—————— —————— ——————

Barbara glanced to the right as she passed the street, curious about the other driver's mad rush. She couldn't see anything, which surprised her. The other car might have been going fast, but how could it just disappear?

—————— —————— ——————

Brad turned around, stomped on the accelerator, and raced for the highway, sliding to a stop in a hail of gravel. A quick look to the right revealed the Volvo's retreating taillights and light traffic coming west toward him. He turned and brought his speed up slowly, allowing the agent's car to get further ahead. Then he turned on his lights.

Brad's mind raced. He knew the apartment's approximate location and that the area was rural, with large rambling houses surrounded by overgrown lots and fields. If Ed was stalking the agent, what would he do?

The most straightforward answer was an ambush; and since the apartment was north of 104, that suggested a spot somewhere on the south side of the highway.

Up ahead the Volvo's brake lights came on, and the car turned left. Brad pulled onto the shoulder, stopped, and turned off his lights.

Ed looked to the left and squinted at the glare from the approaching headlights. The car slowed rapidly and began to turn. Ed's heart pounded so hard it seemed audible to him. He knew it had to be the nosy Ms. Post, the one who had humiliated him, the one who could wreck everything they had worked so hard for. Why Brad couldn't see the danger, he had no idea. They were so close to their goal now. This one final danger had to be dealt with; and if the job fell to him, so be it.

The car pulled up to the stairs and stopped. Ed stuck his M-16 through the shrubs, brought the scope up, and trained it. He smiled as the crosshairs neatly quartered the agent's head. The metal jacket bullet would have no trouble punching through the rear window before exploding the woman's brain. Then Ed stopped as he realized there was a better way: hit her just as she opened her door, almost safe but not quite.

The car door opened, and the woman got out. She pressed something in her palm, and the headlights flashed and the horn honked. Then she began a leisurely walk across the drive. Ed shifted the rifle to keep the crosshairs lined up, forcing himself to take shallow breaths.

Brad stepped out, slipped on his night vision goggles, and turned them on, bringing the hidden world of deep shadow to grainy, green life. He checked his automatic, making sure he had a round chambered and flicked the safety off.

The Gathering Storm

Brad saw a house to his right. A light streamed from an upper-story window, brilliant green in his goggles, but the lower story was hidden by the tall shrubs that lined the sidewalk. Brad looked across the street. Ms. Post was nearing the stairs to her apartment.

Brad couldn't see Ed's van but knew his brother had to be nearby, but where? The woman was halfway up the stairs now. Brad's eyes followed the shaggy hedge. There! A long, thin object was sticking through. He raced soundlessly down the street to the corner of the lot and through a gap in the hedge.

Brad spotted his brother immediately. Ed's prone shape shifted slightly as he tracked his target. Brad knew he only had seconds. He dashed through the heavy grass without any regard for the noise he was making. Ed turned his head, surprise evident on his face.

"Drop it!" Brad shouted.

Ed resumed his aim. "No! I have to stop her!"

Brad was almost there, but even as he dove through the air, he knew he was too late. Ed let out a pungent oath just before he got hit. Brad gasped as the impact knocked the wind out of him. Despite the pain, he twisted the rifle out of Ed's grip and threw it aside. Then he grabbed a handful of shirt and drew back his fist, before finally checking himself. After a few long seconds, Brad let go.

"Get up," he ordered in a harsh whisper. "So help me, if you weren't my brother, I'd kill you. Do you realize what you could have done?"

"But she's trying to stop us!"

Brad slapped him hard. "Keep your voice down," he said through clenched teeth. "Now, come with me."

"What about my van?"

"Let me worry about that." Brad jerked his brother to his feet. "Come on."

He picked up the M-16 and out of habit reached down to flip the safety on. To his surprise he found it was already on. On this slender thread had hung the continued existence of his militia. He shook his head and guided Ed toward the street.

3 1 4

They returned to the Suburban then rode around to where Ed had left his van, and Brad gave him explicit instructions. He followed Ed back to the garage, and after putting the van back inside, they went into the office.

"Sit down!" Brad ordered.

He propped the M-16 in the corner and punched in Hawk's number. Only then did he breathe a sigh of relief. Despite everything, their operation was still a go.

Chapter Thirty-two

Brad hadn't slept well Sunday night, but excitement covered his initial weariness—that and lots of black coffee. The day he had planned for had finally arrived; soon they would strike a blow for freedom that the world would not forget. But first he had to assemble his team, and one member was missing.

Brad looked out the window in the door. There were only a few cars in the garage parking lot—Hawk's and Greg's, plus one left overnight by a customer. Brad's Suburban was in back.

"What time is it?" Brad asked.

"About five minutes since the last time you asked," Hawk said. "Almost 6:00," he finally added.

Brad turned and glared at him. "Not funny. Paul said he'd be here by 5:30. I want to be out of here before my regular mechanics start showing up."

"Relax, Brad. We've got over an hour. Besides, what's so unusual about your garage working on a phone company truck?"

"The phone company does its own maintenance."

"So, who else besides you knows that?"

Ed looked past Brad. "Someone just drove in."

Brad turned back. "There he is," he said.

He opened the door as Paul approached. "Where were you?"

"Sorry," Paul said. "Typical crazy Monday. One of the guys called in sick, and they tried to assign me to his area. Took a while to get it straightened out."

"Then we're set to go?"

Paul grinned. "We are now." He looked over at the van. "Hey, would you look at that?"

"Think it'll pass inspection?" Greg asked.

"It would fool me. You do good work."

"Thanks. I appreciate you getting the decals."

"Don't mention it. Is the missile installed?"

"Come and see."

They gathered around the end of the van, and Greg opened the back doors. The business end of a TOW missile was pointed right at them, looking much like a giant machine gun on its stubby tripod legs.

"Sweet!" Paul said. He turned to Ed. "Think you can spike the president with that?"

Ed beamed at him. "You bet!"

"Let me show you the vent," Greg said. He pointed behind the TOW to some angled sheet metal that led up to an overhead hole. "The deflector directs the blast up through that vent in the roof."

Brad glanced inside. "What's it covered with?"

"A plastic insert, painted to match the truck."

"What about the screen?"

"See this?" Greg pointed to a roll of thin plastic mesh wound tightly around a rod. He pulled the end down and attached two hooks to eyelets on the floor of the van. "Now come over here." He led them back to the door beside Brad's office. "What do you see?"

Brad peered closely at the taut screen. Even this close it looked like the inside of a maintenance truck with shelving units lining both sides. There was no sign of the deadly missile.

"That is spooky," Brad said, almost in a whisper. He looked at Greg. "Very nice."

Greg smiled. "As long as the feds don't get any closer than about twenty feet, you should be fine. But, I recommend you keep the back doors closed until just before party time."

Brad laughed. "Right." Then his smile disappeared. He turned to Hawk, Ed, and Paul. "Guys, chances are we won't be coming back." He clinched his teeth. "But, this is worth doing. Someone has to stand up for liberty before it's too late. Last chance. Are you with me?"

"You bet!" Ed said immediately.

"You can count on me," Paul said.

"I'm in," Hawk added.

Brad felt a tightness in his throat. He took a deep breath. "Are you ready to go?" he asked Paul.

"Let's do it."

"Hawk, you and Ed get in the back. I'm riding shotgun."

They climbed into the van, and Greg shut the doors. Brad waited for him to turn around.

"Uh, watch over things while we're gone," he said. He hesitated, not knowing exactly what to say. "I appreciate everything you've done for the cause. Take care of yourself."

"You do the same," Greg said.

Brad shook hands with him, then walked to the truck and got in. He heard the sound of the garage door rattling up.

"OK," he said to Paul. "Time to get this show on the road."

⚞⚟ ⚞⚟ ⚞⚟

Harold Mitchell paced back and forth in the presidential suite of *Air Force One,* the white-over-blue Boeing 747 which the Air Force designated a VC-25A. The so-called "Flying Oval Office" took up four thousand square feet of the huge aircraft, including the suite, a combination conference/dining room, and an office area for senior advisors, which was where Vincent Walters was now waiting. This thought brought a smile to the president's lips.

"What's funny?" Nancy Mitchell asked. She was seated on a cozy couch that had been one of her contributions to the suite's décor.

Harold looked at her. "Just thinking of Vince cooling his heels outside. He's probably gnawed his fingernails up to the elbows by now."

"He's worried about your safety, dear." She paused. "I am too."

He looked into her eyes and saw the love they held.

She patted the couch. "Come here."

He crossed the room and sat beside her, sinking back into the comfortable upholstery. He put his arm around her, and she snuggled against his side. He squeezed her arm and took her hand.

"Thank you," he whispered.

"For what?"

"For standing by me. I know it's been hard, and I'm sorry. I love you, dear, and this really isn't fair to you."

She looked into his eyes. "We'll see it through—just like always."

"Do you wish I had backed off?" He glanced toward the door. "Like Vince wanted?"

She shook her head. "No. I'm scared—I admit that, but I know this is something you have to do." She squeezed his hand. "I'm with you all the way."

Harold felt a tightness in his chest.

A knock sounded on the door.

Harold cleared his throat. "Come in."

Vince opened the door. "We're beginning our approach into Grand Rapids."

Harold forced a smile. "Very well. I'll be out shortly."

Vince left and closed the door.

Harold glanced at his watch and saw it was almost 8:45. His schedule said he would arrive in Grand Rapids at 9:10, and that meant his foot would touch the top of the stairs at that moment and not one minute before or after. From that point his day was scheduled to the last tick of the clock until they again boarded *Air Force One* for the trip back to

The Gathering Storm

Andrews Air Force Base. Harold sighed. He knew it was going to be a long day.

———— ———— ————

Harold Mitchell stood at the top of the stairs and waved at the crowd below. He felt a little self-conscious as he scanned the costly array of resources gathered around the presidential plane, resources required because of his decision to give a speech in Grand Haven. Off to the left stood the presidential motorcade, with his black limousine sandwiched between the cars of the other dignitaries and his army of Secret Service agents, all sworn to protect his life.

A band broke into "Hail to the Chief," and the marine guards at the foot of the stairs came to attention. Harold took Nancy's arm, and they started down the steps. As they approached the bottom, the marines saluted. Harold returned the honor. A young girl in a white dress approached, clearly nervous, and extended a large bouquet of roses to the first lady.

"Thank you, dear," Nancy said as she took them.

Up ahead, Harold saw the governor of Michigan approaching with the mayor of Grand Rapids at his side.

Well, now it begins, Harold thought to himself.

———— ———— ————

Paul reached behind Brad's seat and picked up a long-handled tool with heavy cutters.

"What's that for?" Brad asked.

"To cut the cable," Paul said.

"How will you get at it?"

"There's a junction box about a hundred feet from here. The cable comes up inside it. Be right back."

He got out and starting walking east. Brad watched him in the side mirror until he disappeared through a gap in some bushes. A few minutes later Paul emerged and jogged back to the truck. He opened the driver's door, stowed the cutter, and got in.

Brad jumped as Hawk slid open the tiny window in the sheet metal partition behind the seats.

"What's happening?" Hawk asked.

Paul turned to him. "Something tells me I'm about to get a work order," he said with a grin.

A moment later his beeper chirped. Paul looked at the display then radioed in. He made a few notes on a form and acknowledged the assignment.

"Well, what do you know. There's a cable break somewhere east of Spring Lake, and I'm supposed to check it out."

"How bad is it?" Brad asked.

"Spring Lake, Grand Haven, and Ferrysburg are cut off from the rest of Michigan; and somehow, I suspect I won't find the problem until after—say—10:30."

Brad laughed. "How surprising. Now all we have to do is wait." He turned back to the window. "Is the TOW ready to go?" he asked Ed.

"Absolutely! Once the president gets in range, he's dead meat."

Brad glanced at his watch and saw it was 9:30. He turned back to Paul. "Guess it's time for me to get in the back."

"Right," Paul agreed. "We better look official, in case the feds come snooping around."

"OK, close it," Brad told Hawk.

The window slid shut. Brad checked to make sure the opening was invisible, then got out. Paul followed him to the back and opened the doors. Brad peered into the dim interior. The TOW was pointed right at him. Brad shifted his gaze to Hawk and Ed, then climbed up into the truck. The light cut off as Paul closed and locked the doors. After a few seconds a battery-powered lantern clicked on.

"Now we wait," Hawk said.

Brad felt the thrill of excitement in the pit of his stomach. "Right. It won't be long now."

⚊⚋⚊ ⚊⚋⚊ ⚊⚋⚊

Barbara and Sam waited until the helicopter touched down at the Grand Haven YMCA ball field, then ran out to it. The side door slid open, and Art helped them aboard and secured Barbara's M-16. She hurried forward into the cockpit and started strapping in. Craig smiled at her and waited while she slipped on her headset and plugged into the intercom circuit.

"You're getting to be a real pro at that," he said into his mike. "Are you sure I can't interest you in a Coast Guard career?"

She smiled at him. "I'm doing fine where I am, thank you. Carry on."

"Aye, aye, ma'am."

He faced forward, and moments later they lifted off into the bright, blue skies. Craig brought the Dolphin around into a tight left turn over the Grand River and flew down it past the lighthouses and out onto the broad expanse of Lake Michigan.

"What a gorgeous day to be flying," a voice behind them said.

Barbara turned to see Sam standing in the doorway, bracing himself with both hands.

Craig glanced back. "It sure is. What do you want to do first?"

"I'll leave that to our cruise director," Sam said.

"As if we didn't plan it out—in detail," Barbara said.

"Look, unless someone gives me some instruction, we'll be over Milwaukee in about an hour."

Barbara looked back at the receding shoreline. But before she could say anything, Craig brought the helicopter around on a course for the Grand Haven State Park.

"Orbit the pavilion?" he asked.

"Yes, wise guy," Barbara said.

"Where is the president now?" Craig asked.

Barbara glanced at her watch. "Partway through his speech at Grand Center. He's scheduled to leave there at 9:50 and arrive in Grand Haven at 10:30."

"And we're to stick around here, right?"

"Yes."

"OK. There's already quite a crowd down—" He stopped abruptly.

"What?" Barbara asked.

Craig flipped a switch and spoke into his mike "Group Grand Haven, this is Coast Guard Rescue 5934, go ahead."

"Rescue 5934, Group Grand Haven. I have a radio patch for you from Traverse City. Resident Agent in Charge Dan Oliver, for agents Sam Green and Barbara Post. Stand by."

"Rescue 5934, standing by," Craig said.

The radio crackled. "Sam, where are you and Ms. Post?"

"We're orbiting the pavilion at Grand Haven State Park, as per our instructions." Sam paused. "Did I hear correctly? Are you calling us through Traverse City?"

"Yes. The phone lines between here and Grand Haven are down. The Secret Service wanted confirmation you were in position, and this is the only way I could reach you."

"What happened?" Barbara asked.

"The phone company contact said a cable's been cut somewhere around Spring Lake. They have a lineman out investigating."

"I don't like the sound of that—not with the president coming here."

"Yeah, well the Secret Service shares your concern, Ms. Post, but the guy at the phone company wasn't worried. He said these things happen—probably some utility crew cut through it."

"Do you have any other instructions for us?" Barbara asked.

"No, just keep a sharp lookout."

"Will do."

The radio clicked and popped. "Rescue 5934, Group Grand Haven. Your party has disconnected."

Craig keyed his mike. "Group Grand Haven, Rescue 5934, roger; out."

Barbara looked back at Sam.

"I don't think Dan likes long good-byes," he said.

"Hey, Brad!" Paul's voice was muffled by the sheet-metal partition.

Brad crept forward, taking care to keep his head down. He slid open the window and peered out. "Yeah?"

"We've got company coming down 104 from the east."

"Feds?"

"Smells like it. It's a black Suburban with tinted windows. You guys hang tight. I'm going out to do my lineman thing."

Brad felt an icy pang in his stomach. "OK. Take care."

"Thanks. I will."

Brad closed the window and duck waddled back to Hawk and Ed.

"Kill the light," he said. "I doubt it can be seen, but no point in taking chances."

Hawk punched the switch, plunging the back of the truck into inky blackness. Brad leaned against the side and listened. At first all he could hear was the crunch of Paul's boots. Then the distant roar of a powerful engine drifted in and quickly grew louder. Soon Brad heard the unseen vehicle brake and pull off the road. A door opened and closed, but the engine kept running.

Brad patted his holstered automatic to reassure himself it was there. If Paul's ruse failed, the feds would pay dearly. Brad strained to hear what they were saying, but all he could hear was an occasional word. The conversation went on for a long time, so long he fully expected to hear approaching footsteps. Finally, a door opened, then closed, and the other vehicle drove away. A few moments later Brad heard the van's front door open. He wiped the sweat off his hands, worked his way forward, and opened the window. Paul was smiling, but clearly relieved.

"It was a Secret Service agent," Paul said.

"What took so long?" Brad asked.

"He was very thorough. Examined my ID, then radioed someone to check me out with the phone company and make sure I was really assigned to work here—the whole nine yards. The guy didn't say, but it's obvious the feds are worried about the phone service to Grand Haven being cut off. He even asked me if I had found out what the problem was."

"What did you tell him?"

"Only that I was still checking." He glanced at his watch. "It's 10:05 now, and the paper said the president arrives in Grand Haven at 10:30. I'd say we're golden."

Brad took a deep breath. "It looks like it."

"When do you want to open up the back?"

"How's the traffic?"

"Let me check." He stepped away for a few moments. "It's pretty light," he said when he returned, "and nothing official looking."

"OK. I'm going to pull down the screen. I'll knock on the side when we're ready for you to open the doors."

"Roger that."

The president tried to relax as his limousine purred down Interstate 96 outside Grand Rapids. He held Nancy's hand, grateful for her reassuring presence—as always. But the next stop would be the make-or-break.

"I think it went well," Vince said.

Harold couldn't help a snort of derision. "The press was sure out for blood!" He was referring to the questions shouted at him as he entered and left the auditorium.

"Nothing we can do about that. We have to stay focused on Grand Haven."

"I know, I know."

Nancy shifted and squeezed his hand.

All Harold could think about was giving the speech, enduring the luncheon, and heading back to the airport.

The limousine began to slow as the long line of vehicles took the exit for Highway 104.

"It's getting packed down there," Sam said.

"Looks like the president's going to get a good turnout," Barbara said.

"Got another radio patch," Craig announced. He flipped a switch.

"Group Grand Haven, Rescue 5934, go ahead."

"Hello, Sam?"

"Right here, Dan."

"Got an update for you. A Secret Service agent checked out the lineman working on the cable, so the break's legit. How are things in Grand Haven?"

"No problems," Sam said. "We're observing with binoculars, and everything looks normal."

"Well, keep a sharp watch. The motorcade has just turned onto 104, so the president should arrive on time."

"Will do."

A few moments later Group Grand Haven reported that the caller had disconnected.

Brad looked out through the screen at the westbound traffic on Highway 104. Behind him, Ed and Hawk were checking over the TOW missile.

"Is it ready?" Brad asked.

"Roger," Ed replied. "Self-test says all systems are go."

Paul stood outside, looking east.

Brad raised his voice. "See anything?"

Paul turned around. "Not yet."

"Can you see us through the screen?"

"Negative. Looks just like the inside of a maintenance truck."

Barbara's nagging thought would not go away. What had started out as an unlikely possibility began to take on credibility when she considered other facts.

"Sam?" she said, unable to keep silent.

"Yes?"

"What if a local militia has that Montana militia TOW? We never did find it, and with that Oklahoma suspect calling someone up here, there could be a connection."

"What are you getting at?"

"A TOW could turn a limo into a smoking hulk, and the location of that cable break would make an excellent launch point. Sam, I don't believe in coincidence."

"I don't know . . ."

"Sam, think about it."

"What do you want to do?"

"Fly out 104 and check it out."

"Oh, no! Our orders are to orbit the park until the president is on his way back to Grand Rapids."

"What if they hit him on the highway?"

"You're forgetting our boss."

"Look, we've completed our preliminary observations and reported. Nothing else can happen until the president gets here. We can fly out 104 and be back before the motorcade gets here."

The intercom remained silent.

"Sam!"

"OK. I only hope Dan doesn't fire us both."

—◆— —◆— —◆—

"Isn't it beautiful?" Nancy said.

Harold looked out his window and smiled. "Yes, it is. I had forgotten what spring is like around here."

"I wish we could stay for a while."

He patted her hand. "So do I, but we have a job to do."

"Yes, I know."

—◆— —◆— —◆—

"There they are!" Brad said, louder than he intended.

Ed stooped behind the sight and adjusted his aim. "Wow! Would you look at that line of cars!"

"Can you see the president's limo?" Hawk asked.

Ed squinted in concentration. "Just a minute. There! Got it!"

"Is it in range?" Brad asked.

Ed shook his head. "Not yet, but it won't be long."

The launching tube made tiny movements as Ed followed his target.

—◆— —◆— —◆—

Barbara looked ahead through the bubble canopy. In the distance she could see a long line of black cars—the presidential motorcade.

"Where are we?" she asked.

"On the east side of Spring Lake," Craig said. "We should be somewhere near that cable break."

Barbara looked down. "That looks like a phone company truck."

"Yes, it does," Joel said. "And there's the lineman."

Barbara looked where he was pointing. "I see. He's just standing there."

"Could be watching the motorcade," Craig said.

Barbara's stomach began to tighten. "Or he could be a lookout. Can you drop down at little? I want to see inside the back of that truck."

"Roger."

The helicopter entered a steep diving turn. Barbara hurried back and grabbed her M-16. Art opened the door a crack, and Barbara stuck the rifle out and peered through the telescopic sights.

"What do you see?" Sam asked.

"Nothing. Just the inside of the truck."

"Are you sure?"

"Yes. Wait! Something moved—like a shimmer!"

"Hey!" Barbara shouted. "The lineman's running back to the truck! Craig! Put us down!"

"Roger!"

Ed looked up at the circling helicopter. "What are we going to do?"

"Get back on your target!" Brad shouted. "Is the president's limo in range?"

Ed peered through the sight. "Yes, just barely."

"Then fire!"

Ed pressed the trigger. A little over a second later a silvery blur shot out of the launch tube with a deafening roar and a white plume of smoke. The missile ripped through the plastic screen and coasted on. At first Brad thought it had misfired, but then white exhaust trails erupted from the TOW's sides.

"Keep the crosshairs on the target!"

"I have him! He's history!"

—✦— —✦— —✦—

"Too late!" Sam said.

A requirement of the TOW leapt to Barbara's mind, a product of her training on the missile. She lifted the M-16 and aimed. "Not if I can distract him!"

All she could see through the ripped plastic was the end of the launch tube. Barbara took a deep breath and pulled the trigger, hoping the round would at least scare the missile's operator. She fired again. On the third round, the M-16 jammed.

—✦— —✦— —✦—

Ed looked down in horror as a slug ripped a jagged hole in the floor.

"Get back on that sight!" Brad screamed.

Ed hesitated, then did so.

—✦— —✦— —✦—

Barbara dropped the rifle and followed the missile's white exhaust trail. To her horror, she saw it was almost halfway to the motorcade. Disaster was only seconds away.

"Craig! Ram the truck!"

"Roger! Joel! Drop the gear!"

The helicopter whirled to the right, turbines screaming, as Craig banked in a tight turn. Barbara lurched to the cockpit door and gaped at the ground hurtling toward them. Time slowed to a crawl. They dipped lower. The helicopter flew straight at the truck, then started pulling up. The van was huge now, and Barbara was sure they would crash. The helicopter lurched and metal screamed. Craig fought for control.

Joel scanned the instruments. "Nothing vital hit!" he said. "But the front gear is junk!"

Craig banked the helicopter around to the east. Barbara's throat tightened, and tears blurred her eyes. The missile's smoke trail had reached the president's limousine. A moment later it streaked past, exploding well beyond the motorcade. The distraction had worked. Barbara breathed a sigh of relief. She looked back at the truck and saw the V-shaped gouge in its roof.

"The lineman is making a break for it!" Sam shouted.

Barbara leaned into the cockpit. "Set us down!"

"Roger!" Craig said. He glanced back. "Jackson!"

"Yes, sir?" Art said over the intercom.

"Standby to evacuate the aircraft!"

"Aye, aye, sir!"

Craig brought the helicopter into a hover, then descended rapidly. The rear landing gear hit with a thump. "Everybody out!" Craig shouted. He turned his head to Joel. "You too!"

Barbara heard the door slide open. She ripped off her headset and yanked her Glock from its holster. Sam stood at the door waiting, gun in hand.

"You first, ma'am," Art said.

Barbara jumped down and ran out from under the rotor blades. A man jumped down from the back of the truck, brought up his gun and fired.

Barbara fell to the ground and squeezed off a shot. The man spun around and crumpled.

Sirens screamed in the distance. Barbara jumped up and started running toward the side of the truck. Reaching it, she turned to the back and held out her gun. The first black Suburban screeched to a halt, and all the doors flew open. Men in dark suits tumbled out, guns drawn. Another car roared past, lights flashing.

Barbara pounded on the side of the truck. "ATF!" she shouted. "Come out with your hands up!"

She heard rustling sounds inside. Finally a man jumped down, turned, and faced her. Barbara recognized the escaped hijacker. Then another man stepped down—Mike Hawkins. Barbara covered them while the

Secret Service agents took over and led them away. Then she walked over to the fallen man and looked down into his sightless eyes. It was Brad Anderson. Barbara's eyes fell on the mangled red mess that had been his chest. She heard someone running and turned.

"Are you all right?" Craig asked.

She saw his look of concern but wasn't sure how to answer. "I guess so. I'm just glad it's over."

Sam finished talking to an agent and came over. "They got the lineman," he said. "After they secure the scene, they're taking the motorcade on into Grand Haven."

"The president is going ahead with his speech?"

"That he is."

Barbara looked at the distant limo. "I admire his courage."

<hr />

Craig took Barbara's hand as they walked up the stairs. The Group Grand Haven conference room was empty when they entered. Barbara and Craig sat down at the table. It was after three o'clock now, and *Air Force One* was safely on the ground at Andrews Air Force Base.

Joel sat on the other side of Craig. "They keep sitting on the same side," he said.

Sam sat on the other side of Barbara. "Yeah, I know. Can't do a thing about it."

"I wouldn't advise you trying," Barbara said.

"Trying what?" Dan asked. He closed the door and took a chair at the head of the table.

"Oh, nothing," Barbara said.

Although Dan was obviously relieved, he also seemed tense. "That was excellent work, people." He looked at Craig. "And Lieutenant, we can't thank you enough."

"It was a team effort, sir," Craig said.

"And, it was Barbara's idea to check out the highway," Sam added.

Dan remained silent for what seemed a long time. Then he finally said, "Well, for the country's sake, I'm glad you did, Ms. Post." He paused. "Good work."

"Thank you, Dan," Barbara said.

He nodded. "Now, let me bring you up-to-date. We just raided Anderson's Automotive and found a fully equipped armory in the basement. I also have agents searching Hawkins' gun store, as well as their residences. Then we go after the other militia members. I think we can write off the Grand Haven Militia as the first casualty of the president's new initiative." He glanced at his watch and stood up. "I hate to cut this short, but I have to get back to the office. I expect full reports from both of you by eight o'clock tomorrow."

"You'll have them," Barbara said.

Dan hurried out.

"We've got paperwork too," Craig said to Barbara. "I'll call you later."

"That's our cue to leave," Sam told Joel.

"Roger that." He punched Craig in the shoulder. "Carry on, sir." He and Sam left the room.

"Well, that was considerate, I guess," Craig said.

Barbara laughed. "We must thank them."

Craig became serious. "How are you doing?"

Barbara exhaled slowly. "I'm glad we stopped them, but I'm pretty wiped out." She sighed. "If it wasn't for my report, I'd go home and crash right now." Then her smile returned and she took his hand. "Thank you—for everything."

They stood. He kissed her gently. "I'll call you," he said.

Chapter Thirty-three

Barbara smiled at the reassuring pressure of Craig's hand around hers as they strolled across the grass in Bicentennial Park. Although it was only two days since the attempted assassination, it seemed more like a month with all she had been doing. She still remembered her surprise when Craig had called to relay Susan's invitation to a picnic, but this in no way hindered her acceptance.

"It's nice of Susan to do this," Barbara said.

"I think it's her way of thanking you for what you did for William," Craig said.

"I was glad to do it. William's a good kid. I only wish Susan would reach out for the help she needs."

"I know, but I believe she's beginning to come around. Don't say anything to her, but she told me she's coming to church next Sunday."

"That's a good first step."

A shout came from up ahead. "Hi, Ms. Post!" William raced up to them and slid to a stop.

"Howdy, pardner." Barbara traded high fives with him.

"Uh, howdy!"

Barbara grinned. "Gotta work on that accent some."

"I'm trying! Did you and Uncle Craig stop those bad guys all by yourselves?"

"Ms. Post can't talk about that," Craig said.

"But . . ."

"Have you seen the news reports?" Barbara asked.

"Well, yes," William said.

"That's about all there was to it. Your Uncle Craig rammed the militia truck, causing the missile to miss the president."

"But, what was it like? Were you scared?"

"Maybe we can talk about it later." She saw the disappointment in his eyes. "Yes, I was scared."

"And so was I," Craig said. "Now, were you sent over here to do something?"

Williams eyes grew very wide. "Oh, yes! I was supposed to come and get you." He turned and pointed. "We're over there."

"Lead the way."

As they approached, Elizabeth turned in her wheelchair and waved. "Barbara, so nice to see you, dear."

"I'm happy to see you, Elizabeth."

Susan removed the foil covering from a platter and stood up.

"Thank you for coming," she said to Barbara.

"I appreciate you inviting me."

Susan looked around. "Please sit down. I think it's ready. Hope everyone likes lasagna."

"One of my favorites," Barbara said.

She and Craig sat next to Elizabeth. After Craig offered the blessing, Susan started the plates around. The food was excellent. For dessert Susan served a chocolate pudding cake, heavy on the chocolate, with scoops of homemade ice cream.

Barbara put her plate down. "That was wonderful."

"Glad you enjoyed it." A hint of a smile touched her lips. "If you and Craig have things to do, we'd understand."

"Thank you."

Craig grabbed a blanket and helped her stand.

William jumped up. "Now can you tell me about . . ."

"William," Susan said, "sit back down. I don't think Uncle Craig needs any help right now."

"But . . ."

"How about some more cake and ice cream?"

Barbara grinned as she witnessed the boy's abrupt shift in focus.

"Shall we?" Craig whispered.

"Sure thing, pardner." Barbara saw Elizabeth's approving smile.

Craig put his arm around her as they walked slowly toward the musical fountain. The cool breeze only heightened Barbara's joy at being next to the one she loved. A familiar face crossed their path in the gathering dusk. The young man waved, and Barbara finally realized it was the fountain operator.

Craig picked a spot with a good view but a reasonable distance from the powerful sound system. "This OK?" he asked.

"Just fine," Barbara replied.

Craig spread the blanket. They sat down, and a few minutes later the fountain's voice boomed its greeting.

"What's tonight's show?" Barbara asked.

Craig squeezed her hand. "Let's wait and see."

After the introduction finished, jets of water shot heavenward in a blaze of red, white, and blue, and the first song began:

The eyes of Texas are upon you all the
live long day

The eyes of Texas are upon you, you
cannot get away

Do not think you can escape them at
night or early in the morn

The eyes of Texas are upon you 'till
Gabriel blows his horn

Barbara turned to Craig. "You set that up, didn't you?" She saw him grinning in the fountain's glow.

"Yep."

She smiled. "We need to work on your accent, pardner."

Craig pulled her close. Their lips touched, and suddenly the evening was cool no longer.